Public lives and private secrets collide at . . .

THE
COTTAGE

PRAISE FOR
DANIELLE STEEL

"A LITERARY PHENOMENON . . . and not to be
pigeonholed as one who produces a predictable
kind of book." —*The Detroit News*

"THE PLOTS OF DANIELLE STEEL'S NOVELS TWIST
AND WEAVE as incredible stories unfold to the glee
and delight of her enormous reading public."
—*United Press International*

"Ms. Steel's fans won't be disappointed!"
—*The New York Times Book Review*

"One counts on Danielle Steel for
A STORY THAT ENTERTAINS AND INFORMS."
—*The Chattanooga Times*

"Steel writes convincingly about universal human
emotions." —*Publishers Weekly*

"STEEL IS AT THE TOP OF HER BESTSELLING
FORM." —*Houston Chronicle*

"FEW MODERN WRITERS CONVEY THE PATHOS
OF FAMILY AND MARITAL LIFE WITH SUCH
HEARTFELT EMPATHY."
—*The Philadelphia Inquirer*

"It's nothing short of amazing that even after
[dozens of] novels, Danielle Steel can still
come up with a good new yarn."
—*The* (Newark) *Star-Ledger*

Also by Danielle Steel

ANSWERED PRAYERS

SUNSET IN ST. TROPEZ

THE KISS

LEAP OF FAITH

LONE EAGLE

JOURNEY

THE HOUSE ON
HOPE STREET

THE WEDDING

IRRESISTIBLE FORCES

GRANNY DAN

BITTERSWEET

MIRROR IMAGE

HIS BRIGHT LIGHT:
THE STORY OF NICK TRAINA

THE KLONE AND I

THE LONG ROAD HOME

THE GHOST

SPECIAL DELIVERY

THE RANCH

SILENT HONOR

MALICE

FIVE DAYS IN PARIS

LIGHTNING

WINGS

THE GIFT

ACCIDENT

VANISHED

MIXED BLESSINGS

JEWELS

NO GREATER LOVE

HEARTBEAT

MESSAGE FROM NAM

DADDY

STAR

ZOYA

KALEIDOSCOPE

FINE THINGS

WANDERLUST

SECRETS

FAMILY ALBUM

FULL CIRCLE

CHANGES

THURSTON HOUSE

CROSSINGS

ONCE IN A LIFETIME

A PERFECT STRANGER

REMEMBRANCE

PALOMINO

LOVE: POEMS

THE RING

LOVING

TO LOVE AGAIN

SUMMER'S END

SEASON OF PASSION

THE PROMISE

NOW AND FOREVER

PASSION'S PROMISE

GOING HOME

DANIELLE STEEL

THE
COTTAGE

A Dell Book

THE COTTAGE
A Dell Book

PUBLISHING HISTORY
Delacorte hardcover edition published March 2002
Dell mass market edition/February 2003

Published by Bantam Dell
A division of Random House, Inc.
New York, New York

ISBN 0-440-23681-9

Manufactured in the United States of America
Published simultaneously in Canada

OPM   10 9 8 7 6 5 4 3 2 1

To my very wonderful children,
Beatie, Trevor, Todd, Sam, Nick,
Victoria, Vanessa, Maxx, and Zara,
who are the light of my life,
the joy of my days,
the comfort of my life,
the solace in sorrow,
my light in the dark,
and the hope of my heart.
No greater joy than you,
and when you have children one day,
may you be as lucky as I have been
to love and be loved by you.

> *with all my love,*
> *Mom/d.s.*

THE
COTTAGE

Chapter 1

The sun glinted on the elegant mansard roof of The Cottage, as Abe Braunstein drove around the last bend in the seemingly endless driveway. The sight of the imposing French manor would have taken his breath away, if the driver had been anyone but Abe. It was a spectacular home, and he had been there dozens of times before. The Cottage was one of the last legendary homes of Hollywood. It was reminiscent of the palaces built by the Vanderbilts and Astors in Newport, Rhode Island, at the turn of the century. This one was in the style of an eighteenth-century French château and was opulent, handsome, graceful, exquisite in every aspect of its design. It had been built for Vera Harper, one of the great stars of silent movies, in 1918. She had been one of the few early stars to conserve her fortune, had married well more than once, and had lived there until she died at a ripe old age in 1959. Cooper Winslow had bought it from her estate a year later. She had had no children and no heirs, and had left everything she had, including The Cottage, to the Catholic Church. He had paid a handsome sum for it even then, because his career had been booming at the time. His acquisition of The Cottage had caused a considerable stir. It had been quite an extraordinary house and property for a young man of twenty-eight, no matter how major a star he was. Coop had had no embarrassment about living in the palatial home, and was comfortable that it was worthy of him.

The house was surrounded by fourteen acres of park and impeccably manicured gardens in the heart of Bel Air; it had a tennis court, an enormous pool paved in blue and gold mosaic, and there were fountains located in a number of places on the grounds. The design of the grounds and gardens had allegedly been copied from Versailles. It was quite a place. Inside the house were high-vaulted ceilings, many of them painted by artists brought in from France to do the work. The dining room and library were wood-paneled, and the boiseries and floors in the living room had been brought over from a château in France. It had provided a wonderful setting for Vera Harper, and had been a spectacular home for Cooper Winslow ever since. And the one thing Abe Braunstein was grateful for was that Cooper Winslow had bought it outright when he purchased it in 1960, although he had taken two mortgages out on it since. But even they didn't hamper its value. It was by far the most important piece of property in Bel Air. It would have been hard to put a price on it today. There were certainly no other houses comparable to it in the area, or anywhere else for that matter, except maybe in Newport, but the value of the estate in Bel Air was far greater than it would have been anywhere else, despite the fact that it was now somewhat in disrepair.

There were two gardeners pulling weeds around the main fountain as Abe got out of his car, and two others working in a flower bed nearby, as Abe made a mental note to cut the gardening staff in half, at the very least. All he could see as he looked around him were numbers, and dollar bills flying out windows. He knew almost to the penny what it cost Winslow to run the place. It was an obscene amount by anyone's standards, and certainly by Abe's. He did the accounting for at least half the major stars in Hollywood, and had learned long since not to gasp or wince or faint or make overt gestures of outrage when he heard what they spent on houses and cars and furs and diamond necklaces for their girlfriends. But in comparison to Cooper Winslow, all of their extravagances paled. Abe was convinced that Coop Winslow spent more than King Farouk. He'd been doing it for nearly fifty years, he spent money like water, and hadn't had an important part in a major movie in more than twenty years. For the last ten, he'd been reduced to minor character parts, and cameo appearances, for which he was paid very little. And for the most part, no matter what the movie or the role or the costume, Cooper always seemed to play the dashing, charming, fabulously handsome Casanova, and more recently the irresistible aging roué. But no matter how irresistible he still was on screen, there were fewer and fewer parts for him to play. In fact, as Abe rang the front door bell and waited for someone to answer, Coop hadn't had any part at all in just over two years. But he claimed he met with directors and producers about their new movies every day. Abe had come to talk turkey with him about that, and about cutting back his expenses radically in the near future. He had been living in debt and on promises for the past five years. And Abe didn't care if he made commercials for his neighborhood butcher, but Coop was going to have to get out and work—and soon. There were a lot of changes he was going to have to make. He had to cut back dramatically, reduce his staff, sell some of his cars, stop buying clothes and staying at the most expensive hotels around the world. Either that, or sell the house, which Abe would have preferred.

He wore a dour expression as he stood in his gray summer suit, white shirt, and black and gray tie, as a butler in a morning coat opened the front door. He recognized the accountant immediately and nodded a silent greeting. Livermore knew from experience that whenever the accountant came to visit, it put his employer in a dreadful mood. It sometimes required an entire bottle of Cristal champagne to restore him to his usual good spirits, sometimes an entire tin of caviar too. He had put both on ice the moment Liz Sullivan, Coop's secretary, had warned Livermore that the accountant would be arriving at noon.

She had been waiting for Abe in the paneled library, and crossed the front hall with a smile as soon as she heard the bell. She had been there since ten that morning, going over some papers to prepare for the meeting, and she'd had a knot in her stomach since the night before. She had tried to warn Coop what the meeting was about, but he'd been too busy to listen the previous day. He was going to a black-tie party, and wanted to be sure to get a haircut, a massage, and a nap before he went out. And she hadn't seen him that morning. He was out at a breakfast at the Beverly Hills Hotel when she arrived, with a producer who had called him about a movie with a possible part in it for him. It was hard to pin Coop down, particularly if it involved bad news or something unpleasant. He had an instinctive sense, a kind of finely tuned supersonic radar that warned him almost psychically about things he didn't want to hear. Like incoming Scud missiles, he managed to dodge them with ease. But she knew he had to listen this time, and he had promised to be back by noon. With Coop, that meant closer to two.

"Hello, Abe, it's nice to see you," Liz said warmly. She was wearing khaki slacks, a white sweater, and a string of pearls, none of which flattered her figure, which had expanded considerably in the twenty-two years she'd worked for Coop. But she had a lovely face, and naturally blonde hair. She had been truly beautiful when Coop hired her, she had looked like an advertisement for Breck shampoo.

It had been love at first sight between them, not literally, or at least not from Coop's side. He thought she was terrific, and valued her flawless efficiency, and the motherly way she had taken care of him from the first. When he hired her she had been thirty years old, and he was forty-eight. She had worshipped him, and had a secret crush on him for years. She had given her life's blood to the impeccable running of Cooper Winslow's life, working fourteen hours a day, sometimes seven days a week, if he needed her, and in the process, she had forgotten to get married or have kids. It was a sacrifice she had willingly made for him. She still thought he was worth it. And at times she was worried sick about him, particularly in recent years. Reality was not important to Cooper Winslow. He considered it a minor inconvenience, like a mosquito buzzing around his head, and he avoided it all costs. Successfully, from his perspective at least, most of the time. Nearly always in fact. Coop only heard what he wanted to hear, i.e., only good news. The rest he filtered out long before it reached either his brain or his ears. And so far, he had gotten away with it. Abe had come that morning to deliver reality to him, whether Coop liked it or not.

"Hello, Liz. Is he here?" Abe asked, looking stern. He hated dealing with Coop. They were opposites in every way.

"Not yet," she said with a friendly smile, as she led him back to the library, where she'd been waiting for both of them. "But he'll be back any minute. He had a meeting about a lead part."

"In what? A cartoon?" Liz very diplomatically did not respond. She hated it when people said rude things about Coop. But she also knew how irritated the accountant had been with him.

Coop had followed absolutely none of his advice, and his precarious financial situation had become even more so, disastrously so in fact, in the past two years. And Abe's last words to Liz on the phone the day before had been "This has to stop." He had come on a Saturday morning to deliver the message, and it annoyed him no end that as usual, Coop was late. He always was. And because of who he was, and how endearing he could be when he chose to, people always waited for him. Even Abe.

"Would you like a drink?" Liz asked, playing hostess, as Livermore stood by stone-faced. He had a single expression he used in every situation, none. It seemed to suit his part. Although rumor had it that once or twice, when Cooper teased him mercilessly about something, he had actually smiled. But no one had actually seen him do it, so it was more legend than fact. But Coop swore he did.

"No, thanks," Abe said, looking almost equally expressionless as the butler, although Liz could see that irritation was creeping in at a rapid speed.

"Iced tea?" There was still an ingenue quality about her as she tried to put him at ease.

"That would be fine. How late do you think he'll be?" It was twelve-oh-five. And they both knew that Coop would think nothing of being an hour or two late. But he would come armed with a plausible excuse, and a dazzling smile, which made women go weak at the knees, but not Abe.

"Hopefully, it won't be long. It's just a preliminary meeting. They were going to give him a script to read."

"Why?"

His more recent parts had been walk-ons, or showed him walking in or out of a premiere, or at a bar draped over some girl. Almost every part he played was in black tie. And he was as charming on the set as he was in real life. So much so that even now, the perks in his contracts were legendary. He somehow always got to keep his costumes, and negotiated his wardrobe, custom made at all his favorite tailors in Paris,

London, and Milan. In addition to which, much to Abe's chagrin, he continued to buy more, wherever he went, along with antiques, crystal, linens, and staggeringly expensive art for his house. The bills were stacked up on Abe's desk, along with the bill for his most recent Rolls. Rumor had it he currently had his eye on a limited-edition, turbo-powered convertible Bentley Azure for half a million dollars. It would be a handsome addition to the two Rolls, a convertible and a sedan, and the custom-built Bentley limousine he had in the garage. Coop viewed the cars and wardrobe not as luxuries, but as the necessities of life. Those were the basics, the rest was cream.

A houseman appeared from the kitchen with two glasses of iced tea on a silver tray. Livermore had disappeared. The young man hadn't even left the room when Abe looked over at Liz with a frown.

"He's got to fire the staff. I want to do it today." Liz saw the houseman glance back over his shoulder with a look of concern, and she smiled reassuringly at him.

It was her job to keep everyone happy and pay what bills she could. Their salaries were always top on her list, but even those had to slide for a month or two at times. They were used to it. And she herself hadn't been paid in six months. She'd had a little trouble explaining that to her fiancé. She always caught up when Coop did a commercial or got a small part in a film. She could afford to be patient. Unlike Coop, she had a nest egg socked away. She never had time to spend money, and she had lived frugally for years. Coop was always generous with her, when he could.

"Maybe we can let them go slowly, Abe. This is going to be hard on them."

"He can't pay them, Liz. You know that. I'm going to advise him to sell the cars and the house. He won't get much for the cars, but if he sells the house, we can pay off the mortgage, and his debts, and he can live decently on the rest. He can buy an apartment in Beverly Hills, and be in good shape again." He hadn't been in years.

But the house, Liz knew, was part of Coop, like an arm or a leg or an eye. It was his heart. It had been part of his identity for more than forty years. Coop would rather have died than sell The Cottage. And he wouldn't part with the cars, she was sure. The idea of Coop behind the wheel of anything but a Rolls or a Bentley was unthinkable. His image was part of who he was, all of who he was in fact. And most people had no idea that he was in dire financial straits. They just thought he was casual about paying his bills. There had been a little problem with the IRS a few years before, and Liz had seen to it that all the proceeds from a movie he made in Europe had gone to them instantly. It had never happened again. But things were tough these days. All he needed was one great film, Coop said. And Liz echoed that to Abe. She always defended Coop, and had for twenty-two years. It was getting harder to do so lately because of the irresponsible way he behaved. That was just Coop, they both knew well.

Abe was tired of the games he played. "He's seventy years old. He hasn't had a part in two years, or a big one in twenty. If he did more commercials, it would help. But it still won't be enough. We can't do this anymore, Liz. If he doesn't clean this mess up soon, he's going to wind up in jail." Liz had been using credit cards to pay credit cards for over a year, as Abe knew, and it drove him insane. There were other bills that didn't get paid at all. But the idea of Coop in jail was absurd.

It was one o'clock when Liz asked Livermore to bring Mr. Braunstein a sandwich, and Abe looked as though there was smoke about to come out of his ears. He was furious with Coop, and only his devotion to his job kept him sitting there. He was determined to do what he had come to do, with or without Coop's help. He couldn't help wondering how Liz had stood him for all those years. He had always suspected they'd had an affair, and would have been surprised to learn that wasn't the case. Coop was smarter than that, and so was Liz. She had adored him for years, and never gone to bed with him. Nor had he asked. Some relationships were sacred to him, and he would never have tainted theirs. He was a gentleman after all, and at all times.

Abe finished his sandwich at one-thirty, and she had drawn him into a conversation about the Dodgers by then, his favorite team. She knew he was a passionate baseball fan. Putting people at ease was one of the things Liz did best. He had almost forgotten the time, as Liz turned her head. She knew the sound of his car on the gravel, although Abe hadn't heard a thing.

"There he is," she smiled at Abe, as though announcing the imminent arrival of the three kings.

And as always, Liz was right. Coop was driving the Bentley Azure convertible the dealer had just loaned him for several weeks. It was a splendid machine, and suited him to perfection. He was playing a CD of *La Bohème,* as he came around the last curve, and stopped the car in front of the house. He was a breathtakingly handsome man, with chiseled features and a cleft chin. He had deep blue eyes, smooth, fair skin, and a full head of immaculately trimmed and combed silver hair. Even with the top down, he didn't have a hair out of place. He never did. Cooper Winslow was the epitome of perfection in every detail. Manly, elegant, with a sense of extraordinary ease. He rarely lost his temper, and seldom looked unnerved. There was an air of aristocratic grace about him, which he had perfected to a fine art, and came naturally to him. He was from an old family in New York, with distinguished ancestors and no money, and his name was his own.

In his prime, he played all the rich-boy, upper-class parts, a sort of modern-day Cary Grant, with Gary Cooper looks. He had never played a villain or a single rough part, only playboys and dashing heroes in impeccable clothes. And women loved the fact that he had kind eyes. He didn't have a mean bone in his body, he was never petty or cruel. The women he dated adored him, even long after they left him. He somehow nearly always managed to engineer it so that they left him, when he had had enough of them. He was a genius at handling women, and most of the women he had affairs with, those he remembered at least, spoke well of him. They had fun with him. Coop made everything pleasant and elegant, for as long as the affair lasted. And nearly every major female star in Hollywood, at some point, had been seen on his arm.

He had been a bachelor and a playboy all his life. At seventy, he had managed to escape what he referred to as "the net." And he looked nowhere near his age.

He had taken extraordinarily good care of himself, in fact he'd made a career of it, and didn't look a day over fifty-five. And when he stepped out of the magnificent car, wearing a blazer, gray slacks, and an exquisitely starched and laundered blue shirt he'd had made in Paris, it was obvious that he had broad shoulders, an impeccable physique, and seemingly endless legs. He was six feet four, also rare in Hollywood, where most of the movie idols had always been short. But not Coop, and as he waved at the gardeners, he flashed not only a smile which showed off perfect teeth, but a woman would have noticed that he had beautiful hands. Cooper Winslow appeared to be the perfect man. And within a hundred-mile radius, you could see how charming he was. He was a magnet to men and women alike. Only a few people who knew him, like Abe Braunstein, were impervious to his charm. But for everyone else, there was an irresistible magnetism, a kind of aura about him that made people turn and look, and smile with awe. If nothing else, he was a spectacular-looking man.

Livermore had seen him coming too, and opened the door as he approached, to let him in.

"You're looking well, Livermore. Did anyone die today?" He always teased him about his somber mood. It was a challenge to Coop to make the butler smile. Livermore had been with him for four years, and Coop was immensely pleased with him. He liked his dignity, his stiffness, his efficiency, and his style. It lent his home precisely the kind of image he wanted to achieve. And Livermore took care of his wardrobe impeccably, which was important to Coop. It was a major part of the butler's job.

"No, sir. Miss Sullivan and Mr. Braunstein are here, in the library. They just finished lunch." He didn't tell his employer they'd been waiting for him since noon. Cooper wouldn't have cared anyway. As far as Coop was concerned, Abe Braunstein worked for him, and if he had to wait, he could charge him for that too.

But as Cooper strode into the room, he smiled winningly at Abe, and looked faintly amused, as though they shared a long-standing joke. Abe didn't fall for it, but there was nothing he could do. Cooper Winslow danced to his own tune.

"They served you a decent lunch, I hope," he said, as though he were early instead of nearly two hours late. His style generally threw people off guard, and made them forget they'd been angry at him for being late, but Abe refused to be distracted and got right to the point.

"We're here to talk about your finances, Coop. There are some decisions we have to make."

"Absolutely," Coop laughed as he sat down on the couch and crossed his legs. He knew that within seconds, Livermore would bring him a glass of champagne, and he was right. It was the vintage Cristal he always drank, chilled to the perfect temperature. He had dozens of cases of it in his cellar, along with other fabulous French wines. His cellar was legendary, as was his taste. "Let's give Liz a raise," he beamed at her, and her heart went out to him. She had some bad news for him too. She'd been dreading telling him all week, and had put it off until the weekend.

"I'm firing all your domestic help today," Abe said without ceremony, and Cooper laughed at him, as Livermore left the room expressionlessly. It was as though nothing had been said at all. Cooper took a sip of the champagne, and set the glass down on a marble table he'd bought in Venice when a friend's palazzo had been sold.

"There's a novel idea. How did you come up with that? Shouldn't we just crucify them, or maybe shoot them perhaps? Why fire them, it's so middle class."

"I'm serious. They've got to go. We just paid their salaries, they hadn't been paid in three months. And we can't pay them again, we can't keep up this kind of overhead, Coop." There was a sudden plaintive note in the accountant's voice, as though he knew that nothing he could say or do would make Cooper take him seriously. He always felt as though someone had pressed the "mute" button when he was talking to Coop. "I'm going to give them notice today. They've got to be out of here in two weeks. I'm leaving you one maid."

"How marvelous. Can she press suits? Which one are you going to leave me?" He had three maids, as well as a cook, and the houseman who'd served lunch. Livermore, the butler. Eight gardeners. And a driver he used part-time for important events. It took a lot of staff to run his enormous house, although he could have done without most of them. But he liked being well served, and indulging himself.

"We're leaving you Paloma Valdez. She's the cheapest one," Abe said practically.

"Which one's she?" Coop glanced at Liz. He couldn't remember anyone by that name. Two of them were French, Jeanne and Louise, he knew who they were, but Paloma didn't ring any bells with him.

"She's the nice Salvadorian I hired last month. I thought you liked her," Liz said, as though speaking to a child, and Coop looked confused.

"I thought her name was Maria, at least I've been calling her that, and she didn't say anything. She can't run this whole house. That's ridiculous," he said pleasantly, as he glanced back at Abe. Coop looked remarkably unruffled by the news.

"You have no choice," Abe said bluntly. "You have to fire the help, sell the cars, and buy absolutely nothing, and I mean nothing, not a car, not a suit, not a pair of socks, not a painting or a place mat for the next year. And then maybe you can start to dig yourself out of the hole you're in. I'd like to see you sell the house or at the very least rent the gatehouse, and maybe even part of this house, which would bring some money in. Liz tells me you never use the guest wing in the main house. You could rent that out. We could probably get a big price for it, and for the gatehouse. You don't need either of them." Abe had put considerable thought into it, he was very conscientious about what he did.

"I never know when people are coming from out of town. It's ridiculous to rent out part of the house. Why don't we just take in boarders, Abe? Or turn it into a boarding school? A finishing school perhaps. You come up with the oddest ideas." Coop looked vastly amused and as though he had no intention of doing any of it, but Abe was glowering at him.

"I don't think you have a full understanding of the situation you're in. If you don't follow my suggestions, you're going to have to put the whole house on the market and sell it in six months. You're damn near bankrupt, Coop."

"That's ridiculous. All I need is a part in one major film. I got a terrific script for one today," he said, looking pleased.

"How big is the part?" Abe asked mercilessly. He knew the drill.

"I don't know yet. They're talking about writing me in. The part can be as big as I want."

"Sounds like a cameo to me," Abe said, as Liz winced. She hated it when people were cruel to Coop. And reality always seemed cruel to him, so much so that he never listened to it. He just shut it out. He wanted life to be pleasant and fun and easy and beautiful at all times. And for him it was. He just couldn't pay for it, but that never stopped him from living the way he wanted to. He never hesitated to buy a new car, or order half a dozen suits, or buy a woman a beautiful piece of jewelry. And people were always willing to do business with him. They wanted the prestige of having him wear or use or drive their things. They figured he would pay for whatever it was eventually, and most of the time he did, when he could. Somehow, in time, the bills got paid, mostly thanks to Liz.

"Abe, you know as well as I do, that with one big film, we'll be rolling in money again. I could get ten million dollars for a picture by next week, or even fifteen." He was living in a dream.

"Make that one, if you're lucky. Or more like five hundred thousand, or three or two. You can't pull in the big money anymore, Coop." The only thing he didn't say was that Cooper Winslow was over the hill. Even Abe had boundaries about what he felt he could say to him. But the truth was he'd be lucky to get a hundred thousand dollars, or maybe two. Cooper Winslow was too old to be a leading man now, no matter how handsome he was. Those days were over for good. "You can't count on a windfall anymore. If you tell your agent you want to work, he can get you some commercials, for fifty thousand dollars, maybe a hundred if the product is big. We can't wait for big money to come in, Coop. You've got to cut back until it does. Stop spending money like water, reduce the staff down to next to nothing, rent out the gatehouse and part of this house, and we'll take another look at things in the next few months. But I'm telling you, if you don't, you'll be selling this house before the end of the year. I think you should. But Liz seems to think you're determined to stay here."

"Give up The Cottage?" Coop laughed even more heartily this time. "Now that is an insane idea. I've lived here for more than forty years."

"Well, someone else will be living here if you don't start tightening the belt. That's no secret, Coop. I told you that two years ago."

"Yes, you did, and we're still here, aren't we, and I'm neither bankrupt nor in jail. Maybe you need to take mood elevators, Abe. They might help that dismal point of view." He always told Liz that Abe looked like an undertaker, and dressed like one. Coop didn't say it, but he strongly disapproved of Abe wearing a summer suit in February. Things like that bothered him, but he didn't want to embarrass him by commenting on it. At least he wasn't suggesting Coop sell his wardrobe too. "You're serious about the staff, aren't you?" Coop glanced at Liz, and she was looking at him sympathetically. She hated knowing how uncomfortable he would be.

"I think Abe's right. You're spending an awful lot on salaries, Coop. Maybe you should cut back just for a little while, until the money starts rolling in again." She always tried to allow him his dreams. He needed them.

"How can one Salvadorian woman possibly run this entire house?" Coop said, looking momentarily stunned. It was a truly absurd idea. To him at least.

"She won't have to, if you rent out part of it," Abe said practically. "That'll solve one problem at least."

"Coop, you haven't used the guest wing in two years, and the gatehouse has been closed for nearly three. I don't think you'll really miss either one," Liz gently reminded him, sounding like a mother trying to convince a child to give up some of his toys to give to the poor, or eat his meat.

"Why on earth would I want strangers in my house?" Cooper asked, looking bemused.

"Because you want to keep the house, that's why," Abe said doggedly, "and you won't be able to otherwise. I'm dead serious, Coop."

"Well, I'll think about it," Coop said, sounding

vague. The whole idea just didn't make sense to him. He was still trying to imagine what his life would be like without help. It didn't sound like much fun to him. "And you're expecting me to cook for myself, I assume," he said, looking nonplussed.

"Judging by your credit cards, you're out for dinner every night anyway. You'll never miss the cook. Or the rest of them. We can get a cleaning service in from time to time if things get out of hand."

"How charming. A janitorial service perhaps? Maybe we could get a crew of convicts on parole, that might work." There was a spark in Coop's eyes again, and Abe looked exasperated.

"I've got their checks, and letters giving them all notice," Abe said, looking grim. He wanted to be sure that Coop understood he was really going to fire them. There was no other choice.

"I'll talk to a realtor on Monday," Liz said in a soft voice. She hated upsetting him, but he had to know. She couldn't just do it without warning him. But she thought renting out the two guest facilities was actually not a bad idea. Coop wouldn't miss the space, and they could get a very high price for the rent. She thought it was one of Abe's better ideas. And it would be a lot easier on Coop than selling the place.

"All right, all right. Just make sure you don't bring some serial killer into my house. And no children for God's sake, or barking dogs. In fact, I only want female tenants, and damn attractive ones. I should audition them myself," he said, only half-joking. Liz thought he was being exceptionally reasonable not to make a fuss about it, and she was going to try to find tenants as soon as she could, before he balked. "Is that all?" he asked Abe, as he stood up, signaling that he'd had enough. That had been a strong dose of reality for Coop at one go. And it was obvious he wanted Abe to leave.

"It'll do for now," Abe answered, standing up. "And I meant what I said, Coop. Do not buy *anything*."

"I promise. I'll make sure that all my socks and underwear have holes in them. I'll let you inspect them the next time you come."

Abe didn't respond as he walked to the door. He handed the envelopes he'd brought to Livermore and asked him to distribute them to the staff. They all had to be gone in two weeks.

"What a disagreeable little man," Coop said with a smile at Liz after Abe left. "He must have had a miserable childhood just to think like that. He probably spent his boyhood years pulling the wings off flies. Pathetic, and God, someone should burn his suits."

"He means well, Coop. I'm sorry, it was a tough meeting. I'll do my best to get Paloma trained in the next two weeks. I'll have Livermore show her how to handle your wardrobe."

"I shudder to think what that's going to look like. I suppose she'll be putting my suits in the washing machine. I might start a whole new look." He refused to be daunted by it, and continued to seem vaguely amused as he glanced at her. "It'll certainly be quiet here with just you and me and Paloma, or Maria, or whatever her name is." But he saw a strange look in Liz's eyes as he said it. "What's that about? He's not firing you too, is he?" For a fraction of a second, she saw a look of panic, and it nearly tore her heart out. And it took her an eternity to answer him.

"No, he isn't, Coop... but I'm leaving...." She said it in a whisper. She had told Abe the day before, which was the only reason why he wasn't firing her too.

"Don't be silly. I would rather sell The Cottage than have you leave, Liz. I'll go out and scrub floors myself to keep you."

"It's not that..." there were tears in her eyes, "I'm getting married, Coop."

"You're *what*? To whom? Not that ridiculous dentist in San Diego?" That had been five years earlier, but he lost track of things like that. He couldn't even conceive of losing Liz, and it had never occurred to him she might get married. She was fifty-two years old and it seemed not only like she'd been there forever, but always would be. She was family after all these years.

There were tears rolling down her cheeks as she answered. "He's a stockbroker in San Francisco."

"When did he come into the picture?" Coop looked shocked.

"About three years ago. I never thought we'd get married. I told you about him last year. I just figured we'd go on dating forever. But he's retiring this year, and he wants me to travel with him. His kids are grown up, and he finally said now or never. I figured I'd better grab the chance while I still have it."

"How old is he?" Coop looked horrified. It was the one piece of bad news of the day he had never expected to hear, and which had shaken him up.

"Fifty-nine. He's done very well. He has a flat in London, and a very nice house in San Francisco. He just sold it and we're moving to an apartment on Nob Hill."

"In San Francisco? You'll die of boredom, or get buried in an earthquake. Liz, you'll hate it." He was reeling from the impact. He couldn't begin to imagine managing without her. And she was blowing her nose and couldn't stop crying.

"Maybe I will. Maybe I'll come running back. But I thought I should at least get married once, just so I can say I've done it. You can call me anytime, Coop, wherever I am."

"Who's going to make my reservations, and talk to my agent? And don't tell me Paloma, whoever the hell she is!"

"The agency said they'd handle as much as they can for you. And Abe's office will handle all the bookkeeping. There's really not much else I do here," other than field calls from his girlfriends, and keep his press agent fed with fresh information, mostly about who he was dating. He was going to have to start making his own phone calls. It was going to be a new experience for him. She truly felt as though she had betrayed him, and was abandoning him.

"Are you in love with this guy, Liz, or just panicked?" It hadn't occurred to him in years that she still wanted to get married. She had never said anything to him, and he never asked about her dating life. It was rare for her to mention it to him, or to even have time to date anyone. She was so busy juggling Coop's appointments, his purchases, parties, and trips, she had hardly seen the man she was going to marry in the last year, which was why he had finally put his foot down.

He thought Cooper Winslow was a narcissist and an egomaniac, and he wanted to save Liz from him.

"I think I'm in love with him. He's a good person, he's nice to me. He wants to take care of me, and he has two very nice daughters."

"How old are they? I can't imagine you with kids, Liz."

"They're nineteen and twenty-three. I really like them, and they seem to like me. Their mother died when they were very young, and Ted brought them up himself. He did a nice job of it. One of them works in New York, and the other one is at Stanford in premed."

"I can't believe this." He looked absolutely shattered. The day had become instantly disastrous for him. He didn't even remember he was about to rent out his gatehouse and his guest wing. He didn't care about that now, only about losing Liz. "When are you actually marrying him?"

"In two weeks, right after I leave here." She started crying again as soon as she said it. It suddenly seemed like a terrible idea, even to her.

"Do you want to do it here?" he said generously.

"We're doing it at a friend's house in Napa," she said through her tears.

"It sounds awful. Are you having a big wedding?" He was truly stunned. He had never expected this.

"No. Just us and his daughters and the couple whose house we're getting married at. If it were any bigger, I'd have invited you, Coop." She hadn't had time to plan a wedding. She was too busy taking care of him. And Ted didn't want to wait any longer. He knew if he did, she'd never leave Coop. She felt responsible for him.

"When did you decide all this?"

"About a week ago." Ted had come down for the weekend and put a lot of pressure on her. And their decision coincided perfectly with Abe's decision to fire everyone. In a way, she knew she was doing Coop a favor. He couldn't afford her either. But she knew it was still going to be hard for both of them to say goodbye to each other. She couldn't imagine leaving him, and it broke her heart to do it. He was so innocent and so helpless—in his own inimitable way. And she had spoiled him over the past twenty-two years. She constantly worried about him and mothered him. She knew she would lie awake nights in San Francisco, fretting about him. It would be a tremendous adjustment, for both of them. Taking care of Coop had replaced the children she'd never had and finally stopped wanting years before.

He still looked shell-shocked when she left the house, and before she did, she answered the phone. It was Pamela, his latest romance. She was twenty-two years old, young even by his standards. She was a model, and aspiring to be an actress. He had met her at a shoot he had done for *GQ*. They had hired half a dozen models to stand beside him adoringly, and she had been the best looking of the lot. He'd only been dating her for about a month and she was totally infatuated with him, although he was old enough to be her grandfather, but he didn't look it fortunately. He was taking Pamela to The Ivy for dinner, and Liz reminded him to pick her up at seven-thirty. He gave her a big hug before she left, and reminded her to come back to him if she hated being married. And secretly, he hoped she would. Coop felt as though he were losing his younger sister and best friend.

Liz started crying again as she drove away. She loved Ted, but she couldn't imagine what life would be like without Coop. Over the years, he had become her family, her best friend, her brother, her son, her hero. She adored him. And it had taken every ounce of courage and strength she had to agree to marry Ted, and then to tell Coop. She hadn't been able to sleep for the past week, and she had felt sick about it all morning before Coop came home. She was grateful Abe had been there to distract her. And as she drove out the main gate, she nearly hit a car driving by. She was totally unnerved. Leaving Coop would be like leaving the convent or the womb. She just hoped she had made the right decision in the end.

Coop was still standing in the library when she left, and poured himself another glass of champagne. He took a sip, and then, still holding the glass, he walked slowly upstairs to his bedroom. He passed a small woman in a white uniform on the way. There was a large stain on the front of her dress that looked like tomato sauce, or soup. She was wearing her hair in a long braid down her back, and she was wearing sunglasses, which caught his attention, as she vacuumed noisily on the stairs.

"Paloma?" he asked cautiously, as though seeing her for the first time, and wishing he hadn't. She was wearing leopard sneakers, which made him wince.

"Jess, Mr. Weenglow?" There was something very

independent about her. She didn't remove the sunglasses, but stood staring at him from behind the dark lenses. It was impossible to guess how old she was, but he assumed somewhere in her middle years.

"It's Winslow, Paloma. Did you have some sort of accident?" He was referring to the spot on her uniform, which looked as though someone had thrown a pizza at her.

"We had essspagghetti for lunch. I dropped my spoon on my juniform. And I don't have another one here."

"Looks delicious," he said as he wandered past her, still shell-shocked over Liz, and wondering what it was going to be like when Paloma was caring for his wardrobe. And as he closed the door to his bedroom, Paloma stood staring at him, and then rolled her eyes. It was the first time he had ever spoken to her, but even from the little she knew of him, she'd never liked him. He went out with women young enough to be his children, and seemed entirely self-involved. She couldn't think of a single thing to like about him, and shook her head disapprovingly as she continued to vacuum the stairs. She wasn't looking forward to being alone in the house with him either. She felt as though she'd drawn the short straw when she found out she was the only one not being fired by the accountants. But she wasn't going to argue about it. She had a lot of relatives in San Salvador to support and she needed the money. Even if it meant working for the likes of him.

Chapter 2

Mark Friedman signed the last of the papers, standing in the empty house with the realtor, and it nearly broke his heart when he did. The house had only been on the market for three weeks. They'd gotten a good price for it, but that meant nothing to him. As he stood looking around him at the bare walls and empty rooms where he and his family had lived for ten years, it was like seeing the last of his dreams disappear.

He had been planning to keep the house, and live in it, but Janet had told him to sell it as soon as she had gotten to New York. He knew then, that no matter what she had said in the weeks prior to that, she was never coming back to him. She had told him that she was leaving him only two weeks before she left. And her lawyer had just called his. His entire life had unraveled in the past five weeks. Their furniture was already on its way to New York, he had given everything to her and the kids. He was staying in a hotel near his office, and he was waking up every morning, wishing he were dead. They had lived in Los Angeles for ten years, and been married for sixteen.

Mark was forty-two years old, tall, lean, blond, blue

eyed, and until five weeks earlier had been convinced he was happily married. He and Janet had met in law school, and got married as soon as they graduated. She had gotten pregnant almost instantly. Jessica was born on their first anniversary, and was now fifteen. Jason was thirteen. Mark was a tax attorney in a major law firm, and they had transferred him from New York to Los Angeles ten years before. It had been an adjustment at first, but they came to love it eventually. He had found the house in Beverly Hills within weeks, even before Janet and the kids arrived from New York. It had been perfect for them, with a big backyard, and a small pool. The people who had just bought it wanted to close as soon as they could, they were expecting twins in six weeks. And as Mark thought about it as he took a last walk around, he couldn't help thinking that their life was just beginning, and his was over. He still couldn't believe what had happened to him.

Six weeks earlier, he had been a happily married man with a beautiful wife he was crazy about, a job he loved, a nice house, and two gorgeous kids. They had no money worries, they were all in good health, and nothing bad had ever happened to them. Six weeks later, his wife had left him, the house was gone, his family was living in New York, and he was getting a divorce. It was almost too much to believe.

The realtor left him alone as he wandered through the empty rooms. All he could think of were the good times they'd shared. There had been nothing wrong with their marriage from his perspective, and even Janet admitted that she'd been happy with him.

"I don't know what happened," she said tearfully when she told him. "Maybe I was bored...maybe I should have gone back to work after Jason was born...." But none of that explained to Mark adequately why she had left him for another man. She had admitted to Mark five weeks earlier that she was madly in love with a doctor in New York.

A year and a half before, Janet's mother had gotten very sick. First a heart attack, then shingles, and finally a stroke. It had been an endless seven months of Janet commuting back and forth to New York. Her father was devastated and developing Alzheimer's, her mother went from one medical crisis to the next. He took care of the kids whenever Janet was gone. The first time she went, after the heart attack, Janet was gone for six weeks. But she called him three or four times a day. He had never suspected a thing, and it hadn't happened immediately, Janet had explained, it had happened over time. She had fallen in love with her mother's doctor. He was a great guy, had been wonderfully supportive and sympathetic and kind to her. They had dinner one night, just casually, and it had taken off from there.

She had been involved with him for a year, and she said it was tearing her apart. She kept thinking she'd get over it, that it was a passing thing. She assured Mark that she had tried to end it several times. But they were hooked on each other, it had become an obsession for both of them. Being with Adam, she told Mark, was like being addicted to a drug. He suggested therapy and couples counseling, but Janet refused. She didn't say it to him then, but she had made up her mind. She said she wanted to move back to New York, and see where things went. She needed to be out of the marriage, for the time being at least, so she could explore the affair honestly. And as soon as she got to New York, she told Mark she wanted a divorce, and asked him to sell the house. She wanted her half of the money out of it, so she could buy an apartment in New York. Mark stood staring at their bedroom wall, as he thought about the last conversation he'd had with her. He had never felt so lost and alone in his life. Everything he'd believed and counted on and thought would always be there for him no longer was. And the worst thing was that he hadn't done anything wrong, at least he didn't think he had. Maybe he worked too hard, or didn't take her out to dinner often enough, but it was all so comfortable, and she had never complained.

The second worst day of his life, after the day she told him about the affair, was when they told the children they were splitting up. They had wanted to know if he and Mom were getting divorced, and he had said honestly that he wasn't sure. But he realized now that Janet had known even then. She just didn't want to tell them yet, or him.

The kids had cried endlessly, and for no apparent reason, at first Jessica had blamed it all on him. None of it made sense to them. At fifteen and thirteen, it made even less sense to them than it did to Mark. At least he knew why Janet was leaving him, whether he deserved it or not. But to the kids, it was a mystery that defied any explanation. They had never seen their parents argue or disagree, and they rarely had. Maybe over where to hang what on the Christmas tree, and once Mark had had a fit when Janet had totaled his new car, but in the end, he apologized and told her he was glad she hadn't been hurt. He was a pretty easy-going guy, and she was a decent person too. Adam was just more exciting than Mark. According to Janet, he was forty-eight years old, had a lively practice, and lived in New York. He kept a sailboat on Long Island, and had been in the Peace Corps for four years. He had interesting friends and a fun life. He was divorced, and had never had kids. His wife hadn't been able to have any, and they didn't want to adopt. And he was crazy about the idea of Janet's kids. He even wanted two more of their own, which Janet had not mentioned to Mark, or the kids. They knew nothing about him yet. She was going to introduce him into their lives once they got settled in New York, and Mark suspected she had no intention of telling them that Adam was the reason she'd left him.

In comparison, Mark knew he was dull. He liked his work, and estate planning was something he enjoyed and did well, but it wasn't something he could discuss at length with her. She had wanted to go into criminal law, or child advocacy, and tax law had always bored her to tears. She and Mark played tennis several times a week, they went to movies, hung out with the kids, went to dinner with friends. It had been a comfortable, ordinary life for all of them. And now, nothing was comfortable anymore. The emotional anguish he felt was almost a physical pain. He had had a knife in his gut for the past five weeks. He had just started going to a therapist, at the suggestion of his doctor, when Mark called and asked for sleeping pills, because he said he could no longer sleep. His life had become a living hell. He missed her, he missed his kids, he missed his life. In the blink of an eye, everything and everyone was gone, and now so was the house.

"Ready, Mark?" the realtor asked gently as she stuck her head in the bedroom door. He was just standing there, staring into space, lost in his own thoughts.

"Yeah, sure," he said, and walked out of the room, with one last glance back. It was like saying goodbye to a lost world, or an old friend. He followed her out of the house and she locked the door. He had given her all his keys. The money was being deposited into his account that afternoon, and he had promised to wire Janet her half. They had gotten a good price for it, which meant nothing to him now.

"Are you ready to start looking for something for you?" the realtor asked hopefully. "I have some great small houses for you up in the hills, and there's a little gem in Hancock Park. There are some nice apartments around right now too." February was always a good month to look. The holiday doldrums were over, and some great listings came on the market in the spring. And with the sale of the house, and the price he'd gotten for it, she knew he had money to spend. Even his half was more than enough to buy himself a handsome new place. And he had a good job. Money wasn't a problem for Mark. Just everything else.

"I'm fine at the hotel," he said, slipping into his Mercedes after thanking her again. She had done a great job, and closed the sale smoothly and in record time. He almost wished she hadn't been so efficient, or had even lost the sale. He hadn't been ready to move on. It was something to talk about with his new therapist, grist for the mill. He had never been to a therapist before, and he seemed like a nice guy, but Mark wasn't sure it would help. Maybe with the sleep problem, but what could he do about the rest? No matter what they said in the counseling sessions, Janet and the kids were still gone, and without them he had no life. He didn't want a life. He wanted them. And now she belonged to someone else, and maybe the kids would like him better too. It was a devastating thought. He had never felt as hopeless in his life, or as lost.

He drove back to the office, and was back at his desk by noon. He dictated a stack of letters, and went over some reports. He had a partners' meeting that afternoon. He didn't even bother eating lunch. He had lost ten pounds in the last five weeks, maybe twelve. All he could do now was keep moving, putting one foot after the other, and try not to think. He did his thinking at night, when it all came back to him, and he heard her words again and again, and thought about the kids and how much they had cried. He called them every night, he had promised to come and visit them in a few weeks. He was taking them to the Caribbean over the Easter vacation, and they were going to come out to LA in the summer, but now he had nowhere for them to stay. Just thinking about all of it made him feel sick.

When he saw Abe Braunstein in a meeting about new tax laws late that afternoon, the accountant was stunned. Mark looked like he had a terminal disease.

He usually looked healthy and young and athletic, he was always in good spirits, and even though he was forty-two, Abe always thought of Mark as a nice kid. He looked like the boy next door. Now he looked like someone had died. And he felt as though he had.

"Are you all right?" Abe asked with a look of concern.

"Yeah, I'm fine," Mark answered vaguely, looking numb. His face even looked somewhat gray. He seemed exhausted and pale, and Abe was genuinely worried about him.

"You look like you've been sick. You've dropped a lot of weight." Mark nodded, and didn't respond, and then after the meeting, he felt like a jerk for not reacting to Abe's concern. Abe was going to be the second person he'd told, the first being his therapist. He hadn't had the guts, or the stomach, to tell anyone else. It was too humiliating, it made him seem like such a loser, and he worried that people would think he'd been a shit to her. He wanted to explain, and he was torn between wanting to whine, and needing to hide.

"Janet left," Mark said cryptically as they left the meeting side by side. It was nearly six o'clock. He hadn't heard half of what was said, and Abe had noticed that too. Mark looked like he was having an out-of-body experience, and felt like it. But at first, Abe didn't get his drift.

"On a trip?" he asked, looking confused.

"No. For good," Mark explained, looking grim. But in a way, it was a relief to tell the truth. "She left three weeks ago. She moved to New York with the kids. I just sold the house. We're getting a divorce."

"I'm sorry to hear that," Abe said, feeling sorry for him. The poor guy looked destroyed. But he was young, he'd find another wife, maybe even have more kids. He was a good-looking guy, Abe had always thought. "That's really rough. I didn't know." He hadn't heard a thing, although he did a lot of accounting work with Mark's firm. But they usually talked about tax law, or their clients, not about themselves. "Where are you living now?" It was funny how men asked each other what they were doing, not how they felt.

"In a hotel two blocks from here. It's kind of a dump, but it's okay for now."

"Do you want to go out and get something to eat?" Abe's wife was expecting him at home, but Mark looked as though he needed a friend. He did, but he felt too lousy to go anywhere. Closing on the house had made everything seem even worse. It was tangible evidence that his life with Janet was over for good.

"No, thanks." Mark managed to force out a smile. "Maybe another time."

"I'll give you a call," Abe promised, and left. He didn't know whose fault the divorce was, but it was obvious that Mark wasn't happy about it. He obviously didn't have anyone else. And Abe wondered if she did, she was a great-looking girl. They had looked like the all-American couple, the boy and girl next door. Both blond, both blue eyed, and their kids looked like poster children for the American way of life. They all looked like they were off a farm in the Midwest, although he and Janet had grown up within blocks of each other in New York. They had gone to all the same high school dances, but never met. She had gone to Vassar and he to Brown, and they finally met at Yale Law School. It was the perfect life. But no more.

Mark stayed at the office shuffling papers on his desk until eight o'clock that night, and then finally went back to the hotel. He thought about picking up a sandwich on the way, but he wasn't hungry. Again. He had promised both his doctor and his therapist that he would try to eat. Tomorrow, he promised himself. All he wanted to do now was go to bed and stare at the TV. And maybe eventually sleep.

The phone was ringing when he reached his room. It was Jessica. She had had a good day at school, and gotten an A on a quiz. She was a high school sophomore, but she hated her new school. And so did Jason, he was in eighth grade. The adjustment was hard on them. Jason was playing soccer, and Jessica was on the varsity field hockey team. But she said the boys in New York were all geeks. And she was still blaming Mark for everything she didn't understand about the divorce.

He didn't tell her the house had closed that day, or that they would never see it again. He just promised that he would come to New York soon, and told them to say hi to Mom. And after he hung up, he just sat there in bed, staring at the TV, with tears rolling silently down his cheeks.

Chapter 3

Jimmy O'Connor was lean and athletic and strong. He had broad shoulders and powerful arms. He was a golfer and a tennis player. He had gone to Harvard and been on the ice hockey team. He had been a superb athlete in school, and still was. And he was a great guy. He had gone to graduate school, and got a master's in psychology at UCLA, while he did volunteer work in Watts. He had gone back the following year to get a degree in social work, and had never left Watts. At thirty-three, he had a life and a career he loved, and still managed to get a little time in for sports. He had organized a soccer team and a softball team for the kids he worked with. He placed kids in foster care, and removed them from abusive homes, homes where they were beaten or molested or abused. He carried children who had had bleach poured on them, or been burned, in his own arms to emergency rooms, and more than once he had brought them home until the right foster home could be found. The people he worked with said he had a heart of gold.

He had classic black Irish looks, jet-black hair, ivory skin, and huge dark eyes. There was an almost sensual quality to his lips, and he had a smile that knocked women off their feet. It had knocked Maggie off hers. Margaret Monaghan. They were both from Boston, met at Harvard, and had come to the West Coast together when they graduated. They'd been living together since junior year. And grousing about it every inch of the way, they had gone to City Hall and gotten married six years before. Mostly to get their parents off their backs. It didn't make much difference to either of them, they claimed, and then grudgingly they admitted to each other that it was not only okay, it was nice. Getting married had been a good thing.

Maggie was a year younger than Jimmy and the smartest woman he'd ever known. There wasn't a woman like her in the world. She had a master's in psychology too, and was thinking about getting a Ph.D. She wasn't sure. And like him, she worked with inner-city kids. She wanted to adopt a flock of them, instead of having kids of their own. He was an only child, and she was the oldest of nine. She was from good, solid Boston Irish stock, originally from County Cork. Her parents had been born in Ireland and had powerful brogues which she imitated flawlessly. Jimmy's family had left Ireland four generations before. He was a distant cousin of the Kennedys, which she had teased him about mercilessly when she found out, and called him "Fancy Boy." But she kept the information to herself, she just liked to rattle his cage. About anything and everything. He loved that about her. Brilliant, irreverent, beautiful, brave, with fiery red hair and green eyes, and freckles everywhere. She was his dream woman, and the love of his life. There wasn't a single thing he didn't like about her, except maybe the fact that she couldn't cook and didn't care. So he cooked for both of them, and was proud of the fact that he was a pretty decent cook.

He was packing the kitchen, and his frying pans, when the building manager rang the bell and walked in. He shouted out a greeting so Jimmy would know he was there. He didn't like to intrude, but he had to show the place. It was a tiny apartment in Venice Beach. They had loved living there. Maggie liked to roller blade down the streets, everyone did there. And they loved the beach.

Jimmy had given notice the week before, and was moving at the end of the month. He didn't know where. Just not there. Anywhere but there.

The building manager was showing the apartment to a young couple who said they were getting married. They were both wearing jeans and sweatshirts and sandals, and to Jimmy they seemed innocent and young. They were in their early twenties, had just graduated from college and had come from the Midwest. They were in love with LA and they thought the apartment was great. They thought Venice was the best. The building manager introduced them to Jimmy, and he nodded and shook hands, and went back to his packing, and left them to look at the apartment on their own. It was small, and in good order. There was a small living room, and a tiny bedroom, barely bigger than the bed, a bathroom you had to stand on each other's shoulders to use together, and the kitchen where he was packing. It had worked for them, they hadn't needed more space than that, and Maggie had always insisted on paying her half of the rent and couldn't afford more. She was stubborn about things like that. They had split all their expenses in half since the day they met, even after they were married.

"I'm not going to be a kept woman, Jimmy O'Connor!" she had said, imitating her parents' brogue, as her flame-colored hair danced around her face. He wanted to have babies with her just so he could have a house full of kids with red hair. They'd been talking about getting pregnant for the past six months, but Maggie also wanted to adopt. She wanted to give kids a better life than they might have had otherwise.

"How about six and six?" Jimmy teased. "Six of ours, six adopted. Which ones do you want to support?" She had conceded that she might be willing to let him support the kids, some of them at least. She couldn't afford to have as many as they wanted. But they had often talked about five or six.

"Gas stove?" the prospective tenant asked with a smile. She was a pretty girl, and Jimmy nodded, without saying more. "I love to cook." He could have told her he did too, but he didn't want to engage in conversation with them. He just nodded and kept on packing, and five minutes later they left. The building manager called out thank you and Jimmy heard him close the door, and then muffled voices in the hall. He wondered if they were going to take the apartment. It didn't really matter. Someone would. It was a nice place, the building was clean, and they had a good view. Maggie had insisted on a view, although it had stretched her budget, but there was no point living in

Venice if you didn't have a view, she had said with the brogue again. She played with the brogue a lot. She had grown up with it, and it was familiar to her, and always amused him. Sometimes they went out for pizza and she spent the entire dinner pretending to be Irish, and everyone was fooled. She had taught herself Gaelic too. And French. And wanted to learn Chinese, so she could work with immigrant children in the Chinese neighborhoods. She wanted to be able to talk to the kids.

"He's not very friendly," one of the new tenants whispered. They had conferred in the bathroom and decided to take the place. They could afford it, and they loved the view, even if the rooms were small.

"He's a good guy," the building manager said protectively. He had always liked them both. "He's had a tough time," he said cautiously, not sure if he should tell them, but they'd hear it anyway from someone else. Everyone in the building loved the O'Connors, and he was sorry to see Jimmy go, but he understood. He would have done the same thing.

The new tenants had wondered if he was being evicted or asked to leave, he had looked so unhappy and almost hostile as he packed up his stuff.

"He had a beautiful young wife, a terrific girl. Thirty-two years old, with bright red hair, smart as a whip."

"Did they break up?" the woman asked innocently, feeling slightly more sympathetic. Jimmy had looked almost fierce to her as he shoved his skillets into a cardboard box.

"She died. A month ago. Terrible thing. A brain tu-

mor. She started having headaches a few months ago,
she said they were migraines. Three months ago they
put her in the hospital for tests, brain scans, I guess.
MRIs, CAT scans, whatever they do. She had a lot of
tests. They found a brain tumor, they tried to operate
but it was too big, and it had spread all over the place.
She was dead in two months. I thought it was going to
kill him too. I've never seen two people more in love.
They never stopped laughing and talking and kidding
around. He just gave me notice last week. He says he
can't stay, it makes him too sad. I feel so bad for him,
he's such a good man." The building manager had
tears in his eyes.

"How awful!" the woman said, feeling tears sting
her eyes too. It was a terrible story, and she had noticed photographs of the two of them all around the
apartment. They looked happy and in love in the pictures. "What a terrible shock for him."

"She was very brave. Right up until the last week,
they went on walks, he cooked dinner for her, he carried her down to the beach one day because she loved
it so much. It'll be a long time before he gets over it, if
he ever does. He'll never find another girl like her."
The building manager, who was both known and
beloved for his gruffness, wiped a tear from his eye,
and the young couple followed him downstairs. But
the story haunted them for the rest of the day. And late
that afternoon, the building manager slipped a note
under Jimmy's door to tell him the young couple had
taken the apartment. He was off the hook in three
weeks.

Jimmy sat staring at the note. It was what he had

wanted, and what he knew he had to do, but he had nowhere to go. He no longer cared where he lived. It didn't matter to him. He could have slept in a sleeping bag on the street. Maybe that was how people became homeless. Maybe they no longer cared where they lived, or if. He had thought of killing himself when she died, just walking into the ocean without a murmur or a sound. It would have been an enormous relief. He had sat on the beach for hours the day after she died, and thought about it. And then, as though he could hear her, he could imagine her telling him how furious she would be, and what a wimp he was. He could even hear the brogue. It was nightfall when he went back to the apartment, and sat for hours crying and wailing on the couch.

Their families had come out from Boston that night, and the rosary and funeral had eaten up the next two days. He had refused to bury her in Boston. She had told him she wanted to stay in California with him, so he buried her there. And after they all went home, he was alone again. Her parents and brothers and sisters had been devastated over their loss. But no one was as distraught as he, no one knew how much he had lost, or what she meant to him. Maggie had become his whole life, and he knew with absolute certainty that he would never love another woman as he had her, or perhaps at all. He couldn't conceive of another woman in his life. What a travesty that would be. And who could possibly be like her? All that fire and passion and genius and joy and courage. She was the bravest human he had ever known. She hadn't even been afraid to die, she just accepted it as her fate. It was he who had cried and begged God to change his mind, he who had been terrified, who couldn't imagine living on without her. Unthinkable, unbearable, intolerable. And now here he was. She had been gone for a month. Weeks. Days. Hours. And all he had to do now was crawl through the rest of his life.

He had gone back to work the week after she died, and everyone treated him like broken glass. He was back at work full-time with the kids, but there was no joy in his life now, no spirit, no life. He just had to find a way to keep putting one foot in front of the other for the rest of his life, to keep breathing, to keep waking up every morning, with absolutely no reason why.

Part of him wanted to stay in the apartment forever, and another part of him couldn't bear waking up there without her one more time. He knew he had to get out. He didn't care where. Just out. He had seen the name of a realtor in an ad, and called them. All the agents were out. He left his name and number, and went back to packing. But when he got to her half of the closet, he felt as though Mike Tyson had reached out and punched him in the chest. It took his breath away. The sheer reality of it was so powerful it sucked the air out of his lungs and the blood out of his heart. He just stood there for a long moment. He could smell her perfume, and feel her presence beside him as though she were standing in the room next to him.

"What the fuck am I supposed to do now?" he said out loud as tears sprang to his eyes, and he held on to the door frame. It was as though a supernatural force had almost knocked him down. The power of her loss was so great he could hardly stand up.

"Keep going, Jimmy," he heard the voice in his head. "You can't quit now." He could still hear the brogue.

"Why the hell not?" But she hadn't. She had never given up. She had fought right till the end. She had worn lipstick and washed her hair the day she died, and wore the blouse he loved best. She had never given up. "I don't want to keep going!" he shouted at the voice he could hear, the face he would never see again.

"Get off your bloomin' arse!" he could hear as plain as day, and suddenly he laughed through his tears as he stood there staring at her clothes.

"Okay, Maggie . . . okay . . ." he said, as one by one he took down her dresses and folded them carefully into a box as though she'd come back for them someday.

Chapter 4

Liz came back to The Cottage on Sunday, to meet with the realtor, the day after Coop had agreed to rent the gatehouse and the guest wing. She wanted to move ahead as soon as possible, before he changed his mind. The income they would generate would make a big difference for him. And she wanted to do everything she could for him before she left.

She had agreed to meet the realtor at eleven, and when they both reached The Cottage, Coop was out. He had taken Pamela, the twenty-two-year-old model, to brunch at the Beverly Hills Hotel, and had promised to take her shopping on Rodeo Drive the next day.

She was absolutely gorgeous, but she had nothing to wear. And spoiling women was one of the things Coop did best. He loved shopping for them. Abe was going to have a coronary when he saw the bill. But Coop never worried about that. Coop had promised to take her to Theodore and Valentino and Dior and Ferre, and wherever else she fancied, and to Fred Segal after that. It was going to be a fifty-thousand-dollar shopping spree for sure, or more. Particularly if they stopped off at Van Cleef or Cartier, if anything caught his eye in the windows. And it would never occur to Pamela to tell him that his generosity was excessive. For a twenty-two-year-old girl from Oklahoma, this was a dream come true, and so was Coop.

"I'm amazed that Mr. Winslow is willing to have tenants on the property, particularly in a wing of the main house," the real estate agent mentioned to Liz, as she let her into the guest wing. She was fishing for some piece of gossip she could share with future tenants, which didn't please Liz. But it was also inevitable, and a necessary evil if they were going to rent. They were at the mercy of how people interpreted it. And those interpretations were never kind about major movie stars, or celebrities of any sort. It was part of the deal.

"The guest wing has a separate entrance of course, so they'll never run into Coop. And you know, he travels so much, I don't think he'll know they're there. Having tenants is protection for him, if people realize that there are people living on the property full-time. Otherwise, there could be break-ins or all kinds of problems. This is really a security bonus for him." It was an angle the realtor hadn't thought of, but it did make sense. Although she was suspicious that there was more to it than that. Cooper Winslow hadn't had a lead in a major movie in years. She couldn't remember the last one she'd seen, although he was certainly still a big star, and caused a huge stir wherever he went. He was one of the great Hollywood legends of all time, which was going to help her rent the two facilities he was leasing, and get a stiff price for them as well. This was high, high prestige, and the estate was the only one like it in the country, if not the world. With a handsome movie star in residence, at least some of the time. Maybe if the tenants were lucky, they would catch a glimpse of him on the tennis court or at the pool. She was going to put that in the brochure.

The door to the guest wing creaked open, and Liz wished she had sent a crew in to dust and clean before they'd gone in. But there hadn't been time, and she wanted to move fast. But generally speaking, it looked fine. It was a beautiful wing of the house. It had the same high ceilings the rest of the house had, and elegant French windows leading out to the grounds. There was a lovely stone terrace framed with hedges, and antique marble benches and tables Coop had bought in Italy years before. The living room was full of handsome French antiques. There was a small study next to it, which could serve as an office, and up a short flight of stairs an enormous master bedroom all done in pale blue satin with mirrored Art Deco furniture he had picked up in France.

There was an enormous white marble bathroom next to the master bedroom, and a dressing room with more closets than most people needed, although they wouldn't have been enough for Coop. And on the other side of the living room, there were two small, but adequate bedrooms, decorated in bright English floral chintz and antiques. And there was a wonderful country kitchen with a big dining table in it, which the realtor said reminded her of Provence. There was no dining room, but Liz pointed out that they didn't really need it, since the living room was so large, a table could be set up there, or the tenants could eat in the kitchen, which was cozy and fun and informal. There was a massive old French stove, a ceramic fireplace in the corner of the room, and beautiful antique painted tiles on the walls. All in all it made a perfect apartment for someone, on the grounds of the most beautiful estate in Bel Air, and they had full access to the tennis courts and the pool.

"How much does he want for it?" The realtor's eyes were shimmering with excitement. She had never seen a better place, she could even imagine another movie star renting it, just for the prestige. Perhaps someone staying in town to make a movie, or spending a year in LA. The fact that it was furnished would make it a real bonus for someone. And beautifully furnished at that. With fresh flowers, and a little dusting, the guest wing would really come to life, and the realtor could see that too.

"How much do you suggest?" Liz asked. She wasn't sure. She hadn't had any dealings with the rental market in years, and had lived in the same modest apartment herself for more than twenty years.

"I was thinking at least ten thousand a month. Maybe twelve. For the right tenant, we could push it to fifteen. But surely no less than ten." It sounded good to Liz, and with the gatehouse, it would give Coop a comfortable cushion every month, if they could keep his credit cards out of his hands. She was seriously worried about what mischief he'd get up to after she was gone, with no one to monitor him, or even scold him if need be. Not that she had such perfect controls on him, but she could at least remind him from time to time not to get in any deeper than he was.

As soon as Liz locked the front door to the guest wing, they drove to the north end of the property to where the gatehouse stood secluded in a seemingly secret garden. It was in fact nowhere near the front gate, and had so much greenery and land around it, that it appeared to be on an estate of its own. It was a beautiful little stone house with vines growing up one side, and it always reminded Liz of an English cottage. It had a magical feeling to it, and inside there were both elegant wood paneling and rough-hewn stone walls. It was an interesting juxtaposition of two worlds, and entirely different from the elegant French decor of the guest wing.

"Oh my God, this is fabulous!" the realtor said enthusiastically, as they walked past a rose garden that surrounded the house, and stepped inside. "It's like being in another world."

In the gatehouse, the rooms were small and well proportioned with beam ceilings, and the furniture was heavier and English, with a long, handsome leather couch that Coop had bought from an English club. The house had a wonderful cozy feeling, and a huge fireplace in the living room. It had a decent-sized country kitchen, full of antique cooking implements on the walls, and there were two average-sized bedrooms upstairs, done in manly stripes, with George III furniture that Coop had collected for a while. There were beautiful needlepoint rugs in all the rooms, and a small elegant dining room with antique silver set out on the sideboard. The china in the cupboard was Spode. It was a perfect little English cottage, and you could have imagined yourself anywhere but Bel Air. It was closer to the tennis courts than the main house, but it was farther from the pool, which was almost directly outside the guest wing. So each place had its virtues and conveniences and own style.

"This is an absolutely perfect place for the right tenant," the realtor said with unabashed glee. "I'd love to stay here myself."

"I've always thought that too," Liz smiled at her. She had once asked Coop if she could borrow it for a weekend, but in the end she never had. And like the guest wing, it was perfectly appointed with linens and drapes, china, and all the cooking utensils and flatware anyone could possibly need.

"I can get at least ten thousand a month for this one too," the realtor said, looking pleased. "Maybe more. It's small, but it's absolutely beautiful, and has incredible charm." It had an entirely different feeling from the guest wing, which seemed grander and more luxurious because of the scale, but was very homey too. There were just higher ceilings, and a lot more room, because the living room and the master bedroom and kitchen were all so large. But they were both beautiful properties, and the realtor felt certain she could have them rented in no time at all. "I'd like to come out and take some pictures of both places next week, I don't even want to show them to other brokers yet. I want to see who we have on our own books looking for furnished rentals. Properties like these don't come along every day, and I want to find the right tenants for Coop."

"That would be very important for him," Liz said solemnly.

"Are there any restrictions I should know about?" the realtor asked, making a few quick notes on a pad, about size, facilities, and number of rooms.

"To be honest, he's not crazy about kids, and he wouldn't want anything damaged. I don't know how he'd feel about a dog. But other than that, I think as long as someone is respectable and can pay the rent, there won't be any problem." She didn't tell her that he only wanted female tenants.

"We have to be careful about the kid thing, we don't want to get reported to the rental board for discrimination," the realtor warned her. "But I'll keep it in mind when I show it. These are both pretty sophisticated rentals, and the rent is a pretty big ticket. That will keep out the riffraff," unless of course they rented it to rock stars. That was always a less predictable element, and the realtor had had some problems with them, as everyone else had.

The real estate agent left the property shortly after noon, and Liz drove back to her own apartment, after checking that everything was all right at the main house. All of the staff were still somewhat in shock after being given notice by Abe the previous afternoon, but given the irregularity of their paychecks, it wasn't totally unexpected. Livermore had already announced that he was going to Monte Carlo, to work for an Arab prince. He'd been hounded by him for months, and had called that morning to accept the job that had been a standing offer to him. He didn't seem particularly upset to be leaving Coop, and if he was, as usual, he showed no sign of it. He was flying to the South of

France the following weekend, which was going to be a major blow to Coop.

Later that afternoon, Coop came back to the house with Pamela. They'd had a long lunch and sat at the Beverly Hills Hotel pool, chatting with some of Coop's friends, all of them major Hollywood figures. Pamela couldn't believe the crowd she was suddenly traveling in, and she was so impressed she could hardly speak when they left the hotel, and came back to The Cottage. They were in bed together half an hour later, with a bucket of Cristal chilling at his bedside. The cook served them dinner in bed on trays, and at Pamela's insistence, they watched videos of two of his old films. And he drove her home afterwards, because he had an appointment with his trainer and acupuncturist early the next morning. Besides which, he preferred to sleep alone. Even sleeping with a beautiful young woman in his bed sometimes disturbed his sleep.

By the next morning, the realtor had prepared two folders with all the details of both rentals. She got on the phone bright and early, and called several of her clients who were looking for unusual rentals. She set up three appointments to show the gatehouse to bachelors, and another to show the guest wing to a young couple who had just moved to LA and were remodeling a house that was going to take at least another year, if not two, to finish. And shortly after that, her phone rang. It was Jimmy.

He sounded serious and quiet on the phone, and explained that he was looking for a rental. He didn't care where, just something small and easy to manage, with a decent kitchen. He wasn't cooking these days, but he realized that at some point he might like to start again. Other than sports, it was one of the few things that relaxed him. He also didn't care whether or not the place was furnished. He and Maggie had the basics, in terms of furniture, but they hadn't loved any of it, and he wouldn't have minded leaving it all in storage. In some ways, he thought it might remind him less of her, and be less painful, if even the furniture was different. In fact, as he thought about it, he realized he preferred it. The only reminder of Maggie he was taking with him were their pictures. Everything else that had been hers he was boxing up and putting away, so he didn't have to look at it every day.

The realtor asked if he had a preference of location, but he didn't. Hollywood, Beverly Hills, LA, Malibu. He said he liked the ocean, but that would remind him of her too. Everything did. It would have been hard to find something that didn't.

And when he didn't make a point about price, the realtor decided to take a chance, and told him about the gatehouse. She didn't mention the price to him, but described it, and after a moment's hesitation, he said he'd like to see it. She made an appointment with him for five o'clock that afternoon, and then asked him what part of town he worked in.

"Watts," he said, sounding distracted, and as though to him there was nothing unusual about it, but the realtor looked instantly startled at her end.

"Oh. I see." She wondered if he was African American, but obviously couldn't ask him, and also wondered if he could afford the rent. "Do you have a budget, Mr. O'Connor?"

"Not really," he said quietly and then glanced at his watch. He had to run to an appointment with a family about two of their foster children. "I'll see you at five then." But she was no longer quite so certain that he'd be the right tenant. Someone who worked in Watts was not going to be able to afford Cooper Winslow's gatehouse. And when she saw him late that afternoon, she was certain of it.

Jimmy arrived driving the beat-up Honda Civic that Maggie had insisted they buy, although he had wanted to spring for something a lot more jazzy when they moved to California. He had tried to explain to her that living in California was all about having a great car, but in the end, as usual, she convinced him otherwise. There was no way they could do the kind of work they did, and drive an expensive car, no matter how easily he could afford it. The fact that he came from money, very old money, and quite a lot of it, had always remained a well-kept secret, even among their friends.

He was wearing worn jeans with frayed edges and a torn knee, a faded Harvard sweatshirt that he'd had for a dozen years, and a battered pair of workboots. But in the places where he visited families, there were often rats and he didn't want to get bitten. But in contrast to his clothes, he was clean shaven, intelligent, obviously well educated, and had a recent haircut. He was an interesting conglomeration of conflicting elements, which confused the agent completely.

"What sort of work do you do, Mr. O'Connor?" she

asked chattily as she unlocked the door to the gate-house. She had already shown it three times that afternoon, but the first man she'd shown it to said it was too small, the second one thought it was too isolated, and the third one really wanted an apartment. So it was still free and clear, although she was certain now that Jimmy couldn't afford it. Not on a social worker's wages. But she had to show it to him anyway.

As they came through the hedge, she heard him catch his breath. It looked like an Irish cottage, and reminded him of the trips to Ireland he'd taken with Maggie. And the moment he stepped into the living room, he felt as though he could have been in Ireland or England. It was a perfect little house for a bachelor, it had a manly, unpretentious, unfussy feel to it, and he seemed pleased when he saw the kitchen. And he seemed satisfied with the bedroom too. But what he said he liked most of all was the feeling that he was out in the country somewhere. Unlike the man who had seen it that afternoon, he liked the isolation. It suited his mood.

"Will your wife want to see it?" the realtor asked, probing delicately to see if he was married. He was a good-looking guy, in great shape, and as she glanced at the sweatshirt, she wondered if he actually had gone to Harvard, or just bought the shirt at the Goodwill.

"No, she . . ." he started to say in answer to the question about his wife, and then didn't. "I'm . . . I'd be living here alone." He still couldn't bring himself to say "widowed." It sliced right through his heart like a knife each time he tried it. And "single" sounded pathetic and dishonest. At times, he still wanted to say he was married. He would have still been wearing his wedding band if he'd had one. Maggie had never given him one, and the one she'd worn had been buried with her. "I like it," he said quietly, walking through all the rooms again, and opening all the closets. Being on the estate seemed a little grand to him, but he wondered if he could tell people he was housesitting, or paid to work on the grounds, if he brought anyone home from work.

There were a lot of stories he could tell if he had to, and had over the years. But what he liked best about it was that he knew Maggie would have loved it. It was just her kind of place, although she would never have agreed to live there, because she couldn't afford her share. It made him smile, thinking of it, and he was tempted to take it. But he decided to wait and sleep on the decision, and promised to call the realtor the next day. "I'd like to think about it," he said, as they left, and she was sure he was just saving face. From his car and his clothes and his job, she knew he couldn't afford it. But he seemed like a nice man, and she was pleasant to him. You never knew who you were dealing with. She had been in the business long enough to know that. Sometimes the people who looked the least reputable or the most poverty stricken turned out to be the heirs of enormous fortunes. She had learned that early on in the business, so she was gracious to him.

As Jimmy drove home, he thought about the gatehouse. It was a beautiful little place, and it seemed like a peaceful retreat from the world. He would have loved to live there with Maggie, and wondered if that would bother him. It was hard to know what was best anymore. There was nowhere he could hide from his sorrow. And when he got home, he went back to his packing, just to distract himself. The apartment was already fairly empty. He made himself a bowl of soup, and sat staring silently out the window.

He lay awake for most of the night, thinking about Maggie, about what she would advise him. He had thought of taking an apartment on the edge of Watts, which would be practical certainly, and the dangers didn't alarm him particularly. Or maybe just an ordinary apartment somewhere in LA. But as he lay in bed that night, he couldn't stop thinking about the gatehouse. He could afford it, and he knew she would have loved it. He wondered if, for once in his life, he should indulge himself. And he liked the story about working on the grounds of the estate in exchange for reduced rent at the gatehouse. It seemed a plausible story. And besides, he loved the kitchen, the living room and fireplace, and garden all around him.

He called the realtor on her cell phone at eight in the morning, while he was shaving. "I'll take it." He actually smiled as he said it. It was the first time he had smiled in weeks, but he was suddenly excited about the gatehouse. It was perfect for him.

"You will?" She sounded startled. She'd been sure she wouldn't hear from him again, and she wondered if he had understood the price when she quoted it to him. "It's ten thousand dollars a month, Mr. O'Connor. That won't be a problem?" She didn't have the guts to quote him more than that, and she'd been beginning to wonder if it was going to be harder to rent than she had thought. It had a very definite and most unusual flavor.

It wasn't for everyone, living in isolation on an estate, but he seemed to love that about it.

"It'll be fine," he reassured her. "Do I need to drop off a check to secure it, or a deposit?" Now that he'd made up his mind, he didn't want to lose it.

"Well, no ... I ... we'll have to do a reference check first." She was sure that would do him in, but by law, she had to go through the process, no matter how ineligible he seemed.

"I don't want to lose it if someone else comes along in the meantime." He sounded worried. He was no longer as casual about life as he had been. He noticed lately that he got anxious more easily, about things that before he'd never even thought of. Maggie had always done all the worrying for him, now it was all his.

"I'll hold it for you, of course. You have first rights on it."

"How long will the reference check take?"

"No more than a few days. The banks are a little slow with credit checks these days."

"I'll tell you what, why don't you call my banker?" He gave her the name of the head of private banking at BofA. "Maybe he can move things along a little faster." Jimmy was always discreet, but he also knew that once she called him, things would move like greased lightning. His credit was not an issue, and had never been.

"I'll be happy to do that, Mr. O'Connor. Is there a number where I can reach you today?"

He gave her his office number, and told her to leave a message on his voice mail if he was out, and he'd call her back as soon as he got it. "I'll be in all morning."

He had a mountain of paperwork on his desk. And at ten o'clock that morning, she called him.

The credit check had gone exactly as he'd expected. She called the head of private banking, as a matter of routine, and the moment she said Jimmy's name, she was told that without question, there was no problem. His credit was excellent, and they were not able to disclose his balances, but they were of an amount as to put him in the upper echelons of their clients was all they could say.

"Is he buying a house?" the banker asked with interest. He hoped he was, although he didn't say it. After Jimmy's recent tragedy, he would have seen it as a hopeful sign, and he could certainly afford it. If he'd wanted to, he could have bought The Cottage. But he didn't mention that to the realtor.

"No, he's renting a gatehouse. It's quite expensive," she said, just trying to reconfirm what he'd told her, and to make sure there was no misunderstanding. "Ten thousand a month, and we'll need first and last months' rent, and a twenty-five-thousand-dollar security deposit." Once again, he assured her there was no problem. It aroused her curiosity and in a rare burst of indiscretion, she asked him a question. "Who is he?"

"Exactly who he says he is. James Thomas O'Connor. He's one of our most solid clients." It was all he would tell her, and she was more than a little intrigued.

"I was a little concerned because, as a social worker, of course . . . it's a little unusual to pay such a high rent."

"It's a shame there aren't more people like him. Is there anything else I can tell you?"

"Would you mind faxing me a letter?"

"Not at all. Do you need us to issue a check on his behalf, or is he going to do it himself?"

"I'll ask him," she said, as she realized that she had just rented Cooper Winslow's gatehouse. She called Jimmy back, told him the good news, and told him he could have the gatehouse and the keys as soon as he wanted. He promised to drop a check off to her at lunchtime, and told her he wouldn't be moving in for another few weeks, until he vacated his current apartment. He wanted to hang on to the last of Maggie for as long as he could, but he was suddenly excited about the gatehouse. And he knew that wherever he went, he would take her with him.

"I hope you'll be very happy there, Mr. O'Connor. It's a gem of a house. And I'm sure you'll enjoy meeting Mr. Winslow."

As he hung up, he laughed thinking of what Maggie would have said about having a movie star as their landlord. But for once, he was going to indulge in doing something a little crazy. And somehow, in his heart of hearts, he had the feeling that Maggie would not only have approved, she would have loved it for him.

Chapter 5

Mark had had another nightmarish night, nearly without sleep, when he arrived at his office the next morning. And almost moments after he got there, his phone rang. It was Abe Braunstein.

"I'm so damn sorry about what you told me yesterday," Abe said sympathetically. He had been thinking about him the night before, and then suddenly wondered if he was looking for an apartment. He couldn't stay in a hotel forever. "I had a crazy idea last night. I don't know if you're looking for a place to live, or what your needs are, but there's a very unusual place that just came on the market. One of my clients is renting out his guest wing, Cooper Winslow. He's gotten himself in a hell of a bind, of course that's confidential. He's got a fantastic estate in Bel Air, and quite a house. He's renting out his gatehouse, and his guest wing. They started showing both yesterday, and I don't think they're rented yet. I just thought I'd mention it, because it might be a terrific place to live, kind of like being in a country club. Maybe you'd like to see it."

"I haven't given it much thought," Mark said honestly. He really wasn't ready, although living on Cooper

Winslow's Bel Air estate had a certain ring to it, and it might be a great environment for his kids when they came out to visit.

"If you want, I'll pick you up at lunchtime and drive you out to see it. If nothing else, it's worth a look as a tourist. It's quite a place. Tennis courts, swimming pool, fourteen acres of garden in the middle of the city."

"I'd love to see it." He didn't want to be rude to Abe, but he wasn't in the mood to look for apartments, even on Cooper Winslow's estate, but he thought maybe he should, just in case it would be good for the kids.

"I'll pick you up at twelve-thirty. I'll call the realtor and have her meet us out there. It's pricey, but I think you can afford it." He smiled, knowing that Mark was one of the firm's highest-earning partners. Tax law was not exciting, but it had been profitable for him, although nothing about Mark was ostentatious. He drove a Mercedes, but other than that, he was down to earth, and very unassuming, and always had been.

For the rest of the morning, Mark forgot about it. He thought it was a long shot that he would like the guest wing at The Cottage. He was going to see it mostly out of courtesy to Abe, he had nothing else to do at lunchtime. Now that he hardly ever ate, he had more time on his hands. His clothes were hanging off him.

Abe arrived at the office on schedule, and told Mark that the realtor was meeting them at The Cottage in fifteen minutes. And for the entire drive they talked about a new tax law that seemed to have some loopholes in it that interested both of them, so much so that

Mark looked up in surprise when they got to the main gate. The Cottage had a very imposing entrance. Abe knew the code, and let himself in, and they drove along the winding drive through trees, and endless manicured gardens, and Mark laughed out loud when he saw the house. He couldn't even imagine living in a house like that, it looked like a palace to him.

"My God, does he actually live there?" There were marble pillars and marble steps, and an enormous fountain that reminded him of the Place de la Concorde in Paris.

"It was built for Vera Harper. Winslow's had it for over forty years. It costs him an absolute fortune to run."

"I can imagine. How much staff does he have?"

"At the moment, close to twenty. In two weeks, one in the house, and three gardeners. He has eight at the moment. He calls it my scorched-earth policy, and he's not too happy about it. I'm forcing him to sell the cars too, if you need a Rolls or a Bentley. He's an interesting guy, but about as spoiled as they come. I hate to admit it, but the place suits him. We have kind of an armed truce between us." Abe was everything that Coop wasn't, practical, down to earth, frugal, he didn't have an ounce of elegance or style, but he had more compassion than Coop suspected, which was why he was bringing Mark out to see the house. He felt sorry for him, and wanted to help him. He'd never seen the guest wing himself, but Liz had told him it was terrific, and she was right.

Mark whistled as the realtor let him in. He looked up in amazement at the high ceilings, and out the

French windows with pleasure. The gardens were absolutely beautiful. He felt as though he were in an old French château, and the furniture was very handsome too. The kitchen was a little antiquated, but he didn't really care, and as the realtor pointed out, it was warm and cozy. And he was amused by the grandeur of the master bedroom. Blue satin was not what he would have chosen for his bedroom, but it was certainly glamorous, and for a year, while he figured out what he was doing with his life, this would be an easy solution. And the grounds were wonderfully safe and protected for his children. It had a lot to recommend it. He had been thinking lately about moving back to New York to be near his kids, but he didn't want to encroach on Janet, and he had a lot of clients in LA who counted on him. The one thing Mark didn't want to do was make a hasty decision. And having a place to live was one way not to. He would have a home again, even if it wasn't his own. And it was a lot less depressing than living in a hotel, lying awake at night, listening to people flush toilets and slam doors.

"This is quite something." He smiled at Abe, and felt like an innocent as he looked around. It never even dawned on him that people lived this way. His own house had been comfortable and well decorated, but the guest wing looked like a movie set. If nothing else, it would be amusing, and fun to live there. And he had a feeling that his kids would love it when they came to visit, particularly the tennis courts and the pool. "I'm glad you brought me out here." He smiled gratefully at Abe.

"I thought of it last night, and I figured it was worth a look. You can't live in a hotel forever." He had given all his furniture to Janet, so the fact that it was furnished, and so handsomely, was a no-brainer for him. In a lot of ways, it was perfect for Mark.

"How much is it?" Mark asked the realtor.

"Ten thousand a month," she said, without batting an eye. "But there's nothing else like it. A lot of people would pay ten times that just to be here. The Cottage is a unique property, and so is the guest wing. I just rented the gatehouse to a very nice young man this morning."

"Really?" Abe commented with interest. "Anyone we've ever heard of?" He was used to celebrities and the movie stars who were his clients and Coop's friends.

"Actually, no, I don't think so. He's a social worker," she said primly, and Abe looked surprised.

"Can he afford it?" As Coop's accountant, he had a vested interest in asking her those questions. They didn't want to get someone in who couldn't pay the rent.

"Apparently. The head of private banking at BofA says he's one of their most solid clients. He sent me a fax to that effect about ten minutes after I spoke to him, and the tenant dropped off a check for first, last, and security, as I was walking out of the office to come here. I'm dropping the lease off to him tonight. He lives in Venice Beach."

"Interesting," Abe commented, and then turned his attention back to Mark, who was investigating the closets. There were more than he needed. But he particularly liked the two bedrooms for the children, and he thought his kids would love the place. It was elegant and glamorous, but still comfortable, and it was all done in beautiful taste.

Mark was pondering the rent as he looked around, but he knew he could afford it. He just didn't know if he wanted to spend that much on rent. If he did, it would be the first outrageous thing he'd done for himself in an entire lifetime, but maybe it was time for him to do something outrageous. Janet had. She had walked right out the door into the arms of another man. All he was doing was renting an expensive apartment for a year, but one that he would really enjoy living in. He might even start sleeping decently again, on the peaceful grounds. He could swim laps in the pool when he came home from the office, or play tennis, if he could find a partner. He couldn't imagine inviting Cooper Winslow to play with him. "Is he ever around?" he asked the realtor with interest.

"Apparently he travels a great deal, which is why he wants tenants, so there are people living full-time on the property, and not just servants." It was the party line, and Abe recognized instantly that it was probably what Liz had told her. She was always so diplomatic, and so protective of Coop's reputation. Abe didn't want to tell the realtor that there would no longer be servants living there in two weeks.

"That makes sense," Mark nodded. "It's good security for him." But he also knew what Abe had told him in confidence about Coop's financial situation. They shared a lot of information like that about their clients.

"Are you married, Mr. Friedman?" the realtor asked him politely. She wanted to make sure that he didn't have ten children, but that looked unlikely. And the fact that Coop's own accountant had brought him there meant that he didn't need any intense scrutiny in the screening process, which was simpler for all concerned.

"I...uh...no...I'm getting divorced." It nearly choked him to say it.

"Do your children live with you?"

"No, they live in New York." It broke his heart to say that too. "I'm going to be going back to see them as often as possible. They can only come out here during their vacations. And you know how kids are, they want to stay close to their friends. I'll be lucky if they come out once a year," he said sadly. But the realtor was relieved, after Liz's warning that Coop wasn't anxious for tenants with children. He was a perfect candidate, a single man, with children who weren't even in the same city, and would hardly ever come to visit. You couldn't ask for better. And he was obviously solvent, if Abe had brought him. And then, as he walked back into the living room, he blurted out, "I'll take it." Even Abe looked startled, but Mark was beaming, and the realtor was delighted. In the two first days on the market, she had rented both of Coop's properties, and at a very decent price. She thought ten thousand was fair for each of them, and Liz had said Coop would be satisfied if she got that much for them. She hadn't wanted to push any higher. And Mark looked ecstatic. Suddenly, he couldn't wait to get out of the hotel, and move in. The realtor told him he could occupy it within a few days, as soon as the credit check was complete, they got his check, and she gave him the keys. Liz had told her she wanted to have both facilities professionally cleaned for the tenants, which she mentioned to him.

"I think I'll move in this weekend," he said happily, as he and the realtor shook hands on the deal, and he thanked Abe profusely for bringing him to see it.

"That was a lot easier and more productive than I expected it to be, and faster." Abe smiled happily as they drove back down the driveway. He had expected him to agonize and have a tougher time making the decision.

"It's probably the craziest thing I've ever done, but maybe I need to be a little crazy once in a while," Mark volunteered. He was always so serious and so responsible, so measured in everything he did. He wondered now if that was why he had lost Janet to another man, who was probably more exciting. "Thanks, Abe. I love the place, and I think my kids will too. We're going to get awfully spoiled living here for a year."

"It'll do you good for a while," Abe said compassionately.

That night Mark called Jessica and Jason in New York, and told them about the guest wing he'd rented from Coop.

"Who's he?" Jason asked, sounding blank.

"I think he's some really old guy who was in movies when Dad was a kid," Jessica explained.

"That's about right," Mark said, sounding pleased. "But the main thing is it's a great house, and we have our own wing, on beautiful grounds, with a tennis court and a pool. I think it'll be fun for you two when you come out." All three of them were on the phone at the same time.

"I miss our old house," Jason said, sounding glum.

"I hate my school," Jessica chimed in. "All the girls are mean, and all the boys are geeks."

"Give it time," Mark said diplomatically. It hadn't been his idea to end the marriage, or move the kids to New York. But he didn't want to say anything critical about their mother. He preferred to keep whatever animosity they felt toward each other between them. It seemed better for the kids. "It takes time to get used to a new school. And I'm going to see you soon." He was flying to New York for a weekend, in February. They had reservations in Saint Bart's in March for their spring break. And he was thinking about chartering a small boat for their Caribbean holiday. He was trying to break out of his familiar mold. "How's Mom?"

"She's okay, she goes out a lot," Jason complained, but they hadn't said a word yet about the new man. Mark was sure she hadn't introduced them to him yet. She was waiting for things to settle down. They had only been there for three weeks, nearly four. It wasn't a long time, although it felt like an eternity to him.

"Why can't we keep our old house?" Jessica asked mournfully, and when he told her it had just sold, they both cried. It was yet another conversation that ended on an unhappy note. They had a lot of those. And Jessica always seemed to be looking for someone to blame, mostly him. She still hadn't figured out that her mother had wanted the divorce. And Mark didn't want to point the finger at her. He was waiting for Janet to step up to the plate and take responsibility for it herself, but so far she hadn't. She had just told them that she and Daddy hadn't been getting along, which was a lie. They'd been fine, until Adam came along. Mark wondered how she was going to sell him to the kids, maybe as someone she'd just met. It was probably going to be years before they figured it out, if they ever did, which depressed him too. His children were going to go on blaming him forever for causing the divorce. And one of his worst fears was that his kids were going to be as crazy about Adam as their mother was, and then they would forget him. He was three thousand miles away, in Los Angeles, and he couldn't see them as often as he liked. He could hardly wait for their vacation in Saint Bart's. He had chosen it because he thought it would be fun for them, and for him too.

He promised to call them the next day, as he always did. And he gave the hotel notice that night that he was moving out on the weekend. He could hardly wait. He loved his new digs. It was the first cheerful thing that had happened to him since Janet had hit him with the news. He felt like he'd been in shock for the last five weeks. And that night, he went out and ate a hamburger before he went to bed. For the first time in weeks, he was actually hungry.

He packed his clothes into two suitcases on Friday night, and on Saturday morning, he drove to the estate. He had the code to the gate and opened it, and when he let himself into the guest wing, it was immaculately clean. Everything had been vacuumed and dusted, and the furniture shone. The kitchen was spotless and there were clean sheets on his bed. And for a surprisingly long moment, it felt like coming home.

After he'd unpacked, he took a walk around the grounds. They were beautifully tended. He went out and bought groceries, and fixed himself lunch, and afterwards he went to lie beside the pool, to soak up some sun. He was in great spirits that afternoon when he called the children. It was the end of the day for them, on a snowy Saturday in New York. And both kids sounded bored. They were tired of being shut in. Jessica was going out with friends that night, but Jason said he had nothing to do. He missed his dad, and his house, and his friends, and his school. There was apparently nothing he liked about New York.

"Hang in, sport, I'm coming to see you in two weeks. We'll find something to do. Have you played any soccer this week?" Mark chatted with him, and Jason continued to complain.

"We can never play because of the snow." Jason hated New York. He was a California kid, and had lived there since he was three. He didn't even remember living in New York before. All he wanted to do was go back to California, which still felt like home to him.

They talked for a while longer, and then Mark finally got off. He checked out where things were in the kitchen, and put a video on that night, and he was amused to see that Cooper Winslow had a walk-on part in it. He was certainly a good-looking man, and Mark wondered when and if they'd meet. He had seen someone drive in behind him in a Rolls-Royce convertible that afternoon, but he was just far enough ahead that all he could see was a man with silver hair, presumably Coop, and a pretty girl next to him in the front seat. Mark realized Coop had a far more interesting life than he. After sixteen years being faithfully married, he couldn't even imagine what it would be like to start dating again, and had no desire to. He had too much on his mind, too many memories, too many regrets, and all he could think about were his kids. For the moment, there was no room for a woman in his life. Room maybe, but no heart. He was just grateful that when he went to bed that night, he slept like a baby, and woke up happy the next morning after dreaming that his children were living with him. That would in fact have made it a perfect life for him. But in the meantime, what he had was an improvement over his room at the hotel. And he'd be seeing them in two weeks. It was something to look forward to, and all he needed now.

He went to cook himself breakfast, and was surprised to discover that the kitchen stove didn't work. He made a note to call the realtor about it, but he didn't really care. He was just as happy with orange juice and toast. He wasn't much of a cook, except when the kids were around, he would cook for them.

And in the main part of the house, Coop was making similar discoveries. His cook had left earlier that week, after finding another job. Livermore was already gone. And both maids were off for the weekend, and leaving the following week. The houseman was already working for someone else. And Paloma didn't come in on weekends. Pamela was cooking breakfast for him, wearing bikini underwear and one of his shirts. She claimed to be a whiz in the kitchen, as witnessed by a mound of rock-hard scrambled eggs and burnt bacon she handed him on a plate in bed.

"Aren't you a clever girl," he said admiringly, with a look of concern as he glanced at the eggs. "I take it you couldn't find the trays?"

"What trays, darlin'?" she asked in her Oklahoma drawl. She was very proud of herself, and had forgotten napkins and silverware. She went back to get them as Coop used a cautious finger to poke the eggs. They were not only hard, but cold. She'd been talking to a girlfriend on the phone while she cooked. Cooking had never been her strong suit, but what she did in bed with him was, and he was pleased. The only problem was, she couldn't talk. Except about her hair, and her makeup and her moisturizer, and the last photo shoot she'd been on. She was extremely limited, but it wasn't her conversation which fascinated him. He just liked being with her. There was something very invigorating about young girls. He had a marvelous way with women her age, he was debonair and fun and worldly-wise and sophisticated, and besides which, he took her shopping nearly every day. She had never had as much fun in her life as she was having with Coop. She didn't care how old he was. She had a whole new wardrobe, and he'd bought her diamond earrings and a diamond bracelet the week before. There was no question about it. Cooper Winslow knew how to live.

He flushed the eggs down the toilet when she went back downstairs to get him a glass of orange juice, and she was proud to see that he had eaten everything.

And as soon as she ate hers, he brought her back to bed with him, where they spent the afternoon. And that night, he took her to Le Dome for dinner. She loved going to Spago with him too. It was a real thrill for her to see everyone stare at them as they recognized him and wanted to see who he was with. Men looked at him enviously, and women raised an eyebrow as they looked at them, and Pamela liked that too.

He drove her back to her apartment that night, after dinner. He'd had a fun weekend with her, but he had a busy week ahead. He was shooting a car commercial, which was a big deal, and they were paying him handsomely for it, and it was going to be Liz's last week.

Coop was actually happy to climb into his bed alone that night. Pamela was a lot of fun, but after a while, she was just a kid. And he no longer was. He needed his beauty sleep. He went to bed at ten o'clock, and slept like a rock, until Paloma threw back the curtains and lifted the shades the next day. He woke up with a start, and sat up staring at her.

"Why on earth are you doing that?" He couldn't imagine what she was doing in his room, and was relieved to note that he'd put on silk pajamas the night before. Otherwise he might have been sprawled naked across his bed. "What are you doing in here?" She was wearing a clean uniform, this time with rhinestone sunglasses, and bright red high-heeled shoes. She looked like a combination between a nurse in the white uniform, and a gypsy fortune-teller, and he wasn't amused.

"Miss Liz said to wake ju up at eight o'clock," she

said, glaring at him. She had a powerful dislike for him and it showed. And Coop hated her too.

"Couldn't you knock on the door?" he barked at her, falling back into his bed with his eyes closed. She had woken him from a sound sleep.

"I try. Ju don' answer. So I come in. Now ju wake up. Miss Liz say ju gotta go to work."

"Thank you very much," he said formally, his eyes still closed. "Would you mind making me breakfast?" There was no one else now who could. "I'll have scrambled eggs and rye toast. Orange juice. Black coffee. Thank you."

She was muttering to herself as she left the room, and Coop groaned. This was going to be a painful alliance, he realized with total clarity. Why in hell did she have to be the one they kept? Couldn't they have kept one of the others? No, of course not, he complained to himself . . . she was cheap. But he had to admit, twenty minutes later when he came out of the shower, and found his breakfast sitting on a tray on his bed, the eggs were good. Better than Pamela's. That was something at least, although she had made huevos rancheros instead of scrambled eggs. He would have complained about her not cooking what he'd asked for, but they were delicious and he devoured it all.

Half an hour later, he was out the door, impeccably dressed, as usual, in a blazer, gray slacks and blue shirt, a navy blue Hermès tie, and his hair as beautifully groomed as it always was. He was a vision of elegance and sophistication as he slipped into his old Rolls, and drove off. And Mark followed him down the drive, on his way to work. He wondered where

Coop was going at that hour, and couldn't imagine it. He was alone for once, which was unusual for him, but so was leaving the house at that hour.

Liz passed them both on the way in, and waved at Coop. She still couldn't believe this was her last week.

Chapter 6

Liz's last days in Coop's employ had a bittersweet quality to them. He had never been as sweet to her, or as generous. He gave her a diamond ring that he said had been his mother's, which was one of those stories she was always skeptical of. But whosever ring it had been, it was beautiful and fit her perfectly, and she promised him she would always wear it and think of him.

He took her to Spago on Friday night, and she had too much to drink, and by the time he dropped her off at her house, she was crying about how miserable she was going to be without him. But he had resigned himself to her departure by then, reassured her that she was doing the right thing, left her at her place and drove home, where he had a new flame waiting for him. Pamela was on location for a magazine in Milan. And he had met Charlene while doing the car commercial he'd just done. She was a spectacular-looking woman, and at twenty-nine, she was old for him. But she had the most extraordinary body he'd ever seen, and he'd seen many of them. Hers was worthy of the Cooper Winslow Hall of Fame.

Charlene had enormous breasts that she insisted were real, and a waist he could circle with both hands. She had long jet-black hair, and she had enormous cat-like green eyes. She said her grandmother was Japanese. She was an amazing-looking girl, and she had been completely bowled over by him. She was more intelligent than Pamela, which was something of a relief. Charlene had lived in Paris for two years, modeling on the side, and going to the Sorbonne, and she had grown up in Brazil. She was a wonderful mélange of international flavors, and she had gone to bed with him by the second day of the shoot. Coop had had a very good week.

He had invited her to spend the weekend with him, and she had accepted with a squeal of delight. He was already thinking of going to the Hotel du Cap with her. She would look fabulous with her top off at the pool. She was in his bed when he got home after his dinner with Liz, and he joined her without ceremony. They spent a very interesting, somewhat acrobatic, night together, and on Saturday they drove to Santa Barbara for lunch, and came home in time for dinner at L'Orangerie. He was enjoying her company, and he was beginning to think it was time to kiss Pamela goodbye. Charlene had a lot more to offer, and she was a more sensible age for him.

She was still there on Monday morning, when Paloma arrived for work. Coop asked her to bring trays for both of them, which she did with a sullen expression of disapproval. She glared at Coop, slammed the trays down on the bed, and stalked out of the room in bright pink high heels. The accessories she wore with her uniform always fascinated him.

"She doesn't like me," Charlene said, looking crestfallen. "I think she disapproves."

"Don't worry about it. She's madly in love with me. Don't be afraid if she makes a jealous scene," he said sarcastically, as they dug into what appeared to be rubber eggs, covered with a thick layer of pepper which made Coop choke and Charlene sneeze. It was a far cry from the huevos rancheros she'd made him the week before. Paloma had won this round, but Coop was determined to have a word with her after Charlene left, and by then it was early afternoon.

"That was an interesting breakfast you served this morning, Paloma." Coop stood in the kitchen, looking coolly at her. "The pepper was a nice touch, but unnecessary. I needed a buzz saw to cut through the eggs. What did you make them with? Rubber cement, or just ordinary paper glue?"

"I donnow what ju talkin' about," she said cryptically, polishing a piece of silver that Livermore had told her had to be polished every week. She was wearing the rhinestone sunglasses again. They were obviously her favorites, and were becoming Coop's too. He was wondering if there was even a remote possibility of bringing her to heel. If not, he was going to have to replace her, no matter what Abe said. "Ju don' like my eggs?" she asked angelically, as he scowled at her.

"You know what I mean."

"Miss Pamela called from Italy this morning, at eight o'clock," Paloma announced nonchalantly, and as she did, Coop stared. Her accent had suddenly disappeared.

"What did you just say?" It wasn't so much what as how.

"I said..." she looked up at him with an innocent grin, "Mees Pamela called ju at eight o'clock." The dialect was back again. She was playing games with him.

"That's not how you said it a minute ago, is it, Paloma? What's the point of all that?" He was visibly annoyed, and she looked a little sheepish, and then covered it with bravado and a shrug.

"Isn't that what you expect? You called me Maria for the first two months I was here." He could still hear the echo of San Salvador, but only faintly, and her English was almost as good as his.

"We hadn't been properly introduced," he excused himself. And although he wouldn't have admitted it to her, he was faintly amused. She had figured she would hide from him by pretending to be barely able to speak English. He suspected she was not only smart, but probably a damn good cook too. "What did you do in your country, Paloma?" He was suddenly intrigued by her. As irritating as she was, she was becoming a human being to him, and he wasn't sure he wanted to be burdened with that. But nonetheless, his curiosity got the best of him.

"I was a nurse," she said, still polishing the silver. It was a loathsome task, and she missed Livermore almost as much as Coop.

"That's too bad," Coop said with a grin, "I was hoping you were going to tell me you were a tailor or a dressmaker. At least then you could take proper care of my clothes. Fortunately, I am not in need of your nursing skills."

"I make more money here. And ju have too many clothes," she said, donning the accent again, like a garment she put on and off at will. It was like playing peekaboo with him.

"Thank you for that piece of editorial commentary. You have some interesting accessories yourself," he said as he glanced down at the pink shoes. "Why didn't you tell me Pamela called, by the way?" He had already decided to make a switch in paramours. But he always remained friends with the previous ones. And he was generous enough that they always forgave him his vagaries and his sins. He was sure Pamela would.

"You were busy with the other one when she called. What's her name." The accent was gone again.

"Charlene," he supplied, and Paloma looked vague. "Thank you, Paloma," Coop said quietly and decided to quit while he was ahead, and left the room. She never wrote a single message down, and only told him about them when she thought of it, which worried him. But she seemed to know who the players were. So far, at least. And she was becoming a more interesting character herself day by day.

Paloma had met Mark the previous week, and she had offered to do some laundry for him, when he told her the washing machine in the guest wing was out of order. And the stove still was too. She had told him that he could use the kitchen in the main house if he needed to. She said Coop never came down to the kitchen himself in the morning, and she gave him a key to the connecting door between the main house and the guest wing. The espresso machine in the guest wing was broken too. Mark had made a list of all of it, and the realtor had promised him it would all be repaired, but with Liz gone, there was no one to take care of it, except Coop himself, which wasn't likely to happen, they both knew. Mark was taking his clothes out to be laundered, and Paloma was doing sheets and towels for him, and with the use of Coop's espresso machine on the weekends, he had no other needs. He was using the microwave instead of the stove, and the only time he'd need the stove would be when he had the kids. He was sure it would be fixed by then, even if he had to take care of it himself, and he told the realtor he was willing to. She said she would see what she could do. But Coop never returned any of her calls, or his. And Coop was scheduled to do another commercial that week, for a brand of chewing gum. It was a ridiculous ad, but the pay was decent enough so his agent had talked him into it. He was working more than usual these days, although no features had surfaced yet. His agent had been beating the bushes for him to no avail. His reputation was too well known in Hollywood, and given the kind of parts he wanted to play, romantic leads, leading men, he was simply too old. He wasn't ready to play fathers or grandfathers yet. And there hadn't been any demand for aging playboys in years.

Charlene stayed at The Cottage with him almost every night that week. She was trying to get work as an actress, but she got even less work than Coop. And the only work she had done so far since she'd come to Hollywood were two X-rated videos, one of which had been shown on TV at 4 A.M. And her agent had finally convinced her that neither of them would look good on her C.V. She had already asked Coop if he could talk to anyone about getting work for her, and he'd said he would see what he could do. She had started out as a lingerie model on Seventh Avenue, after similar modeling in Paris, and she had a fabulous body for that, but he wasn't even sure if she could act, and seriously doubted it. She claimed to have modeled in Paris extensively, but she could never seem to find her book. Her real skills were in an area that was far more appealing to Coop, and had nothing to do with acting, modeling, or TV.

He was enjoying her company immensely. And he was relieved when Pamela told him when she got back from Milan that she'd gotten involved with the photographer on the shoot. Those things had a way of working themselves out, particularly in Coop's world. It was all about bodies and temporary alliances and quick affairs. It was only when he went out with famous actresses that he encouraged the rumors about engagements and wedding bells. But he wanted none of that with Charlene. She was all about having a good time, and seeing that he had fun too. He'd already been on two major shopping sprees with her, which had eaten both checks his tenants had given him, but he thought she deserved it, as he explained to Abe when the accountant called and warned him he'd have to sell the house if he didn't behave.

"You'd better give up starving models and actresses, Coop. You need to find a rich wife." Coop laughed at him and said he'd give it some thought, but marriage had never appealed to Coop. All he wanted to do was play, and that's what he was going to do, or planned to anyway, until his dying day.

The following weekend Mark went to New York to see his kids. He had told Paloma all about them by then. She had done a little cleaning for him, and he'd paid her handsomely. She would have done it for him anyway. She felt sorry for him when he told her his wife had left him for another man, and she started leaving fresh fruit in a bowl on his kitchen table, and some tortillas she'd made. She liked hearing about his kids. It was easy to see he was crazy about them. There were photographs of them all over the place, and others of him and his wife.

But in spite of that, it was a challenging weekend. It was the first time Mark had seen the children since they'd left LA more than a month before. Janet said he should have given them more time to settle in before he came, and she seemed nervous and hostile to him. She was leading a double life, pretending to be unattached when she was with the kids, and continuing her clandestine affair. And Adam wanted to know when he was going to meet her kids. She had promised him it would be soon, but she didn't want them to figure out why she had moved them to New York. She was terrified they'd object to Adam, and start a war with him, out of loyalty to their father, if nothing else. She was looking nervous and strained when Mark saw her, and he wondered what was going wrong. And the kids were unhappy too. But they were thrilled to see their dad.

They stayed at the Plaza with him, and ordered lots

of room service. He took them to the theater, and a movie. He went shopping with Jessica, and he and Jason went for a long walk in the rain, trying to make sense of things. And by Sunday afternoon, he felt as though he had only scratched the surface, and hated leaving them again. He was depressed all the way home on the plane. He was really beginning to wonder if he should move to New York. He was still thinking about it the following weekend, as he lay in the sun at the pool on Saturday, and he noticed that someone was moving into the gatehouse finally. He took a stroll over, and saw Jimmy hauling boxes out of a van by himself, and offered to give him a hand.

Jimmy hesitated for a long moment, and then accepted gratefully. He was surprised himself at how much stuff he had. He had sent most of what he had to storage, but had kept a lot of framed photographs, some trophies, his sports equipment, and his clothes. He had a lot of stereo equipment, some of which was Maggie's. There seemed to be a mountain of stuff he had brought with him, and even with Mark helping, it took them two hours to unload the van, and they were both tired when they stopped. All they'd done was introduce themselves to each other at that point, and Jimmy offered him a beer when they finally sat down, and Mark accepted gratefully. It had been a lot of work.

"You sure have a lot of stuff," Mark said with a grin as he sipped the beer. "Heavy stuff, what's in all that, your collection of bowling balls?" Jimmy smiled and shrugged.

"Damned if I know. We had a two-room apartment

and I sent most of it to storage, and I still had all this."
He had a lot of books and papers, and CDs. It seemed
endless, but it disappeared easily into the drawers and
cupboards and bookcases and closets of the gatehouse. And when he opened the first box, he took out
a picture of her and set it on the mantelpiece and stood
looking at her. It was one of his favorites. She had just
caught a fish in a lake on one of their trips to Ireland,
and she looked victorious and pleased, her bright red
hair tied in a knot on top of her head, her eyes squint-
ing against the sun. She looked about fourteen years
old. It was the summer before she got sick, only about
seven months ago. It seemed like a lifetime ago to him,
as he turned and saw Mark watching him. Jimmy
looked away and didn't say anything.

"Pretty woman. Your girlfriend?" Jimmy shook his
head and took a long time to answer, but finally did
with a knot in his throat. He was used to it now, it felt
like a growth sometimes, the knot that still turned into
tears at the drop of a hat, and felt like it always would.

"My wife," Jimmy said quietly.

"I'm sorry," Mark said sympathetically, assuming
they were divorced, because it seemed like everyone
was now. "How long has it been?"

"Seven weeks tomorrow night," Jimmy said, as he
took a breath. He never talked about it, but he knew
he had to learn how, and maybe this was as good a
time as any to start. Mark looked like a nice guy, and
maybe they'd be friends, living on the same property.
Jimmy tried to keep his voice steady as he lowered his
eyes.

"It's been six for me. I just visited my kids in New

York last weekend. I miss them so damn much. My wife left me for another guy," Mark said in a somber voice.

"I'm sorry," Jimmy said sympathetically. He could see the pain in Mark's eyes, mirrored and magnified only by the pain in his own. "That's tough. How old are your kids?"

"Fifteen and thirteen, a girl and a boy. Jason and Jessica. They're great kids, and so far they're hating New York. If she was going to fall for someone else, I wish it had been someone out here. The kids don't know about him yet. What about you? Kids?"

"No. We were talking about it. We hadn't gotten around to it yet." He was amazed at how much he was willing to say to Mark. It was as though they had some strange invisible bond. The bond of heartache and loss and unexpected tragedy. The brutal blows of life that come as a surprise.

"Maybe it's just as well. Maybe it's easier to get divorced if you don't have kids. Maybe not. What do I know?" Mark said with a blend of compassion and humility, and suddenly Jimmy realized what he thought.

"We're not getting divorced," he said in a choked voice.

"Maybe you'll get back together," Mark said, envying him, but she obviously wasn't around either, so things couldn't be working out for them. And then he saw the look of raw anguish in Jimmy's eyes.

"My wife died."

"Oh my God ... I'm so sorry.... I thought.... What happened? An accident?" He glanced at the photograph again, suddenly horrified that the beautiful young woman holding the fish was gone, not just to her own life, but dead, and it was easy to see how heartbroken Jimmy was.

"A brain tumor. She started having headaches... migraines... they did some tests. She was gone in two months. Just like that. I don't usually talk about it. She would have loved this place. Her family was Irish, born in County Cork. She was Irish to her very core. An amazing woman. I wish I could be half the human being she was." Mark almost cried listening to him, and he could see the tears glistening in Jimmy's eyes. All he could do was look at him sympathetically, and then he helped him haul the rest of the boxes around, and he carried at least half of them upstairs. They didn't say anything to each other for a while, but Jimmy seemed to have regained his composure again by the time all the boxes were in the right rooms and Mark had helped him open some of them. "I can't thank you enough. I feel a little crazy moving to this place. We had a perfectly good apartment in Venice Beach. I just had to get out, and then this came up. It seemed like the right thing to do for now." It gave him a place to recover where he didn't have a thousand memories of being there with her. And under the circumstances, it seemed sensible to Mark too.

"I was living in a hotel two blocks from my office, listening to people cough all night. An accountant I work with does work for Coop and knew he was renting out the gatehouse and the guest wing. I fell in love with the place the minute I saw it, and I think the grounds will be great for my kids. It's like living in a park. I moved in two weeks ago, and it's so peaceful here, I sleep like a baby. Do you want to come see my place? It's completely different from this. You had just rented this place the morning I saw mine. But I think mine will work better for my kids." It was all he thought about, particularly after seeing them the previous weekend, and knowing how unhappy they were in New York. Jessica was fighting constantly with her mother, and Jason seemed to be disconnecting from everyone and isolating. He didn't think either of them were in good shape, and neither was their mom. He had never seen her as stressed. She had blown all their lives to smithereens, and he wondered if she was finding that it wasn't as idyllic as she had thought it would be. She had chosen an arduous, rocky road, not only for them, but herself.

"I'm going to take a shower," Jimmy said with a smile at Mark. "I'll come down to your place in a while, if you'll be home. Do you want to play some tennis this afternoon?" He hadn't played since Maggie died.

"Sure. I haven't looked at the courts yet. I haven't had anyone to play with. I've used the pool though, it's very nice. It's right next to my place. I was going to swim laps every night after work, but I haven't had time."

"Have you seen Coop?" Jimmy asked with an amused grin, and Mark could see he felt better again. The poor guy was in a fragile state after losing his wife.

"Not yet, or not to talk to anyway. Only from a distance, when he drives in and out. He drives some damn nice-looking women. He seems to have a flock of young girls."

"That's his reputation, isn't it? I think that's pretty much what he's done all his life. I haven't seen him in a movie in years."

"I think he's down on his luck, or in a tight spot anyway, which is why you and I wound up as his tenants," Mark said practically. It had worked out well for them.

"I figured that much. Especially in your case," he said to Mark, "why would he rent a wing in his house, if he didn't need the money? This place must cost a fortune to keep up."

"His accountant just fired all the help. Maybe we'll be seeing him out gardening one of these days." They both laughed at the thought, and a few minutes later Mark left and went back to his place. He was glad to have met Jimmy and was impressed by the work that he did with kids in Watts, and he was sorry as hell about his wife. What miserable, rotten luck. It seemed worse than what had happened to him. At least he still had his kids, and Janet had broken his heart and screwed up his life, but at least she hadn't died. Mark couldn't think of anything worse than what had happened to his new friend.

Jimmy turned up half an hour later, looking fresh and clean, with freshly shampooed hair. He was wearing shorts and a T-shirt, and carrying a tennis racket. And he was vastly impressed when he saw the wing where Mark lived. And Mark had been right, it was completely different than his. Jimmy liked his own place better, but he could see why Mark's place would be good for his kids. There was a lot more room to move around. And he suspected they'd be happier close to the pool.

"Coop didn't object to your kids?" Jimmy asked as they walked to the tennis court.

"No. Why?" Mark looked surprised. "I told the realtor they live in New York, and they're not going to be out here much unfortunately, except on vacations. It's easier for them if I go there."

"I got the impression from the realtor that he doesn't like kids. I can see why of course. He's got some pretty nice stuff in both our places. It worked out well for me. We didn't have much furniture, it was kind of beaten up and our apartment was very small. I just put it all in storage. It's kind of nice to have a fresh start for a while. What about you?"

"I let Janet take everything, except my clothes. I thought it would be better for the kids to have all their familiar stuff with them. This place was a godsend for me. Otherwise, I'd have had to go out and buy a load of furniture. I think if I'd had to do that, I'd have stayed at the hotel. For a while anyway. I really wasn't up to furnishing an apartment, or worrying about all that. I just walked into this with my suitcases and unpacked. Presto, magic, I'm home."

"Yeah," Jimmy grinned, "me too." As Mark knew.

They found the tennis court easily, but were disappointed to find that it was in bad shape. They tried to play a game and the surface was broken and too rough. And in the end, they just volleyed some balls back and forth. They enjoyed the exercise, and afterwards, wound up at the pool. Mark swam laps, while

Jimmy lay in the sun for a while, and afterwards Jimmy went back to his place. He invited Mark for dinner that night. He was going to cook a steak on the barbecue, and out of habit, he had bought two.

"Sounds good. I'll bring the wine," Mark volunteered. He showed up an hour later with a bottle of very decent cabernet, and they sat on Jimmy's terrace and talked about life, sports, their jobs, Mark's kids, and the ones Jimmy wished he'd had, and might someday, and they talked as little as possible about their wives. It was still too painful for both of them. Mark admitted that he was reluctant to start dating again, and Jimmy wondered if he ever would. For the moment, he doubted it, but at thirty-three that was a tough decision to make. They both agreed they were just going to drift for a while. And eventually their conversation extended to Coop, what they both thought he was like, who he really was, if anyone. Jimmy had a theory that if you led the Hollywood life for as long as he had, it eventually corroded your reality. It certainly seemed like a plausible theory about Coop, from what they'd both read about him.

At that exact moment, as they sat on Jimmy's patio, Coop was at the main house, in bed with Charlene. She was a veritable smorgasbord sexually, and he had done things with her that he hadn't even thought of in years. It made him feel young again, and challenged, and amused. She had a kittenish quality, which titillated him, and then a moment later, she was a fierce lioness, defying him to conquer her. She kept him busy for most of the night. And the next morning, she sneaked downstairs to cook breakfast for him. She was going to surprise him with a wonderful breakfast, and then make love to him again. She was standing in the kitchen wearing nothing but a thong, and a pair of red satin platform high heels, when she heard a lock turn and a door open, and she turned around to see Mark standing in Coop's kitchen in his underwear, with his blond hair tousled. He looked like a sleepy eighteen-year-old kid, as she stood there without apology or any attempt to cover herself, and just grinned.

"Hi, I'm Charlene," she said, as though she'd been wearing a dressing gown and fluffy slippers. He couldn't even see her face, he was so overwhelmed by her enormous breasts, the thong, and her endless legs. It took him a full minute to find her face.

"Ohmygod...I'm so sorry....Paloma told me Coop never uses his kitchen on the weekends...my stove doesn't work and the espresso machine is broken...I was just going to make a cup of coffee...she gave me the key...." He was practically stuttering, and Charlene didn't look the least upset. More than anything, she seemed friendly and amused.

"I'll make you a cup of coffee. Coop is asleep." Mark suspected she was probably an actress or a model Coop had brought home, or a girlfriend of his. He'd seen a blonde with him weeks before, and Mark didn't know who either of them was. Sexual talent in some form or other he assumed.

"No, really, I'll go....I'm terribly sorry...." She just stood there, smiling at him, with her breasts practically in his face.

"It's okay." She didn't seem the least bothered to be standing naked in front of him. And if it hadn't been so embarrassing he would have laughed at the scene. He felt completely inept standing in front of her, and while he continued to look mortified, she made him a cup of coffee and handed it to him. "Are you the tenant?" she asked comfortably, as he held the steaming cup, trying to retreat.

"Yes, I am." Who else would he be? A cat burglar? A stranger off the street? "I won't come in here again. I'll buy a new coffee machine. Maybe it's best if you don't tell Coop," he said nervously. She was a stunning-looking girl.

"Okay," she said amiably, as she took out a container of orange juice and poured a glass for Coop, and then she glanced at Mark before he left. "Do you want orange juice?"

"No, thanks...really. I'm fine. Thanks for the coffee," he said, and disappeared as quickly as he could. He locked the door to the main house again, and then stood grinning in the hallway off his living room where the communicating door was. He couldn't believe the scene he'd just been in. It was like something in a very bad movie. But she sure had one hell of a figure, and incredibly long raven-black hair.

He was still laughing to himself, and the scene seemed to get funnier as he thought about it. And once he was dressed, he couldn't resist walking up to the gatehouse to tell Jimmy. He had already vowed to himself he was going out to buy a new coffee machine that afternoon.

Jimmy was sitting on the patio, drinking a mug of coffee and reading the newspaper, when he looked up and saw Mark grinning at him. He smiled easily, and Mark looked unable to contain his amusement.

"You will never guess where I had coffee this morning, or with whom."

"Probably not, but from the look on your face, it must have been good." Mark told him about Paloma and the key, the broken stove and the coffee machine, and that he had walked in on Charlene, standing virtually naked, wearing a G-string and a pair of platform shoes, looking totally unembarrassed as she made coffee for him.

"It was like a scene in a movie. Christ, imagine if I'd run into him. I'd probably have gotten evicted."

"Or worse." But Jimmy was grinning too. It was the funniest vision, imagining Mark in his underwear, with a naked woman serving him coffee.

"She offered me orange juice too. But I figured I was pushing my luck, staying another minute."

"Do you want another cup of coffee, though I'll admit, the service is a little more mundane here."

"Yeah, sure." They were like the two new kids on the block who had found each other, and their circumstances were sufficiently similar to form a bond between them. And there was something easy and pleasant about being neighbors. They both had their own friends and lives, but they had both been avoiding their own circles lately. Their tragedies had set them apart, and made them feel awkward even with their closest friends. They had isolated themselves, and now they had each found a partner in their isolation. It was far easier than being with the people who knew them when they were married. It was like starting with a clean slate, even though they had shared their stories. But their old friends' pity was sometimes hard to take.

Mark went back to his place half an hour later. He had brought some work home from the office. But they met up again at the pool later that afternoon. Mark had bought himself a new coffee machine, and Jimmy had finished unpacking by then. He had put up half a dozen pictures of Maggie in key locations. Oddly enough, it made him feel less lonely if he could see her face. Sometimes, late at night, he was terrified he'd forget how she looked.

"Did you get your work done?" Jimmy asked Mark comfortably from a lounge chair.

"Yeah," Mark smiled at him, "and I bought a new coffee machine. I'm going to give that key back to Paloma in the morning. I'll never do that again." The vision of Charlene in her thong still made him smile.

"Would you have expected less of him?" Jimmy asked, referring to their landlord.

"Probably not. I just didn't expect front-row seats to his sex life."

"I suspect that would keep you pretty busy." Jimmy looked as amused as he did, and they were chatting quietly half an hour later, when they both heard a gate creak open and slam shut, and a moment later, there was a tall man with silver hair, smiling at them. He was wearing jeans and a perfectly pressed white shirt, no socks, and brown alligator loafers. He was a vision of perfection, and they both jumped like two kids who had been caught doing something they shouldn't. In fact, they had both been given access to the pool, and the only reason Coop had come out was to meet them. He had seen them from his terrace. Charlene was upstairs, in the shower, washing her hair.

"Don't let me disturb you. I just thought I'd come down and say hello. As long as you're my guests, I wanted to meet you." They both had the same feeling of amusement to be called his "guests." For ten thousand a month, they were not his "guests," but his tenants. "Hello, I'm Cooper Winslow," he said with a stunning smile, as he shook hands first with Jimmy and then Mark. "Which of you lives where? Did you know each other before?" He was curious about them, as they were about him.

"I'm Mark Friedman, I live in the guest wing. And no, we met yesterday while Jimmy was moving in."

"I'm Jimmy O'Connor," he said easily, as he shook hands with the handsome man towering above him. They both had the feeling of being new boys at school meeting the headmaster for the first time. And both were aware that Coop had come honestly by his reputation for being charming. He looked easy and pleasant, and elegant, and impeccably tailored. Even the perfectly pressed jeans fit every inch of his well-toned body and seemingly endless legs. And if either of them had had to guess, they would never even have pegged him at sixty, he looked far younger. And it was inconceivable that he was seventy. It was no mystery why women adored him. Even in blue jeans, he exuded style and glamour. He was every inch the Hollywood legend, as he lowered himself into a chair and smiled at them.

"I hope you're both comfortable in your respective houses."

"Very much so," Mark was quick to answer, praying that Charlene hadn't told him about that morning. He was afraid she had and that was why Coop had come out to see them. "It's a remarkable place," he said admiringly, trying not to think of the woman in the G-string who had served him coffee. And sensing that that was what he was thinking, Jimmy was grinning, with eyes full of mischief. It was a wonderful story.

"I've always loved it here," Coop said, referring to The Cottage. "You'll have to come up to the main house sometime. Maybe for dinner one night," and then he remembered he no longer had a cook or a butler or anyone to serve properly. He was going to have to call caterers now if he wanted to invite people to dinner. There was no way he would have trusted Paloma to produce anything but pizza or tacos, no matter how good her English was now. With or without an accent, she was a rebel and frighteningly independent. If he asked her to serve dinner, there was no telling how she'd behave. "Where are you both from?"

"I'm originally from Boston," Jimmy answered. "I've been here for eight years, since graduate school. I love it."

"I've been here for ten," Mark explained. "I came out from New York." He was about to add "with my wife and children," but he didn't. It sounded too pathetic, particularly if he had to explain why they were no longer with him.

"You both made the right decision. I'm from the

East too, I can't stand the weather there anymore, particularly the winters. It's a much better life here."

"Particularly on a property like this," Jimmy said admiringly. He found himself fascinated by Cooper Winslow, as he sat and chatted with them. He seemed totally at ease in his own skin, and he was obviously used to attention and adulation. There was no question that he was entirely aware of how dazzling he was. He had made his living off it for half a century. They were impressive statistics, particularly given the way he looked, at his age.

"Well, I hope you'll both be happy here. Let me know if you need anything." Mark wasn't about to complain about the stove or the coffee machine. He had already decided to have them fixed himself and take the appropriate amount off his next rent check. He didn't want to open the conversation about his morning coffee, on the off chance that the woman with the huge breasts had told Coop, even though she'd promised she wouldn't. Mark was afraid to trust her.

Coop smiled winningly at both of them again, chatted for a few more minutes and then left them, as the two much younger men stared at each other once he was gone. They waited several minutes before speaking, to give him a chance to go back into his own house, so he wouldn't overhear them.

"Holy shit," Mark spoke first. "Do you believe what he looks like? I'm going to hang up my spurs forever. Who could ever compete with that?" He had never been so impressed by any man in his life. Cooper Winslow was the best-looking man he'd ever seen. But

Jimmy looked less impressed when he answered pensively.

"There's only one problem," he said in a whisper. He didn't want Coop to hear him. "It's all about him. You can't help but wonder if there's a heart there, or if it's just charm and good looks and a great tailor."

"Maybe that's enough," Mark said, thinking of Janet. She would never have left a man with the looks, wit, and charm of Cooper Winslow. Mark felt like a total geek beside him. All his insecurities had leapt to the surface the minute Coop appeared.

"No, it isn't," Jimmy said wisely. "The guy's a shell. Nothing he says means anything. It's all about beauty and bullshit. And look at the women he gets. Thirty years from now, do you want a bimbo in a thong serving you breakfast, or a real person you can talk to?"

"Can I take a minute to think that over?" Mark said, and they both laughed.

"Yeah, okay, it's probably fun for a while, but then what? It would drive me insane." Maggie had been such a whole person. Smart, real, beautiful, fun, sexy. She had been everything he'd ever wanted. The last thing Jimmy wanted was a bimbo. And all Mark wanted was Janet. But on the surface, Cooper Winslow looked like he had all his bases covered. Even Jimmy had to admit he was impressive. "Actually, he can keep the woman with the tits. Given a choice, I want the loafers. They were terrific."

"You keep the loafers. I'll take the bimbo. Thank God, he didn't mention my encounter with her in his kitchen this morning," Mark said with a look of relief.

"I knew that was what you were thinking." Jimmy

laughed at him. He liked Mark. He was a nice guy, and he had decent values. Jimmy had enjoyed talking to him, and the prospect of their friendship. It was off to an interesting beginning, and he felt so sorry for him. He could easily relate to the trauma he'd been through, particularly missing his kids. "Well, now we've met him. He looks like a movie star, doesn't he?" Jimmy said, thinking back on the brief meeting. "I wonder who presses his clothes? Mine have been wrinkled since I left home. Mag wouldn't iron anything. She said it was against her religion." She had been a staunch Roman Catholic, and a vehement feminist. The first time he'd asked her to do a load of laundry, she damn near hit him.

"I've been taking everything including my underwear to the dry cleaner," Mark admitted willingly. "I ran out of shirts last week, and had to buy six new ones. Housekeeping isn't my forte. I've been paying Paloma to do a little cleaning for me. Maybe if you ask her, she'd do it for you too." She had been incredibly kind to him. And she seemed not only willing and capable, but intelligent and wise. He'd talked at length about his kids with her, and everything she'd said had been sympathetic and sensible. He respected her a great deal.

"I'm okay," Jimmy added with a smile. "I'm a real artist with a vacuum and a bottle of Windex. Maggie didn't do that either." Mark didn't want to ask what she did do. She'd obviously had enough virtues for Jimmy to be crazy about her. And later that afternoon, Jimmy told him they'd met at Harvard. She was obviously a very bright young woman.

"Janet and I met in law school. But she never practiced. She got pregnant as soon as we got married, and she stayed home with the kids."

"That's why we hadn't had kids yet. Maggie was always torn between giving up her career, and staying home with children. She was very Irish that way. She thought mothers should stay home with their babies. I figured we'd work it out sooner or later." What he hadn't figured on was what had happened instead.

They went back to talking about Coop again after a while, and at six o'clock, Jimmy went back to the gatehouse. He had promised to meet friends for dinner. He invited Mark to come along, but Mark said he was going to shuffle some papers. He had more reading to do about new tax laws. But when they went their separate ways, they both decided it had been a good weekend. They had each made a new friend, and they were happy in their new homes. And they were both amused at having met Cooper Winslow. He hadn't disappointed either of them. Coop was everything he was said to be. The perfect Hollywood legend.

Jimmy and Mark promised to get together for dinner one night the following week. And as Jimmy walked up the path to the gatehouse, Mark walked into the guest wing, and smiled to himself again, thinking of his morning coffee, and the woman who had handed it to him. Lucky, lucky Cooper Winslow.

Chapter 7

Liz called Coop the morning after he had met Jimmy and Mark at the pool, and he was delighted to hear her. She had been married for a week, and was still on her honeymoon, but she was worried about him.

"Where are you?" he asked, smiling at the sound of her voice. It still seemed strange not to see her face every morning.

"In Hawaii," she said proudly. She was using her married name every chance she got, and even though it felt strange, she loved it, and was sorry now she hadn't done it sooner. Being married to Ted was like a dream.

"How plebeian," Coop teased her. "I still think you should ditch him and come back. We can have the marriage annulled in a minute."

"Don't you dare! I like being a respectable, married woman." Far more than she had ever thought she would.

"Liz, I'm disappointed in you, I thought you had more character than that. You and I were the last hold-outs. This leaves only me."

"Well, maybe you should get married too. It's really

not that awful. There are even minor tax benefits, or so I'm told." In truth, she loved it, and she had married the right man. Ted was wonderful to her. And Coop was happy for her, in spite of the inconvenience she had caused him.

"That's what Abe says. That I should get married. He says I need to find a rich woman. He's so unspeakably crude."

"It's not a bad idea," she teased him. She couldn't imagine Coop getting married. He had far too much fun playing the field. She couldn't see him settling down with one woman. He'd have to have a harem to keep him amused.

"I haven't met a rich woman in ages, in any case. I don't know where they're hiding. Besides, I prefer their daughters." Or in recent years, granddaughters, but neither of them said it. He had been involved with his share of heiresses, and a number of very wealthy women of more respectable ages over the years, but Coop had always preferred the young ones. There had even been an Indian princess, and a couple of very wealthy Saudis. But no matter who they were, or how wealthy, Coop always tired of them. There was always a more beautiful, more exciting one just around the corner. And he always turned just one more corner. Liz suspected he always would, and if he lived to be a hundred, he'd still be turning yet one more corner. He loved being free.

"I just wanted to be sure you were behaving," Liz said adoringly. She really did miss him. She had enormous affection for him. "How is Paloma doing?"

"She's absolutely fabulous," Coop said, sounding

convincing. "She makes rubber eggs, puts pepper on my toast, she turned my cashmere socks into baby booties, and she has exquisite taste. I've actually come to love her rhinestone glasses. Not to mention the fuchsia pumps she wears with her uniform, when she isn't wearing the leopard sneakers. She's a gem, Liz. God only knows where you found her." But the truth was, much as she irritated him, he was enjoying the animosity that had developed between them.

"She's a nice woman, Coop. Teach her, she'll learn. She worked with the others for a month, some of it must have rubbed off."

"I think Livermore had her locked up in leg irons in the basement. I may have to try that. Oh and by the way, I met my houseguests yesterday."

"Houseguests?" Liz sounded startled. She didn't know about them.

"The two men who are living respectively in the gatehouse and the guest wing." His tenants.

"Oh, *those* houseguests. How are they?"

"They seemed respectable. One is a lawyer, and the other one is a social worker. The social worker looks like a kid, and went to Harvard. The lawyer looks a little nervous, but he was perfectly pleasant. They seem reasonable and well behaved, as long as they don't start throwing beer bottles into the pool, or adopt undesirable orphans. They don't look like heroin addicts, or criminals. I'd say we got lucky."

"Sounds like it. The realtor assured me they were nice people."

"She could be right. I'll reserve judgment till they've been here a little longer. But for the moment, I don't foresee any problems." It was a great relief to her, she had been worried about it, which was also why she had called him. "Why are you calling me anyway? You should be making mad, passionate love on the beach with that plumber you married."

"He's not a plumber, he's a stockbroker. And he's playing golf with a client."

"He brought clients on your honeymoon? Liz, that's a very bad sign. Divorce him immediately." Coop was laughing, and Liz was relieved to hear him sound happy.

"He ran into the client here," she said, laughing. "I'll be home in a week. I'll call you. Now, behave yourself, don't buy any diamond bracelets this week. You'll give Abe Braunstein an ulcer."

"He deserves one. He's the most humorless, tasteless man on the planet. I should send you a diamond bracelet, just to annoy him. At least you deserve it."

"I'm wearing the beautiful ring you gave me when I left," she reminded him. She was always grateful to him. "I'll talk to you when I get back. Take care, Coop."

"I will, Liz. Thanks for calling." He enjoyed talking to her, and hated to admit it, but he missed her. Terribly. He had felt adrift ever since she left. His house and his life were like a ship without a rudder. He still couldn't imagine what he would do without her.

And when he checked his appointment book that morning, he saw her careful handwriting in it. He was expected at a dinner party at the Schwartzes' that night. They were the social stars of Hollywood, and had been for two decades. He was a major producer, and she had been an actress and great beauty in the fifties. Coop didn't want to go, but he knew they'd be upset if he didn't. He was far more interested in spending another night with Charlene, and he didn't want to take her with him. She was a little bit too racy for that circle. Charlene was the kind of girl he played with, not someone he wanted to be seen with at formal dinner parties. He had many categories of women. Charlene was an "at home" girl. The major movie stars he reserved for premieres and openings, where they would double their impact on the press by being seen together. And there were a whole flock of young actresses and models he enjoyed going out with. But he preferred going to the Schwartzes' parties alone.

They always had a roomful of interesting people, and he never knew who he'd meet there. It was more effective to be alone, and they enjoyed having him as a bachelor. He was fond of both Arnold and Louise Schwartz, and he called Charlene and told her he couldn't see her that night, and she was a good sport about it. She said she needed a night off anyway, to wax her legs and do her laundry. She needed her "beauty sleep," she said, which was the one thing he knew she didn't need. She had no problem staying up all night, and looking ravishing in the morning. And he was always willing to ravish. But tonight belonged to the Schwartzes.

He met with a producer at lunch, had a massage afterwards, and a manicure. He had a nap, and a glass of champagne, when he woke up, and at eight o'clock, he was wearing his dinner jacket as he stepped out the front door. The driver he hired when he went out was waiting in his Bentley, and Coop looked more handsome than ever in the well-cut tuxedo with his silvery hair.

"Good evening, Mr. Winslow," the driver said pleasantly. He had driven Coop for years, and he drove other stars as well. He made a good living doing freelance driving. It made more sense for Coop than having a full-time driver. Most of the time he preferred driving himself.

When Coop got to the Schwartzes' enormous mansion on Brooklawn Drive, there were a hundred people already standing in the front hall, drinking champagne and paying homage to the Schwartzes. She looked stylish in a dark blue gown, and was wearing a fabulous collection of sapphires. And all around her, Coop saw the usual suspects, ex-presidents and first ladies, politicians, art dealers, producers, directors, internationally known lawyers, and the usual smattering of movie stars, some more current than Coop, but none as famous. He was instantly surrounded by a flock of adoring admirers of both sexes. And an hour later, they went in to dinner, as Coop followed the herd.

He was seated at the same table as another well-known actor of a similar vintage, and there were two famous writers at their table, and an important Hollywood agent. The head of one of the major studios was also seated there, and Coop made a mental note to speak to him after dinner. He had heard they were making a feature that was perfect for him. He knew the woman on his right, she was one of the better-known Hollywood matrons, whose parties tried to rival Louise Schwartz's but didn't. And on his left was a young woman he had never met before. She had a delicate, aristocratic face, big brown eyes, ivory skin, and dark hair pulled back in a bun, like a Degas ballerina.

"Good evening," he said pleasantly. He noticed that she was small and lithe, and he wondered if she actually was a dancer. And as a brigade of waiters served the first course, he asked her, and she laughed. It wasn't the first time someone had asked her that, and she claimed she was flattered. She knew who he was, and had been excited to find him sitting next to her. Her place card said Alexandra Madison, which meant nothing to him.

"Actually, I'm a resident," she said, as though that explained everything, but to him, it didn't mean a thing.

"A resident of where?" he said, with a look of amusement. She was not his usual profile, but she was strikingly pretty, and he saw that she had lovely hands, with short nails, and no polish on them. She was wearing a white satin gown, and had a young girl's face and figure.

"At a hospital. I'm a physician."

"How interesting," he said, looking momentarily impressed. "What kind? Anything useful?"

"Not unless you have children. I'm a pediatrician, a neonatologist to be exact."

"I detest children. I eat them for dinner," he said with a wide smile that showed off the perfect white teeth he was known for.

"I don't believe you," she said with a giggle.

"Truly. And children hate me. They know I eat

them. I only like them when they turn into grown-ups. Particularly women." At least he was honest. He had had a lifelong distrust of children, and an aversion to them. He generally tried to choose women who didn't have them. They complicated everything, and had spoiled many an evening for him. Women without children were much more fun to be with, from his standpoint. You didn't have to rush home to pay baby-sitters. They weren't sick at the last minute. They didn't spill their juice all over you, or tell you they hated you. It was one of the many reasons why he pre-ferred younger women. Over thirty, most women seemed to have kids. "Why couldn't you be something more entertaining? Like a lion tamer. Or actually, be-ing a ballerina would suit you. I think you should consider a career change now, before you get in any deeper." Alexandra was having fun sitting next to him. She was impressed with him, but she was enjoying playing with him, and in spite of her unfortunate choice of jobs, and severe hairdo, according to Coop, he liked her.

"I'll have to give it some thought. What about being a veterinarian? Would that be better?" Alexandra asked innocently.

"I don't like dogs either. They're filthy. They get hair all over your trousers, they bite, snap, and smell. Almost as bad as children. Not quite, but a close sec-ond. We'll have to think of an entirely different career for you. What about acting?"

"I don't think so," she laughed, as a waiter spooned caviar onto her blini. Coop loved the food at the

Schwartzes' dinners, and Alexandra looked comfortable there too. She had an aura of ease and grace about her, as though she had grown up in dining rooms like this one. It was written all over her, despite the fact that she wasn't wearing important jewels. Just a string of pearls, and a pair of pearl and diamond earrings. But something about her spelled money. "What about you?" She turned the tables on him. She was above all intelligent, and he liked that about her too. At the dinner table at least, it provided a challenge. "Why are you an actor?"

"I find it amusing. Don't you? Imagine being able to play pretend every day, and wear beautiful clothes. It's actually very pleasant. Far nicer than what you do. You wear an ugly wrinkled white coat and children throw up all over you, and scream the minute they see you."

"That's true. But the ones I deal with are too small to do much damage. I work in the neonatal ICU, mostly with preemies."

"Ghastly," he said, pretending to be horrified. "They're probably the size of mice. You could get rabies. This is much worse than I suspected." He was having a delightful time with her, and a man across the table glanced at him with a look of amusement. It was like watching fine art as Coop turned the charm full force on a woman. But Alexandra was a good match for him. She was sensible, and smart enough not to let Coop lure her or make her feel ill at ease. "What else do you do?" Coop continued to quiz her.

"I fly my own plane, and have since I was eighteen. I love to go hang gliding. I've parachuted out of an airplane, but I promised my mother I wouldn't, so I no longer do. I play tennis, ski. I used to race motorcycles, but I promised my father I wouldn't. And I spent a year doing health care work in Kenya before med school."

"You sound relatively suicidal. And your parents seem to interfere a great deal in your athletic pursuits. Do you still see them?"

"When I have to," she said honestly, and he saw in her eyes that she was telling the truth. She was a girl with an amazing amount of poise and spirit. He was fascinated by her.

"Where do they live?" he asked with interest.

"Palm Beach in the winter. Newport in the summer. It's very boring and predictable, and I'm something of a rebel."

"Are you married?" He had seen that she wasn't wearing a ring, and he didn't expect a positive answer. She didn't feel married to him. He had excellent radar for these things.

"No." She hesitated for a moment before she answered. "I almost was," she volunteered. She didn't usually say that, but he was so outrageous, it was fun being honest with him. He was easy to talk to, and very quick.

"And? What happened?"

The ivory face turned icy, although she continued smiling. But her eyes were full of sorrow suddenly. No one but Coop would have seen it. "I was jilted at the altar. The night before actually."

"How tasteless. I hate people who do rude things like that, don't you?" He was stalling for time. He could see that saying it had hurt her, and for an instant he was sorry that he had asked. She had been so bluntly truthful with her answer. He hadn't expected her to do that. "I hope he fell into a pit of snakes after that, or a moat full of alligators. He deserved it."

"He did, more or less. The moat full of alligators, I mean. He married my sister." It was heavy stuff for a first meeting. But she assumed she'd never see him again, so it didn't matter what she said to him.

"That is rude. And do you still speak to her?"

"Only when I have to. That's when I went to Kenya. It was a very interesting year. I enjoyed it." That was her signal to him that she didn't want to discuss the matter further, and Coop didn't blame her. She had been painfully honest with him, far more than he would have dared with a stranger. And he admired her for it. He told her about his last safari after that, which had been fraught with miseries and discomforts. He had been invited to a game preserve, as their guest, and by his estimation, they had tortured him with every horror they could think of. He had hated every minute of it, but listening to him tell it, he made it sound funny, and he had her roaring with laughter at his description of the scene.

They had a wonderful time sitting beside each other, and they both ignored their other neighbors. She was still laughing at him when the meal came to an end, and he was sorry when she got up and went to talk to some old friends she had spotted at another table. They were friends of her parents, and she thought she should speak to them, but she told Coop how much she had enjoyed meeting him, and she meant it. He had made it a memorable evening for her.

"I don't have time to go out much. And Mrs. Schwartz was sweet to invite me. She's a friend of my parents. I only came because I was able to get the night off, but most of the time, I'm stuck at the hospital. I'm glad I did come." She shook his hand firmly, and a moment later, Louise Schwartz was tittering beside him.

"Watch out, Coop," she warned him. "She's a handful. And if you take her out, her father will kill you."

"Why? Is he in the Mafia or something? She looks perfectly respectable to me."

"She is. That's why he'd kill you. Arthur Madison." It was a name that anyone would have recognized. It was the oldest steel fortune in the country, and the biggest. And she was a doctor. An interesting combination. Abe Braunstein's words rang in his ears as Louise said it. She was not only a rich woman, but possibly one of the richest. And totally simple and unassuming, and one of the brightest girls he'd ever met. Better than that, she had a lot of spirit. It would have been difficult not to be attracted to her, or amused, or challenged at least. Coop watched her with interest as she spoke to a number of people. She had scored a hit with Cooper. He ran into her again as he was leaving. He had timed his exit perfectly to match hers, and pointed to the waiting Bentley.

"Can I give you a lift?" He sounded friendly, and harmless. He had calculated that she was roughly thirty, and had been correct in his estimation. He was exactly forty years older than she was, but at least he didn't look it, or feel it. And the funny thing was that he wasn't drawn to her because of who she was. He actually liked her. She was clearly a woman who would not tolerate any nonsense. Better yet, or worse, she'd been hurt, and he could see that she was cautious. And who she was, or who her father was, only added depth and color to the picture. She appealed to him immensely, and would have, with or without her father, or his money. Odd as it was, Coop mused as he watched her, he liked Alexandra for herself.

"I've got my car, but thank you," she said politely, smiling at him. And as she said it, one of the valet parkers brought up her old beat-up Volkswagen, and she smiled at him.

"I'm impressed. Very humble. I admire your discretion," he teased her about her car.

"I just don't like wasting money on cars. I hardly ever drive it. I never go anywhere. I'm always working."

"I know, with those dreadful mouse babies. What about beauty school? Have you ever thought about that?"

"It was actually my first career choice, but I couldn't pass the exams. I kept flunking crimping." She was as quick and as irreverent as he.

"I enjoyed meeting you, Alexandra," he said, looking her in the eye with the blue eyes and the cleft chin that made him a legend, and irresistible to women.

"Call me Alex. I enjoyed meeting you too, Mr. Winslow."

"Maybe I should call you Dr. Madison. Would you prefer that?"

"Absolutely." She grinned at him, as she slid into

her battered car. It didn't bother her in the least to have come to the Schwartzes' in a car that looked like it should have been abandoned by the side of a highway somewhere, or perhaps had been. "Goodnight," she called to him with a wave as she drove away, and he called after her.

"Goodnight, Doctor! Take two aspirin and call me in the morning." He could see that she was laughing as she drove down the driveway, and he was smiling as he got into the back of the Bentley. He reminded himself to send Louise flowers in the morning. A lot of them. He was so glad that he had decided not to see Charlene that night. He had had a wonderful evening with Alex Madison. She was a most unusual girl indeed, and a very interesting prospect for him.

Chapter 8

The morning after the dinner party, Coop sent Louise Schwartz an enormous arrangement of flowers. He thought of calling her secretary for Alex Madison's phone number, but decided to call the hospital directly to see if he could locate her on his own. He asked for the neonatal ICU, and they went down a list of residents before giving him her pager number. He paged her, but she didn't respond. They said she was on duty, but couldn't be called to the phone. He was surprised to find he was disappointed when he didn't hear back from her.

And two days later, he was out in black tie again. He was invited to the Golden Globes as usual, although he hadn't been nominated for anything in more than twenty years. But like all the other major stars, he added excitement and color to the event. He was going with Rita Waverly, one of the biggest stars Hollywood had seen in the past three decades. He liked going to major events with her. The attention they got from the press was staggering, and they had been linked romantically from time to time over the years. His press agent had leaked that they were getting married once, and she got annoyed with him. But they had been seen together too often now for anyone to believe the rumor again. But just being seen with her made him look good. She was an incredible-looking woman, in spite of her age. Her press kit said she was forty-nine, but Coop knew for a fact she was fifty-eight.

He picked her up at her apartment in Beverly Hills, and she emerged wearing a white satin bias-cut gown that was wallpapered to a figure that had not only been starved in recent years, but had experienced every possible kind of surgery except for prostate and open heart. She had been nipped and tucked and pulled and yanked and chopped with staggeringly good results. And resting on her considerable cleavage, which had also been enhanced surgically, was a three-million-dollar diamond necklace, borrowed from Van Cleef. And as she walked out of her building, she was trailing a floor-length white mink coat. She was the epitome of a Hollywood star, just like Coop. They made a handsome couple, and when the press saw them at the Golden Globes, they went wild. You would have thought they were both twenty-five years old and had won the Oscar that year. The press ate them up, as they always did.

"Over here!!!...Over here!!!...Rita!!!...Coop!!!" Photographers shouted for better angles, while fans waving autograph books screamed, and a thousand flashes went off in their faces, as they beamed. It was a night to feed their egos for the next ten years. But they were both used to it, and Coop laughed as they were stopped every few feet by TV camera crews asking them what they thought of this year's nominees.

"Wonderful...truly impressive work...makes you proud to be in the business..." Coop said expertly as Rita preened. With the endless adulation and all eyes on them, it took them nearly half an hour to get to their seats. They were at tables, and would be eating a meal before the televised awards began. And Coop was visibly attentive to her, leaning gently toward her, handing her a glass of champagne, carrying her coat.

"You almost make me sorry I didn't marry you," Rita teased, but she knew as well as he did, it was all for show, although he was fond of her. But they were good for each other's reputations, and even the hints of romance over the years had always brought them back into the main focus of the public eye for a time. The truth was they had never even come close. He had kissed her once, just for the hell of it, but she was so narcissistic he knew he couldn't have stood her for more than a week, nor she him. They were both smart about that.

As soon as the show began, and the cameras scanned the audience, they zoomed in instantly, and at considerable length, on them.

"Holy shit!" Mark suddenly exclaimed as he sat in the gatehouse with Jimmy, drinking a beer, and watching TV. Neither of them had anything better to do, and Mark had suggested they watch the awards. He had even joked about it, wondering if they'd see Coop, but neither of them had expected to see quite so much of him, or his date. The cameras seemed to stay on them forever, and eat them up. "Look at that!!" Mark pointed and Jimmy grinned.

"Who is that? Rita Waverly? Jesus, he really does know everyone, doesn't he?" Even Jimmy was impressed. "She looks pretty good for her age." It reminded him instantly that Maggie used to love watching all the Hollywood stuff, the Golden Globes, the Oscars, Grammys, Emmys, even the awards for soap operas. She loved being able to identify all the stars. But identifying Coop and Rita Waverly was hardly challenging, blind babies would have known who they were.

"That's quite a dress," Mark commented, as the camera moved on to someone else. "Pretty cool, huh? When was the last time you had a landlord you saw on national TV?"

"I think I had one in Boston who got arrested for a felony, and I saw him for a split second on the evening news. I think he was selling crack." They both grinned, and Jimmy popped open another beer. Their friendship had become convenient and comfortable, they lived close to each other, were both personable and intelligent, and other than their work, had nothing much else in their lives. They had recent grief and loneliness in common, and neither of them was ready to date. It helped pass the evenings to share a steak and a few beers a couple of times a week. And once Coop vanished from the screen, they settled in to watch the Golden Globes. Jimmy had just put a bag of popcorn in the microwave.

"I'm beginning to feel like half of the Odd Couple," Jimmy smiled as he handed the open steaming bag of popcorn to Mark. They were playing this year's nominees for best theme song from a dramatic movie, and Mark glanced up at him with a grin.

"Yeah, me too. But it works for now at least. Someday I'd like to get ahold of Coop's address book and audition some of his cast-offs, but not yet." And Jimmy had practically taken a vow of celibacy for life. He had no intention of betraying Maggie's memory in the foreseeable future, or ever perhaps. Their friendship was a blessing for both of them for the time being. And their camaraderie filled their empty nights.

Alex Madison was on duty at the hospital that night, to pay penance for the evening she'd spent at the Schwartzes' when she met Coop. She had traded Monday for tonight with another resident, who had a date with the girl of his dreams. It had been an easy switch.

She had already had a busy, stressful evening, when she walked through the waiting room looking for the parents of a two-week-old preemie who had been a code blue earlier in the day, but had been stabilized again. She wanted to reassure them that their baby's vital signs were stable, and he had gone to sleep. But she realized as she stepped into the empty waiting room that they must have gone out to eat. And as she looked around, she glanced at the TV that was droning on, as it always did, and was startled to see Coop. The cameras had just zeroed in on him, and she stood there grinning as she spoke out loud in the empty room.

"I know him!" He was looking incredibly handsome, and very charming as he hovered over Rita Waverly, and handed her a glass of champagne. It was an odd feeling realizing he had done the same for her, with just that look, at the Schwartzes' only two days before.

Coop was certainly a splendid-looking man, and Rita Waverly looked good too. "I wonder how much plastic surgery she's had," Alex said out loud again, without realizing it. It was funny to think how distant their world was from her own. She spent her days and nights saving lives, and comforting parents whose babies hovered on the brink of death. And people like Coop and Rita Waverly spent their time looking beautiful and going to parties, wearing furs and jewels and evening gowns. She hardly ever had a chance to wear makeup, and she was wearing wrinkled green pajamas with a huge stamp on her chest that said "NICU." She was unlikely to appear on any best-dressed lists, but she had chosen this, and liked her life the way it was. Not for anything would she have gone back to her parents' rarified, pretentious, hypocritical world. It often made her realize that it was a good thing she hadn't married Carter. Now that he had married her sister, and was emblazoned in the social register, he was as snobbish and arrogant as all the other men she detested in her old world. Coop was an entirely different breed. He was a movie star, a celebrity. At least he had an excuse for looking and behaving the way he did. It was his job to be that way. But not hers.

A moment later, after watching him until the camera moved away from him again, she went back to her safe, protected environment, full of incubators, and tiny babies on monitors and tubes. And she forgot about Coop and the Golden Globes again. She didn't even see his message on her pager until the next day. He was the last thing on her mind.

But as amused as Mark and Jimmy and Alex had been to see Coop on television, Charlene was considerably less so, as she sat scowling at the TV. He had told her two days before that he couldn't take her to the Schwartzes' because they needed him as an extra man. And he had assured her that she would have been bored to death, which was what he always said when he wanted to go somewhere alone. But going to the Golden Globes with him would have been just her cup of tea. And she was furious with him for not taking her, and going with Rita Waverly instead. But professionally at least, going with Charlene would have done nothing for him.

"Bitch!" she spat petulantly at the TV. "She must be eighty years old," she said out loud, as Alex had in the waiting room. There was something about seeing people you knew on television that made you want to speak to them. And there was a lot she would have liked to say to Coop. She had seen him put an arm around Rita and lean close to her and whisper in her ear. Rita Waverly was laughing at something he said, as the cameras moved off to another star sitting nearby.

Charlene left half a dozen messages for him, and was seething when she finally reached him on his cell phone at 2 A.M.

"Where the hell are you, Coop?" She sounded halfway between a tantrum and tears.

"And good evening to you too, my dear." He sounded calm and undisturbed.

"I'm at home in bed, where are you?" He knew

what she was upset about. It had been predictable, but unavoidable. Not in a million years would he have taken her to an event as highly publicized as the Golden Globes. As far as he was concerned, their relationship wasn't serious or important enough to warrant publicity. Besides which, being seen with Rita Waverly did him a great deal more good. He enjoyed Charlene, and others like her, immensely but privately. He had no desire whatsoever to show her off to the world. But he assumed correctly that she had seen him on TV.

"Is Rita Waverly with you?" she asked, a tone of hysteria creeping into her voice. She was going to turn ugly soon, Coop knew. Those kinds of inquiries always encouraged him to move along quickly to the next candidate on his list. Beautiful or not, Charlene's moment in the sun was almost up. There were always others waiting for him in the wings. It was time to turn the corner again.

"Of course not. Why would Rita be here?" He sounded innocent, and was.

"You looked like you were going to fuck her any minute when I saw you on TV." The time had come.

"Let's not be rude," he said, as though speaking to a naughty child who had just attempted to stomp on his foot. When in doubt, Coop always removed himself, or stomped first. But he had no need to do that to Charlene. He knew that all he had to do was quietly disappear. "It was a very boring ordeal," he said with a well-staged yawn. "It always is. It's work, my dear."

"So where is she?" she asked. She'd drunk almost an entire bottle of wine as she tried to reach him all night. But quite reasonably he had turned his cell phone off at the awards, and had forgotten to turn it on again until he got home.

"Who?" He genuinely had no idea who she meant. She sounded more than a little drunk. She'd gotten upset waiting to talk to him.

"Rita!" Charlene said insistently.

"I have no idea where she is. In her own bed, I assume. And I, dear lady, am going to sleep. I have an early call tomorrow for a commercial. I'm not as young as you. I need my sleep."

"The hell you do. If I were there, we'd be up all night, and you know it."

"Yes," he smiled, "I'm sure we would, which is why you're not here. We both need some sleep."

"Why don't I come over now?" she asked, slurring her words. She was sounding even drunker than she had at first, and she was still drinking while they talked.

"I'm tired, Charlene. And you sound under the weather too. Why don't we let it go for tonight." Boredom had crept into his voice.

"I'm coming over."

"No, you're not," he said, sounding firm.

"I'll climb over the gate."

"The security patrol would pick you up, which would be embarrassing for you. Let's both get some sleep and talk about it tomorrow," he said gently. He didn't want to get into a fight with her, especially if she was drunk and upset. He was smarter than that.

"Talk about what tomorrow? Are you cheating on me with Rita Waverly?"

"What I'm doing is entirely none of your business, Charlene, and the term 'cheating' presumes some kind of commitment on either of our parts, and there is no such thing between us. Now, let's keep a little perspective here. Goodnight, Charlene," he said firmly, and promptly hung up. His cell phone rang again almost immediately and he let it go to voice mail, and then she tried his house. She called for the next two hours, and he finally switched off the phone, and went to sleep. He hated possessive women who made scenes. It was definitely time for Charlene to vanish out of his life. He was sorry Liz was no longer around. She had always been so good at that. If Charlene had been more important to him, he'd have sent her a diamond bracelet or some similarly impressive gift to thank her for the time they'd spent together. But she hadn't been around long enough to warrant it. And in her case, he knew, it would only have encouraged her. Charlene was the kind of girl you had to cut off suddenly, and stay away from after that. It was a shame she had made a scene that night, he mused to himself, as he drifted off to sleep. If she hadn't, he would have been perfectly happy to keep her around for at least another two or three weeks, but surely no longer than that. But after tonight, she was destined for a speedy exit. In fact, he knew, as he heard his phone ring in the distance for the hundredth time, she was already gone. Bye, Charlene.

Coop mentioned her discreetly to Paloma the next morning when she served his breakfast on a tray. She was doing better than she had for the first few days, although she had served him hot peppers with his poached eggs, and even after spitting them out, his mouth burned all day. She said it was a treat for him, and he had begged her not to "treat" him again.

"Paloma, if Charlene calls, please tell her that I'm out, whether or not I'm at home. Is that clear?"

Paloma stared at him through narrowed eyes. He had finally learned to see her through the rhinestone sunglasses. And in any case, her whole face gave her away. Most of the time, her entire body read disapproval, contempt, and rage. She referred to him as a "dirty old man" to her friends. "You don't like her anymore?" She no longer bothered to use the accent on him. She had other tricks up her sleeve instead. She loved challenging him in a myriad of ways.

"That's not the point. It's simply that our...our little interlude...has come to an end." He would never have had to explain that to Liz, nor did he want to explain it to his maid. But Paloma seemed determined to be the champion of the underdog, and defender of all womanhood, rather than Coop.

"'Interlude'? 'Interlude'? Does that mean you're not sleeping with her anymore?" Coop winced.

"That's crude, but correct, I'm afraid. Please don't put her calls through to me again." He couldn't have said it more clearly to her. And half an hour later, she told him he had a call.

"Who is it?" he asked distractedly. He was reading a script in bed, and trying to figure out if there was a part in it for him.

"I don't know. Sounds like a secretary," she said vaguely, and he picked up the phone. It was Charlene. She was sobbing and hysterical, and said she wanted to see him immediately. She said she was going to have a nervous breakdown if he didn't, and it took him an hour to get off the phone. He told her he didn't think their relationship was good for her, and it seemed wiser not to see each other for a while. He didn't tell her that these were precisely the kind of histrionics he avoided in his life, and he had no intention of seeing her again. She was still crying, but less hysterically, when he finally got off the phone. And he went to find Paloma immediately. He was still in his pajamas, when he found her in the living room, vacuuming. She was wearing a new pair of purple velvet sneakers and matching sunglasses, with rhinestones of course. She didn't hear a word he was saying to her, and he turned the vacuum off and stood there glaring at her, as she looked unconcerned.

"You knew exactly who that was," he said accusingly. It was rare for him to lose his cool with anyone, but Paloma brought out the worst in him. He wanted to strangle her, and Abe, for firing the rest of the staff and leaving him with her. Any benevolence he'd begun feeling for her instantly disappeared. As far as he was concerned, she was a witch.

"No. Who?" she said innocently. "Rita Waverly?" She had seen him at the Golden Globes too, and told all her friends watching it, what an asshole he was. He wouldn't have been pleased with her reviews.

"It was Charlene. That was a rotten thing to do. It upset her terribly and me too. She was hysterical, which is not how I like to start my day. And I warn you, if she shows up here, and you let her in, I'm going to throw you both out of this house, and call the police and tell them you broke in."

"Don't get so nervous," she said with a quelling look at him.

"I'm not nervous. I'm angry, Paloma. I specifically told you, I don't want to speak to Charlene."

"I forgot. Or maybe I didn't know who she was. Okay, I won't answer the phone again." Her final victory, and yet another task she no longer had to do, which only made him angrier.

"You *will* answer the phone, Paloma. And you will not tell Charlene if I'm here. Is that clear?"

She nodded, and turned the vacuum on again, in open defiance of him. She did defiance extremely well. And passive aggression too.

"Fine. Thank you," he said, and stomped back upstairs, and when he went back to bed, he couldn't concentrate on the script. Other than his fury at Paloma, he was extremely annoyed at Charlene. She was being tiresome and hysterical and rude. He hated women who hung on like that. When the romance waned, they had to know how to leave elegantly. But elegance was clearly not Charlene's strong suit. He could sense easily that she was going to be difficult. He was still irritated when he finally got out of bed, showered, shaved, and dressed.

He was having lunch at Spago with a director he'd worked with years before. Coop had called and suggested lunch, he wanted to find out what he was up to. You never knew when someone was making a movie with a great part for him. Thinking about it forced Charlene from his mind at least. And it was only on his way to Spago that he remembered he had never heard from Alex, and he decided to page her again. He left his cell phone number on her pager.

He was surprised and pleased when she answered him immediately this time. He had just put his cell phone on the seat next to him when she called.

"Hello, this is Dr. Madison. Who's this?" She didn't recognize the number, and had her official voice on, as he smiled.

"It's Coop. How are you, Dr. Madison?"

She was surprised to hear his voice, and in spite of herself, pleased. "I saw you on the Golden Globes last night." So had half the world, and all of Hollywood.

"I didn't think you had time to watch TV."

"I don't. I was walking through the waiting room, looking for one of my patients' parents, and there you were, with Rita Waverly. You both looked great," she said with sincerity. She had a young voice, and the same openness he had liked about her when they met. There was no artifice about her, only beauty and brains, unlike Charlene. But the comparison was unfair. Charlene would have been at a disadvantage with the likes of Alex Madison. Alex had everything going for her, looks, charm, intelligence, breeding. She came from another world. And in contrast, there were things Charlene did that women like Alex knew nothing about. There was room in Coop's world for both of them, or there had been until the night before. But there would be women like Charlene in his world again, Coop knew. There were a lot of them. It was women like Alex who were rare and few and far between. "I think you might have paged me yesterday," she said candidly. "I didn't recognize the number, and I didn't have time to return the call. I didn't even see it till today. But when it came up again just now, I thought I'd better call. I was afraid you might be a consulting physician. I'm glad you're not." She sounded relieved.

"So am I, particularly with those little miniature rug rats you play doctor to. I'd rather be a barber than do what you do." Although in truth, he respected her more than he was willing to admit. But his feigned horror at what she did was part of his game, and she knew it too.

"How was last night? Was it fun? Rita Waverly sure is beautiful. Is she nice?" The question made him smile. "Nice" was not a word he would have chosen to describe Rita Waverly, and she would have been insulted if he had. Nice was not a highly prized virtue in Hollywood. But she was important and powerful and beautiful and glamorous, even if slightly long of tooth.

"I think 'interesting' is more appropriate. Amusing. She's very much a movie star," he said diplomatically.

"Like you," Alex tossed the ball back to him, and he laughed.

"Touché. What are you doing for the rest of the day?" He liked talking to her, and he wanted to see her again, if he could pry her away from the hospital and her duties in the ICU. He wasn't sure he could.

"I'm working till six o'clock, and then I'm going to go home and sleep for about twelve hours. I have to be back here at eight o'clock tomorrow morning."

"You work too hard, Alex," he said sincerely, sounding concerned.

"Residency is like that. It's a form of slavery, I think all you have to do to pass eventually is prove you can survive."

"It all sounds very noble," he said blithely. "Do you suppose you could stay awake long enough to have dinner with me tonight?"

"With you and Rita Waverly?" she teased, but it had none of the malice he had gotten from Charlene the night before or earlier that morning. Alex wasn't like that. She seemed all innocence and decency and good spirits. It was very refreshing for Coop, who was so tired of jaded women. Alex was like a breath of fresh air in his very sophisticated existence. She was an entirely different creature, and the fact that she was Arthur Madison's daughter hadn't been forgotten either. A fortune of that magnitude couldn't be ignored.

"I could ask Rita, if you like," he said sensibly, "but I thought you might have dinner alone with me, if you can make it."

"I'd like to," she said honestly, she was flattered to be invited to dinner by Coop. "But I'm not sure I could stay awake long enough to eat."

"You can sleep on the banquette and I'll let you know what I ate. How does that sound?"

"Unfortunately, very realistic. Maybe if we do something early, quick, and simple. I haven't slept in about twenty hours." Her work ethic was inconceivable to Coop, but he nonetheless admired her for it.

"It will be interesting to try and meet those specifications. I accept the challenge. Where shall I pick you up?" He wasn't going to take no for an answer.

"How about my place?" She gave him an address

on Wilshire Boulevard, in a good but not overly luxurious building. She was entirely self-supporting. She didn't actually live on her resident's salary, but she tried to add very little to it, so as not to set herself too radically apart from the others. She had a very small studio apartment. "I could be ready by seven. But I really don't want to stay out late, Coop. I have to be wide awake and fully conscious while I'm working tomorrow."

"I understand," and he respected her for it. "I'll pick you up at seven, and we'll go someplace simple and easy. I promise."

"Thank you," she said, smiling at the prospect. She couldn't believe she was actually going to have dinner with Cooper Winslow. If she had told someone, she was certain they wouldn't have believed her. She went back to work after that, and Coop went to his lunch at Spago. It proved entertaining but fruitless.

Things had been more than a little thin for him of late. He'd been offered another commercial, for men's underwear this time, and he had refused to do it. He never lost sight of the importance of his image. But Abe's threats had remained clear in his mind. Much as he hated to be driven by financial concerns, he knew he had to make some money. All he needed was one great, big, fat movie, and a leading role at that. It never seemed impossible to Coop, or even unlikely. It was just a question of timing. And in the meantime, there were cameos and commercials. And girls like Alex Madison. But he wasn't after her money, he told himself. He just liked her.

Coop picked Alex up promptly at seven on Wilshire

Boulevard, and she came bounding out the door before he could walk into the lobby. The building looked respectable, though a little worn, and she admitted to him in the car that her apartment was relatively awful.

"Why don't you buy a house?" he questioned her, as they drove along in his favorite Rolls. Money was certainly no object for her, but she seemed very discreet, and he noticed that she wore no jewelry and dressed simply. She was wearing black slacks, and a black turtleneck sweater and a secondhand Navy peacoat. He was wearing gray slacks, a black cashmere sweater, and a leather jacket, and black alligator loafers. He had sensed that she would dress down, and he was taking her to a Chinese restaurant. And when he told her, she was delighted.

"I don't need a house," she said in answer to his question. "I'm never home, and when I am, I'm sleeping, and I don't know if I'm going to stay here. When I finish my residency, I'm not sure where I'll go into practice, although I wouldn't mind staying in Los Angeles." The one place she knew she wasn't going to go was back to Palm Beach, to her parents. That was a closed chapter for her. She only went for major holidays and state occasions, and as seldom as she could.

Coop had a fascinating evening with her. They talked about a thousand different subjects, Kenya again, and Indonesia, where she had done extensive traveling after college. And Bali, which was one of her favorite places, along with Nepal, where she'd gone trekking. She talked about the books she liked to read, most of which were surprisingly serious. And she had very eclectic taste in music. She knew a lot about antiques and architecture. And she was interested in politics, particularly as it related to medicine, and she was surprisingly knowledgeable about recent legislation on the subject. He had never known anyone like her. She had a mind like a finely tuned machine, and she was far better than any computer. He had to work hard to keep up with her, and he liked that. And when he asked, she told him she was thirty. She assumed he was somewhere in his late fifties, early sixties. She knew he'd been making movies for a long time, but she didn't know how old he'd been when he started. She would have been startled to realize that he had recently turned seventy, and he certainly didn't look it.

She had a delightful evening with him, and she said so as he drove her home. It was only nine-thirty, and he'd been careful not to keep her out late, or he knew she'd be reluctant to see him again, if he dragged her around till midnight and she felt like death the next morning. He knew she had to get up at six-thirty.

"You were a good sport to come out with me," Coop said generously. "I would have been very disappointed if you hadn't."

"That's nice of you, Coop. I had a great time, and the dinner was delicious." Simple, but good, and just spicy enough, the way she liked it. And he had been extremely good company, even better than she'd expected. She had feared he would be all glitter and flash and charm, and very much a product of his business. She was surprised to find him intelligent and warm, and well informed. She didn't have the feeling that he was playing a part, but rather that he was in fact a worthwhile human being, which surprised her.

"I'd like to see you again, Alex, if you have time, and aren't otherwise encumbered." He hadn't asked her until then if she had a boyfriend. Although other men had never stopped him. He had enough faith in himself to dispose of the best of them, and generally he had, without much trouble. He was, after all, Cooper Winslow. And he never forgot it.

"I'm not 'encumbered' actually. I don't have enough time to be. I'm not a very reliable date, I'm afraid. I'm either on duty, or on call."

"I know," he smiled, "or sleeping. I told you, I like a challenge."

"Well, I am one, in more ways than one," she admitted. "I'm a little gun-shy about serious relationships. A lot gun-shy actually."

"Thanks to your brother-in-law?" he asked gently, and she nodded.

"He taught me some painful lessons. I haven't ventured out too far in deep waters since then. I tend to stay at the shallow end, with the kiddies. I can handle that. I'm not so sure about the other stuff."

"You'll risk it for the right man, you just haven't met him yet." There was some truth to what he said, but honesty in what she had too. She was terrified of getting hurt again, hadn't had a serious relationship since her broken engagement, and dated very little.

"My life is my work, Coop. As long as we both understand that, then I'd love to see you."

"Good," he sounded pleased. "I'll call you." Though it wouldn't be too soon, he had good instincts about those things. He wanted her to miss him, and wonder why he wasn't calling. He knew exactly how to play

women. And Alex was open and easy to read, and she
had explained herself to him.

She thanked him without kissing him, and he
watched to make sure she got into the building safely.
He waved as he drove away, and she looked pensive
as she rode up in the elevator. It was hard to know if he
was for real, and she was skeptical. It would be so easy
to fall for someone as smooth and charming as he was,
and then God knew what would happen. As she let
herself into her apartment, she wondered if she should
go out with him again, or if it was too risky. He was a
very experienced player.

Alex took her clothes off and dumped them in a
heap on a chair, along with the surgical pajamas she'd
worn all day, and the ones she'd worn the day before,
and the day before that. She never had time to do laundry either.

Coop was very pleased with himself as he drove
home. It had gone exactly the way he had wanted it to.
And whatever his intentions, or hers, it had been a
good beginning. He would just have to see which way
the wind blew, and how he wanted to play it. But Alex
Madison was definitely an option.

He wasn't worried about it, and Alex didn't have
the energy to be. She was asleep before he even got
home to The Cottage.

Chapter 9

Charlene called Coop half a dozen times that night, and again, at least another dozen times, the next morning. But this time, Paloma didn't trick him into taking the calls. She knew he would have killed her. He finally took a call from her two days later. He was trying to let her down gently, although not speaking to her for two days was not Charlene's idea of gentle.

"What's up?" Coop asked casually when he took the call. "How are you?"

"I'm crazed, that's how I am," she said, sounding frantic. "Where the hell were you?"

"I was on location, doing a commercial." It was a lie, but it calmed her down for a minute.

"You could at least have called me," she said, sounding injured.

"I thought of it," he lied, "but I didn't have time. And I thought we both needed space. This isn't going to go anywhere, Charlene. I think you know that."

"Why not? We were great together."

"Yes, we were," he conceded gracefully. "But if nothing else, I'm too old for you. You need to find someone your own age to play with." It never even occurred to him that she was only a year younger than Alex.

"That's never stopped you before." She knew from the tabloids and people who knew him, that he'd been out with girls who were even younger than she. "That's just an excuse, Coop." She was right of course, but he would never have admitted that to her.

"It doesn't feel right," he tried another tack. "It's awfully hard making relationships work in our business." But that wasn't plausible either. They both knew he'd been out with every actress and starlet in Hollywood, sometimes for long periods of time. He just didn't want to pursue it with Charlene. He thought she was vulgar, at least in the way she dressed, and a little obsessive. What's more, she bored him. He was far more intrigued by Alex. And not entirely indifferent to her fortune. It wasn't his main attraction to her, but it certainly added incentive to lust and fascination. Charlene had none of that to offer. And he also wisely sensed that if he wanted to date Alex, he would have to keep his nose relatively clean. Appearing in the tabloids with a girl who had started as an actress in porn videos was not going to further his cause with Alex. And for the moment, Alex was the object of his current interest. Charlene was history, and an extremely brief, undistinguished chapter. He had had many like her, and he always tired of them quickly. And the few exotic elements she had, like a Japanese grandmother, and having lived in Paris and grown up in Brazil, simply didn't make up for what she lacked in distinction. Besides which, he had discovered, she had a vicious temper, and she seemed a little unbalanced to him. She was not taking the hint and disappearing gracefully, she was hanging on to him like a pit bull with a bone in its teeth, which was something Coop hated. He much preferred swift, painless endings to the dogged, desperate pursuit Charlene was inflicting on him. He resented her for it, and felt trapped and claustrophobic every time he talked to her.

"I'll call you in a few days, Charlene," he said finally, but that only enraged her.

"No, you won't. You're lying."

"I don't lie." He sounded greatly offended. "I have a call on the other line, I'll call you back."

"You're a liar!" she screamed, and he quietly disconnected. He didn't like anything about the way she was behaving. Overnight, she had become a major problem. But there wasn't much he could do about it. She'd give up eventually, but in the meantime, she was being very unpleasant, and Coop was annoyed at her.

He called Alex that afternoon, but she had three emergencies back to back, and she didn't get back to him till that evening. And all he got was a message on his voice mail from her. She'd been going to bed at 9 P.M. when she called, and said she had to be up at four the next morning. Establishing a relationship with her was not going to be easy, but it was definitely worth it, in Coop's eyes.

He finally connected with Alex the following afternoon. She only had a few minutes to talk, and she was on duty for the next several days, but she agreed to come to dinner on Sunday. Although she warned him she'd be on call then.

"What does that mean? They call you for advice?"

he asked hopefully, and somewhat naively. He couldn't remember ever dating a doctor, although he had dated several nurses, and a chiropractor once.

"No," she laughed easily, and he loved the sound of her laughter. Everything about Alex was honest and open. "It means I have to leave in a matter of seconds, if they page me."

"I may have to confiscate your pager in that case."

"There are days when that would be extremely appealing. Are you sure you want me to come to dinner if I'm on call?"

"Absolutely sure. I'll make you a doggie bag if you have to leave."

"Would you rather wait till I have a day off free and clear? I have one next week, if you'd prefer that," she offered fairly.

"No, I want to see you, Alex. I'll make something simple you can take with you."

"You're going to cook?" She sounded vastly impressed, and so was he. The only thing he could cook was toast for caviar, or boil water for tea.

"I'll figure out something." Life without a cook was a new challenge for him. He was thinking of calling Wolfgang Puck and having him send over some pasta and a salmon pizza. He liked that idea, and on Saturday, he called Wolfgang, who promised to send over a simple meal for two, and a waiter. It was perfect.

Alex arrived at five o'clock Sunday afternoon, on schedule, in her own car, as she said she needed it in case they called her back to work. She came chugging down the driveway, and was most impressed when she saw The Cottage. Unlike girls like Charlene, she had seen houses of its ilk before, in fact she had lived in several of them. Her parents' house in Newport looked very much like The Cottage, only bigger, although she didn't say that to Coop, she didn't want to be rude. She thought the property itself and the gardens were lovely, and she was excited about using the pool. Coop had told her to bring a bathing suit, and she had just gotten into the water, and swam in long, smooth strokes to the far end and back, as Coop watched her, when Mark and Jimmy arrived in shorts, after a game of tennis, or a game of "lob" as they had come to call it on the damaged court. They were surprised to see Coop and a very pretty young woman, and she was surprised to see them chatting with Coop when she surfaced from under the water.

She swam to the side of the pool, and Mark looked at her admiringly. She was a beautiful girl, and far more interesting looking than the one who had made him coffee. He was still hoping she had never told Coop about their early morning meeting.

"Alex, I'd like to introduce you to my houseguests," Coop said grandly, as he introduced them by name, and she smiled at them.

"What a wonderful place to stay," she said, smiling at them. "You're very lucky." They agreed with her, and a few minutes later, got into the pool with her. Coop rarely swam. Although he had been captain of the swimming team in college, he was happier sitting by the side of the pool, alternately chatting with them, and talking to Alex, and entertaining everyone with his outrageous stories about Hollywood.

They stayed by the side of the pool until six o'clock, and Coop took her inside to show her the house, and let her change back into dry clothes. Wolfgang's waiter was busy in the kitchen by then, and Coop said they would eat at seven. It was all wonderfully civilized, and they settled down in the library, while he offered her a glass of champagne, but she said she couldn't, in case she had to go back on duty. Being on call meant she couldn't touch alcohol, but Coop didn't seem to mind. And they were both relieved that so far at least, her pager had remained silent.

"Your houseguests seem very nice," Alex said comfortably as Coop sipped a glass of Cristal, and the waiter from Spago served delicious hors d'oeuvres, and disappeared back into the kitchen to finish the meal. "How do you know them?"

"They're friends of my accountant's," Coop said easily, which was a half-truth, but it explained their presence on his grounds.

"It's nice of you to let them stay here. They seem to love it." Mark had said he was barbecuing that night, and had invited Coop and Alex to join them, but Coop had said they had other plans. Mark had showed an obvious interest in Alex, and he'd commented on her to Jimmy in an undertone after she and Coop went back into the main house.

"Nice-looking girl," he said, and Jimmy said he hadn't noticed. He was still wandering around in a blur much of the time, and had no interest in women. Mark was coming back to life more quickly, and he was getting increasingly angry at Janet. It suddenly made other women seem more attractive to him. But his grief was a lot different than Jimmy's. "I'm surprised Coop is interested in her."

"Why?" Jimmy looked surprised. He hadn't paid much attention to her looks, but she was obviously intelligent, and Coop had said she was a doctor. She seemed appropriate to him.

"Big brain, small boobs. Not his usual profile, from what I've seen," Mark explained.

"Maybe there's more to him than we think," Jimmy suggested. There had been something vaguely familiar about her. He wasn't sure if it was just a type he had often seen back in Boston, or if he'd ever met her. He hadn't asked what kind of medicine she practiced, and Coop had monopolized most of the conversation with his stories. And they were always amusing. He was easy to be with, and both Mark and Jimmy could see why women liked him. He was infinitely charming, undeniably good-looking, and his wit was sharp and quick.

Coop and Alex had sat down to dinner by then, and Mark had started the barbecue. It was the first time he had used it, the week before they had used Jimmy's, and the steaks he'd made had been delicious. Mark was making hamburgers and Caesar salad. And things were going pretty well, until he put too much fuel on the charcoal and flames started leaping skyward, and seemed to get rapidly out of control.

"Shit, I haven't done this in a while," he apologized, trying to dampen the flames and save their dinner. But a minute later, there was a minor explosion. Coop and

Alex heard it from the dining room, where they were having an elegant dinner, courtesy of Wolfgang. They were having Peking duck, and three different kinds of pasta, with a big tossed salad and homemade bread.

"What was that?" Alex asked, looking worried.

"The IRA, I think," Coop suggested, seeming unconcerned, as they went on eating. "My houseguests probably blew up the guest wing." But as Alex looked over his shoulder out the window, she could see billows of smoke coming through the trees, and the next thing she saw were flames as a small bush caught fire.

"Oh my God, Coop.... I think the trees are burning."

He was about to tell her not to worry about it, when he turned to look and saw the same thing.

"I'll get a fire extinguisher," he said practically, without knowing if he even had one, and if so, where it was kept.

"You'd better call 911." She pulled her cell phone out of her bag without hesitating, and called them as Coop ran outside to see what had happened.

Mark was standing at the barbecue outside the guest wing, looking mortified, as he and Jimmy tried to squelch the flames with towels. It was a totally unsuccessful effort, and by the time the fire trucks roared through the gate ten minutes later, there was a good-sized blaze going. Alex was horrified, and Coop was worried about the house. It took the firemen less than three minutes to put it out. No great damage had been done, except that several of the neatly trimmed hedges had been scorched pretty badly. But by then, the firemen had spotted Coop, and for the next ten minutes he was signing autographs, and exchanging war stories with them, including his experiences as a volunteer firefighter in Malibu thirty years before.

He offered them each a glass of wine, which they declined, but they were still standing around admiring him and enjoying his stories half an hour later, while Mark continued to apologize, and Coop assured him there was no harm done, when Alex's pager went off, and she called the hospital on her cell phone while the others talked.

She walked away from the center of conversation so she could hear better. Two of their preemies had coded, and one had died. The resident on duty had his hands full and needed her to come in. A new patient was on its way in, a preemie that was hydrocephalic. She glanced at her watch as she approached the group again. She had promised to be back at the hospital in fifteen minutes, or less, if she could.

"What's your specialty?" Jimmy asked quietly as the others continued chatting. Coop had noticed neither her page, nor the conversation on the cell phone. He was too busy talking to the firemen and entertaining the entire group, but Jimmy had been intrigued by the questions he'd heard her ask on her cell. She sounded competent in the extreme.

"Neonatology. I'm a resident at UCLA."

"It must be interesting," he said pleasantly, as she caught Coop's attention and told him she had to leave.

"Don't let these two arsonists scare you off," Coop said with a grin in Mark's direction. Coop was being remarkably relaxed about the entire episode, which impressed Alex no end. Her father would have had a fit.

"They didn't," she smiled at him, "what's a little bonfire among friends? The hospital called me. I have to go in."

"They did? When? I didn't hear anything."

"You were busy. I've got to be there in ten minutes. I'm really sorry." She had warned him, but it was always disconcerting when it happened. And she'd been having a nice time with him.

"Why don't you just have a quick bite to eat before you go. It looks like an awfully good dinner."

"I know. I'd love to stay, but they need me. They've just had two emergencies, and there's another one on its way in. I've got to run," she said apologetically. She could see that Coop was disappointed, and so was she, but she was used to it. "I had a great time anyway. I loved the swim." She had been there for almost three hours, which was practically a record when she was on call. She said goodbye to Jimmy and Mark, and Coop walked her back to her car, as the firemen packed their gear on the trucks, and she promised to call him later. He was back in the group two minutes later, smiling and at ease.

"Well, that was short and sweet," he said with a rueful look at his tenants. They had grown accustomed to being called "houseguests." And he seemed to actually believe they were.

"What a nice woman," Mark said admiringly, sorry that she was Coop's, or seemed to be, and not available for closer inspection, although she was a little young for him. But she was even younger for Coop.

Like most of the women he dated, he could have been her grandfather.

"Would you gentlemen like to join me for dinner?" he suggested to Jimmy and Mark, whose hamburgers had turned to ashes in the ill-fated barbecue. "Wolfgang Puck sent over a very creditable meal, and I hate to eat alone," he said pleasantly, as the last of the firemen drove away.

Half an hour later, Coop and his "houseguests" were enjoying Peking duck, the assortment of pastas, and the salmon pizza, and Coop was regaling them with more of his stories. He poured the wine liberally, and by the time the two younger men left at ten o'clock, they had had a lot to drink, and they felt as though they had a new friend in Coop, or a very old one. The wine had been exceptional, and the dinner delicious. And he seemed no worse for wear when they left him.

"He's a great guy," Mark commented to Jimmy as they walked toward the guest wing.

"He's a character certainly," Jimmy agreed, realizing through the haze that surrounded him that he was going to have a hell of a headache in the morning, but at the moment it seemed worth it to him. It had been a very amusing evening. More than he could ever have dreamed it would be. Hanging out with a famous movie star seemed totally surreal.

The two friends said goodnight to each other, Mark went back to the guest wing, and Jimmy to the gatehouse, as Coop sat in the library, smiling to himself, sipping a glass of port. He'd had a very pleasant evening, although different than he'd expected. He was sorry that Alex had had to leave so early, but his two tenants had been fun, and surprisingly good company. And the firemen had added a little spice to the evening.

As Alex sat in her office at the hospital, sipping a cup of coffee, it was midnight before she had time to call Coop, and by then, she was sure it was too late to call. She hadn't had the evening she had expected to have either. The hydrocephalic baby had come in and was in a lot of trouble. And the first one that had coded earlier was doing a lot better. The one they had lost was a heartbreak for all of them. She wondered if she'd ever get used to that, but it was the nature of her business. And as she settled down on a cot in her office to get some sleep, she wondered what it would be like if she ever took Coop seriously, if one even could. It was hard to know who he really was behind the charm, and the wit, and the stories. She wondered if it was all a facade, or if there was someone real inside. It was hard to say, but she was tempted to find out.

She realized too that the age difference between them was considerable, but he was such an extraordinary man, she really didn't care about his age. There was something about Coop that made her want to ignore all the possible risks of being involved with him. He was enchanting and mesmerizing and captivating. She kept trying to remind herself that going out with him might not be such a wise idea. He was older, he was a movie star, and he had been involved with innumerable women over the years. But all she could think of was how dazzling and immensely appealing he was. The lure of him seemed to outweigh the downsides in her mind. She was hooked. And as she drifted off to sleep, she heard little warning bells go off in her head, but for the moment, she decided to ignore them all and see where things went.

Chapter 10

Mark was in a deep sleep, assisted by the wine he had drunk with Jimmy and Coop, when he heard the phone ring. He started to wake up, and then decided he was imagining it. He had had a lot to drink, and he knew if he opened his eyes, he would have a serious headache, so he kept his eyes closed and went on sleeping. But it continued ringing. He opened an eye finally and saw that it was 4 A.M. He turned over with a groan, and then realized he wasn't dreaming. The phone really was ringing, and he couldn't imagine who was calling him at that hour. He reached for the phone, and lay on his back with his eyes closed. The headache was already starting.

"Hello?" His voice sounded gruff, and the room was spinning. And for an instant, all Mark could hear was crying. "Who is this?" He wondered if it was a wrong number, and then his eyes flew open as he came fully awake. It was his daughter, calling from New York. "Jessie? Baby, are you okay? What happened?" He thought maybe something terrible had happened to Janet, or Jason. But all Jessica could do was cry. They were sobs of anguish, she sounded like a

wounded animal, or the way she had as a little girl
when their dog died. "Talk to me, Jess...what is it?"
He was panicked.

"It's Mom...." She went back to sobbing.

"Did she get hurt?" He sat up in bed and winced.
He felt like someone had hit him in the head with a
brick, but his adrenaline was pumping. What if she
was dead? He felt sick at the thought of it. Even if she
had left him, he still loved her, and would have been
heartbroken if she died.

"She has a *boyfriend*!" Jessica wailed, as he realized
it was seven o'clock in the morning in New York, but
only four in California. "We met him last night, and
he's a total jerk!"

"I'm sure he's not, sweetheart," Mark said, trying to
be fair, but in some part of him, he was relieved that
Jessica didn't like him. Mark hated him. He had destroyed their family and stolen Janet. How great a guy
could he be after all that? Not very, in Mark's estimation. And apparently in Jessie's as well.

"He's a creep, Dad. He tries to act like he's really
cool, and he orders Mom around like he owns her. She
says she just met him a few weeks ago, but I don't believe her. I know she's lying. He keeps talking about
stuff they did six months ago, and last year, and Mom
keeps acting like she doesn't know what he's talking
about, and trying to make him stop talking about it.
Do you think that's why she wanted us to move to
New York?" The ceiling had fallen in on Jessica, and
Janet had been very foolish to lie to the children. He
had wondered how she was going to handle it, and

when. Well, she'd done it, and badly, judging by Jessie's sobs.

"I don't know, Jess. You have to ask her."

"Is that why she left you?" They were heavy questions for the middle of the night, and not any he wanted to answer, surely not with a hangover of the degree he was developing. He already had a headache of mammoth proportions. "Do you think she had a boyfriend? Is that why she went to New York all the time when Grandma was sick, and after she died?"

"She told me she was worried about Grampa. And Grandma was very sick for a long time, she needed to be there," he said honestly. He thought Janet should level with her about the rest, eventually. If she didn't, Jessica would never trust her. And he couldn't blame her. He didn't trust her anymore either.

"I want to come back to California," Jessica said bluntly, sniffing loudly. But she was no longer sobbing.

"So do I," Jason said, echoing her words. He had gotten on the extension. He wasn't crying, but he sounded badly shaken. "I hate him, Dad. You would too. He's a real asshole."

"New York hasn't improved your language. You have to discuss all this calmly with your mother, not in the heat of the moment. And much as I hate to say it, you have to give this guy a chance." It was unlikely that they would be enthusiastic about anyone their mother dated. Or that he did, if he ever found anyone he wanted to date. He wasn't there yet. "He may turn out to be a very nice guy, no matter how long she's known him. And if he's important to your mom, you may have to get used to him. You can't make your minds up after five minutes." He was trying to be reasonable with them, for their sake as well as hers, but they didn't want to hear it. But stoking the fires against the man their mother was in love with, and had left him for, was only going to make the children more unhappy. If she married Adam eventually, they would have to accept him. There was no other choice.

"We had dinner with him, Dad," Jason said unhappily. "He treats Mom like he can make her do whatever he tells her, and she acts really dumb around him. She yelled at us after he left, and then she cried. I think she really likes him."

"Maybe she does," Mark said sadly.

"I want to come home, Dad," Jessica said, sounding agonized. But there was no home to come back to. They had sold it. "I want to go to my old school, and live with you," she insisted.

"Me too," Jason echoed.

"Speaking of which, shouldn't you guys be leaving for school right about now?" It was almost seven-thirty in New York, and he could hear Janet saying something to them from the background. He wasn't sure, but it sounded like she was shouting. She would have been shouting even louder if she'd known what they'd been saying to him, but he suspected she had no idea. He wondered if she even knew that he was on the line, and they had called him.

"Will you talk to Mom about our coming back to California?" Jessica asked in an undertone, confirming his suspicions that their mother didn't know who they were calling.

"No. You two have to give it a chance there. It's too

soon to do anything hasty. I want you both to settle down and try to be reasonable. And right now, I want you to go to school. We'll talk about this later." Much later. When the hangover was no longer hammering right behind his eyes.

They still sounded miserable when they got off the phone, and for the first time in two months, Jessica told him she loved him. But he knew it was only because at the moment she hated her mother. Eventually, the furor would die down, and they might even like Adam once they got to know him. Janet said he was a wonderful man. But in his heart of hearts, Mark still hoped they would hate Adam, out of loyalty to him. Given what Janet had done, it was hard not to feel that way.

Mark lay in bed thinking after he hung up, and wondering what he should do. For the moment, nothing, he decided. He was going to sit tight and see what happened. He rolled over in bed and tried to get to sleep again, but his head was pounding, and he was worried about them. It was six o'clock when he finally gave in to his own anxieties, and called their mother. She sounded nearly as unhappy as the children had earlier that morning.

"I'm glad you called," she said, surprised to hear him. "The kids met Adam last night, and they were awful to him."

"I'm not surprised. Are you? It's too soon for them to accept the idea that you're dating. And maybe they suspect you've known him for a while."

"That's what Jessica accused me of. You didn't tell her, did you?" she asked, sounding panicked.

"No, but I think you should, eventually. Otherwise, one of you will slip sometime, and they'll figure it out. They already suspect it, from things he said."

"How do you know?" She sounded startled, and he decided to be honest with her.

"They called me. They were pretty unhappy."

"Jessie slammed into her room and locked the door halfway through dinner, and Jason wouldn't even talk to him, or me. Jessie says she hates me." Mark could hear tears in Janet's voice.

"She doesn't hate you. She's hurt and angry, and she's suspicious of you. And she's right. We both know that."

"That's none of her business," Janet said hotly, feeling guilty.

"Maybe not, but she thinks it is. Maybe you should have waited to bring him around." She didn't want to tell Mark that Adam had been putting pressure on her to introduce him to the children, and she had acceded to his wishes. She didn't think they were ready either, but he said he refused to stay hidden any longer. If she was serious about him, he wanted to meet them. And it had been a disaster. She and Adam had had a huge fight afterwards, and he had stormed off, slamming the door behind him. It had been a nightmarish evening.

"What am I going to do?" Janet asked, sounding worried and anxious.

"Wait. Go easy on them. Give them time." She didn't want to tell him that Adam wanted to move in immediately, he didn't want to wait until they got married, and she wasn't sure she could stall him. She didn't want to lose him. Or her children. She felt pulled in all directions.

"This isn't as easy as you think, Mark," she said in a plaintive tone that made her sound like the victim, and they both knew she wasn't.

"Just don't screw our kids up in the process," he warned her. "I don't know how you can expect me to be sympathetic about this, or the kids for that matter. The truth is you did break up our marriage for him, and sooner or later, the kids are going to know that. That's a lot for them to swallow." It had been a lot for him to swallow, except that he had loved her, and still did. "They have a right to be angry. At both of you." It was the fairest thing he could say. He hated the fact that he was always the peacemaker, but he always seemed to be able to see all sides of a problem, not just his own. It was one of his great strengths, and failings, vis-à-vis her.

"Yeah. Maybe so. But I'm not sure he understands that. He doesn't have children, and he doesn't understand a lot about them."

"Then maybe you should have found another guy. Like me, for instance." She didn't answer, and he felt foolish for having said it. The wine and the port and the brandy weren't helping, nor was his headache. His hangover was already in full swing and he hadn't even gotten up yet. It had been a busy morning for him so far.

"I guess they'll calm down eventually," Janet said hopefully, but Adam wasn't going to tolerate it if they didn't. He wanted them to like him, and he was insulted by the way they'd behaved, and threatened her about it.

"Stay in touch," Mark said, and then hung up. He lay in bed for another two hours after that, unable to sleep, with his head pounding. It was nearly nine when he got up, and after ten when he got to the office. And the kids were back on the phone with him at lunchtime. They had just gotten home from school, and they were insistent that they wanted to come and live with him, but he told them he wasn't going to do anything hasty. He wanted them to calm down and at least try to be fair to their mother. But all Jessica could say was that she hated her, and she'd never speak to her again if she married Adam.

"We want to come and live with you, Dad," Jessica insisted. She was relentless.

"And what if I go out with someone you don't like? You can't keep running away from things like this, Jessie."

"Are you dating, Dad?" She sounded shocked. She hadn't even thought about that prospect, nor had Jason.

"No, but I will someday, presumably, and you might not like her either."

"You didn't leave Mom for her. I think Mom left you for Adam." He realized that if he hadn't known the truth himself, it would have been a brutal piece of information for him. Kids certainly didn't hesitate to throw bombs or information. But he did know. And Jessica's suspicions were accurate. He didn't want to tell her the truth, but he didn't want to lie to her either. "I'll run away if you make us live with her, Dad."

"Don't threaten me, Jess. That's not fair. You're old enough to know better. And you're getting your brother worked up. We'll talk about all this when we go on vacation together. You may feel differently about it by then. You may decide you like him after all."

"Never!" she said vehemently.

For the next two weeks, it was a constant battle. Tears, threats, calls in the middle of the night. Adam had actually been foolish enough to tell them he wanted to live with them and their mother. By the time Mark picked them up in New York, they were waging a full-scale war on their mother. And it was all they talked about during the vacation. And Janet had her hands full with Adam. He was telling her that if she didn't let him move in, he would feel that she was choosing her children over him. He said he had waited long enough for her. He wanted a life with her now, and her children. But her children didn't want him. And as a result, they didn't want Janet either. At the end of the vacation, Mark sat down with Janet, and told her he had no idea how to make them settle down and stay with her. Jessica was threatening to call a child advocacy lawyer, and ask the court to send her to her father. And she was old enough not only to do it, but to have the court listen, and so was Jason.

"I think you have a major problem on your hands here," Mark told her honestly. "There's no way to de-escalate this right now. What about letting them come back to LA till the end of the school year? You can renegotiate with them then. But I think you're only going to make things worse now if you force them to stay here. They are not willing to listen, or compromise."

She had handled the entire situation abominably, and she was paying the piper, and they both knew it. She felt torn in opposite directions, loyalty to Adam, and loyalty to her children. And the two factions were in direct conflict one hundred percent of the time.

"Will you send them back to me at the end of the school year?" she asked, looking panicked. She didn't want to lose her children. Or Adam. And he had not only told her he wanted to marry her as soon as the ink on the divorce was dry, but he wanted her to get pregnant. He wanted them to have a baby, maybe two. She couldn't even imagine selling that to her children. But she'd deal with that later. Right now they were threatening to move out and go back to their father.

"I don't know what I'd do," Mark said honestly about the following school year. "It depends what they want." She had created an incredible mess for herself, and Mark almost felt sorry for her. But he was torn by his own feelings too. She had damn near killed him when she left him, and the worst of it was that he still loved her, but he didn't tell her that. She was completely obsessed with Adam, enough so to jeopardize not only her marriage, but her relationship with her children. In Mark's eyes, she'd made a very bad bargain. He wouldn't have sacrificed anything for his children, and they knew it, which was why they wanted to come and live with him.

"Can you get them back into their old school?" Janet asked, dabbing at her eyes. She had never expected anything like this to happen, or she might not have left him. And now she had Adam on her hands, ready for a full-scale battle, to force her to allow him to move in with them.

"I don't know. Maybe. I'll try to get them into their old school," Mark said, mulling it over.

"Is your place big enough?" She was almost resigned to the idea. She could see that she had no other choice, unless she stopped seeing Adam, or hid him from them, and she knew he wouldn't let her do that.

"It's perfect for them," Mark reassured her. He described the grounds of The Cottage to her, and she cried as she listened. She knew she was going to be miserable without them, but maybe if they went to stay with Mark for a few months, they might ease into it when they got back. She hoped so. "I'll see what I can do when I go back, and I'll call you." Both children pounced on him after he'd talked to Janet, and wanted to know what their parents had agreed on. "Nothing yet," he said sternly to both of them, "we'll see what happens. I don't even know if I can get you back into school. And whatever happens, I want you to be nice to your mother in the meantime. This is hard for her too. She loves you."

"If she loved us, she'd have stayed with you," Jessica said bluntly with eyes full of anger. She was a pretty blonde teenager with a heart full of scars now. Mark just hoped he could minimize any future damage. He didn't want their divorce to destroy his children. That was the last thing he wanted.

"It doesn't always work that way, Jess," he said sadly. "People change...lives change...you can't always have what you thought you would, or do what you said you would. Life throws curves at you." But they didn't want to hear it. They were still furious with their mother, and her boyfriend.

He flew back to California that night, and spent the next week negotiating with their school to let them back in. They had been gone for less than three months, and they were in an excellent school in New York, so they hadn't lost any ground. And by the end of the week, their old school in Los Angeles had agreed to take them back. The rest was simple. All he had to do was hire a babysitter to keep an eye on them while he was at the office, and drive them to their after-school activities and sports. He didn't think that was going to be a problem, and he called Janet over the weekend.

"We're all set. They can start on Monday if they want, but I figured you'd want at least another week with them, to make your peace with them. It's up to you when you send them."

"Thanks, Mark. Thanks for being so decent. I guess I don't deserve it. I'm going to miss them so much," she said, and started to cry again. This whole chapter had been an agony in their lives, and now for their children.

"They'll miss you too. Once they stop being pissed off at you, they'll probably want to come back to school in New York after the summer."

"I'm not so sure. They're pretty emphatic about Adam, and he has very definite ideas. It's hard for him to start parenting with teenagers, particularly since he's never had children." From Mark's perspective, it sounded like a miserable situation, and he didn't envy Janet. He and the kids were calling the shots, and she was bouncing like a ball between them. She had never done well in stressful situations. He had always handled everything for her. Except her affair with Adam. She had managed that on her own, and screwed up everyone's life in the process.

She told the children on Sunday, and they didn't even have the grace to pretend they were sorry they were leaving. They both cheered, and Jessica started packing half an hour later. They would have gladly left the next day, but Janet insisted they spend another week with her. And she told them they would have to come home for the summer. She and Adam had already agreed to get married in July, when the divorce was final, but she didn't tell them that. She was afraid they'd never come back if she told them the news. She'd have to figure that out later.

It was an agonizing week for her, knowing they were leaving, and the following Saturday, she put them on a plane to California. Mark had decided not to hire a babysitter for them, he told her he had made an arrangement with his landlord's housekeeper. She was going to babysit for them. He was going to drive them to their activities himself, and shorten his workday if he had to. They were worth it.

Janet stood in the airport looking devastated when they left. They had hugged her before they left her, and Jason hesitated for a long moment. Even if he didn't want to stay, he felt sorry for her. But Jessica never even looked back. She just kissed her mother, said goodbye, and walked straight down the gangway. She could hardly wait to get to California, and see her dad.

And the scene at the other end was one of unreserved jubilation. Mark was waiting for them as they got off the plane, and the kids gave a whoop of joy. There were tears in his eyes as he held them. Things were finally beginning to look up for him. He had lost Janet irreversibly, maybe through his own fault, maybe not, but he had his kids back. That was all he wanted.

Chapter 11

Alex's work schedule was a whole new world for Cooper Winslow. He had never known another woman like her. He'd been involved with career women before, and even a couple of lawyers, but never a doctor. And not a resident. His dating life with her consisted of pizzas, fast food, and Chinese take-out, and nearly every meal, movie, and evening was interrupted by calls from the hospital. She couldn't help it. It was why most residents had no personal life, and most of them dated doctors or nurses, or other med students or residents. Dating a famous movie star was a whole other experience for her. But she was clear about the demands on her time, and she did the best she could to juggle. Coop did his best to adjust to it. He was excited about her. And most of the time, he forgot about her fortune. Every now and then, it crossed his mind, and it only enhanced the package further. Like a red ribbon on a Christmas gift. But he tried not to think about it. His only concern was how her parents would feel about him. So far, he hadn't dared discuss it with her.

Things were moving slowly between them, partially because of the number of hours and days she worked, and in part because she'd been badly burned, and was extremely cautious. She didn't want to make another mistake, and she had no intention of moving quickly with Coop. He had kissed her after the fifth date, but they had gone no further, and he didn't press her. He was smarter than that, and far more patient. He wasn't going to sleep with her until she begged him for it. He knew instinctively that if he pushed her, she might back off or bolt, and he didn't want that to happen. He was more than willing to wait until she was ready for him to make a move. He was exquisitely patient.

And Charlene had finally disappeared off his screen. After two weeks of his not responding to her calls, she had stopped calling. Even Paloma approved of Alex. It would have been hard not to. But Paloma felt sorry for her, and wondered if she knew what she was getting into, although Coop was behaving for the time being. Even when he wasn't with Alex, he stayed at home at night and read scripts, or went out with friends. He went to another, smaller dinner at the Schwartzes', but Alex couldn't make it this time, she was working. And he didn't mention her to them. He didn't think it was a good idea for people to know they were dating. He wanted to keep every possible breath of scandal from her. He knew how proper and decent she was, and she would have hated being dragged through the tabloids, as a member of a chorus line he was now trying to avoid. She knew of his reputation to some extent, he had been a glamorous playboy around

Hollywood for decades after all, but he preferred to keep the details from her.

And at the places where they dined, they were unlikely to catch the attention of the tabloids. He hadn't taken her to a decent restaurant yet, simply because she never had the time or the energy for an elegant evening. She was always working. It was a major victory when they went to a movie. And she enjoyed coming to The Cottage whenever she was off on the weekends. She swam in the pool, and she cooked dinner for him one night, and then had to leave before she could eat it with him. She was used to it, but it was a major adjustment for Coop. He had had no idea what he was getting into. But it seemed challenging, and she was so bright and intelligent, the obstacles and inconveniences seemed worth it to him.

She enjoyed chatting with Mark when she ran into him at the pool. He talked a lot about his kids, and shared with her one night, the problems he was having with them and Janet, and Adam. He admitted to Alex that he didn't really want them to like the man who had destroyed his marriage, and at the same time he didn't want his kids to be unhappy. Alex felt sorry for him, and liked talking to him.

She saw less of Jimmy than she did of Mark. He seemed to work almost as hard as she did. He visited foster homes on some evenings, and coached a softball team in the projects. But Mark always said what a great guy he was, and he told her what he knew about Maggie. Her heart went out to him as she listened, but Jimmy never talked about his wife when Alex saw him. He kept to himself a lot of the time, and he seemed uncomfortable around women. He hated the fact that he was single again. In his heart, he was still married. And by then, she had figured out that they were both tenants, although Coop never admitted it to her, and she never questioned him about it. She figured it was none of her business what his financial arrangements were with them.

She had dated Coop for three weeks when he invited her to go away for a weekend. She said she would see if she could get the time, although she doubted it, and was amazed when she found she could arrange it. Her only condition was separate rooms at the hotel. She wasn't ready to commit her body to the relationship yet. She wanted to take her time, and move slowly, but she was immensely attracted to him. And she told Coop she would pay for her own hotel room. They were going to stay at a resort he knew in Mexico, and she was excited about it. She hadn't taken a vacation since she started her residency, and she loved to travel. Two days of sun and fun with him sounded like heaven to her. And she assumed that by going to Mexico, they would avoid any noise in the tabloids. No one would know what they were up to. It was a naive assessment on her part, and Coop didn't disabuse her of it. It suited his purposes not to. He wanted to go away with her, and didn't want to discourage her from going by frightening her about the press. He wanted to keep everything simple and pleasant.

They left on a Friday night, and the hotel was even more beautiful than he had promised her it would be. They had connecting rooms, and an enormous living room and patio, their own pool, and a little private beach just beyond it. They never saw anyone, except when they wanted to. And in the late afternoon, they went into town, wandered into shops, and sat at outdoor cafés drinking margaritas. It felt like a honeymoon, and on the second night, just as he had hoped she would, she seduced him. She wasn't even drunk when she did it. She wanted to. She was falling in love with him. No man had ever been as kind to her, as thoughtful, or as gentle. He was not only a wonderful companion, and a great friend, but the perfect lover. Cooper Winslow knew his way around women. He knew what they wanted, what they liked to do, and how they liked to be treated, as well as what they needed. She had never enjoyed shopping with anyone as much as she did with Coop, she had never talked as easily to anyone, never laughed as much, had never been as spoiled. She had never known anyone like him.

She was also surprised by how many autographs he signed, and how many people stopped him to take his photograph. It seemed like the whole world knew him. But none as well as she did. Or at least that was what it felt like to her. He seemed surprisingly willing to share not only his life and his history, but his innermost secrets with her. And she reciprocated easily. She was entirely open with him.

"What are your parents going to think about us?" Coop asked after they made love for the first time. It had been a memorable experience. And they sat in their private pool afterwards, naked in the moonlight, with music in the distance. It had been the most romantic night of her life.

"God knows," she said, looking pensive. "My father's never liked anyone in his life, man or woman, including his children and my mother. He's suspicious of everyone. But it's hard to imagine him not liking you, Coop. You're respectable, you're well born, you're polite, intelligent, charming, successful. What's to object to?"

"He may not like the difference in our ages." For a start.

"That's possible. But some days you look younger than I do." She smiled at him in the moonlight, and they kissed again. He hadn't told her that there was also a difference in their circumstances, that she was solvent, and he wasn't. It pained him to admit it. It wasn't a reality he faced often. But it was nice knowing she wasn't financially dependent on him. That had always been an issue for him. He had never wanted to take on a wife, when his own circumstances weren't stable, and most of the time, they weren't. Even when he had money, it slipped right through his hands. He didn't need help spending it, and most of the women he had known had been fearfully expensive. Alex wasn't, and she had her own anyway, so it wasn't an issue. For the first time in his life, he was actually thinking about marriage. In a vague, distant way of course, but it no longer terrified him to the same degree. Much to his own amazement, he could actually contemplate settling down with her, without wanting Dr. Kevorkian to officiate at the wedding. He had always thought he would have preferred suicide to marriage. The two had always seemed equally lethal, and synonymous to some degree. But with Alex, everything was different.

And he said so, in the magical Mexican night, as he kissed her.

"I'm not there yet, Coop," she said softly, always honest with him. She loved him, but didn't want to mislead him. She was by no means ready for marriage, both because of her medical career, and her previous brush with disaster as she approached the altar. She didn't want another disappointment, but Coop seemed like the one man who wouldn't do that to her.

"I'm not there yet either," he whispered. "But at least it doesn't give me shingles when I think about it. For me, that's an improvement." She liked the fact that they were both cautious about marriage. So much so, that he had never done it before. When she'd asked him about it, he had said that he'd never found the right girl. But now he was beginning to think he finally had. Alex was a woman worth having for a lifetime.

The weekend they shared was magical, and when they flew back to LA, they were both starry-eyed and sorry to leave each other.

"Do you want to stay at the house with me?" he asked as he drove her home from the airport, and she looked pensive as she thought about it.

"Want to, yes. But probably shouldn't." She still wanted to move slowly. She was afraid to get used to it, and then have something go wrong that would spoil it. "I'm going to miss you tonight though."

"So will I," he said, and meant it. He felt like a new man. He insisted on carrying her bag up to her apartment. He had never seen it, and he was shocked when he did. He was stunned by the stacks of discarded hospital scrub suits, lying in piles, the medical books stacked sky high on the floor, the bathroom with no frills and no amenities. All she had was soap, toilet paper, and towels. She hardly had any furniture, no curtains, no rugs, no decor. "For God's sake, Alex, it looks like a barracks." She had never bothered to decorate it. She didn't have time, and she didn't care. All she did was sleep there. "If anyone sees this, they're going to condemn it." All he could do was laugh at the way she lived. She was so exquisite and so delicate, but all she had cared about for years was being a doctor. He had seen gas stations that were more inviting. "I think you should throw a match into this place and move in with me immediately." But he knew she wouldn't. She was far too cautious and independent to do that. Not for a while at least. But in spite of the unmade bed and the grim decor, he spent the night with her, and got up with her when she left for work at six o'clock the next morning. And when he got back to The Cottage, he truly missed her. He had never felt that way before about any woman.

Paloma came in later that morning, and when she saw the look on his face, she was intrigued. She was beginning to think he really was in love with the young doctor. It almost made her like him better. Maybe he had a heart after all.

He was out at a series of appointments all afternoon, and posed for the cover of *GQ*. It was six o'clock when he got home, and he knew Alex was still working. She was going to be at the hospital until the next morning. She had to pay her dues for the trip to Mexico. She was going to have to work for several days to pay people back for the shifts they had taken for her.

He had just settled down in the library with a glass of champagne, and put some music on, when he heard a terrifying sound at the front door. It sounded like a machine gun, or a series of explosions, as though part of the house were falling down, and he got up to look out the window. At first he didn't see anything, and then he caught a glimpse of a young boy, and Coop's eyes opened wide with amazement. The little hooligan was riding a skateboard down the marble steps, and using it to do exotic jumps, and land on the marble that stretched out around it. He did it again and again, and with a few quick strides, Coop reached the front door and yanked it open with a look of fury. The marble had been there since 1918, unblemished, and the juvenile delinquent skateboarding on it was going to destroy it.

"What the hell do you think you're doing? I'm going to call the police if you don't get out of here in the next three seconds. How did you get on this property?" The alarms should have gone off when he climbed over the gate, and hadn't. Coop couldn't imagine any other way for him to get there. The boy stood staring up at him in terror and amazement.

All he could think of to say was, "My father lives here," in a strangled voice as he clutched his skateboard to his chest. He had never contemplated for an instant the damage he might do to the marble. It just looked like a good place to practice jumps, and he'd been having a great time doing it, until Coop opened the door and shouted at him, threatening to have him arrested.

"What do you mean your father lives here? I live here, and thank God, I'm not your father!" Coop said, still in a fury. "Who are you?"

"I'm Jason Friedman." The boy looked like he was shaking, and he dropped the skateboard with a clatter, which made them both jump. "My father lives in the guest wing." He had arrived the night before from New York, with his sister. And he loved the place. He had spent all afternoon exploring it, after he got back from school. The night before, Mark had introduced him and Jessica to Jimmy, and they'd had dinner with him. Jason had only heard about Coop from his father. And Coop was in Mexico for the weekend when they arrived. And to add insult to injury, Jason looked at him, and added, "And now I live here too, and so does my sister. We got here yesterday, from New York." All the boy wanted was not to get arrested. He was willing to offer name, rank, and serial number, and any information Coop wanted to prevent that from happening.

"What do you mean, you 'live' here? How long are you staying?" He wanted to know how long he had to endure the presence of the enemy within his borders. He vaguely remembered Liz telling him that Mark had children who would come to visit from New York occasionally, but only for a few days and very rarely.

"We left our mom in New York, and we came to live with our dad. We hated her boyfriend." It was more information than Jason would have offered normally, but Coop was more than a little daunting.

"I'm sure he hated you too, if you took a skateboard

to his marble steps. If you ever do that again, I will personally whip you."

"My father wouldn't let you," Jason said fiercely. He had decided the man was crazy. He knew he was a movie star, but first he had threatened to have him arrested, and now he was threatening to whip him. "You'd end up in jail. But anyway," he backed down slightly, "I'm sorry. I didn't hurt them."

"You could have. Have you actually moved here?" That was the most horrifying piece of information he'd had so far, and he hoped the boy was lying. But he had a gnawing terror that he wasn't. "Your father didn't tell me you were moving in."

"It was kind of a last-minute decision, because of the boyfriend. We just got here yesterday, and we started back at our old school today. My sister's in high school."

"I don't find that reassuring," Coop said, looking at him with anguish. This couldn't be happening to him. These two children couldn't have come to live in his guest wing. He was going to have to evict them. As quickly as possible before they burned the place to the ground, or damaged something. He was going to call his lawyer. "I'll speak to your father," he said menacingly, "and give me that," he said, reaching for the skateboard, but Jason took a big step back from him, unwilling to give it up. It was his prize possession, and he'd brought it with him from New York.

"I said I was sorry," Jason reminded him.

"You said a great many things, mostly about your mother's boyfriend." Coop was all aristocratic grandeur as he looked down at him from the top step. He was a tall man, and Jason was standing on the marble which led to the steps. From where he stood, Coop looked like a giant.

"He's an asshole. We hate him," Jason volunteered about the boyfriend.

"That's very unfortunate. But that doesn't mean you can come to live in my house. Not by a long shot," he said, glowering at him. "Tell your father I'll speak to him in the morning." And with that, he walked back into the main house and slammed the door, as Jason skated hell-for-leather back to the guest wing, and recounted a modified version of the encounter to his father.

"You shouldn't have skated on the steps, Jase. It's an old house, and you could have damaged them."

"I told him I was sorry. He was a real shithead."

"He's a nice guy actually. He's just not used to having kids here. We have to go a little easy on him."

"Can he make us leave?"

"I don't think so. That would be discrimination, unless you do something awful and give him reasonable cause. Do me a favor, try not to." Both kids had loved the place when they saw it. And Mark was thrilled to have them with him. They had been beside themselves with joy when they saw their old friends at school. Jessica was already on the phone, with everyone she knew. And Mark had been cooking dinner. They had met Paloma in the courtyard that afternoon, and she loved them. But her employer was significantly less enchanted. He still didn't know that Paloma occasionally did laundry and some minor housekeeping for Mark in her spare time.

Coop had poured himself a stiff drink the minute he slammed the door, and sat down to page Alex. She called him five minutes later. She could hear in his voice that something terrible had happened.

"My house has been taken over by aliens," he said in a voice that was so shaken it didn't sound like him.

"Are you all right?" She sounded worried.

"No, I'm not. Mark's children have moved in. I've only met one of them, but he's a juvenile delinquent. I'm going to start eviction proceedings immediately. But I may have a nervous breakdown in the meantime. The boy was skateboarding on my front steps, doing jumps off the marble." She laughed when he said it, and was relieved that it was nothing serious. But Coop sounded as though the house had fallen in.

"I don't think you can evict them. There are all kinds of laws to protect people with children," she said sensibly, amused by how upset he was. He truly hated kids, just as he'd said he did.

"I need laws to protect me. You know how I hate children."

"I guess that means we won't be having any, huh?" She was teasing him, but it occurred to him that that could be a major obstacle for her. He hadn't thought about it, but she was young enough to want children. And he was in no mood to think about it now.

"We can certainly discuss it," he said reasonably. "Your children would be civilized at least. Mark's aren't. Or at least not this one. He says his sister is in high school. She probably smokes crack and deals drugs at her school."

"It may not be quite as bad as all that, Coop. How long will they be there?"

"It sounds like forever. Tomorrow would be too long. I'm going to call him in the morning and inquire."

"Well, try not to get yourself in a state over it." But she could hear that he already was.

"I'm becoming an alcoholic. I think I have a severe allergy to anyone under the age of twenty-five. He can't possibly intend to have his children live here. And what if I can't throw them out?"

"We'll make the best of it, and teach them to behave."

"You're sweet to say that, my love. But some people cannot be taught. I told him I'd whip him if he skateboarded on my steps again, and he said he'd have me put in jail." They were definitely off to a rocky start. But threatening to whip him had hardly been the politically correct thing to say.

"Just tell Mark to keep them out of your hair. He's a nice guy. I'm sure he'll understand."

The next day, when Coop called him, Mark apologized profusely for any disturbance Jason had caused. He explained the circumstances to Coop, all of them, and said that he was sure the kids would go back to Janet at the end of the school year. More than likely, they would only be there for three months.

It sounded like a death sentence to Coop. All he wanted to hear was that they were leaving the next day. But there wasn't a chance. Mark swore they would behave, and Coop resigned himself to living cheek by jowl with them. He knew he had no other choice. He had called his attorney before calling Mark, and Alex had been right. He was stuck with Jason and Jessica, and even the letter of apology Mark forced Jason to write barely mollified Coop. He was furious that Mark had somehow snuck them in on him. Coop didn't want to run a high school or a nursery, or a Cub Scout troop, or a skateboard park. He didn't want children within a hundred miles of his house, or his life. He just hoped their mother's romance ended quickly, and they'd go back to her soon.

Chapter 12

After Coop's initial run-in with him, Mark told Jason to stay away from the main wing of the house at all times, and only use his skateboard on the driveway. Jason saw Coop drive in a few times, but there was no further incident, at least for the first two weeks of their living there. They were happy to be back in LA with their old pals, loved their school, and thought their new home was really "cool," in spite of what they referred to as their crabby landlord. He continued to take a dim view of them, but both the realtor and his attorneys had told him there was nothing he could do. There were strong laws to prevent people from discriminating against children. And Mark had warned him that he had kids and they'd be out from time to time. He had a right to live there with his children, even now that they were in residence full-time. Coop had no other option than to get used to it, and complain if they did something they shouldn't. And other than Jason using his front steps as a skateboard ramp on the first day he was there, so far at least there had been no other problems.

It was only on the first weekend Alex spent at the

house with him, that they both woke up at noon, and heard what sounded like a convention in full progress at his pool. It sounded like there were five hundred people shouting to each other. There was loud rap music coming from somewhere, and Alex couldn't help smiling as she lay in bed listening to the lyrics. They were absolutely filthy, but very funny, and totally irreverent about grown-ups and what kids thought of them. It was quite a message to Coop.

"Oh my God, what is that?" Coop asked with horror as he raised his head from his pillow, looking stunned.

"It sounds like a party of some kind," Alex said with a stretch and a yawn, as she cuddled up beside him. She had traded four shifts just to be there, and things were going well between them. Coop was adjusting well to her busy life, and he hadn't enjoyed any woman as much in years. And in spite of their considerable age difference, she was very comfortable with him. Even after giving it some careful thought, his age wasn't an issue for her. He seemed younger, and far more interesting, than most men her age.

"It must be the aliens again. I think another UFO just landed." He had had sightings of teenagers in the past three weeks, but Mark seemed to be keeping them in good control, until that morning. Coop was not yet aware that Paloma was doing occasional babysitting for them. "They must be deaf. You could hear that music in Chicago for chrissake." He got out of bed and looked out the window. "Oh my God, Alex, there are thousands of them." She got out of bed to look with him, and there were twenty or thirty teenagers, laughing and shouting and throwing things, at the pool.

"Looks like a party," Alex confirmed, "must be someone's birthday." She thought it was nice seeing healthy, happy kids having fun. After all the agony and tragedy she saw in her daily life, it looked blissfully normal. But standing next to her, Coop looked horrified.

"Aliens don't have birthdays, Alex. They hatch at the most inconvenient time, and then they come to Earth to break everything in sight. They were sent here to destroy us and Planet Earth."

"Do you want me to go out and tell them to turn down the music?" she asked helpfully with a broad grin. She could see that it really upset him. He loved his peaceful, orderly life, and he loved having everything beautiful and elegant around him. The songs they were listening to qualified as neither, and she felt sorry for him.

"That would be lovely," he said gratefully, as she stepped into shorts and a T-shirt and slipped her feet into sandals. It was a beautiful spring day, and she promised to make breakfast as soon as she got back. He thanked her, and went to take a shower and shave before breakfast. He always looked impeccable, and he even looked handsome and in relatively good order when he woke up. Unlike Alex, who always woke up feeling as though she'd been dragged behind a horse on a rope all night. Her hair was all over the place, and with the hours she worked, she was always exhausted. But she had youth on her side, and she looked like a kid herself as she went out to the pool, to deliver his message to Mark.

When she got to the pool, she saw that Mark was there, and Jessica was at the hub of a flock of girls in bikinis and one-piece bathing suits, giggling and screaming. The boys were being "cool" and ignoring them, and Mark was trying to organize a game of Marco Polo from the pool.

"Hi, how've you been? I haven't seen you in a while," he said pleasantly when he saw her. He'd been beginning to wonder if Coop had stopped seeing her. But Mark hadn't seen any other women there either. Things had been relatively quiet for weeks.

"I've been working. What's the occasion? Someone's birthday?"

"Jessie just wanted to get together with her old friends and celebrate being back here." She was ecstatic to be living with her father, and for the moment she was refusing to speak to her mother, much to Mark's dismay. But so far at least, he hadn't been able to sway her. He kept telling Janet to give her time, but Jessica seemed to be relentlessly unforgiving. At least Jason was willing to talk to her, but he made no bones about the fact that he was thrilled to be living with his father.

"I hate to bug you about it, they look like they're having so much fun," Alex said apologetically, "but Coop is having a little problem with the noise. Do you think they could turn the sound system down a little?" Mark looked startled, and then winced, realizing how bad it had gotten. He was so used to the chaos of having kids around, he hadn't noticed. And he realized he probably should have warned Coop of the gathering, but he was afraid now to even mention the kids to him.

"I'm sorry. Someone must have turned the volume up while I wasn't looking. You know how kids are." She did, and she was happy to see that they were good, clean, wholesome kids. There wasn't a tattoo or a Mohawk in sight. Just a lot of earrings and the occasional nose pierce. Nothing scary. And none of them looked like delinquents or druggies, contrary to what Coop would have told her if he'd seen them. They were just ordinary "aliens," in Alex's opinion.

Mark got out of the pool and went to turn the sound down on the stereo, and Alex stood smiling as she watched the kids for a minute. She saw that Jessica was a pretty girl, with long, straight blonde hair and a lovely figure, and she was giggling uncontrollably in the midst of her girlfriends, as several young boys eyed her with lust. She seemed to be oblivious to them. And then, Alex saw Jason approach with Jimmy. He was wearing a catcher's mitt and holding a baseball, and he was wearing a big grin as they talked earnestly about something. Jimmy had just taught him how to put a spin on the ball with unfailing precision. It was an art Jason had never previously mastered, but Jimmy made it easy for him.

"Hi," Alex said pleasantly, as they stopped where she was standing. Jimmy looked awkward for a minute, and then introduced her to Jason. There was always something guarded about Jimmy's eyes, as though even looking at people now was painful. Alex could see the toll his loss had taken on him. He looked like someone who had suffered a trauma. He had that familiar shell-shocked look she saw in the eyes of parents who had just lost their babies. But when he was talking to Jason, he seemed more at ease than when he was in the midst of adults. "How've you been?" she asked casually. "Been to any good fires recently?" The last time she'd seen him was when Mark had nearly caused a forest fire with the barbecue, and they'd paged her to come back on duty. "That was quite an experience." They both smiled at the memory. And she still had an unforgettable vision of Coop signing autographs for the firemen while the bushes were burning. It made her laugh to think of it.

"I got a very good dinner out of it," Jimmy said with a shy smile. "I think we ate yours after you left. Too bad you had to go back to work. But if you hadn't, we wouldn't have gotten dinner," he said sensibly, and then grinned at his own memory of the evening. "It was quite an evening. I haven't been that hungover since I was in college. I couldn't even go in to work until eleven o'clock the next morning. He serves some pretty exotic stuff, and a lot of it."

"Sounds like I missed a good time," she smiled at him, and then turned her attention to Jason and asked him what position he played. He said he was a shortstop.

"He throws a good ball," Jimmy praised him, "and he's a hell of a hitter. We lost three balls this morning, over the fence. Definite home runs, right out of the park."

"I'm impressed. I can't hit a ball to save my life," she confessed.

"Neither could my wife," he said, without thinking. The words were out of his mouth before he could stop them. And she could see in his eyes that they had hurt him. "Most women can't hit a ball, or throw one. They have other virtues," he said, trying to bring the comment back to the world at large and get it away from Maggie.

"I'm not sure I have those virtues either," Alex said easily, sensing that it had been an uncomfortable moment for him. "I can't cook to save my life. But I make a mean peanut butter sandwich, and I order a great pizza."

"That'll do it. I'm a much better cook than my wife was." Damn. He had done it again. She could see him retreat behind a wall after he made the comment, and he lapsed into a distracted silence as she chatted with Jason, and then the boy wandered off to see his sister and her friends.

"They're nice kids," Alex said, hoping to put him at ease again. She could see what a hard time he was having, and she wanted to tell him she was sorry, but she didn't want to upset him more than he already was.

"Mark is out of his mind with joy to have them out here. He really missed them," Jimmy said, trying to drag himself back from the precipice. He was constantly falling into an abyss of grief. Everything he said or did reminded him of Maggie. "How's our landlord handling it?"

"He's in deep therapy, and on mood-altering medication," she said solemnly, and Jimmy burst into laughter. It was a wonderful sound, and in sharp contrast to what she suspected he was feeling most of the time.

"That bad, huh?"

"Actually, worse. Last week, he almost coded." It was hospital-ese for a code blue, when all of a patient's systems failed, their heart stopped, and they stopped breathing. But Jimmy seemed to understand. "I think he might make it, but I had to brush up on my CPR training. We've got him on a respirator now, speaking of which, I'd better get back. I came out here to ask them to turn down the music."

"What's it going to be?" Jimmy asked casually.

"It's been rap up to now, with some pretty juicy lyrics." She grinned at him.

"No, breakfast, I mean. Peanut butter, or pizza?"

"Hmmm...now that's an interesting question. I hadn't thought about it. Personally, I'd opt for pizza, used, leftover. I live on it. With doughnuts for dessert, preferably stale. I think Coop has more mundane taste, maybe eggs and bacon."

"Can you handle it?" Jimmy asked solicitously. He liked her, he got a sense of enormous warmth and compassion from her. He wasn't sure what she did, but he remembered it was something with babies. And he suspected she was good at it. She was obviously smart, and seemed like a very caring person. He hadn't figured out yet what she was doing with Cooper Winslow. It seemed like an odd match to him, but there was no accounting for people's choices of partners and playmates. They never seemed to follow the path you'd expect them to. Coop was old enough to be her father and then some. She didn't look like the kind of woman to be lured by celebrity or glamour. It made him wonder if there was more to Coop than he suspected, or maybe, bad news, less to Alex. In spite of the evening Jimmy had spent with him, he didn't think much of Cooper. Charming and handsome without a doubt, but not a lot of substance or depth.

"Can I call 911 to deliver breakfast?" Alex asked, continuing the banter. He was a sweet guy, and she felt sorry for him.

"Sure, just have Coop sign for it," he said unkindly, and then was instantly apologetic. He had no reason to be nasty about the guy, and he knew it. "Sorry, that was uncalled for."

"It's okay, he has a great sense of humor, even about himself. It's one of the things I like about him."

It made him want to ask her what else there was to like, other than his looks, but he didn't.

"Well, I'd better get back. I guess we won't be using the pool today. Coop definitely couldn't handle this scene. We'd have to restrain him." They both laughed, and she waved at Mark and went back to the main wing, where she found Cooper looking petulant, and struggling with breakfast. He had burned muffins to a crisp, and had broken the yolks on all four of the eggs he was frying. The bacon was burned beyond recognition, and he had spilled orange juice all over the table.

"You can cook!" she said with amazement, and a broad smile as she took stock of the chaos. She couldn't have done much better. She was far more skilled in the ICU than in the kitchen. "I'm impressed."

"Well, I'm not. Where the hell were you? I thought the aliens had taken you hostage."

"They're nice kids, Coop. I don't think you need to worry. I was just chatting with Mark and Jimmy, and Mark's son, Jason. All the kids out at the pool look polite and wholesome and well-behaved." He turned to stare at her then, with a spatula in his hand, as the eggs burned.

"Oh my God... it's the pod people... they've exchanged you... you're one of them... who are you really?" He had the wide-eyed look of horror you only saw in science fiction movies and she laughed at him.

"I'm still me, and they're fine. I just thought I'd tell you so you don't worry."

"You were gone so long, I figured you'd run off with them, so I made my own breakfast... *our* breakfast," he corrected, and then looked around him with dismay. "Do you want to go out to eat? I'm not sure any of this is edible." He looked a little discouraged.

"I guess I should have ordered a pizza."

"For breakfast?" He looked appalled, and rose to his full height with a look of indignation. "Alex, your eating habits are dreadful. Don't they teach you anything about nutrition in med school? Pizza is not an appropriate breakfast, even if you are a physician."

"Sorry," she said humbly, and put two more muffins in the toaster, and then cleaned up the spilled orange juice and poured two more glasses.

"This is women's work," he said with a look of chauvinistic relief. "I think I'll leave you to it. Just give me orange juice and coffee." But five minutes later, she produced scrambled eggs, bacon, muffins, juice, and coffee, and brought it to him on a tray on the terrace. She had used his best plates, Baccarat crystal for the orange juice, and folded paper towels in lieu of napkins.

"The delivery is excellent.... You need a little work on table service.... Linen is always a nice touch when you're using good china," he teased her, but he smiled at her as he set down the newspaper.

"Just be grateful I didn't use toilet paper. We do that at the hospital when we run out of napkins. It works fine, so do paper plates and Styrofoam cups. I'll bring some for next time."

"I'm enormously relieved to hear it," he said grandly. She had a way of refusing to be pretentious no matter where she'd grown up, or what her last name was. When they finished the excellent eggs she had prepared for them, it led to a question he'd been meaning to ask her. "How do you suppose your family would feel about me, Alex? About us, I mean." He looked worried, and it touched her. She had a growing feeling that he was serious about her, and she didn't really mind. So far at least, she liked everything about him, but it was early days yet. They had been going out for barely more than a month, and a lot of things could change, problems could come up, as they got to know each other better.

"What difference does it make? They don't run my life, Coop. I do. I decide who I want to spend time with."

"And they have no opinions on the subject? That seems unlikely." From everything he'd read about her father, Arthur Madison had opinions about everything on the planet, and surely about his daughter. And from what Coop knew, most of what Arthur Madison thought and did was not overly warm and cozy. He would be the perfect candidate to object to her being involved with Cooper Winslow.

"My family and I don't get along," Alex said quietly. "I keep them at a very healthy distance. That's one of the reasons why I'm out here." Her parents had criticized her all her life, and her father had never had a kind word for her. Her only sister had run off with her fiancé the night before their wedding. There was very little she liked about any of them, if anything. And as far as Alex was concerned, her mother had ice water in her veins, and had given up on life years before. She let her husband do and say anything he wanted, even to his children. Alex had always felt she had grown up in an entirely loveless household, where everyone was out for themselves, no matter who it hurt in the process. And no amount of money and history changed that. "They are actually the aliens you talk about. They came here from another galaxy, to stamp out life on Planet Earth, as they see it. They have a tremendous advantage in doing so, they have no hearts, medium-sized brains which process only the obvious, and they have an embarrassing amount of money, which they use almost exclusively to their own advantage. Their plot to take over the world has gone relatively well. My father seems to own most of it, and he doesn't give a damn about a single human being other than himself. To be perfectly blunt with you, Coop, I don't like them. And they don't like me much either. I won't play the game with them, and I don't buy their bullshit, never have, never will. So whatever they think about us, if they eventually hear about it, and I assume they will, I really could care less what they think about it."

"Well, that certainly spells things out, doesn't it?" He was a little taken aback by the vehemence of her speech, and it was easy to see how much they'd hurt her, particularly her father. Coop had always heard he was both ruthless and heartless. "I've always read that your father is very philanthropic."

"He has a great PR man. My father only gives to causes that will do him some good, or lend him prestige. He gave a hundred million dollars to Harvard. Who cares about Harvard when there are children starving all over the world, and people dying of diseases that could be cured, if someone put up the money to do it? He doesn't have a real philanthropic bone in his body." But she did. She gave away ninety percent of her income from her trust fund every year, and lived on as little as she was able. She allowed herself small luxuries, like the studio apartment on Wilshire Boulevard, but very seldom. She felt she had a responsibility to the world because of who she was, not in spite of it, which was why she had spent a year working in Kenya. It was also where she had realized that her sister had done her a huge favor by stealing her fiancé, although she hated her for the betrayal it had been. But she and Carter would have killed each other. It had taken her years to realize that he was just like her father, and her sister was just like her mother. All her sister wanted was the money and the name and the security and the prestige of being married to someone important. She didn't know who he was, or care. And all Carter wanted was to be the most important man on the planet. Her father was all about himself, and so was Carter. And they weren't close enough to discuss it anymore, but Alex had suspected for years that her sister was unhappy. Alex was sorry for her, she was an empty, lonely, vapid, useless human being.

"Are you telling me that if it comes out in the tabloids, or elsewhere, that we're involved, your father won't care about it?" he asked incredulously. That came as a surprise to Coop.

"No, I'm not. I'm telling you he'll probably care a great deal. But *I* don't care what he thinks about it. I'm a grown woman."

"That was my point though," he said, looking even more worried. "He probably wouldn't like you being involved with a movie star, let alone someone of my vintage." Or reputation. He had been a notorious playboy for years after all. Alex was sure that even her father knew that.

"Possibly," she said, offering only minimal reassurance. "He's three years younger than you are." That piece of information smarted, and didn't seem like good news to Coop, nor had anything she'd said, except for the fact that she seemed indifferent to her father's opinions. But if he got angry enough, her father might cause her or Coop some real problems. He wasn't sure how, but people as powerful as Arthur Madison usually found ways to do it.

"Could he cut off your money?" Coop asked, sounding nervous.

"No," she smiled calmly, as though it was decidedly none of Coop's business. But she suspected he didn't want to be responsible for her family causing her discomfort. It was sweet of him to worry about it. "Most of what I have came from my grandfather. The rest is already set up in an irrevocable trust by my father. And even if they could cut me off, I wouldn't give a damn. I earn my own living. I'm a doctor." And the most independent woman he'd ever met. She wanted nothing from anyone, and surely not from him. She didn't need Coop, she just loved him. She wasn't even emotionally dependent on him, she enjoyed his company, and she was able to walk at any time, if need be. It was an enviable position to be in. Young, smart, free, rich, beautiful, and independent. The perfect woman. Except that Coop would have liked it if she were a little more dependent on him. He had no guarantees with Alex, and no hook in her. She was there by choice, until further notice. "Does that answer all your questions?" she asked Coop, as she leaned over to kiss him, with her long dark hair falling over her shoulders. She looked like one of the teenagers at the pool, in her bare feet, shorts, and T-shirt.

"Enough so, for the time being. I just don't want to cause problems for you with your family," he said, sounding kind and responsible, "that would be a high price to pay for a romance."

"I've already paid that price, Coop," she said, looking pensive.

"So I gather." It sounded like she had gotten the hell out of Dodge years before, probably when her sister ran off with her fiancé.

The rest of the day passed pleasantly. They read the paper, lay in the sun on the terrace, and made love in the middle of the afternoon. The teenagers calmed down eventually, and they hardly heard them. And after they left the pool, she and Coop went out for a swim before dinner. Everything at the pool had been cleaned up and put back in place, and appeared to be in good order. Mark had done a good job policing them, and made them tidy up everything before the party was over.

And that night, she and Coop went to a movie. Heads turned as he paid for tickets at the box office, and two people asked him for autographs while he bought popcorn. She was getting used to being noticed by people wherever they went, and amused when they asked her to step aside while they snapped his picture, usually while one or more of their group posed with him.

"Are you famous?" they would ask her bluntly.

"No, I'm not," she smiled humbly at them.

"Could you move over please." She obliged, as she laughed and made faces at him from behind the camera. But it didn't bother her, she thought it was funny, and loved to tease him about it.

They went to a deli for a sandwich afterwards, and got home early. She had to get up at six, and be at the hospital by seven. The weekend had worked out well, and she was happier than ever with him. She was careful not to wake him when she got up. He didn't even hear her leave, and he smiled when he saw her note next to his razor.

"Dearest Coop, Thanks for a great weekend... peaceful and relaxing... If you'd like an autographed picture, call my agent...talk to you later. Love you, Alex."

The funny thing was he loved her too. He hadn't expected to, he had thought she would just be a diversion, because she was different from the other women he normally dated. But he was stunned to realize how much he liked her. She was so real, and so decent, and so loving. He had no idea what to do about it, if anything. Ordinarily, he would have just enjoyed it for a few weeks or months, and moved on to the next one. But because of what she represented, and what she had, he found himself thinking about the future. Abe's words hadn't been entirely lost on him. And if he wanted a rich wife, which he wasn't even sure he did, Alex was perfect. Everything about her made sense for him. And being married to Alex wouldn't be embarrassing, it had a lot to recommend it. At times, he almost wished she wasn't who she was, because he couldn't pretend to himself that she wasn't one of the richest young women in the country. And he wasn't sure what he would have felt about her, other than just enjoying her for a short time, if she wasn't. It complicated things, and colored them. More than she was, he was suspicious of his own motives. And yet, in spite of all that, he realized that he loved her, whatever that meant, or would mean in the future.

"Why don't you just relax and enjoy it?" he asked his own reflection in the mirror as he picked up his razor.

The uncomfortable thing about her was that she made him question himself, and challenge his own conscience. Did he love her? Or was she just a very rich girl who could solve all his problems forever if he married her? If her father even let her. He didn't completely buy her theory that she didn't give a damn what her father said, and his opinion meant nothing to her. She was after all a Madison, which implied a certain responsibility as to who she married, whose children she had, and what she did with her money.

And that was another thing...children...he still hated the thought of having children, even rich ones. He thought they were a pain in the neck and he had no desire to have any. Ever. But she was far too young to give up the idea of having children. They hadn't talked about it seriously, but it was clear even to him that she expected to have some one day. It was all very complicated, and convoluted, in his mind, if not Alex's. And worst of all, he didn't want to hurt her. He had never worried about that before, with any of the women he dated. Alex brought the best out in him, and he wasn't at all sure he liked it. Being responsible and respectable was an enormous burden.

The phone rang while he was shaving, and he didn't answer it. He knew Paloma was there somewhere, but wherever she was, she didn't pick it up, and it went on ringing. He thought it might be Alex. She was working for the next several days to make up for the weekend. He ran to answer the phone with shaving cream still on his face, and was irritated the instant he heard her. It was Charlene, and she sounded breathless.

"I called you last week, and you didn't return my call," she began by sounding angry, and went straight to accusation.

"I didn't get the message," he said honestly. "Did you leave me a voice mail?" he asked, wiping off the rest of the foam on a towel.

"I talked to Paloma," she said, sounding righteous. Just hearing her irritated him. His brief fling with her seemed light-years from where he was at the moment, with Alex. He was having a respectable romance with an honorable woman, not a sexual circus with a girl he scarcely knew. The two women, and his feelings for them, were worlds apart, and entirely different.

"That explains it," Coop said pleasantly. He wanted to get her off the phone as soon as possible. He never wanted to see her again, and didn't plan to. He was very pleased the tabloids had never gotten wind of her, but they had hardly ever gone out. He had spent most of his time with her in his bedroom. "She never gives mc messages except when she feels like it, and that's not often."

"I have to see you."

"I don't think that's a good idea," he said bluntly. "And I'm leaving town this afternoon." That was a lie, but it usually discouraged women when he said it. "I don't think we have anything more to say to each other, Charlene. It was fun, but that's all it was, for both of us." He had only seen her for a few weeks, between Pamela and Alex. It was hardly grounds for histrionics and drama.

"I'm pregnant." She had believed him when he said he was going out of town, and figured she'd better tell him while she had the chance to. There was a long, thoughtful silence on Coop's end. He'd been there before, and it had always been relatively easy to take care of. A few tears, a little emotional support, and money to pay for the abortion. And it was over. He assumed this would be no different.

"I'm sorry to hear that. I don't mean to be rude, but are you sure it's mine?" Women always hated it when he asked that, but some weren't sure, in which case, he was usually less sympathetic. And in Charlene's case, it seemed a fair question. He knew she had had quite an active romantic career before him, possibly during, and surely after. Sex was the mainstay of Charlene's life, and her primary means of communication. The way some women used food, or shopping. She was a very active young woman.

She was outraged. Incensed virtue itself when she answered. "Of course I'm sure it's yours. Would I call you if it weren't?"

"That's an interesting question. But in that case, I'm very sorry. Do you have a good doctor?" Her announcement had instantly caused him to feel distant, and sound guarded. He was feeling threatened.

"No. And I don't have any money."

"I'll have my accountant send you a check to cover everything." These days it wasn't a big deal. In the old days, it had meant driving across the Mexican border, or flying to Europe. Now, it was as routine as having your teeth cleaned, as far as Coop was concerned at least. And it was neither dangerous nor expensive. "I'll send you the names of some doctors." It was a ripple on the ocean of his life, but hardly a tidal wave. Worse things could have happened. Like a public scandal, which he did not want at the moment, because of Alex.

"I'm having the baby," she said, and to Coop's ears, sounded dogged and stubborn. She was dangerous and menacing from his perspective. All he wanted was to protect himself, and Alex, and all Charlene was in his mind was a threat. He had never loved her. He felt utterly threatened not only by what she said, but the tone of her voice. And more than a human dilemma, her plight seemed more like a threat for blackmail. It was hard for him to feel anything toward her. And every protective feeling he had was not for her, but for Alex. He didn't want her upset by this nightmare.

"I don't think that's a good idea, Charlene," he said, trying to maintain distance between them. He couldn't help thinking too that as brief as their affair had been, she could have taken care of it without even telling him. Instead, she wanted to pull him into the drama with her. But having the baby of a celebrity appealed to some women, and so did pressing them for money. She seemed to have a sense of entitlement that terrified him, and an agenda he had no desire to share with her. "We don't know each other that well. And you're too young and attractive to get tied down with a baby. They're a lot of trouble." It was a tack that made sense and had worked for him in the past, but Charlene seemed to have no intention of backing off. In truth why would she want to have a baby with a relative stranger? Except in this case, the stranger was Cooper Winslow.

"I've had six abortions. I can't have another one, Coop. And besides, I want our baby." *Our* baby, therein lay the key. She was trying to pull him into the soup with her. He couldn't help wondering if she was even pregnant, or if this was a ploy for money. "I want to see you."

"That's also not a good idea," and it was the last thing he wanted. All he needed was a hysterical meeting with her. What she really wanted was to get him back, and to make him feel obligated to her, but he didn't. He didn't for a moment believe that she was sincere about any of this, and he wasn't about to do anything to jeopardize his relationship with Alex. The affair with Charlene had lasted a mere three weeks. The one with Alex might last a lifetime. "I can't tell you what to do, but I strongly feel you should have the abortion." He wasn't foolish enough to beg her. He would have preferred to strangle her, and the baby, if there was one. He was not yet even convinced she was pregnant, nor if she was, that it was his baby.

"I'm not having an abortion!" she said plaintively, and then started crying. She told him how much she loved him, and that she had thought they would be together forever, that she thought he loved her too, and what was she going to do now with a fatherless baby?

"Precisely," he said coolly. He was determined not to let her know he was worried. "No baby deserves a father who won't recognize him. I'm not going to marry you. I'm not even going to see you or the baby. I don't want to be a father. And I never gave you the impression that I loved you, Charlene. We were two adults who had sex together for a few weeks, and nothing more. Let's not get confused here."

"Well, that's how babies are made," she said, and suddenly giggled. He felt like he was in a very bad movie, and he didn't like it. He liked her even less for causing him this much discomfort. "It's your baby too, Coop," she said, almost cooing.

"It's not my baby. It's not anyone's baby at this point. It's a nothing, it's a cell the size of the head of a pin, and it means nothing. You won't even miss it." He knew that wasn't entirely true, because hormones would cause her to believe that she loved it. But he was refusing to address that.

"I'm Catholic." He winced as she said it.

"So am I, Charlene. But if that made any difference to either of us, we wouldn't have been sleeping with each other out of wedlock. I don't think you have a choice here. You can either be sensible, or very, very foolish. And if you choose to be foolish, I'm not going to be a party to it. If you have this baby, you do so without my support or my blessing." He wanted her to know that from the beginning, and he intended to be unwavering about it. He thought it was better that she should know it, and not harbor any illusions about him.

"You *have* to support it," she said practically. "The law says so." She was very clever. "And I can't work while I'm pregnant. I can't model or act with a big, fat stomach. You have to help me." He could hardly help himself at the moment, and he had no desire whatsoever to support her. "I think we should get together and talk about it." She sounded suddenly almost cheerful. He suspected that she thought she could eventually suck him into it, and maybe even into marrying her, if she had the baby. But all it did was make him hate her. In his mind, she was threatening not only his finances, but his relationship with Alex, which meant a great deal to him.

"I'm not going to see you," he said in a tone of icy determination. He was not going to let her do this to him.

"I think you should, Coop," she said, with a menacing tone in her voice. "What will people think if they find out you won't take care of me or our baby?" She made it sound like he had walked out on seven children and a ten-year marriage. She was a girl he had slept with for a few weeks, and she had turned into a blackmailer and a nightmare.

"What will people think if they find out you're blackmailing me?" he asked with an edge to his voice he could no longer suppress when he answered.

"This isn't blackmail, it's fatherhood," she said blithely. "This is what people do, Coop. They get married and have babies. Or sometimes, they have babies and get married." She made it sound inevitable and he wanted to slap her. No one had ever done this to him before, not as cold-bloodedly or as blatantly. Every woman he'd ever gotten pregnant had been reasonable about it. Charlene wasn't, nor was she prepared to be. This was a golden opportunity for her.

"I'm not going to marry you, Charlene, whether you have the baby or not. Let's get that very clear right now. I don't give a damn what you do. I'll pay for an abortion, but that's all I'm going to do. And if you expect me to support you, you'll have to sue me." But he had no doubt now that she would. As publicly as possible, most likely.

"I'd hate to do that, Coop," she said regretfully. "It

would be such bad publicity for both of us. It could really hurt our careers." He didn't want to anger her further by telling her she didn't have one, and the truth was, at the moment, he didn't either. No one was hiring him anyway, except for cameos, and the occasional commercial. But he still didn't want to be pulled into a scandal with her. He had never been involved in anything like that. He might have been known as frivolous, or a playboy, but no one had ever had anything truly scandalous to say about him. And if she had her way, Charlene was going to change that. And because of his current affair with Alex, her timing was appalling. Arthur Madison was really going to love that one. "Can't I just see you for lunch before you leave?" She sounded pitiful and innocent. She went from shark to minnow and back again in a matter of seconds. And for an instant he almost felt sorry for her, and then went back to feeling threatened.

"No, you can't. I'll send you a check this morning. And what you do about it is up to you, but rest assured I'm not going to warm up to this, or change my mind. I will not be involved in this insanity, if you have my baby."

"See?" she sounded satisfied. "You're already thinking about it as your baby too. It's our baby, Coop. And it's going to be a beautiful baby." She was waxing poetic, and he wanted to throw up as he listened.

"You're insane. Goodbye, Charlene."

"Bye, Daddy," she whispered and hung up, as he sat staring at the phone in horror. This truly was a nightmare.

He wondered what she was going to do about it, if

she would realize he wasn't willing to play ball with her, and have the abortion, or if she would insist on having the baby. If she did, it was likely to cause one hell of an ugly scandal, especially with Alex. Ordinarily, he wouldn't have said anything to her, but there was so much at stake, that he decided, given the possibilities with Charlene, he was better off making a clean breast of it with Alex. Charlene was a loose cannon, and there was no telling what she would do. He knew there were two things he had to do immediately, no matter how much he disliked them.

First he had to send Charlene a check to cover the cost of an abortion. And then he had to find Alex and tell her. He walked naked through his bedroom, and grabbed his checkbook. He jotted off a check in an amount he thought was suitable. And then he called Alex at the hospital and left her a message to call him when she had a free moment. He was not looking forward to telling her, but it seemed the wisest thing to do under the circumstances. He just hoped she wouldn't end the affair with him when he told her.

Chapter 13

When Alex got Coop's message, she called him back half an hour later. She'd been busy doing paperwork on a new intake, and after that they had another new admission, a preemie with a heart valve problem. It was presumably reparable, but the baby needed close supervision. And she sounded busy and distracted when she called him.

"Hi, what's doing?"

"Busy morning?" He was nervous, but he didn't want her to know it. Suddenly, he realized how much she meant to him, and not just because of her fortune. He genuinely didn't want to hurt her, or lose her.

"Not too busy. Things are moving, but they're not insane yet." She seemed to be in full control of what she was doing, but she was always happy to hear from him, and to chat with him, when she had a minute. It had been nice of him to call her.

"Have you got time for a quick lunch?" he asked, trying to sound casual.

"I'm sorry, Coop. I can't get out of here. I'm the senior resident in charge here. I'm stuck for the duration."

She was on duty until the following morning. "I can't leave the building."

"You don't have to. Why don't I come by for a cup of coffee?"

"Sure, that would be fine, if you don't mind my being stuck here. Is something wrong?" He sounded all right, but he had never offered to come by the hospital before. She wondered if he missed her.

"No, I just wanted to see you." The way he said it almost made her nervous. He had said he'd come by at noon, and as soon as she hung up, an emergency distracted her. She was still tying up loose ends and signing forms when the technician at the front desk told her there was someone to see her.

"Is that who I think it is?" the woman asked when she called Alex in her office. Her voice was filled with wonder, and Alex laughed as she answered.

"I guess so."

"Damn, he's pretty," she said admiringly, just out of his earshot, and Alex smiled as she put down her papers.

"Yes, he is. Tell him I'll be right there." It was a good time to take a break, and she hurried out in her scrubs with her white coat over it. She was wearing socks and clogs, with her stethoscope at a crazy angle around her neck, and a pair of rubber gloves hanging out of her pocket. She was wearing her hair pulled back in a braid, and as usual, she never bothered to wear makeup when she was working. She looked like a teenager in costume as she hurried out to see him.

"Hi, Coop," she said breezily, with a big smile, as people hanging around the ICU tried to stare at him discreetly. She was used to it by now, and he looked as impeccable as ever, in a tweed sport jacket and a beige turtleneck, with perfectly pressed khaki slacks and brown suede loafers. He looked like he'd stepped out of a fashion magazine and she felt like she'd been dragged through a bush backwards.

She told the tech at the front desk that she was going to the cafeteria to grab something to eat, and to page her if they needed her. "If I'm lucky, they might even give me ten uninterrupted minutes." She stood on tiptoe to kiss his cheek, and he put an arm around her as they got into the elevator to go to the basement. Alex smiled as the doors closed and she saw everyone staring at them. He was quite a vision. "You just increased my importance around here by about four thousand percent. You look terrific." He pulled her closer to him affectionately as she said it.

"So do you. You look very official with all that stuff hanging off you." She was wearing her pager, her stethoscope, and there was a clamp she had forgotten clipped to her pocket. The tools of her trade made her look more like a grown-up. Or if it was a Halloween costume, it was a very good one. It impressed him to see her there, and the easy way she had breezed past the desk and instructed one of the nurses before she addressed him. She was really something. Which made him even more nervous as he contemplated what he was about to tell her. He had no way of knowing what her reaction would be. But he knew he had to tell her before someone else did. Thanks to Charlene, things could get dicey.

They both selected sandwiches and put them on a

tray, and Alex poured them each a cup of coffee. "This stuff is pretty dangerous," she warned him, pointing to the coffee. "Legend has it there's rat poison in it, and I believe them. I'll take you over to the ER after lunch, if you think you need it."

"Thank God you're a doctor," he said, as he paid for their lunch, and followed her to a small corner table. Mercifully, there was no one else around them, and no one seemed to have recognized him in the cafeteria so far. He wanted a few minutes of peace with her. And she was already eating her sandwich, before he had unwrapped his. He took a few minutes to assemble his composure, and she saw that his hands were shaking when he poured sugar in his coffee.

"What's up, Coop?" She was calm and quiet and sympathetic, and her eyes were gentle.

"Nothing...no...that's not true...something came up this morning." She watched his eyes as she waited for him to explain it. She could see now that he was worried. He hadn't touched either his sandwich or his coffee.

"Something bad?"

"Something annoying. I wanted to talk to you about it." She couldn't even begin to imagine what it was. His eyes told her nothing. He took a breath, and launched into what he feared would rapidly become troubled waters. "I've done a few foolish things in my life, Alex. Not many, but some. And I've had a very good time most of the time. I haven't hurt anyone. I generally play on a level playing field, with people who understand the ground rules." As he said it, she began to panic. She felt sure he was about to tell her it was over between them. This sounded like the intro-duction. She had been there before, but not in a very long time. She hadn't allowed herself to care about anyone since then. Until Cooper. She had been falling for him since she met him. And now this sounded like a farewell speech. She sat back in her chair and watched him. If nothing else, she was going to take her lumps with dignity and courage. And he could see that she was backing off as he watched her. It was self-protection. But he continued. He had to. "I've never taken advantage of anyone. I don't mislead women. Most of the people I've gotten involved with did so with their eyes open. I've made a few mistakes, but generally, I have a pretty clear slate. No casualties, no victims. And when it's over, it's been goodbye and thank you, on both sides. As far as I know, no one hates me. Most of the people I've been involved with like me, and I like them. And the mistakes have been short-lived and quickly corrected."

"And now? Is this a mistake, Coop?" She wondered if he was correcting it now, and she had to fight back tears as she listened, but he looked shocked when she asked the question.

"Us? Of course not! Is that what you think I'm say-ing? Oh, baby...this isn't about us. This is about something stupid I did before I met you." She looked immensely relieved as he held her hands and contin-ued. "I'll try to get through this quickly," particularly if there was a chance they might get interrupted. That would be awful. He *had* to tell her. "I went out with a young woman shortly before we met. I probably shouldn't have. She's a simple girl, an aspiring actress, and her only roles so far have been in porn videos and trade shows. She doesn't have a lot going for her, but I thought she was a sweet girl, and we were both playing. She knew the ground rules. She's not an innocent. She's been around the block more than a few times. I never misled her. I never pretended to care about her. It was a sexual interlude for both of us, and nothing more, and it ended very quickly. Even I can't stay involved for long with a woman I can't talk to. It seemed like a very simple thing, and completely harmless."

"And?" Alex couldn't stand the suspense. Clearly, he wasn't telling her he was in love with the girl, but what was he saying?

"She called this morning. She's pregnant."

"Shit," Alex said simply, but with a feeling of immense relief. "At least it's not terminal. She can fix that." She was enormously relieved that he wasn't telling her he was in love with the woman, and she smiled reassuringly at Coop, who felt like a thousand-pound weight had been taken off his shoulders. She hadn't stood up and walked out, or told him she never wanted to see him again, but she also didn't know the whole story.

"That's the other half of the problem. She wants to have the baby."

"Now that is a nasty little problem. But I can see why it would appeal to her. Celebrity baby. Is she blackmailing you, Coop?" Alex was practical, intelligent, and perceptive, which made it easier to talk to her than he'd expected.

"More or less. She wants money. She says in her line of work, she can't work while she's pregnant. I guess they don't do porn videos with pregnant women," he said grimly, and Alex squeezed his hands to give him comfort. "She wants me to support her and the baby. I told her I don't want a baby, hers or anyone else's . . . except yours possibly," he amended with a rueful smile. He felt utterly foolish to be confessing all this to her, but he had wanted to make a clean breast of it to Alex. "I didn't tell her about you, or she'd really be up in arms. She already was. She sounds crazy. One minute she's crying, the next she's threatening, and then she's talking in saccharine tones about 'our baby.' Nauseating, and somewhat terrifying. I have no idea what she's going to do, or if she'll actually have the baby. Or call the tabloids. She's a loose cannon, and she's fully loaded, if you'll pardon the pun. I sent her a check to pay for an abortion, but that's all I'm willing to do for the moment, and I said so. The entire affair lasted three weeks. It shouldn't have happened at all. I should have known better at my age. But I was bored, and she was amusing. But what's happening now is definitely *not* amusing," he said, looking remorseful. "I'm so sorry, Alex, to bring this mess into our lives. But I wanted to tell you. I thought you had a right to know, particularly if she goes to the tabloids. She could do that. They'd love it."

"So would she probably," Alex said, sounding sympathetic. "Are you sure she's pregnant? She might just be trying to see what she can get out of you. She doesn't sound like a very nice person."

"She isn't. I don't know if she's really pregnant or not, or even if it's mine. I wore protection, but to give you the ugly details, it broke on one occasion. I guess from her perspective, she got lucky." At least he knew it hadn't been a setup, just the fates conspiring against him.

"You can have DNA tests eventually, particularly if she's willing to do amnio. They can test her then. But that's a way down the road. How pregnant is she?"

"I think she said two months or something."

He and Alex had been together for six weeks, so he was being truthful when he said he'd been involved with her right before Alex. Right before. Like two weeks before, or less. But Alex reminded herself that what he had done before her was none of her business.

"What are you going to do, Coop?" Alex asked, still holding his hands in hers. She loved the fact that he'd been honest with her, and if anything, she felt closer to him. She knew that these things happened. Particularly in his world, to men who were celebrities and were easy targets for extortion and blackmail and greed.

"I don't know yet. There's nothing much I can do for the moment, except wait and see what she does. I just wanted to warn you that there could be a land mine down the road for us, if she goes public with it."

"Would you marry her if she has the baby?" Alex asked, looking worried.

"Are you crazy? There's no way. I hardly know her. And other than great legs, and other similar attributes, what I do know, I don't like." At least not anymore. "I'm not in love with her, never was, and never will be. And I'm not foolish or noble enough to marry her under these circumstances. At worst, I'll have to pay her child support, at best the whole thing will vanish. I told her I would never see the child, and I meant it."

But that was a whole other kettle of fish, involving responsibility and morality. She knew he would have to review the situation later, if she really did have the baby. But at least he wasn't in love with the woman, and didn't intend to marry her. In essence, it affected nothing between Coop and Alex. Except for some noise that could come up later in the tabloids, and that didn't worry Alex. All she cared about was how he felt about her.

"I hate to say it," Alex said, as Coop held his breath and waited for what was coming. "And I'm sure you don't feel that way about it, but it doesn't sound like a big deal, Coop. These things probably happen to men in your shoes with a fair degree of regularity. It's unpleasant but it's not earth-shattering. I feel a lot better knowing about it, and I just don't see that it's such a big problem. Embarrassing maybe, if it comes out. But things like this happen all the time. I feel a lot better," she beamed at him, "I thought you were about to tell me it was over." In fact, life was just beginning for them.

"You're amazing." He sat back, as he exhaled, and took a long, grateful look at her. "I truly love you. I was afraid you'd tell me to get lost and throw me back in the river."

"Not likely." Neither of them had eaten lunch, they had been so intent on what he was saying. "I think there's a distinct possibility you're a keeper." He felt the same way about her, and he was about to tell her so, when her pager went off, and she glanced at it.

"Shit!" she said, taking a swig of coffee as she stood up. "Someone's coding...I gotta go...don't worry, everything's fine...I love you...I'll call you later...." She was halfway across the cafeteria at a dead run before he knew what had happened. And he stood up and called out to her as everyone around him stood staring.

"I love you!" he shouted. She turned back with a smile and waved, as a man wearing a hairnet cleaning tables with a wet cloth grinned at him.

"Right on!" Coop smiled at him, and walked out of the cafeteria with a light heart and a spring in his step that hadn't been there when he'd walked in. Alex was a remarkable woman, and in spite of what had happened, she was still his.

Chapter 14

Jimmy was sitting in his kitchen going over a stack of papers he'd brought home from work, and trying to decide if he wanted to cook dinner. He never seemed to eat dinner anymore, except when friends from work talked him into it, or Mark came by with a steak and a six-pack. He didn't care if he ate or not, if he lived or didn't. He was just getting through the days. And the nights were endless.

It had been three months since Maggie died, and he was beginning to wonder if it would ever get better. There was no end in sight to the grief he was feeling. And at night, he lay in bed and cried. He never fell asleep until 3 or 4 A.M., and some nights he was awake until daylight.

He knew that moving into the gatehouse had been a good thing, but what he also knew now was that he had brought Maggie with him. She went with him everywhere, in his heart, in his head, in his bones, in his body. She was part of him now, part of every thought and reaction. Part of the way he looked at things, and what he believed, and wanted. Sometimes he felt more Maggie than Jimmy. He saw everything through her eyes. She had taught him so much. He wondered sometimes if that was why she had died. Because she had taught all the lessons she was meant to. But thinking that still didn't make it any easier for him. He missed her unbearably, and the pain he felt night and day was barely tolerable. Nothing made it better. He managed to stave it off for a few hours sometimes, like when he hung out with Mark, or went to work, or coached softball to the kids he worked with. But it was always waiting there for him, like an old friend, the pain that lurked everywhere and waited to overtake him. It was a fight he couldn't seem to win. For the moment, the pain was still winning.

He had just decided not to bother cooking anything, when he heard a knock on the door, and got up to answer it. He was looking tired and disheveled, and smiled when he saw it was Mark. Jimmy saw less of him now, because Mark was busy with his children. He had to cook dinner for them, and help them with homework. But he often called Jimmy and invited him to join them for dinner. Jimmy liked Jessica and Jason, and being with them was fun. But that made him lonely too. It reminded him that he and Maggie should have had children, and now he would never have her babies, or her arms to hold him ever again.

"I just bought groceries," Mark explained, "I thought I'd stop by and see if you want to come for dinner." Sometimes, Mark knew, it was better to drop in on him. It was good to get in his face and drag him out of his cave. Jimmy isolated a lot, and Mark knew he was having a tough time about Maggie. Even more so lately. It was as though with the nice weather, and the feeling of spring everywhere, he was even more lonely for her.

"Naw...it's okay...but thanks....I brought a mountain of shit home from work. I'm always out doing home visits, and I never seem to be able to get anything done in the office." He looked pale and tired to Mark, and he felt sorry for him. It had been a rough stretch for Jimmy, and Mark knew it. He'd had a tough time too, but things had gotten better for him when his kids came back to California to live with him. He just hoped something happened soon to make things easier for Jimmy. He was a bright, good-looking guy, and a nice one. They hadn't even had time to lob tennis balls at each other lately. The kids were keeping him too busy, and he never seemed to have any free time.

"You've got to eat anyway," Mark said practically, "why not let me cook for all of us? I have to feed the kids in a few minutes. I'm making ribs and burgers." It was almost a steady diet for them. He had promised the kids he'd buy a cookbook and learn how to make something else.

"Honest, I'm fine," Jimmy said, looking tired. He knew Mark was trying to be a good Samaritan, and he appreciated it. He just wasn't in the mood to see people. He hadn't been in months, and it was getting worse lately. He had stopped working out, and hadn't been to a movie since the last one he'd been to with Maggie. It was as though by living a full life now, he would have felt he was being unfaithful to her.

"Oh, by the way, I almost forgot..." Mark said with a broad grin. "I have a little tidbit about our landlord." He handed Jimmy a copy of one of the tabloids. He had seen it at the grocery store, and bought it to show Jimmy. It was too bad, but Mark had to admit, it amused him. The guy was a real shaker and mover. "Page two." Jimmy opened the tabloid and his eyes grew wide.

"Holy shit." There was a picture of Coop that covered half the page, and another photograph next to it of a sexy woman with long, black hair, and Asian eyes. The article was full of alleged details and innuendos about their passionate love affair, their love child, gossip about him, and a list of the many well-known women he'd been involved with. "My, my," Jimmy said with a grin, as he handed the paper back to Mark. "I wonder if Alex has seen it? It's not much fun to be going out with a guy who gets himself in that kind of trouble. And she looks like a pretty straight shooter."

"I don't think it's a big deal with them," Mark surmised, "she's only been around for about ten minutes. And they don't seem to last longer than that with Coop. I think I've seen three so far since I moved in here. Keeps things interesting though, doesn't it?"

"For him at least. I'll bet he's real thrilled about the baby." Jimmy couldn't help laughing at him. "Imagine having him as your father."

"He'll be close to ninety when the kid goes to college," Mark added.

"Yeah, and he'll probably be sleeping with coeds," Jimmy ventured. It was an uncharitable exchange, but the tabloid article titillated them both, and as Mark left, Jimmy promised to come to dinner on the weekend.

Coop wasn't nearly as amused as he discussed the

article with Alex when they had dinner that night. He was profoundly upset by it, and the fact that the news was out. And he was very glad he had warned Alex beforehand.

"Look, you've been in the tabloids a million times. It's part of your business. If you weren't who you are, no one would give a damn who you sleep with."

"It was filthy of her to go to the tabloids." He was livid, but Alex was calm.

"But predictable probably." Alex tried to soothe him by assuring him that it didn't matter to her. And eventually, everyone would forget about the baby, if they ever heard about it in the first place. "Not everyone reads the tabloids," she reminded him. He was relieved that she was so philosophical about it. It made things a lot easier for him.

They went out for pizza that night, and Alex did everything she could to distract him. But it wasn't easy. He was in a glum mood, and then when they got back to his place, he remembered something he had wanted to ask her. He invited her to go to the Academy Awards with him, and she was startled and delighted, and then looked suddenly worried.

He gave her the date, and she was pensive. "I'll have to see if I can get the night off. I think I'm working."

"Can you trade it?" He knew the drill now.

"I'll try. I've been doing a lot of trading lately. I'm using up all my tickets."

"This is a big one," he said, hoping she would come. Not only did he want to share it with her, but he wanted to be seen with her. She lent an aura of respectability to him, and at the moment he needed that to counter the dirt Charlene was spewing. But he didn't want to explain that to Alex. Those were the inner machinations of Hollywood, and he thought he'd spare her the details.

She was spending the night with him again, although she had been reluctant to at first. But he was so uncomfortable in her apartment and it was always such a mess, it was easier just staying with him. Her studio was more like a giant laundry basket than an apartment. Coop had taken to calling it "the hamper." And she enjoyed being at The Cottage. She loved being able to swim at night, and didn't mind running into Mark's children. There was something so peaceful and relaxing about the place. It was easy to see why Coop loved it and had hung on to it through thick and thin.

Two days later, she told him she had made another trade to get off for the Academy Awards, and then she panicked when she realized she had nothing to wear, and no time to shop for it. The only evening dress she had was the one she had worn to the Schwartzes' the night she met him. And she needed something fancier if she was going to the Academy Awards with Cooper Winslow.

"I never thought I'd be doing something like that," she said with a giggle as she cuddled up to him that night. He was pleased she was going with him. There was another article about Charlene in one of the other tabloids. The flak was hot and heavy. But aside from that, he also loved the idea of sharing a major event with Alex. "I have nothing to wear, you know. I may have to go in scrubs and clogs. I don't have much time off between now and then to go shopping, if any."

"Leave that to me," he said mysteriously. He knew a lot more about clothes than she did. He had been paying for women's wardrobes for years, and selecting them for them when they didn't know how. It was one of his many skills. And he was generous to a fault.

"If you buy something, I'll pay for it," she reminded him. She had no intention of becoming a kept woman. And unlike the other women he had gone out with, she was perfectly able to pay for her own extravagances, and intended to do so. But she appreciated his offer to find something for her.

She fell asleep that night dreaming of being at a ball, and wearing an enormous gown that swirled around her as she danced and danced with a handsome prince who looked just like Coop. He was the handsome prince. And she was beginning to feel like a fairy princess. The fact that one of the townsfolk was having his baby didn't seem to matter to her at all.

Chapter 15

The night of the Academy Awards came faster than Alex expected. It was two weeks after he'd invited her, and it was later than usual this year, in the third week of April. And true to his word, Coop had found her a fabulous dress at Valentino. It was midnight blue satin and the most elegant thing she'd ever seen, bias cut, and it showed off her flawless figure. All it needed, when she tried it on, was to be shortened. He had borrowed a sable jacket for her from Dior, and a sapphire necklace that took her breath away, with matching bracelet and earrings.

"I really do feel like Cinderella," she said as she modeled it for him. He had also hired a hairdresser and makeup artist, to do her hair and makeup. And in order to save time, she dressed at his place.

She arrived from the hospital in scrubs, and three hours later, she emerged. Presto magic, a fairy princess. Better than that. She looked like a young queen as she came down the stairs from the master bedroom. He was waiting for her in the front hall, and he beamed when he saw her. She looked elegant and beautiful and very striking. She looked every inch the aristocrat she was, and when she looked in the mirror, she was surprised to see that she was reminded of her mother. Her mother had gone to balls dressed like that when Alex was a little girl. She even remembered a blue dress a little like it. But even her mother had never owned sapphires like the ones Coop had borrowed from Van Cleef and Arpels. They were enormous, and they suited Alex to perfection.

"Wow!" he said, and then bowed when he saw her. He was wearing one of the many dinner jackets he owned, that he had made by his tailor in London. He was wearing perfect patent leather pumps, and sapphire studs and cuff links that were his own, and not borrowed. They had been the gift of a Saudi princess, whose father had banished her to God knows where, rather than let her marry Coop. Coop often said that she had been sold into white slavery rather than allowed to become Mrs. Winslow. It made a good story, and the sapphire studs and links were very impressive. "You look incredible, my love," he said, as they exited together.

Nothing he had told her had prepared her for the fanfare of the award ceremony. It was still broad daylight when they got there. There was a long red carpet going in, and an endless wagon train of limousines waiting to disgorge their contents. Beautiful women in expensive gowns, wearing dazzling jewels, were the norm, and photographers were pressing and shoving to take their pictures. Many of them were well-known actresses, and Coop usually attended the Oscars with one of them, but this year it meant more to him to go with Alex. They were the epitome of aristocratic respectability as they made their way slowly down the red carpet. Alex was wearing staggeringly high blue satin heels, and she was grateful for Coop's arm to keep her upright. And she smiled shyly as hundreds of cameras took their picture. Coop hadn't said it to her, but she reminded him of Audrey Hepburn in *Breakfast at Tiffany's*. She was beautiful, elegant, and distinguished. And as she turned toward yet another bank of cameras, as Coop waved at them like a visiting head of state, there was a whoop at the guest wing of The Cottage.

"Oh my God!...That's her!...It's...what's her name...you know...Alex!!! And him!" Jessica was pointing as all heads in the room turned. Jimmy was watching with them, as he had the Golden Globes with Mark, and Coop and Alex had gotten out of the limousine, and were walking slowly into the Oscars. "She looks gorgeous!" Jessica was more excited to see her than any movie star, because she knew her.

"She sure looks good," Mark said, as they all stared at Alex. "I wonder where she got the necklace."

"It's probably borrowed," Jimmy said sensibly, still wondering what she was doing with him. He thought she was foolish to be dating a man like Coop, and deserved better. All she'll ever be is "flavor of the month" to him, he had said to Mark, but Mark thought she was smart enough to know that, although neither of them really knew her, but they liked her.

"I never realized how pretty she is, she looks good all dressed up like that," Mark commented. He had only seen her in shorts and T-shirts at the pool, and the night he had set the bushes on fire. But dressed as she was, he had to admit she was pretty impressive. He was beginning to look around and see women, unlike Jimmy who still felt as though he were brain-dead. Any interest he'd once had in the opposite sex seemed to have died with Maggie. But Mark hadn't started dating yet either. He was just looking. He had no time to anyway, he was too busy keeping track of his children.

Coop and Alex walked off the screen then, and went in to the Oscars. They saw them again later, once they were seated, and the cameras panned on them. They got a close-up of Alex laughing and whispering something to Coop, which made him laugh in answer. They seemed to be very happy together. And later on, the fans at The Cottage saw them going in to the *Vanity Fair* party at Morton's. She was wearing the sable jacket and looked as glamorous as any movie star. Maybe better, because she was real.

She had a fabulous time that night and thanked Coop profusely as they rode home in the back of the chauffeured Bentley. The turbo convertible Azure had gone back long since, because Coop couldn't afford to buy it. But the Bentley limousine had been his for years, and it looked very elegant as they came and went at the Oscars.

"What an incredible evening," she yawned happily. It was three o'clock in the morning. She had seen every star she'd ever heard of, and although she'd never been starstruck as a young girl, she had to admit it was exciting. Particularly, seeing it all with Coop, who told her all the little inside stories and lurid gossip, and introduced her to everyone she had ever seen in a movie.

She really did feel like Cinderella. "I guess now I'm going to turn back into a pumpkin," she said as she leaned against him. He had been very proud of her, and said so. "I have to be at the hospital in three hours. Maybe I should just stay up."

"It's an option," Coop said, smiling at her. "You were perfect, Alex. Everyone thought you were a new star. You'll probably have a dozen producers sending you scripts tomorrow."

"Not likely," she said, laughing as she got out of the car at The Cottage. It was wonderfully peaceful, and nice to get home after a long evening. But she'd had a better time than she would have ever dreamed of, thanks to Coop, who saw to it that it was memorable for her, right down to her hair and makeup and the borrowed sapphire necklace.

"I ought to buy it for you," he said regretfully as she handed it back to him, and he put it in the safe, along with the matching earrings and bracelet. "I wish I could." It was three million dollars, as Alex had seen from the price tag. Rather a big ticket. But it was the first time Coop had admitted to her that some things were beyond his means. Although that one would have been out of reach for many. It didn't surprise her, and she wouldn't have accepted it anyway. It was a nice thought, and it had been fun to wear it. Louise Schwartz had been wearing a similar one, although it was noticeably bigger, which was hard to imagine. And Coop knew Louise had the same one in rubies. Louise had been wearing a spectacular gown, also by Valentino, who had made it especially for her.

"Well, Princess, shall we go up to bed?" Coop

looked at her as he took off his jacket and loosened his tie. He was incredibly handsome, and looked as impeccable at the end of the evening as the beginning.

"Am I a pumpkin yet?" Alex asked sleepily, as she carried her shoes in her hand and walked up the stairs with her satin gown trailing behind her. She looked like a very tired princess.

"No, my darling," Coop said softly, "and you never will be."

It was like a fairy tale being with him, and at times it had a feeling of unreality to it. Alex had to remind herself that she worked in a hospital with sick preemies, and lived in a studio apartment filled with dirty laundry. Although she had other options, but she had long since decided not to use them. The glamour in her life, and the extravagance, was provided only by Coop.

She was asleep in his arms in less than five minutes, and when the alarm went off at five, she almost turned over and went back to sleep, but Coop pushed her gently out of bed and told her he'd call her later. Twenty minutes later, she was grinding down the driveway in her ancient car, and wide awake. The night before seemed like a dream. Until she saw herself in the morning papers. There was a big photograph of her with Coop on their way into the Oscars.

"She looks like you," one of the nurses said as she ogled it, and then looked up wide-eyed when she saw the name under the picture. Alexandra Madison. Coop had forgotten to tell them she was a doctor, and Alex had teased him about it. She told him she had worked hard for her title, and expected him to use it.

"Can't I just tell them you're my psychiatric nurse?"

he had teased her back. She looked radiant in the photographs, and Coop was holding her hand and beaming. It was a message to the world that all was well with him, and he wasn't hiding. It was exactly the message he had wanted to convey, and his press agent congratulated him later that morning.

"Good for you, Coop," he said. Without saying a word, it countered all the filth and rumors in the tabloids. The subliminal message was, so what if he had gotten a minor porn actress pregnant, he was still who he was, and involved with respectable women.

There was another photograph of them in the afternoon paper. And when Coop called her, he told her that several of the gossip columnists had called him, from the respectable press, not the tabloids.

"They wanted to know who you are."

"And did you tell them?"

"Of course. And this time, I remembered to tell them you're a doctor," he said proudly. "They also wanted to know if we're getting married. I told them it was much too early to comment, but that you are the special woman in my life and I adore you."

"Well, that should keep them busy," she smiled as she sipped a Styrofoam cup filled with cold coffee. She had been working for twelve hours by then, but fortunately it had been a relatively easy day. She was more tired than she'd expected. She wasn't used to carousing all night and working all day. Coop had slept till eleven, and then had a massage, a manicure, and a haircut. "Did they ask about the baby?" she inquired, sounding concerned. She knew how much that upset him.

"Not a word." And he hadn't heard anything from Charlene either. She was too busy talking to the tabloids.

But two weeks later, he heard from her lawyer. It was early May, and she claimed to be three months pregnant. She wanted support for the duration of the pregnancy, and she was ready to start negotiating child support and palimony with him.

"Palimony? For a three-week fling? She's crazy," Coop complained to his lawyer. But she was claiming she was so sick she couldn't work until after she had the baby. According to her attorney, she was unusually nauseous. "Apparently not too nauseous to give interviews. Christ, this woman is a monster."

"Just pray the baby isn't your monster," his lawyer told him. And they agreed that whatever Coop offered her temporarily, had to be offset by a promise from her to have an amniocentesis that included a DNA test. "What are the chances it's yours, Coop?"

"I guess about fifty-fifty. As good as anyone's. I slept with her, the condom broke. Depends how my luck is running these days. What would be the odds in Vegas?"

"I'll have to check on that for you," his lawyer said, sounding somber. "I hate to be crude, but as one of my clients put it, 'You stick it in, you pay forever.' I hope you're being careful now, Coop. That was a very pretty woman I saw you with at the Oscars."

"And a smart one," Coop said proudly. "She's a doctor."

"And hopefully not a gold digger like the last one. The prospective mom is good-looking too. Eurasian or something, isn't she? But whatever she is, she has a heart like a cash register. I hope the rest of her was worth it."

"I don't remember," Coop said discreetly, and then hastened to defend Alex. "My doctor friend is anything but a gold digger. With her family background, she doesn't need anything from me. Not by a long shot."

"Really? Who are they?" he asked with interest.

"Her father is Arthur Madison. None other." The attorney whistled.

"Now that is interesting. Have you heard from him yet about the baby?"

"No, I haven't."

"I'll bet you will, sooner or later. Does he know you're dating his daughter?"

"I'm not sure. He and Alex don't seem to talk much."

"Well, it's no secret now. The two of you are in every paper in the country."

"Worse things could happen." And had. Charlene was in all the tabloids.

And a week later, so was Alex. They were rehashing the same news, only now they added Alex's photos to Charlene's and Cooper's. She looked like a young queen in the tabloids, and the headlines were predictably ugly. Mark kept buying all of the papers to show Jimmy, and Jessica was enamored with Alex, whom she ran into at the pool regularly, whenever she wasn't working. The two had struck up an easy friendship, and Alex liked her, although she didn't say anything to Coop. She knew how he felt about them, and he had enough on his plate for the moment.

He was getting calls from Abe these days too, reminding him that he was spending too much money, and concerned over the child support he was going to have to pay Charlene. "You can't afford it, Coop. And if you miss a payment, she'll put you in jail. That's how those things work, and from the look of her, she'll do it."

"Thanks for the good news, Abe." He was spending less money than he usually did on Alex because she had simple tastes, but his overhead was still too high, according to Abe. He kept assuring Coop that the reckoning was coming.

"You'd better marry the Madison girl," he said, chuckling, wondering if that was why Coop was going out with her. Given who she was, it was hard to imagine Coop didn't have an ulterior motive, and he was still examining his own conscience. He was daily more convinced that he loved her.

And Liz had also called him about the furor in the tabloids. She was outraged.

"What a rotten situation! You never should have gone out with her, Coop!"

"Now you tell me," he chuckled ruefully. "How's marriage?"

"I love it, although San Francisco takes a little getting used to. I'm always cold, and it's awfully quiet."

"Well, you can leave him, and come back to me. I always need you."

"Thank you, Coop." But she was happy with Ted, and loved his daughters. She was only sorry she had waited so long to get married. She realized now how much she had sacrificed for Coop. She would have loved to have children of her own, but it was too late for that now. At fifty-two, she had to content herself with Ted's daughters. "What's Alex like?"

"An angel of mercy," he said, smiling, "the girl next door. Audrey Hepburn. Dr. Kildare. She's terrific. You'd love her."

"Bring her to San Francisco for a weekend."

"I'd love to, but she's always working, or on call. She's the senior resident. It's a big responsibility." It was an odd match for him, Liz couldn't help thinking, but she was obviously very pretty. And the papers said she was thirty, which was the outer limit of the age he liked them. Anything between twenty-one and thirty was fair game for Coop.

Liz also asked him how much he was working. She hadn't seen him in anything lately, not even a commercial. He'd been calling his agent, but nothing seemed to be brewing, for the moment. But as his agent reminded him, he wasn't getting any younger.

"I've been working less than I'd like to, but I've got some irons in the fire. I just talked to three producers this morning."

"What you need is one big juicy part to get everyone's motors going again. Once they see you in a big part, they'll all want you. You know what sheep producers are, Coop." She didn't want to say it to him, but he needed a big part playing someone's father. The trouble was Coop still wanted to be the leading man, and no one wanted to hire him for that. But Coop just couldn't see himself as any older, which was why he was so comfortable with Alex. He never even thought about being forty years older than she was. And neither did Alex. She had pondered the issue initially and as she got to know him and fell in love with him, she dismissed it.

They were lying on his terrace talking about nothing in particular that weekend, when her pager went off. She was on call, but when she glanced down at it, she saw that it wasn't the hospital. She instantly recognized the number, and waited half an hour to pick up her cell phone. Coop was stretched out in a deck chair in the shade next to her, reading the paper, and only listening with half an ear to her conversation.

"Yes, that's right. I had a good time. How are you?" He had no idea who she was talking to, but the exchange didn't sound friendly, and she was frowning. "When?...I think I'm working...I can see you for lunch at the hospital, if I'm covered. How long will you be here?...Fine...see you on Tuesday." He couldn't tell if she was talking to a friend or someone like a lawyer, but whatever it was, she didn't look as though she'd enjoyed it.

"Who was that?" Coop looked puzzled.

"My father. He's coming to LA on Tuesday for meetings. He wants to see me."

"That should be interesting. Did he say anything about me?"

"Only that he saw that I was at the Oscars. He never mentioned you by name. He'll save that for later."

"Should we take him to dinner?" Coop offered generously, although it still unnerved him to think that the man was younger than he was, and far more important. Arthur Madison was not only made of money, but of power.

"Nope," Alex said, glancing at him. She was wearing dark glasses, so he couldn't read her expression, but it was definitely not warm and fuzzy, nor was she enthusiastic about seeing her father. "Thanks anyway. I'll see him for lunch at the hospital. He's flying back after his meeting." Coop knew he had his own 727.

"Maybe next time," he said pleasantly. But he could see that she wasn't looking forward to the meeting. And ten minutes later, she got called to the hospital for an emergency.

She didn't come back until dinner. And when she did, she went out to the pool for a swim and ran into Jimmy and Mark and his children. And for the first time since she'd met him, she thought Jimmy looked more cheerful. And the kids were delighted to see her. Jessica told her how beautiful she'd looked at the Oscars.

"Thank you. It was a lot of fun," Alex said easily after swimming around the pool for half an hour. Jessica was in the pool with her and Mark, and Jason and Jimmy were throwing a baseball. Jimmy was telling him how to correct his throw and Jason was listening intently.

And ten minutes later, Jessica was quizzing Alex about what all the stars had been wearing, when Alex heard a whizzing sound overhead, and Jason threw the ball right through Coop's main living-room window.

"Shit!" Mark said under his breath, as the two

women stared and Jimmy gave a whoop of excitement.

"Great throw!" he shouted at Jason before he realized where it had landed. The sound of tinkling glass punctuated his exclamation as Mark and Alex exchanged a look, and Jason looked panicked.

"Uh-oh," Jessica added, and within instants, Coop was at the pool in barely controlled fury.

"Are we trying out for the Yankees, or just indulging in a little idle vandalism?" He addressed them generally, and Alex was embarrassed for him. There was no doubt about it. He hated mess and disruptions and children.

"It was an accident," Alex said calmly.

"Why in God's name are you throwing baseballs at my windows?" Coop shouted at Jason. He had seen the catcher's mitt, and it was no mystery who had done it. The boy looked near tears in the face of Coop's outrage, and he was sure he was going to get in big trouble with his father, who had warned him about not rocking the boat by upsetting Mr. Winslow. He had already had one run-in with him with his skateboard.

"I did it, Coop. I'm really sorry." Jimmy stepped forward. "I should know better." It broke his heart to see how upset his young friend was, and there wasn't much Coop could do to Jimmy. "I'll replace it."

"I should hope so. Although I don't believe you. I think it was young Mr. Friedman who did it." He glanced from Jason to Mark and then back to Jimmy, as Alex got out of the pool and grabbed a towel.

"I'll replace it if you want, Coop," Alex said generously. "No one meant to do it."

"This isn't a ballpark," he said angrily. "Those windows take forever to make, and they're damn near impossible to install." They were curved and had been blown specially for the house. It was going to cost a fortune to replace it. "Keep your children under control, Friedman," Coop said unpleasantly and disappeared back into the main house as Alex looked apologetically at the others.

"I'm really sorry," she said softly. It was a side of him she didn't like to see, but he had warned her often enough that he hated children.

"What an asshole," Jessica said loudly.

"Jessie!" Mark said sternly, as Jimmy looked at Alex.

"I agree with her, but I'm really sorry. I should have taken him out on the tennis court to throw balls. It never occurred to me he'd throw one through a window."

"It's okay," Alex said sympathetically. "He's just not used to kids. He likes everything peaceful and perfect."

"Life isn't like that," Jimmy said simply. He dealt with kids every day, and nothing was ever peaceful or perfect or the way you expected, that was what he loved about it. "At least mine isn't."

"Neither is mine," Alex said realistically, "but his is. Or he likes to think it is." They were all thinking of the mess in the tabloids. "Don't worry about it, Jason. It's just a window. Not a person. You can always replace things, not people." And as she said it, she could have cut her tongue out, as she glanced at Jimmy.

"You're right," he said softly.

"I'm sorry . . . I didn't mean that. . . ." She was horrified.

"Yes, you did. And you're right. We all forget that
sometimes. We get so attached to our stuff, our
'things.' It's the people that matter. The rest is all bullshit."

"I deal with that every day," she said and he
nodded.

"I learned that lesson the hard way," he said honestly and smiled at her. He liked her. He couldn't understand what she was doing with a man who was all
about show and pretense. Everything about her
seemed honest and real. "Thanks for being nice to
Jason. I'll take care of it."

"No, I will," Mark interjected. "He's my son. I'll pay
for it. Just be careful next time," he said to Jason, and
then glanced at Jimmy. "And that goes for you too."

"Sorry, Dad," Jimmy said, looking apologetic, and
they all laughed as Jessica and Jason watched them.
Jason figured he had gotten off pretty easy, except for
Mr. Winslow yelling at him, but everyone else had
been pretty decent. He had expected his dad to kill
him when he saw the ball sail through the window. "It
was a great throw though, Jason. I'm proud of you."

"Let's not go that far," Mark added. He didn't want
to give Coop an excuse to evict them. "Let's keep our
ball sports on the tennis court from now on. Deal?"
Both Jason and Jimmy nodded, as Alex put her shorts
back on over her wet bathing suit and pulled on her
T-shirt.

"I'll see you guys soon," Alex said as she left them,
with her long dark hair wet behind her. Both men

watched her go, and Mark commented as soon as she was out of earshot.

"Jessie's right. He is an asshole. And *she* is a great woman. He doesn't deserve her, no matter how good he looks. He's going to make mincemeat of her."

"I think he's going to marry her," Jessica added with interest, joining into the conversation. She wished her father would go out with someone like Alex.

"I hope not," Jimmy added, as he put an arm around Jason, and the four of them went home to the guest wing. Mark was doing another barbecue for them, and Jimmy had agreed to stay for dinner.

And upstairs, in the main house, Alex was scolding Coop, who was still fuming.

"He's just a kid, Coop. Didn't you do things like that when you were a boy?"

"I was never a boy. I was born wearing a suit and a tie, and sprang full-blown into manhood, with good manners."

"Don't be such an asshole," she teased as he kissed her.

"Why not? I enjoy having tantrums. Besides, you know how much I hate children."

"What if I told you I was pregnant?" she asked, with a look that nearly made his jaw drop.

"Are you?"

"No. But what if I were? You'd have to put up with skateboards and broken windows and dirty diapers and peanut butter and jelly sandwiches all over the furniture. It's something to think about."

"Must I? I'm getting nauseous. You, Dr. Madison,

have a vicious sense of humor. I hope your father beats you when he sees you."

"I'm sure he will," Alex said coolly. "He usually does."

"Good, you deserve it." It was a meeting he would have given almost anything to be at. But Alex hadn't invited him, and she didn't intend to. "When are you seeing him?"

"On Tuesday."

"Why do you suppose he wants to see you?" Coop asked with obvious curiosity. He was convinced it was about him.

"We'll see," Alex said with a smile, as they walked slowly arm in arm up to his bedroom. She had a sure cure for his tantrums. In fact, the incident with the baseball was already nearly forgotten as she kissed him. And a moment later, the broken window was the farthest thing from his mind.

Chapter 16

Alex could have predicted the way the meeting with her father went on Tuesday, or at least to some degree. It was the way meetings with him always went. Nothing ever changed in her dealings with him.

He arrived five minutes early, and he was waiting in the cafeteria for her when she arrived. He was tall and slim, with gray hair and blue eyes, and he looked stern. He always had to have an agenda when he saw her. He could never just talk to her and ask her how she was. Instead, he seemed to go down some kind of mental list, as though he were running a board meeting, and in some ways he was. The only affectionate thing he said to her that even indicated that they were related was that her mother sent her love. And her mother was no warmer than he, which was why she had tolerated being married to him for all those years. But it was her father who had total control. Except over Alex. It was the bone of contention between them, and had been a raging battle all her life.

It took him exactly ten minutes to get down to business with her, and he didn't waste any time.

"I wanted to speak to you about Cooper Winslow,

Alex. And I didn't want to do it on the phone." It made no difference to her. Their exchanges were so distant and so bloodless, being face-to-face added nothing at all.

"Why not?"

"I thought this was a sufficiently important matter, to warrant our meeting in person." For Alex, the fact that he was her father would have been enough to warrant seeing him, but that didn't even occur to him. There always had to be a reason. "It's a delicate matter, and I'm not going to beat around the bush." He never did, but then again, neither did she. She would have hated to admit it, but in some ways she was not unlike him. She was ruthlessly honest, not only about others, but also about herself. She had principles that she adhered to and she was very clear about what she believed. The major difference between them was that Alex was kind, and he was not. Arthur Madison wasted no time on emotions, and never minced words. And if something unpleasant had to be done, he was the first one to volunteer. He just had.

"How serious is this affair between you?" he asked bluntly, his eyes narrowing on hers. He knew her well, and he was reading her face. He knew she wouldn't lie to him, but it was unlikely that she would tell him how she felt either. She felt that it was her business and not his.

"I don't know yet," she said carefully, and in fact it was true.

"Are you aware that the man is up to his neck in debt?" Coop had never said it to her, but the fact that he had tenants had suggested to her that things were tight. And he was no longer getting a lot of work, in fact hadn't in years. But she had assumed, incorrectly, that he had some money put away. And of course, The Cottage was worth a great deal. Her father knew it was the only asset he had, and there was an enormous mortgage on it.

"I don't discuss his financial affairs with him," she said succinctly. "They're none of my business, any more than mine are his."

"Has he asked you about your income, or your inheritance?"

"Of course not, he's much too polite for that," she countered honestly. Coop was far too well bred to discuss her money with her.

"And too shrewd. He has probably done a thorough check on you, just as I did on him. I have a file an inch thick on him on my desk. And it's not good news. He's been in over his head for years, he has a mountain of bad debts. His credit is nonexistent, I don't think he could borrow a book at the library, if he tried. And he has a knack for attracting rich women. He's been engaged to at least five."

"He has a knack for attracting *all* women," Alex corrected him. "What you're saying is that he's after me for my money? Is that correct?" Like him, she cut to the chase. They were an even match. And she was hurt that he was suggesting that Coop only saw her as an easy mark. She was absolutely certain that he loved her, and it was unfortunate that he also happened to be in debt.

"Yes, I am. I think it's entirely possible his motives aren't as pure as you'd like to think, and he's setting you up. Maybe even unconsciously. Maybe he's not even aware of it himself. The man is in a terrible spot. Alex, desperation is not a good thing, for either of you. It might even force him to want to marry you, when he might not otherwise. Aside from that, he's far too old for you. I think you have no idea what you're getting yourself into. I had no idea you were even seeing him, until your mother saw you with him at the Academy Awards. We were both quite shocked. Apparently he went out with someone she knew many years ago. He didn't do anything inappropriate, but he's been around for a very long time. And I assume you know about this illegitimate baby with the porn star. That's just the icing on the cake."

"It can happen to anyone," she said calmly, hating her father for every word he had said, although nothing showed in her face. She had concealed all of her emotions from him for years.

"Those things don't happen to responsible men. He's a playboy, Alex. He's had a life of extravagance and self-indulgence. He hasn't saved a dime. And his debts currently amount to just under two million dollars, not to mention the mortgage on his house."

"If he gets one decent part in a movie," she defended him valiantly, "he could wipe out his debt." She loved him, no matter what her father said.

"The trouble is, he won't. He can't get work. He's too old. And even if he got a windfall, which is unlikely, he's far more likely to spend it, just as he always has. Is that who you want to be married to, Alex? A man who is going to run through money like water, and spend every cent he gets? And possibly yours as well? Just why do you think he's pursuing you? It would be impossible to believe he doesn't know who you are, and who I am."

"Of course he does. I haven't given him a penny, and he hasn't asked me. He's extremely proud."

"He's full of hot air. All hat and no cattle, as they say in Texas. He can't afford to support you or himself. And what about this woman expecting his child? What's he going to do about that?"

"Support her if he has to," she said fairly, "he doesn't even know yet if it's his. She has to submit to tests in July."

"She wouldn't accuse him of it if the baby weren't his."

"She might. I actually don't care about it. It's not pleasant, but it's not the end of the world. These things happen. It matters to me a lot more that he's nice to me, and he is."

"Why wouldn't he be? You're rich and you're single, not to mention the fact that you're a very attractive girl. But frankly, if your last name weren't Madison, I don't think he'd be giving you the time of day."

"I don't believe that for a second," Alex said, looking her father right in the eye. "But we'll never know, will we, Dad? I am who I am, and I have what I have, and I'm not going to select the men in my life by the size of their trust fund. He's from a respectable family. He's a good man. Some people don't have money. That's just the way it is. And I don't give a damn."

"Is he honest with you, Alex? Has he ever told you he's in debt?" He was pressing the point, and trying to undermine everything she felt for Coop, and he for her. But she didn't care. Even if she'd never seen his balance sheet, she knew who Coop was, his quirks, his virtues, and his flaws. And she loved him just as he was. The only thing that worried her was the fact that he didn't want children at his age. That concerned her far more, because she did want them at some point.

"I already told you, we don't discuss financial matters, his or mine."

"The man is forty years older than you are. If you marry him, God forbid, you're going to wind up being his nurse."

"Maybe that's a risk I'll have to take. It wouldn't be the end of the world."

"You say that now. When you're forty, he'll be eighty, twice your age. It's ridiculous, Alex. Be sensible. And be smart. I think the man is gunning for your wallet, not your heart."

"That's a disgusting thing to say," she said heatedly.

"Who can blame him? What if he's trying to provide for his old age, and trying to save himself now, and this is the only way he has? It's too late for him to do it any other way. You're the only meal ticket he has. The girl having his baby isn't going to support him. It's not pretty, Alex, but this book is very easy to read.

"I'm not telling you to stop seeing him, if he means something to you. But for God's sake, be careful, and don't marry him, whatever you do. And if you do, if you're foolish enough to risk it, I can assure you I'm going to do everything I can to stand in your way. I'll talk to him if I have to, and warn him off. He's going to have a very powerful enemy in me."

"I knew I could count on you, Dad," Alex said with

a tired smile. Even if he meant well, he did it in such an ugly, painful way. It was the way he had always dealt with her. It was all about power and control. And when Carter had run off with her sister, hours before her wedding, he had blamed Alex, and told her that if she'd handled him right, he never would have done it to her. Everything was always her fault. Although she'd heard he was less enthused about Carter these days. He had invested a lot of her sister's money in the stock market unwisely, and lost it all. Fortunately, she still had a lot left. But if nothing else, it proved he wasn't very smart.

"I know you think what I'm saying is very unkind, and it is. I was worried about him, and about you. And when I began looking into it, I was horrified by what I found. He may be attractive, and obviously he is, as you say, and charming I'm sure, undoubtedly fun to be with, all of which is very alluring at your age. But the rest is an absolute disaster, and I don't think he'll make you happy in the long run, if he even marries you. He's never gotten married before. He didn't have to. He just has fun and then moves on to the next one. That's not serious, Alex. And it's not what I want for you. To see you paraded around, swept off your feet, and tossed away. Or worse yet, married and used to meet his financial needs. I could be wrong, but I don't think I am," her father said unhappily. But if anything, it didn't warn her off Coop, it only increased her allegiance to him. Her father's speech had had the reverse effect. Hearing about the extent of Coop's debt, she felt sorry for him.

Mercifully, her pager went off at the end of his

speech. It wasn't an emergency, but she used it as an excuse to bring the meeting to a close. They hadn't eaten a thing. What he had to say was far more important, and he felt it was his responsibility. He had discussed the entire matter with her mother, and as usual, she didn't want to get involved. But she had encouraged him to speak to Alex. Someone had to talk to her. And he was always willing to do the dirty work. It had been a very unpleasant hour for both of them.

"I've got to go back to work," Alex said, and he stood up.

"I think you ought to do your best to stay out of the papers with him, Alex. Being seen with him isn't going to do your reputation any good. You'll have every fortune hunter in the world running after you." And so far, mainly due to her own efforts, and the way she lived, she had avoided that. The people she knew at work had no idea who she was, or more important, who her father was, and she liked it that way. "They're all going to smell blood in the water, after Winslow gets through with you." Another lovely image. He saw her as chum for the sharks. She knew her father cared about her, but the way he expressed it was revolting. And the way he perceived the world seemed pathetic to her. He was suspicious of everyone, and all too willing to believe the worst. It was inconceivable to him that, whatever Coop's reputation or financial pressures, he was actually, genuinely in love with her. And she believed he was. "Are you coming to Newport this summer?" he asked in an effort at more pleasant conversation, and she shook her head.

"I can't get away from work," she said, but even if

she could, she would have stayed in LA rather than go there. She had no desire to see her mother, her sister, or Carter, or her father, or any of their friends. She had renounced her passport to that world long since. She was staying in California with Coop.

"Stay in touch," her father said stiffly, as she kissed him goodbye.

"I will. Say hello to Mom." She never came out to see Alex, she never had. She expected Alex to visit her in Palm Beach, although she was perfectly able to travel, and went to visit friends all over the world. But she and Alex had nothing in common. Her mother never knew what to say to her, so she rarely called. She thought her oldest daughter an odd bird, and she'd never understood the need for her medical career. She should have stayed home and married some nice boy in Palm Beach. Even if it hadn't worked out with Carter, there were plenty of others like him, which was precisely why Alex had left. She didn't want a man like him. And for the moment, she was happy with Coop, in spite of everything her father had said.

He walked her to the elevator, and as the doors closed, he turned and walked away, as Alex closed her eyes and rode up to her floor, feeling numb. He always had that effect on her.

Chapter 17

While Alex was meeting with her father, Coop was relaxing under a tree, beside the pool. He was always careful to stay out of the sun, to protect his skin. It was part of the secret of why he never seemed to age. And he loved the peace and quiet of being at the pool in the daytime during the week. There was no one else around. His tenants were at work, and Mark's miserable kids were in school. He was lying there, looking pensive in the shade of the tree, and wondering what her father was saying to her. He was almost certain it was about him, in part at least. And he was sure her father wouldn't approve. He just hoped the old man wouldn't upset Alex too much. But even Coop had to admit her father had cause to be concerned. He wasn't exactly solvent at the moment. And if her father had done an investigation, he was undoubtedly well aware of it.

For the first time in his life, it actually bothered Coop what someone might think of him. For both their sakes, he had been meticulously scrupulous with her, in spite of his financial woes. She was just such a decent person, that it was hard to take advantage of her,

although he'd thought of it. But so far, he had been remarkably good, and had held himself in check. Besides which, he was seriously beginning to suspect he
really was in love with her, whatever that meant to
him. It had meant different things over the years.
Lately, it meant being comfortable and at ease, not
having headaches in the relationship. Sometimes just
liking her was enough. There were so many difficult
women out there, and girls like Charlene.

It was so much easier being with a woman like
Alex. She was fair and kind and funny, and she didn't
ask for much. He liked that about her too. She was
wonderfully self-sufficient, and if he did get desperate
and the bottom fell out of his life financially, he knew
he could turn to her. The money she had was like an
insurance policy for him. He didn't need it yet, but he
might one day. He wasn't with her because of her
money, but he liked knowing it was there. Just in case.
It made him feel safe.

The only thing he didn't like, and which kept him
from making any overt promises, was that she was
young enough to have kids, and probably should have
them one day. That really was too bad, in Coop's eyes.
And a real flaw in their relationship. But you couldn't
have everything. Maybe being Arthur Madison's daughter was enough to compensate for it. He hadn't figured
that out yet. But he would one of these days. She
hadn't pressed him yet, and he liked that about her
too. There was no pressure involved in being with her.
There was a lot about her he liked. Almost too much.

He was thinking about her, as he walked back into
the house, and ran smack into Paloma. She was dust-

ing furniture and eating a sandwich at the same time. And while she did, she was dropping mayonnaise on the rug. And he pointed it out to her.

"Sorry," she said, as she stepped on the spot she'd made with the leopard sneakers.

He had given up trying to train or educate her. They were just trying to survive on parallel paths without killing each other. And he had figured out several weeks before, that she was doing work for the Friedmans too, but as long as she did what she had to do for him, he didn't really care. It wasn't worth the fight. Out of sheer necessity, he was mellowing. Maybe it was Alex's effect on him. The glaziers were working on his living room window that afternoon, although he still wasn't amused about the baseball incident. If he did have children with Alex one day, he hoped they wouldn't be boys. Just thinking about it made him feel sick. Like that damn woman Charlene. At least she wasn't in the tabloids that week.

He was pouring himself a glass of the iced tea he had taught Paloma to make. She left it in a jug in the fridge. And as he did, the phone rang. He thought it might be Alex, but it was an unfamiliar voice, a woman called Taryn Dougherty who said she'd like a meeting with him.

"Are you a producer?" he asked, still holding the glass of iced tea. He'd been a little lax about drumming up work since the incident with Charlene. He had other things on his mind.

"No, actually I'm a designer. But that's not why I called. There's a matter I'd like to discuss with you." He thought she might be a reporter, and was instantly sorry he'd answered the phone, and he'd already admitted who he was. It was too late to say he was the butler and Mr. Winslow was out, which he did sometimes now that Livermore was gone.

"What sort of matter?" he asked coolly. He didn't trust anyone these days. Everyone seemed to want something from him, or Charlene did at least.

"It's a personal matter. I have a letter from an old friend of yours." It sounded too mysterious to him. It was probably a ruse, or a scheme of some kind. Maybe from Charlene. But the woman sounded pleasant at least.

"Who would that be?"

"Jane Axman. I'm not sure you'll remember the name."

"I don't. Are you her attorney?" It was also possible that he owed her money. He got a lot of calls like that too. He always referred them to Abe. Liz used to screen them for him, but now he had to do it himself.

"I'm her daughter." The woman on the phone didn't seem to want to say more, but she insisted that it was important and wouldn't take much time. And he was ever so slightly intrigued. He wondered how attractive she was. He was tempted to tell her he'd meet her at the Beverly Hills Hotel, but he was too lazy to go out. And he was waiting to hear from Alex, after she met with her father. She hadn't called him yet. And he was afraid she might be upset. He didn't want to take her call on a cell phone in the middle of a restaurant.

"Where are you?" Coop asked as though it mattered.

"I'm at the Bel Air Hotel. I just arrived from New York." At least she was staying at a good hotel. It didn't mean much, but it was something, and finally his curiosity got the best of him.

"I'm not far from there. Why don't you come over now?"

"Thank you, Mr. Winslow," she said politely. "I won't take much of your time." She just wanted to see him. Once. And show him her mother's letter. It was a piece of history for them to share.

She was at the gate ten minutes later, and he buzzed her in from the house. She drove up in a rented car, and when she got out, he saw that she was tall and blonde, in her late thirties, he guessed. She was actually thirty-nine. She was a good-looking woman, with a slim figure, and a short skirt. She was very well dressed, and seemed to have a sense of style. There was something familiar about her, but he didn't know what it was. He didn't think he'd ever seen her before. And as she approached, she smiled, and then shook his hand.

"Thank you for seeing me. I'm very sorry to disturb you. I wanted to get this out of the way. I've been wanting to write to you for a long time."

"What are you doing in California?" he asked as he led her into the library, and offered her a glass of wine, which she declined. She asked for a glass of water instead. It was hot outside.

"I'm not sure yet. I had a design business in New York. I just sold it. I've always wanted to do costume design for a movie, but I think that's just one of those crazy ideas. I thought I'd come out here and look around." And meet him.

"That must mean you're not married," he said, handing her the glass of water she'd asked for, in a Baccarat glass. Paloma was using one like it to water the plants.

"I'm divorced. I got divorced, sold my business, and my mother died, all within a few months. It's one of those rare times when you have no encumbrances and can do anything you want. I'm not sure if I like it, or if it scares me to death," but she smiled as she said it. She didn't look as though she would be scared by much. She was extremely poised.

"So what's in this letter? Did someone leave me some money?" He laughed as he said it, and she smiled in response.

"I'm afraid not." She handed him the letter from the woman he no longer remembered, and didn't say another word. The letter was long, and as he read it, he looked up at her several times. And when he finished it, he sat for a long moment, staring at her, not sure what to say next, or what she wanted from him. He handed her back the letter, and looked serious as he did. If it was another blackmail scheme, he wasn't up to it. One of those was enough.

"What do you want from me?" he asked bluntly, and the question made her sad. She had hoped for a warmer response from him.

"Absolutely nothing. I wanted to meet you. Once. And I hoped you'd want to meet me. I'll admit, it's a bit of a shock. It was to me too. My mother never told me. I found the letter, as she intended me to, after she died. My father died years ago. I have no idea if he ever knew."

"I hope not," Coop said solemnly. He was still in shock. But relieved by what she'd said about wanting nothing from him. He believed her. She looked like an honest person, and a nice woman. He would have been attracted to her, but she was a little old for him.

"I don't think it would have mattered to him. He was very good to me. He left me most of his money. He had no other children. And if he did know, he didn't seem to hold it against my mother or me. He was a very kind man."

"How fortunate for you," Coop said, looking closely at her, and suddenly realized why she looked familiar. She looked like him. With good reason. The letter said that her mother had had an affair with Coop forty years before. They were both in a play in London, and the affair had been brief. When the play closed and she went back to Chicago, she had discovered she was pregnant, and she decided, for reasons of her own, not to tell Coop. She didn't feel she knew him well enough to impose on him, as she put it. It was an odd thing for a woman to think when she was having his baby, which she had decided to do, again for reasons of her own. She married someone else, had the baby, a daughter, and never told her that the man she believed was her father actually wasn't. It was Coop. Instead, she left her a letter, which explained it all. And now they were sitting, examining each other. The man who thought he had no children suddenly had two. This thirty-nine-year-old woman who had suddenly appeared, and the one Charlene was carrying, and claimed was his. It was a very odd feeling for a man who hated kids. But Taryn was no kid. She was a grown woman, who appeared to be respectable and intelligent, had money, and looked a great deal like him. "What did your mother look like? Do you have a picture of her?" He was curious to see if he remembered her at all.

"Actually, I brought one just in case. I think it's from about that time." She took it carefully from her purse and handed it to him, and as he looked at it, something jogged in his memory. It was definitely a familiar face. She hadn't left a lifelong impression, but he remembered something about her, and he thought he knew which part she'd played. She'd been an understudy, but the actress she stood in for got drunk a lot, and Coop remembered being on stage with her. But he didn't remember much else. He'd been pretty wild in those days, and drank a lot himself. And there had been a lot of women since. He'd been thirty years old when Taryn was conceived.

"This is very strange," he said, handing the photograph back to her, and looking at his daughter again. She was very good-looking in a kind of classic way, although very tall. He guessed her to be just under six feet. He was six four. And he thought her mother had been tall too. "I don't know what to say."

"That's all right," Taryn Dougherty said pleasantly. "I just wanted to see you, and meet you once. I've had a good life. I had a wonderful father, I loved my mother. I was an only child. I have nothing to reproach you. You never knew. And it was my mother who kept it all a secret, but I don't reproach her anything either. I have no regrets."

"Do you have children?" he asked with trepidation. It was enough of a shock finding out he had a grown daughter, he wasn't ready for grandchildren too.

"No, I don't. I've always worked. And I've never really wanted children, embarrassing as that is to admit."

"Don't be embarrassed. It's genetic," he said with a mischievous grin. "I've never wanted children either. They make a lot of noise, they're dirty, and they smell. Or something like that." She laughed at what he said. She was enjoying him, and she could see why her mother had fallen in love with him, and decided to have his child. He was very charming, and amusing, a gentleman of the old school. Although nothing about him seemed very old, it was hard to believe that he and her mother had been the same age. Her mother had been ill for years. This man seemed years younger than he was. "Will you be here for a while?" he asked with interest. He liked her, and in spite of himself, he felt some kind of bond with her, he just wasn't sure what. It was too new. He needed time to sort it out.

"I think so." She was still unsure of what she wanted to do. But she felt liberated now that she had done this. It had weighed on her ever since she found out. But now that she had met him, she felt free to go on with her life, whether or not she stayed in touch with him.

"Can I reach you at the Bel Air? It might be nice to get together again. Maybe you'd like to come to dinner one night."

"That would be lovely," she said, standing up, and bringing the meeting to a close. She had been true to her word. She had been there for half an hour. She wasn't trying to linger. She had done what she came to do. She had met him. And now she was going back to her own life. And she turned to him then with a serious look. "I want to assure you, in case you're concerned, that I have no intention of talking to the press. This is just between us."

"Thank you," he said, and was touched. She truly was a nice woman. She wanted nothing from him. She just wanted to see who he was. And she liked what she saw. So did he. "It's probably a crazy thing to say, but you were probably a very nice little girl. Your mother must have been a decent woman," particularly for not making trouble for him and shouldering all the responsibilities herself. He wondered if he had cared about her at all. It was hard to say. But he liked her daughter, their daughter, very much. "I'm sorry she died," he said and meant it. It was an odd feeling knowing that while he pursued his own life, unbeknownst to him, he had a daughter somewhere in the world.

"Thank you. I'm sorry she died too. I loved her very much." As she left, he kissed her on the cheek, and she turned to him and smiled. It was the same smile he saw in the mirror every day, and that his friends knew so well. It was uncanny looking at her. He could see the resemblance himself, and her mother must have seen it too. It must have been odd for her. He wondered if her husband ever knew. He hoped not, for his sake.

Coop was quiet for the rest of the day. He had a lot to think about. And when Alex came in at seven, he was still pensive and she asked if he was okay. He asked about her meeting with her father, she said it had been fine, but she didn't say much more than that.

"Was he rough on you?" Coop asked with obvious concern, and she shrugged.

"He is who he is. He isn't the father I'd have chosen if they'd asked me, but he's what I've got," she said philosophically and poured herself a glass of wine.

It had been a long day, for both of them. Coop didn't say anything to her about Taryn until they were eating dinner. Paloma had left some chicken for them, and Alex added some pasta to it, and made a salad. It was enough. And then Coop looked up with a strange expression.

"I have a daughter," he said cryptically. And Alex looked up at him.

"It's too soon for her to know that, Coop. She's lying to you. She's just trying to soften you up." Alex was instantly annoyed at what she thought was yet another of Charlene's tricks.

"It's not her." He seemed almost in a daze. He'd been thinking about Taryn all afternoon. Meeting her had had a powerful effect on him.

"Someone else is having your baby too?" She looked shocked.

"Apparently someone did. Thirty-nine years ago." He told her about Taryn then, and Alex could see how moved he was.

"What an amazing story," she said, somewhat in

awe. "How could her mother keep that secret for all those years? What's she like?" She was intrigued.

"Nice. I like her. She looks a lot like me, I think. Better looking of course," he said gallantly. "I really liked her. She's very..." he searched for the word, "dignified...honorable...something like that. She reminds me of you that way. She's very straightforward and decent. She didn't want anything from me, and she said she wasn't going to talk to the press. She just wanted to meet me. Once, she said."

"Why don't you invite her back?" Alex suggested. She could see that he wanted to.

"I think I will."

But instead, he went to lunch with her at the Bel Air the next day. They told each other all about themselves and were amazed at how similar they were in some ways, how many tastes they shared, right down to their favorite ice cream and dessert, and the kind of books they did and didn't like. It was uncanny how powerful the genetics were. And at the end of lunch, he had an odd idea.

"Would you like to stay at The Cottage while you're here?" he suggested, and meant it. He wanted to spend more time with her. She suddenly seemed like a gift in his life, and he didn't want to turn her away. He wanted her close to him, at least for a few days, or maybe even weeks. And Taryn liked the idea too.

"I don't want to intrude," she said cautiously, but he could see it appealed to her.

"You wouldn't be." He was sorry now that he had tenants in the guest wing and the gatehouse. It would have been nice to have her there. But he had an enormous guest suite in the main house too, and he was sure Alex wouldn't object. He had told Taryn about her, and she thought Alex sounded wonderful, which Coop said she was.

Taryn promised to move in the next day, and he told Alex that night. She was thrilled for him, and excited to meet her. She still hadn't told him what her father had said, and she never would. In retrospect, she realized he had meant well, but she knew it would have broken Coop's heart to hear the horrors her father had to say. He didn't need to know. Her father just didn't understand who Coop was.

And whatever Taryn had brought to him, it was obviously meant to be. She had never seen Coop like that in the few months she'd known him. He seemed remarkably quiet, and totally at peace.

Chapter 18

Taryn moved in to The Cottage with very little luggage, and even less fuss. She was discreet, polite, pleasant, and easy to have around. She asked Paloma for nothing, and was careful not to intrude on Coop. And when Alex met her, the two women hit it off immediately. They were both solid, strong, honest women, who had a penchant for being kind. And Alex could see the resemblance to Coop. Not only physically, but they had the same naturally aristocratic look. It was remarkable. The two things she didn't have in common with him were that she traveled with very little luggage, and she was financially sound. Other than that, they were two peas in a pod. And Coop loved having her around.

They spent days getting to know each other, filling each other in on their pasts, and sharing their views and opinions on everything imaginable. There were differences and similarities that intrigued them both, and Taryn thought him a nice man. After they'd gotten to know each other, she asked him if he was serious about Alex, and he told her he wasn't sure. It was the most honest thing he'd ever said. Even in the short

time he'd known her, Taryn brought the best out in
him, even more than Alex. It was as though she had
come to make him whole. And he brought her something too. Now that she knew he existed, she wanted
to know who he was, and she liked what she saw, although she saw his weaknesses too.

"I have a dilemma about Alex," he confessed.

"Because she's so young?" Taryn asked, as they lay
in the shade at the pool, while everyone else was at
work. She had the same fair skin as he, and like her father, she instinctively avoided the sun, and had the
same flawless alabaster complexion as he. Coop always said it was thanks to his distant British ancestry.
He had "English" skin, and clearly Taryn did too.

"No, I'm used to that, young doesn't bother me," he
grinned. "She's almost too old for me." They both
laughed at that. He had told her about Charlene too.
"Her father is Arthur Madison. You know what that
means. I constantly question my motives about her.
I'm up to my ass in debt." His honesty seemed charming to her. He had never even told Alex that. "Sometimes I worry that I'm after her money. At other times,
I'm sure I'm not. It would be so damn easy and convenient for me. Too easy maybe. The question is,
would I love her if she didn't have a cent? I'm not sure.
And until I am, I'm stuck. It's a hell of a question to ask
yourself."

"Maybe it doesn't matter," Taryn said practically.

"But maybe it does," he said, suddenly honest,
which was an immense relief. She was the one person
he could be totally candid with, because she had no
axe to grind, and he wanted nothing from her. Not her

love or her body or her money. He just wanted her in his life. It was the closest he'd ever been to unconditional love. And it seemed to have happened overnight, almost as though he had known she was out there somewhere, and he was waiting for her to arrive in his life. He needed her. And maybe, in some odd and unexpected way, Taryn needed him. "The minute sex and money get into it, Taryn, it's a mess. It has been in my life anyway." He loved sharing his secrets with her, and was surprised about it himself.

"Maybe you're right. I had a problem with that with my husband too. We built the business together, and in the end, it brought us down. He wanted to take more money out of it than I did. I did the designing so I got the recognition, and he was jealous of that. In the end, he tried to take the business away in the divorce. It was easier to just sell it and move on. And he slept with my assistant, and moved in with her when he left, which damn near broke my heart."

"See what I mean," Coop said, nodding, "money and sex. It screws things up every time. We've got neither one between us, and everything's so simple." And it felt so right. His relationship with her had become precious to him overnight.

"How bad are your debts?" she asked with a look of concern.

"Bad enough. Alex doesn't know. I never told her. I didn't want her to think I was after her money to pay my debts."

"Are you?"

"I'm not sure," he said honestly. "It would certainly be simpler than working my ass off, hustling commercials and God knows what else. But she's so decent, I don't want to take money from her. If she were different, I might. And I don't want money from you," he said pointedly. He didn't want to add that to the mix, or corrupt what they had. He liked things just the way they were. It was clean between them, and he intended to keep it that way. "All I need is a part in a decent movie, a good part, and I'd be back on my feet. But God knows when that will happen, or if. Maybe never again. Hard to say." He seemed philosophical about it.

"Then what?" She was worried about him. He seemed a little vague about his financial affairs.

"Something always turns up." And if not, there was Alex, but that seemed wrong to him. That was what he'd been explaining to Taryn, and as they were talking, he suddenly pointed to her feet.

"Is something wrong?" Taryn asked. She'd just had a pedicure, and her nails were painted pink. She thought maybe he preferred red. But she always wore pink. Red polish looked like blood to her.

"You've got my feet." He stuck his own next to hers and they both laughed. They looked like twins. They had the same long, elegant feet. She stuck her hands out. "And the same hands." There was no denying her, not that he wanted to. He had been thinking of introducing her as his niece. But as time wore on and he got to know her better, he wanted to introduce her as his daughter, and he asked her what she thought.

"Sounds good to me, but not if it's going to screw things up for you."

"I don't see why. We can just say you're big for fourteen."

"I won't tell anyone how old I am," she laughed, and they had almost the same laugh as well, "that works for me too. It's a bitch suddenly being single again at my age. I'm nearly forty, and suddenly I'm back out in the world. I've been married since I was twenty-two."

"How boring," he scolded her and she laughed again. He was fun to be with, and great to talk to. She loved spending time with him, and he with her. They had done nothing else for days, like catching up on an entire lifetime in one gulp. She brought the best out in him, and he in her. "It was time for a change. We'll have to find someone for you out here."

"Not yet," she said calmly. "I'm not ready. I need to catch my breath. I've lost my husband, my business, and my mother, and acquired a father all in the last few months. I need to move slowly for a little while. It's a lot to absorb."

"What about work? Are you going to look for something out here?" He was protective of her now.

"I don't know. I've always wanted to try my hand at costume design, but that's probably a crazy idea. I don't really have to work. We sold the business very well, and Mom left me what she had. My father...my *other* father," she said with a smile, "provided for me very well. I can take my time figuring it out. Maybe I can help you figure out yours. I'm pretty good at sorting things out and making sense of a mess."

"That must have been in your mother's genes. I work it the other way round. I take 'sense' and turn it into a mess. It works for me. Financial chaos is familiar to me." He said it with good humor and humility, which she found endearing too.

"Let me know if you want me to take a look and tell you what I think."

"Maybe you can interpret what my accountant says, although it's pretty plain. He's a one-man band. Essentially he says don't buy anything and sell the house. He's an incredibly boring little man."

"It's the nature of the beast," she said sympathetically.

And when Alex was around, they had fun too. The three of them cooked dinner together, went to movies, and talked endlessly. But when the time was right, Taryn always discreetly disappeared. She didn't want to intrude on them. But she enjoyed Alex immensely and had great respect for the work she did.

Taryn and Alex were lying at the pool talking about it one Saturday morning when Mark and his children came out of the guest wing. Coop was up at the main house on the terrace, reading a book. He had a cold and didn't want to swim.

Alex introduced Taryn to the Friedmans, but didn't say who she was. She didn't have to. Mark asked if she and Coop were related. He said there was an uncanny resemblance between them, and asked if Alex had noticed it. Both women laughed.

"Actually," Taryn said calmly, "he's my father. We haven't seen each other in a long time." It was the understatement of the century and Alex chuckled. She had handled it very well.

"I didn't know Coop had a daughter," Mark said, looking blank.

"Neither did he," Taryn said with a smile, and dove into the pool.

"What did she say?" Mark asked Alex, looking confused.

"It's a long story. They'll tell you about it sometime."

And a few minutes later, Jimmy appeared. It was a hot day, and they all wanted to swim. Mark was talking to Taryn about her business and New York, and the kids were hanging out with friends who had just arrived. Alex asked them not to play their music, since Coop wasn't feeling well, and they hung out at the far end of the pool, talking and laughing. It gave her a chance to talk to Jimmy quietly for a change. There were always other people around.

"How are things?" Alex asked easily, stretched out on a lounge chair as he put sunblock on his arms. Despite his dark hair, he had fair skin. She volunteered to put some on his back, and he hesitated and then thanked her as he turned around. No one had done that for him since Maggie died, and Alex didn't give it a second thought as she handed the tube back to him.

"Okay, I guess. How about you? How's work?" Jimmy asked.

"Busy. Sometimes I think the whole world has preemies, or babies with problems. I never get to see healthy babies anymore."

"It must be depressing work," Jimmy said sympathetically.

"Not really. Most of them get healthy eventually. Some don't. I'm not used to that part yet." She hated it when they lost them. It was so sad for everyone. But the victories were sweet. "The kids you work with don't have an easy road either. It's hard to think about the things some people do to their kids."

"I'll never get used to that either," he admitted. They had both seen a lot in their respective lines of work. And in their own way, they were each saving lives.

"What made you want to become a doctor?" he asked, curious for the first time.

"My mother," she said simply, and he smiled.

"Is she a doctor too?"

"No," Alex grinned, "she leads a totally useless life. She goes shopping and goes to dinner parties and gets her nails done. And that's about it. So does my sister. I wanted to do anything but that, no matter what it took." It had been a little bit more complicated than that, but not much. She had been exceptionally good at science too. "I used to want to be an airline pilot, when I was a kid. But that seemed pretty boring too. It's kind of like being a glorified bus driver after a while. What I do is more fun, and it's different every day."

"Me too," he smiled. "When I was at Harvard, I wanted to play professional ice hockey for the Bruins. But my girlfriend convinced me I'd look like shit with no teeth. I decided she was right. But I still like to skate." He and Maggie used to skate a lot, but he tried not to think about that. "Who's the woman talking to Mark?" he asked with interest, and Alex smiled.

"Coop's daughter. She's staying with him for a while. She just came out from New York."

"I didn't know he had a daughter." Jimmy looked surprised.

"It came as something of a surprise to him too."

"He seems to have a lot of those."

"This was a good surprise. She's really nice." Mark seemed to think so. They had been talking for an hour, and Alex could see Jessica checking her out. Jason was busy trying to drown his friends. "They're good kids," she said about the Friedman children, and Jimmy agreed.

"Yes, they are. He's a lucky guy, with his kids at least. I guess they'll be going back to their mom soon. He's going to miss them a lot." That seemed sad to Alex. He was so happy with them.

"Maybe he'll go back too. What about you? Are you going to stay out here, or go back East eventually?" She knew he was from Boston, and it suddenly occurred to her that he might know her cousin who had gone to Harvard at about the same time.

"I'd like to stay out here," Jimmy said, looking pensive. "Although I feel kind of sorry for my mom. My dad died, and she's alone. And I'm all she's got." Alex nodded, and asked him about her cousin then and he grinned. "Luke Madison was one of my best friends in school. We lived in the same dorm. We used to get drunk together every weekend senior year."

"That sounds like Luke." She laughed.

"I'm ashamed to admit I probably haven't seen him in ten years. I think he went to London when we graduated, and I lost track of him then."

"He's still there. And he has six kids. All boys, I think. I don't see him much either, except at weddings, and I don't go to those a lot."

"Any particular reason?" He was intrigued by her,

and her attachment to Coop. It didn't make sense to him, but he didn't mention it. He wasn't particularly fond of Coop. He wasn't even sure why. It was a kind of instinctive dislike. Jealousy maybe. He was such an obvious ladies' man, and all he seemed to do was indulge himself. It went totally against Jimmy's grain.

"I ate a bad one once... wedding, I mean...." Alex explained and he laughed at her explanation.

"That's too bad. The right ones can be a great thing. Mine was. Not so much the wedding as the marriage. We got married at City Hall. She was a great girl."

"I'm sorry about what happened," Alex said, and meant it. She always felt so sorry for him, but he looked better these days. Not quite so anguished, or so pale. And he had gained a little weight. His evenings with the Friedmans had done him good, and at least he ate. But he particularly enjoyed the kids.

"It's strange. Grief. Some days you think it'll kill you. And other times, it's okay. And you can never tell which when you wake up. A good day can turn to shit. And a day that starts out so badly you want to die can suddenly turn around. It's like pain, or an illness or something, you can never tell which way it's going to go. I think I'm getting used to it. It becomes a way of life after a while."

"I guess there's no remedy except time." It seemed trite, but she suspected it was true. It had been nearly five months. When he'd moved in, he looked half dead himself. "A lot of things are like that, although maybe not as tough. It took me a long time to get over the marriage I nearly had. Years, in fact."

"I think that's different, it's about trust. This is

about loss. It's cleaner. There's no one to blame. It just hurts like hell." He was being amazingly honest about his grief, and Alex suspected it was doing him good to talk. "How much longer do you have in your residency?"

"Another year. It seems like forever sometimes. A lot of days, a lot of nights. I'll probably stay on at UCLA even when I'm through, if they'll have me. They have a terrific neonatal ICU. It's kind of a tough specialty, there aren't a lot of jobs. I was going to be a normal pediatrician originally, but I got hooked on this. High adrenaline, it keeps me focused. I think I'd get bored otherwise." They were still talking about it when Taryn and Mark wandered back. They had been talking about tax laws, and tax shelters, and Mark was surprised by how much she knew about it. And she'd seemed interested in what he'd said. She was almost as tall as he was, and Alex smiled as they approached. They made a handsome pair, and were close to the same age.

"What are you two talking about?" Mark asked as they sat down.

"Work. What else?" Alex grinned.

"So were we." And as they chatted, what seemed like a herd of teenagers got back in the pool. Alex was glad Coop hadn't come down. It would have driven him insane. It seemed fitting that the only child he had had stayed away until she was thirty-nine years old. It was about the right age child for him. She had said as much to Taryn the day before and they both laughed. Coop was incredibly vocal about his dislike of kids.

And five minutes later, the children in the pool

started a lively game of Marco Polo and Mark and Jimmy got in with them.

"He's a good man," Taryn said of Mark. "I gather he was pretty devastated when his wife left. It's lucky for him his kids decided to come back."

"Coop wasn't quite as thrilled," Alex commented and they both laughed. "They're lovely kids," Alex vouched for them.

"What's Jimmy like?" Taryn asked with interest.

"Sad. He lost his wife almost five months ago. I think it's been pretty tough."

"Another one?" It seemed like an epidemic, but Alex shook her head.

"No. Cancer. She was thirty-two years old," she whispered as Jimmy moved closer to them in the pool. He had just scored a point for his team, and threw Jason the ball, who scored yet another point. It was a very loud game, and they were splashing all over the place. And as she watched them, she saw Coop wave. He wanted them to come back up. He was ready for lunch. "I think the master calls." Alex pointed him out to Taryn, and she looked up and smiled. Even at this distance, Alex could see he was proud of her. Taryn had been a lovely addition to his life, and she was glad for him.

"Are you happy with him, Alex?" Taryn asked her. She had been wondering what the relationship meant to her. She had heard a lot about her from Coop.

"Yes, I am. It's a shame he hates kids so much. Otherwise, he's everything I want."

"You don't mind the difference in your age?"

"I thought about it at first, but it doesn't seem to matter. He's like a kid sometimes."

"But he's not," she said wisely. It would matter more in time. A lot more one day.

"That's what my father says."

"He doesn't approve?" She wasn't surprised. Having Cooper as a son-in-law was not every father's dream, unless they were starstruck, which seemed unlikely, knowing who her father was.

"To put it in context, he doesn't approve of anything I do. Or not much. And he's worried about Coop."

"That makes sense. He's led quite a life. Do you care about this girl who says she's having his baby?"

"Actually, I don't. Mostly because he doesn't care about her. And we don't even know yet if it's his."

"And if it is?"

Alex shrugged. "He'll send her a check every month. He says he doesn't want to see the child. He's pretty angry at her."

"I can understand that. It's a shame she's not willing to have an abortion. It would be simpler for everyone."

"It would. But if your mother had done that, you wouldn't be here. I'm glad she didn't, especially for Coop. This means a lot to him," Alex said kindly. She thought it was a blessing for both of them.

"It means a lot to me too. I didn't realize it would. Or maybe I did, and that's why I came. I was curious initially. But now I really like him. I don't know what kind of father he'd have been when I was young, but he's a wonderful friend now." Alex could see too what a positive effect Taryn had on Coop. It was as though he had found a missing piece of himself, a piece he never even knew was lost, but it was.

Taryn and Alex waved to the others, and walked slowly back up to the main house. Coop was waiting for them.

"They sure are loud," he complained. He was feeling lousy with his cold.

"They'll get out of the pool pretty soon," Alex reassured him. "They're going in for lunch."

"What about the three of us going to the Ivy for lunch?" Coop suggested, and both women liked the idea. They went to change and came back twenty minutes later, dressed and ready to go out.

He drove them to North Robertson in the old Rolls, and the three of them chatted and laughed on the way. They sat on the terrace, and enjoyed each other's company. It was an easy, pleasant afternoon, and as Alex looked over at Coop, they exchanged a smile, and she knew that all was well in his world, and hers.

Chapter 19

It was nearly the end of May when Alex was working a two-day shift at the hospital, and the tech at the front desk told her she had a call. She'd had a relaxing weekend with Coop immediately before that, and things were relatively peaceful at work for a change.

"Who is it?" Alex asked, as she reached for the phone. She had just come back from lunch.

"I don't know," the girl said, "it's in-house." Alex figured it was probably another doc.

"Dr. Madison," she said, in her official grown-up voice.

"I'm impressed." She didn't recognize who it was.

"Who is this?"

"It's Jimmy. I had to come in for some lab work, and I thought I'd call. Too busy to talk?"

"No, it's fine. You picked a good time. I think everyone's asleep. I shouldn't say it out loud, but we haven't had a crisis all day. Where are you?" She was happy to hear him, she had enjoyed their most recent chat. He was such a nice guy, and he'd had such rotten luck. It always troubled her. If nothing else, he needed good friends, and she was more than willing to volunteer, if he needed a shoulder from time to time. And he and Mark had become good friends.

"I'm in the main lab." He sounded kind of lost, and she wondered what was happening with his health. Stress probably. And grief.

"Do you want to come up? I can't leave the floor, but I can offer you a cup of our undrinkable coffee, if your stomach's up to it."

"I'd like that," he said. It was what he'd been hoping for when he took the chance and called. He'd felt a little guilty disturbing her. She told him where to go, and he said he'd be right up.

She was watching for him when he got off the elevator, and waved to him from the desk. She was on the phone, talking to a mom who had just taken her baby home, and everything seemed fine. The baby was doing great. It had taken them five months to get her home. She was one of Alex's stars.

"So this is where you do your thing," he said admiringly as he looked around. There was a glass wall behind the desk, where he could see a maze of equipment and incubators and lights and people milling around in scrubs and masks. Alex had one around her neck too, with her stethoscope at a jaunty angle, and the same green scrubs she'd been wearing all day. He was impressed. It was impossible not to be. She was in her element here, and a star in her own right.

"It's good to see you, Jimmy," she said comfortably as she walked him into her tiny office, with the unmade cot she slept on. She only saw parents in the waiting room. "What kind of work were you having done, if it's not rude to ask?" She was concerned about him, particularly here, in her official guise.

"It's just routine. I have to get checked out pretty thoroughly for work every year. Chest X-ray, TB, that kind of thing. I was overdue. They kept sending me notices, and I never had time to come in. They finally told me I couldn't report for work next week unless I did. So here I am. I had to take the afternoon off to do it, because you never know how long it'll take, which is why I've been putting it off. I'll probably have to work Saturday to make up for it."

"Sounds like me," she said, smiling at him. She was relieved to hear that there was nothing seriously wrong with him. And she found herself looking into his dark brown eyes, and as always her heart went out to him. You could still see how much he'd been through. "What exactly do you do?" she asked with interest as she handed him a Styrofoam cup filled with the poisonous brew. He took a sip and grinned instantly.

"You serve the same rat poison we do, I see. We put sand in ours, it gives it that little extra something." She laughed. She was used to it, but she hated their coffee too. "What do I do? Haul kids out of homes where they're having the shit kicked out of them, or being sodomized by their father, uncle, and two older brothers. . . . I put kids in hospitals with cigarette burns all over them. . . . I listen to moms who are basically decent and scared to death they'll freak out and hurt their kids because they've got seven of them and not enough food to go around even with food stamps, and their old man is beating them up. . . . I put eleven-year-old kids in programs who're shooting up, or sometimes nine-year-olds... sometimes I just listen... or I kick a ball around with a bunch of kids. Same thing you do, I guess, trying to make a difference when I can, and a lot of the time, not making any difference and wishing I could." It was amazing stuff, and she was as impressed with him as he was with her.

"I don't think I could do what you do. It would depress the hell out of me, seeing that every day. I'm dealing with tiny little people who come into this world with a couple of strikes against them, and we do the best we can to level the playing field for them. But I think your job would turn me off the human race forever."

"The funny thing is it doesn't," he said, sipping the coffee, and then winced. It was actually worse than what he drank at work, which was hard to believe. "It gives you hope sometimes. You always believe something's going to change, and once in a while it does. That's enough to keep you going till next time. And no matter how you feel about it, you still have to be there. Because if you aren't, things will get worse for sure. And if it gets much worse for any of them..." His voice drifted off and their eyes met, and she had an idea.

"Do you want a tour?" She thought it might be interesting for him.

"Of the ICU?" He looked shocked, as she nodded. "Is that okay?"

"If anyone asks, I'll tell them you're a visiting doc. Just if someone codes, don't step up to the plate." She handed him a white coat. He was medium sized, but powerful, and he barely got his shoulders into it, which made the arms a little short, but no one would notice. They all looked like hell. What mattered there was what they did, not how they looked.

"Not to worry, if someone codes, I'll run like hell."

But nothing untoward happened, they didn't even need her, as she walked him around, and explained what was happening in each case, what the situation was, and what they were doing for the tiny patients who lay in incubators, so small most of them didn't wear diapers. He had never seen as many tubes and machines, or babies so small. Their smallest patient on their service weighed in at just over a pound and a half, but was not expected to live. She'd had babies at less, she explained to Jimmy. Their chances increased exponentially the bigger they were, but the larger babies were in grave danger too. It tore his heart out to see the moms sitting there, touching tiny fingers or toes, and just waiting for something to change. The happiest event had turned into something terrifying, and sometimes they had to live with it for months before they knew how it would unfold. It seemed like inconceivable stress to him, and he was in awe when they came out again.

"My God, Alex, that's incredible. How do you stand the pressure?" If they did anything wrong, even for a split second, or failed to do something they should, someone's life was at stake, and the course of a family's history was forever changed. It was a burden he couldn't have borne, and he admired her tremendously for what she did. "I think I'd be scared to death to come to work every day."

"No, you wouldn't. What you do is just as hard. If you miss something, or don't spot what's happening, or move fast enough, some poor kid could die, or be killed, or be damaged forever. You have to have the same kind of instincts I do. Same idea, different place."

"You have to have a big heart to do this too," he said gently, and she did. He had already figured out that much, which was why he couldn't understand what she was doing with Coop. It was all about him, and Alex was about everyone else. Maybe that was why it worked.

They stood chatting near the desk for a little while, and then they needed her to evaluate a patient and consult with an attending, so he said he'd leave.

"Thank you for letting me come up," he said, still in awe of her. "I'm incredibly impressed."

"It's all about the team," she said fairly, "I'm only a tiny part of it. A very tiny part," she said with humility, as he hugged her, and then left. He waved as the elevator doors closed, and she went back to work.

She didn't see him again until the following Saturday afternoon. Miraculously, she'd gotten another Saturday off, but she had to work on Sunday. And she and Taryn were at the pool with Coop, Mark, and his kids, when Jimmy wandered down from the gatehouse. Taryn was wearing an enormous hat, and as usual, Coop was sitting in the shade of his favorite tree. He attributed his flawless skin and youthful look to never sitting in the sun. And he was pleased to see that Taryn followed suit. He nagged Alex constantly about all the sun she took.

Jimmy looked more rested for once, Alex thought,

automatically assessing him. She treated the rest of the world as though they were patients, and it was hard not to notice how they looked, acted, or moved. She never seemed to be able to put her medical antennae away, and laughed at herself. But Jimmy smiled as soon as he saw her, and shook hands with Coop as Mark and Taryn went on talking about something that seemed to fascinate both of them. And for once, the kids hadn't invited friends over to swim, so things were fairly quiet. With the good weather, it seemed like a constant party at the pool these days, but this time, it was just the actual residents of The Cottage, which was a relief for Coop. The group was big enough without adding to it.

He had been in very good spirits since Taryn moved in. They were spending a lot of time with each other, and he had taken her to lunch at Spago and Le Dome, and all his other favorite haunts. He enjoyed showing her off and introducing her as his daughter. No one seemed surprised, they just assumed they had forgotten he had a grown daughter. And she was a very respectable-looking woman. Coop introduced her to everyone, and she was enjoying her taste of Hollywood. She told Alex all about it whenever they got together. It was a whole new world for her, and she thought it was fun. And sooner or later she had to decide whether or not to go back to New York, or to get involved in something in LA. But she was in no hurry to make the decision. She was having too much fun, and there was no pressure on her.

Alex thought she'd been a good influence on Coop. Although he'd been wonderful before, he somehow seemed more grounded, and more interested in other people's lives suddenly. He wasn't quite as focused on himself. He actually sounded as though it mattered to him when he asked Alex what she'd done at work. But when she explained it to him, he still looked a little blank. The complicated medical interventions she participated in were a little beyond him, as they would have been for most people. But if nothing else, he seemed happy and mellow these days.

He was working a little, but not enough, he said. Abe was still complaining to him. And he had heard from Liz, who was stunned by the number of people living on the property. She worried about how much the Friedman kids might annoy him, and she was touched at his story about Taryn finding him.

"I leave you for five minutes, Coop, and you have a whole new world of people around you." Like Alex, she thought he sounded remarkably peaceful and content. More than she'd ever heard him. And when she asked him about Alex, he was vague. He had his own questions about that, but he didn't share them with anyone. It was occurring to him increasingly that if he just allowed himself to marry her, he would never have to work again. And if he didn't, he would be hustling cameo roles forever. It was so tempting to just let himself go, but he hated to take the easy way out, even at his age. Another, more practical side of him, told him he had earned it. But she was such an honest, decent person, and she worked so hard herself, he actually hated to take advantage of her. He loved her, and the easy life was so tempting. His financial worries would be solved forever, but another part of him was afraid that if he sold out, she would control him. She would have a right to make him do what she wanted, or try to at least, and that was anathema for him. For the moment, it still seemed like an unsolvable problem. And she had no idea what he was wrestling with, she thought their relationship was going fine, and it was for both of them. Except for Coop's bouts with his conscience. Much to his chagrin, it seemed to be growing like a benign tumor inside of him. It had never troubled him before, but Alex had introduced a new element into his life, a kind of white light that had made some things grow and others shrink. And his exchanges with Taryn only seemed to enhance it. They were both remarkable women, and they'd had a profound effect on him. More than he'd ever dreamed of or wanted. Life had been so simple before, without the burden of a conscience. And like it or not, the voices in his head seemed to be there to stay. All he needed now were the answers to their questions. He was searching for them.

By the end of Saturday afternoon, Jimmy had taken Jason somewhere to buy new sports equipment, Jessie was sitting at the far end of the pool, doing her nails with a friend, Taryn and Mark were still chatting quietly, and Coop was asleep under the tree, when Mark turned to Alex and invited the inhabitants of the main house to join them for dinner. Alex's eyes quickly went to Taryn's and she nodded almost imperceptibly, so Alex accepted on all their behalf. And when Coop woke up, and the others had gone, she told him.

"We seem to see an awful lot of them," he complained. Mark and Taryn were trying to play tennis on the damaged court by then, and no one else was around, so she could be honest with him.

"I think Taryn really likes Mark," she explained, "I think it's mutual, and she wanted me to accept. We don't have to go if you don't want to. She can go alone."

"No, it's all right. I'll do anything I have to for my only daughter," he said nobly, with a grin. "No sacrifice is too great for one's children."

In truth, he loved having a nearly forty-year-old daughter, as no one was too clear about her age. But saying that brought Charlene to mind again. There had been some fresh demand for more money through her lawyers. She wanted a bigger apartment in a better neighborhood, preferably somewhere close to him in Bel Air, and she was wondering if she could use the pool, since she was feeling too ill to go anywhere, she claimed. Coop had an absolute fit when his lawyer called him, and said there would be nothing whatsoever given to her until the results of the DNA test came in. It was going to be another five or six weeks before she took it. And until then, and more than likely afterwards as well given the way she'd behaved, she was persona non grata at The Cottage or anywhere else that involved Coop. His irate message had been somewhat cleaned up by his attorney, and duly delivered to the opposition.

Alex felt sorry for him. Understandably, it was a situation he detested. And it put a strain on them as well. She knew he was worried about the financial implications to him. There had been a recent case where a girl had gotten twenty thousand dollars a month in child support from a man she had been involved with for two months. But the father of the baby in that case, as Alex pointed out to Coop reassuringly, was a major rock star with a humongous income. Coop was by no means in that situation. She was particularly aware of that now after talking to her father. Coop never talked about his debts, and he spent money with utter abandon. But she knew that somewhere in the back of his mind, he had to be worried about how much he would have to give Charlene to support the baby, if it was his.

The three of them went downstairs to the guest wing that night, promptly at seven. Taryn was wearing pale blue silk pajamas that were very flattering on her. She had designed them herself for her last season, before she closed her business. And Alex was wearing red silk pants, and a white shirt, with high-heeled gold sandals. She looked more than ever like a model or a ballerina, and not a doctor. It was a far cry from the scrubs and clogs and braid she wore at work, and Jimmy enjoyed the contrast when he joined them for dinner.

Jimmy described his tour of the ICU during dinner, as Taryn and Jessie helped serve the excellent spaghetti carbonara Mark had made. Jimmy had brought the salad. And there was tiramisu for dessert. Coop had brought two bottles of vintage Pouilly-Fuissé. And everyone listened with fascination as Jimmy talked about the work Alex did. She was impressed by how much he'd heard and understood, and only made one small correction, about a baby with a serious heart and lung problem. But he had correctly remembered all the rest.

"He seems to know a great deal about what you do," Coop commented dryly when they went back upstairs. It was after midnight, and Taryn had decided to stay for a while, she was enjoying chatting with Mark and Jimmy. The kids had gone out with friends, and were staying with them. It had been an easy evening. "When did he visit you at the hospital?" Coop asked, sounding cool, and Alex was surprised at his tone. He actually sounded jealous, which was unnecessary, but touched her. It was nice to know how much he cared.

"He had some lab work done this week for work. He came by afterwards for a cup of coffee, and I gave him a tour of the ICU. He must have paid pretty close attention." Closer than she knew. But Coop was more aware of it than she was. He was wise to the ways of men. And he had noticed that evening that Jimmy not only sat next to her, but monopolized her for most of the evening. Alex was completely unaware of it, and kept glancing down the table at Coop, who was seated between Taryn and Mark. But from the head of the table, where Mark had placed him, he had a good view of all the proceedings. He had been watching Jimmy all night.

"I think he has the hots for you," Coop said bluntly, and he didn't seem pleased about it. Jimmy was far closer to her age, and their professional interests weren't entirely unrelated. Coop's were part of a different galaxy, and he wasn't about to start competing with men half his age. It was an indignity he wouldn't tolerate, and had never suffered. He was used to being the only star in his heavens, and it was what he expected. He liked it when everything revolved around him.

"Don't be silly, Coop," Alex chided him. "He's too depressed to have the hots for anyone. He's been a wreck ever since his wife died. He says he still can't sleep, has no appetite. Actually, I was concerned about him when he talked about it the other day. I think he should be on antidepressants. But I didn't say anything, I didn't want to upset him."

"Why don't you prescribe them for him?" Coop said unpleasantly, and Alex put her arms around his neck and kissed him.

"I'm not his doctor. And there's something I want to prescribe for you," she said as she slipped her hands under his shirt and he unbent a little. It was obvious that he hadn't enjoyed the evening, although she had. She liked being with the others, and chatting with them. It was fun having such compatible people close at hand, on the grounds of The Cottage. "Speaking of romances, by the way, I think Mark and Taryn are very attracted to each other. Don't you?"

He seemed to hesitate, and then nodded. He thought Mark was boring. "I think she can do a lot better. She's a fabulous girl, and I want to introduce her to some of the producers I know. She's had a very dull, staid life, and that husband who left her sounds like a jerk. I think she needs a little glamour and excitement." Alex thought he was missing the point. Taryn didn't have stars in her eyes, it was one of the things Alex liked about her. She was real and down-to-earth, and she needed a real person. But it was the ultimate compliment to Taryn that her father wanted to introduce her to his associates and friends. He was justifiably proud of her.

"We'll see what happens," Alex said vaguely.

They went to bed, and Coop made love to her. He felt better afterwards, as though he'd claimed his territory again. It unnerved him having younger men on his turf, particularly as he could see that Alex enjoyed them.

She was gone when he woke up the next morning. She was back at work. And he and Taryn went to Malibu to visit friends. It was nearly ten o'clock that night when Coop called her. She'd had a busy day, and he and Taryn had had fun. There was none of the petulance in his voice that she'd noticed the night before. She told him she'd see him the following night when she got off duty at six o'clock. He had promised to take her to a movie she'd been dying to see, and she was looking forward to it.

She talked to Taryn for a minute too, they almost seemed like one family now. She was going out to dinner with Mark the next day, and Alex was happy for her.

Alex went to bed in her office shortly after that. She always slept in her scrubs when she was on duty. And her clogs were parked right next to her in case she had to hit the deck running. She never fell into a deep sleep when she was at work. She was always half listening for the phone, even in her sleep. It rang at 4 A.M. and she jumped up with a start and grabbed it.

"Madison," she said, clearing her head. She was fully awake within seconds. And she was stunned to hear Mark. She thought something might have happened to one of his kids, or even Coop. But then she realized that if it was Coop, Taryn would have called her. "Is something wrong?" she asked quickly. The hour of the call gave her the answer before he said it.

"There's been an accident," he said, sounding frantic.

"At the house?" Maybe both Taryn and Coop were hurt. But Taryn wasn't with Coop. Mark didn't tell her she was asleep in his bedroom. She'd come down for a drink late in the evening, and his kids had slept at their friends' houses, which had given him unexpected freedom.

"A car accident," he said quickly.

"Coop?" She held her breath, fully aware of how much she loved him. She didn't need an accident to tell her that. She knew it.

"No. Jimmy. I don't know what happened. The other day, we were talking about not having local next of kin to call in case either of us ever got sick. He must have listed me on his papers. They just called me. They took him to UCLA. I think he's in the trauma unit or something. I thought maybe you could go check on him. Taryn and I will be there as soon as we can get there."

"Did they say what kind of shape he's in?" Alex sounded worried.

"No, they didn't. They just said it was serious. He went off the road in Malibu, and went down about a hundred feet. The car was totaled."

"Shit." It occurred to her instantly that it may have been less of an accident than they thought. He had been depressed ever since losing Maggie. "Did you see him today, Mark?"

"No, I didn't." He had seemed fine the night before, but that didn't always mean anything. Often, suicides seemed happier once they made the decision to do it. Euphoric even. But he had seemed normal to her on Saturday night at dinner.

"I'll go down to trauma as soon as I can get someone to cover for me."

She called one of the other residents as soon as she hung up. He was a nice guy she knew well who had covered for her before. She explained the circumstances to him and said she didn't need more than half an hour, to get to trauma and check things out. He said it was no problem, and showed up, sleepy eyed, ten minutes later. By then she had called the trauma unit, and all they could tell her on the phone was that he was in critical condition. He'd been there for an hour, and a team was working on him.

When she got there, she talked to the chief resident, and he told her that Jimmy had broken both legs, one arm, his pelvis, he had a head injury, and he was in a coma. It was not a pretty picture. She went in to see him, and stood at a distance so as not to interfere with what they were doing. They had intubated him, and he was hooked up to a dozen machines. His vitals were irregular, and his face was so cut and bruised, she could hardly recognize him. Her heart ached when she saw him.

"How bad is the head injury?" she asked the chief resident when she saw him again, and he shook his head.

"We don't know yet. He may have gotten lucky. His EEG looks pretty good. But he's in a pretty deep coma.

It all depends on how much brain swelling he gets, and I can't predict that. And if he comes out of the coma." But for the moment, they had decided not to operate to relieve the pressure. They were hoping it was going to come down on its own. Time was of the essence. And luck. Alex walked up next to him, in a quiet moment. They had set his arm and legs by then, and cleaned him up, but he was very, very badly injured.

She walked out to the waiting room, and by the time she got there, Mark and Taryn were there, looking panicked.

"How bad is it?" Taryn asked before Mark could.

"It's bad," Alex said quietly. "It could be worse. And it may get worse before it gets better." She didn't say "if it gets better," but she thought it.

"What do you think happened?" Mark asked her. Jimmy didn't drink a lot and it was unlikely that he'd been driving drunk. But she didn't want to share her suspicions with them. She had with the attending physician, not that it made much difference at this point. But it might later. If he was an attempted suicide, they were going to have to watch him very closely when he came out of the coma.

"You know this guy?" the attending had asked her, and she had said they were friends, and she told him about Maggie. He made a note of it on the chart, with a question mark in a red circle.

She explained to Mark and Taryn as simply as she could what the dangers of the brain swelling meant for him.

"Are you saying he could wind up brain-dead?"

Mark looked horrified. He and Jimmy had become good friends in the past few months, and he didn't want anything terrible to happen to him.

"He could, but we hope he won't. It all depends when and how fast he comes out of the coma. He's got brain waves now, and they've got him on monitors. We'll know right away if there are any changes."

"Jesus," Mark said, as he ran a hand through his hair and looked distraught, and Taryn was sharing the agony with him. "Maybe someone should call his mother."

"I think so," Alex said quietly. There was always the possibility that he could slip away from them, and he was in critical condition. "Do you want me to call?" Those were not easy calls to make, and delivering bad news was part of her job, not that she enjoyed it. But it might be easier for her to do it.

"No. I'll call her. I owe that much to Jimmy." Mark was not a shirker. He went to the phone, and took a number out of his wallet that Jimmy had given him, in case of just such an event. It had never really occurred to him that he might have to use it, it was just a precaution. And now here he was, calling Jimmy's mother to tell her he was in a coma.

"How does he look?" Taryn asked Alex in an undertone after Mark went to use the phone, and Alex looked unhappy.

"He's in bad shape, I'm so sorry this happened to him," she said, as she and Taryn held hands and waited for Mark to come back. He was wiping his eyes when he did, and it took him a minute to regain his composure.

"Poor woman, I felt like an axe-murderer. According to Jimmy, he's all she's got. She's a widow, and he's an only child."

"Is she very old?" Alex asked, concerned for her well-being.

"I don't know, I never asked him," Mark said thoughtfully. "She didn't sound old, but I couldn't tell. She started crying the minute I told her. She said she'd catch the next flight out. She should be here in eight or nine hours."

Alex checked on Jimmy again and there had been no change, and she had to go back to work. She left Mark and Taryn in the waiting room, and before she left, Mark asked if she was going to call Coop. It was 5 A.M. by then, a little early to call him.

"I'll wait a few hours and call him around eight." She gave them her extension and pager number and told them to call her if anything happened. They had their arms around each other, and Taryn had her head on Mark's shoulder when Alex left them.

Things were mercifully quiet on her own service that morning, and as she had said she would, she called Coop just after eight. He was still asleep, and surprised that she had called him so early. But he said he didn't mind. His trainer was coming at nine, and he wanted to get up anyway, and have breakfast as soon as Paloma came in.

"Jimmy had an accident last night," she told him somberly as soon as he was fully awake.

"How do you know?" She found it odd, but he sounded suspicious.

"Mark called me. He and Taryn are downstairs in

the trauma unit. He drove off Malibu Canyon Road, he's got a lot of broken bones and he's in a coma."

Coop sounded duly impressed by the news once she told him. He had seen a lot of ugliness and sorrow over the years, and in spite of hopes and beliefs otherwise, bad things really did happen to good people. "Do you think he'll make it?"

"It's hard to say at this point. It could go either way. A lot depends on the swelling in his brain, and what kind of toll that takes, how fast he comes out of the coma. The broken bones won't kill him." But the rest could.

"Poor guy. He doesn't have a hell of a lot of luck going for him, does he? First his wife, and now this." She didn't tell him that she suspected him of contributing to it. She had nothing to go on, just her gut, and the little she knew of him. "Well, keep me posted."

"Do you want to come down and sit with Taryn and Mark?" She thought he should have volunteered, but it hadn't occurred to him to do that. There was nothing he could do for Jimmy, it was just a matter of waiting. And he hated hospitals anyway. They made him nervous, except when he met Alex downstairs, as he had on occasion.

"I don't see what good it would do them," Coop said sensibly. "And it's too late to cancel my trainer." It seemed an odd excuse to Alex. But he offered it instinctively. He didn't want to see Jimmy with tubes everywhere. He was squeamish about things like that.

"They're pretty upset over it," Alex pressed further, but Coop didn't take the bait. He wanted to avoid the realities of the situation.

"That's understandable," he said calmly. "I discovered years ago, that sitting around hospitals doesn't help anyone. It just gets you depressed and you annoy the doctors. Tell them I'll take them out to lunch if they're still there at lunchtime, but I hope they won't be." He had denial about how serious it was, she knew, which made it easier for him.

"I don't think they want to leave Jimmy alone," nor did she think that they would be in any mood to go out to lunch, but Coop refused to enter the drama with them, or with Alex. It was a place where he absolutely wouldn't go, under any conditions. Being part of it would have been too upsetting for him.

"If what you say is true, and I'm sure it is, Jimmy won't know the difference, if they're huddled in the waiting room miserably, or having lunch at Spago." What he was suggesting seemed in bad taste to Alex but she didn't say anything. It was definitely a different perspective. And she knew from experience that people had odd reactions to stress. Coop seemed to be avoiding it completely.

She called the trauma unit again at ten, and there was no change. The only thing Mark knew was that Mrs. O'Connor was already on a plane. She was expected to arrive at the hospital shortly after noon, if everything went smoothly. And when Alex had an official break, she went down to trauma to see Jimmy. Mark and Taryn were still sitting in the same place. Mark looked terrible, and Taryn had been outside smoking. She said hello to both of them, and then went into the trauma ICU to see Jimmy. They had him isolated and were observing him closely. Alex talked to the nurses for a minute, and if anything, he was in a deeper coma. Things were not looking hopeful for him.

Alex stood silently next to him, and with gentle fingers, touched his naked shoulder. There were monitors taped to it, and wires linked to machines. He had IVs in both arms, and they'd had to give him a transfusion to compensate for internal bleeding. As injuries went, he was in the big leagues.

"Hi, kiddo," she said quietly as one of the nurses walked away and left her with him. They knew she was as capable as they were of keeping an eye on the monitors, and all the data appeared on screens in two other locations. "What the hell are you doing here? I think you'd better wake up now...." Tears stung her eyes as she talked to him. She saw tragedies as great as this every day in her work, but this was different. He was her friend, and she didn't want him to die now. "I know you miss Maggie, Jimmy...but we all love you too...there's a life for you here....Jason is going to be wrecked if something happens to you....You've got to come back now, Jimmy...you just have to...." There were tears sliding down her cheeks as she spoke to him, and she stayed there with him for half an hour, talking firmly but gently to him. And in the end, she kissed his cheek, touched his arm again, and went back to the others in the waiting room.

"How is he?" Mark still looked panicked, and Taryn was exhausted. She had her head back against a chair with her eyes closed. And she opened them and sat up as soon as she heard Alex.

"About the same. Maybe it'll help when he hears his mother."

"Do you really think that'll make a difference?" Taryn looked startled. She had heard that before, but never really believed it.

"I don't know," Alex said honestly. "I've heard people say that they heard people talking to them when they were in comas, and no one thought they could. People have been brought back from the brink of death by stranger things. Medicine is as much an art as a science. I'd be burning chicken feathers and killing goats upstairs if I thought it would help one of my babies. And talking to him can't hurt anything."

"Maybe we all should," Mark said, looking anxious. He was dreading seeing Jimmy's mother. And Alex had increased his level of concern. He had no idea how old she was, and if she was very old and frail, this might be too much for her. "Can we see him?" They had seen him once, for a fraction of a minute, from the doorway, but things seemed less frantic around him now. Alex went to ask, and then beckoned to them. But she was more inured to medical scenes than they were. Taryn only lasted a minute or two, and then she left, with tears running down her cheeks. And Mark staunchly stood beside his friend, and talked to him, as Alex had suggested. But after a few minutes, he was so choked up, he had to stop talking. Jimmy's color wasn't good, and although he wasn't in extremis yet, he looked as though he were dying. It was a distinct possibility, Alex knew, and even Mark could see it.

The three of them sat in the waiting room afterwards, and cried over their friend. It had been an abysmal morning, and they were all frightened and tired.

Alex went back upstairs after that, but before she left, Mark asked her if Coop was coming.

"I don't think so," she said quietly. "He has an appointment this morning." She didn't have the heart to tell them it was with his trainer. She knew it was an excuse Coop had used, and sensed correctly that he was afraid to come. This just wasn't his strong suit.

Alex called trauma and checked on him hourly. And at twelve-thirty, Mark paged her and told her Mrs. O'Connor was there. She had gone straight in to Jimmy the minute she arrived.

"How is she?" she asked with deep concern for the woman she'd never met. Alex knew it was going to break his mother's heart to see him.

"She's a mess. But who isn't?" Mark sounded like he'd been crying. He had been since early that morning, and Alex found it touching, as did Taryn. She hardly knew Jimmy and she was devastated too. It was such a tragedy, but at least if he died, he wouldn't be leaving orphaned children. It was something at least, and very small consolation.

"I'll come down in a few minutes," Alex promised, but it was almost two when she could get away. Someone had finally coded. She apologized for the delay when she got there. "Where's his mom?"

"She's still in there with him, she's been in for almost an hour." They couldn't figure out if it was a good sign or a bad one. But Alex didn't blame her.

Even at thirty-three, he was her baby. It was no different from the moms who sat looking agonized on her service, except she knew him better and had had more time to love him, and more to lose if he died. Alex knew how heartbroken she must be.

"I don't want to intrude," Alex said cautiously, but the other two convinced her to take a look, so she went in, but promised herself she wouldn't introduce herself if it looked too awkward. And what she saw surprised her. There was no old lady in sight, but a very attractive, petite, youthful-looking woman in her early fifties. She looked even less than that, with her dark hair tied in a ponytail, and no makeup. She had traveled from Boston in jeans and a black turtleneck sweater, and she was a prettier, female version of Jimmy, except that her figure was slim and not athletic, and her eyes were huge and blue, instead of dark brown like Jimmy's. But her features were reminiscent of her son's.

She was standing quietly near his head and talking softly to him, just as Alex had that morning. And she glanced up when she saw Alex. She assumed Alex was either a nurse or one of his doctors. They all wore the same scrubs and carried the same equipment.

"Is something wrong?" She glanced up at the monitors with a look of panic, and then back at Alex.

"No, I'm sorry. . . . I'm a friend of Jimmy's . . . I work here. This is an unofficial visit." Valerie O'Connor looked sadly at her, and the two women's eyes held for a long moment, and then she went back to talking to Jimmy.

When she looked up again, Alex was still there, and

Valerie said, "Thank you." Alex left her then and went back to the others. She was grateful at least that his mother was young enough to withstand the shock. She didn't even look old enough to have a son the age of Jimmy. She had had him at twenty and was fifty-three years old, and on a good day she looked ten years younger.

"She looks like a nice woman," Alex said as she sat down beside them, feeling drained. It was much harder dealing with friends than patients.

"Jimmy's crazy about her," Mark said blankly.

"Have you two eaten?" Alex asked, and they both shook their heads. "You should go down to the cafeteria and get something."

"I can't eat," Taryn said, looking sick.

"Me neither," Mark added. He had taken the day off from work, and hadn't left the waiting room in the nine hours they'd been there.

"Is Coop coming?" Mark asked again. He was surprised that he hadn't come, and thought he should be there.

"I don't know. I have to call him," Alex said. She was getting off duty in three and a half hours, and she was thinking about hanging around after she got off work, to see how Jimmy was doing. Mark would have to go home to his kids by then, and Taryn needed to get some rest, she looked exhausted. But she'd been a real trouper.

Alex called Coop when she went back upstairs, he had just come up from a nap at the pool and sounded in good spirits.

"How's it going, Dr. Kildare?" he teased her, which

struck her as inappropriate. She realized then that he didn't understand how serious Jimmy's situation was. So she explained it to him in greater detail. "I know, baby, I know," he said gently. "But I can't do anything about it, so I might as well not get depressed about it. The three of you seem to be upset enough. There's nothing I can add to that. My getting hysterical with you won't help him." He was right but nonetheless it annoyed her when he said that. He seemed to take it all in stride, and she thought he should be there with him, whether he hated hospitals or not. A man that they knew might be dying at any moment, and even with her medical background, she couldn't just ignore it. Maybe life and death were less impressive at his age, or more frightening. Maybe once people you knew died, it no longer seemed so ominous. But his attitude of avoidance seemed shocking to Alex. "Besides, I hate hospitals, except when I come to see you. But all that medical stuff gives me the heebie-jeebies. It's so unpleasant." So is life sometimes, Alex couldn't help thinking. She thought too how much "unpleasantness" Jimmy had had to deal with when Maggie died. He had told her that he had nursed her himself until her last breath, and refused to have a nurse or hospice to help him. He felt he owed it to her, and wanted to do it. But people were different. And Coop wasn't good about things that were neither beautiful nor pleasant. And comas weren't pleasant, nor were accidents or the way Jimmy looked. But by avoiding it, Coop wasn't there to support anyone else.

"What time will you be home?" he asked, as though nothing had happened to Jimmy. "Are we still going to the movies?" But when he said that, something snapped inside her. She just couldn't.

"I can't, Coop. I couldn't think straight. I'm going to hang around here for a while, and see if I can help his mother. Mark and Taryn are going home in a while, and I think it's mean to leave her alone with a comatose son in a strange city. She has no one with her."

"How touching," Coop said with an edge to his voice. "Don't you think you're carrying this a bit far, Alex? He's not your boyfriend for God's sake. At least I hope not." She didn't dignify his comment with a response. If anything, it was insensitive and insulting. His jealousy of Jimmy was misplaced at that point, and totally out of line.

"I'll be home later" was all she said.

"Maybe Taryn will want to go to the movies with me," he said petulantly, and Alex felt a chill run through her. He was behaving like a spoiled brat, not a grown man. But Coop was a child at times, it was part of his charm.

"I don't think she will, but you can always ask her. See you later," Alex said stiffly and hung up. Coop's reaction to the situation was causing her considerable distress.

She finished work at six, and Mark and Taryn were just leaving when she got there. Jimmy's mother was sitting calmly in the waiting room with them. She looked composed but sad, but she was in better shape than they were. It had been a long day for her too, with the shock of the news, and the long flight from Boston before she saw him. But she looked like a quiet, capable, unassuming woman. Mark and Taryn left a few minutes later, and Alex offered to get her soup and a sandwich or a cup of coffee.

"You're very kind," Valerie smiled at Alex, "but I'm afraid I couldn't eat it." In the end, she accepted some crackers and a cup of soup Alex brought her from the nurses' station. "How lucky you know your way around here," she said gratefully as she took the soup from Alex and sipped it. "I can't believe this happened. Poor Jimmy has had such a tough time. First Maggie got sick, and then she died, and now this. I worry about him."

"So do I," Alex said softly.

"I'm very grateful he has such good friends here. Thank God, he had given Mark my number," she said, and the two women chatted for a while. She asked Alex about her work, and she knew about Coop from Jimmy. Mark had explained Alex's situation to her before she got there, so she didn't misunderstand and think Alex was Jimmy's girlfriend. But she knew she wasn't. She kept in very close contact with Jimmy and knew he hadn't seen any women since he lost Maggie. She had been afraid he never would. The two had been perfect for each other, and had an enviable marriage, just as she had. She'd been a widow for ten years and had long since given up meeting any man she cared about. There was no man on earth like Jimmy's father, in her eyes. They had been married for twenty-four years, and she was resigned to having that be enough for one lifetime. No one could replace him, and she had no desire to try.

They sat and talked for a long time, and she asked Alex to go in with her the next time she saw Jimmy.

She confessed that it made her feel braver, and afterwards they talked and she cried. She couldn't imagine what her life would be like if he left her. He was all she had in the world now, although from what she said, she had a busy life. She did volunteer work with the blind and the homeless in Boston. But Jimmy was her only child, and just knowing he was in the world somewhere, even if not at home, made life worth living for her.

It was nearly ten when Alex talked one of the nurses into setting up a bed for Valerie in a back hallway. She didn't want to leave him, although Alex offered to drive her to the gatehouse. But she preferred to stay at the hospital in case something happened.

It was ten-thirty when Alex called Coop, and he was out. Taryn said he had gone to the movies, which seemed strange to Alex.

"I think this whole hospital thing makes him nervous," Taryn explained, but Alex had already figured that out. But it still irritated her that he couldn't at least try to rise to the occasion. He had total denial.

"Tell him I'm going to stay at my place tonight. I have to be back at five, and it's easier to be close by. I don't want to wake him when I get up," Alex explained, and Taryn understood.

"I'll leave him a note. I'm dead myself." Alex had already told her that there was no change in Jimmy's condition. Neither better, nor worse, nor more hopeful than it had been.

And when she went to say goodbye to Valerie, she was already dozing. Alex tiptoed away softly. And as she lay in her own bed that night, she thought of Coop, and tried to identify what she was feeling. It took her a long time, but as she drifted off to sleep, she realized that she wasn't angry at him, she was disappointed. For the first time, in the wake of Jimmy's accident, she had seen a side of Coop she didn't like. And she knew that no matter how much she loved him, she had lost respect for him. Along with Jimmy's accident, for Alex, it was a devastating piece of news.

Chapter 20

Alex called Coop the next morning from work, and he told her she had missed a terrific movie, which stunned her. His denial was in full force. He didn't even ask about Jimmy. She volunteered the information anyway, and said that his condition remained unchanged. He said he was sorry to hear it, but tried to change the subject as quickly as he could.

"The saga continues," he said, sounding almost flip, and she wanted to shake him. Didn't he understand that a man's life was hanging in the balance? What part of this was he missing? All of it, apparently. The realities of Jimmy's situation were too much for Coop.

She said something to Taryn about it later on when she saw her in the trauma unit again. Mark and Valerie were in with him.

"I don't think he relates to difficult situations," Taryn said honestly. She'd been a little startled by his reaction too, and he'd said something to her about resisting "negative energy" over breakfast, that it was a very dangerous thing to let into your experience. But Taryn had the suspicion that he felt guilty about it. No matter how natural his avoidant reaction was to him, he knew it wasn't the right thing, whether he admitted it or not. But what bothered Alex was how he could allow himself to avoid the situation entirely. As a result of his denial, he offered no one any support. And as a result, she felt cheated by him. What she had to accept finally was that it was the best he could do. But it worried her to think about what would happen if something "negative" happened to her one day. Would he deal with it, or go to the movies? It was scary to observe him doing everything he could to run away. It was distressing to watch, and none of what he was doing felt good to her.

She went to The Cottage after work that day, although the others were at the hospital with Valerie. But she didn't want to push Coop too far. He was pleasant and easy when she got home, and had ordered a delicious dinner for them from Spago. It was his way of making up to her for what he didn't do. Coop didn't "do" unpleasant. He did pretty. And easy. And fun. And elegant. And gracious. He had somehow managed to weed out of his life the things he didn't like or that frightened him, and only acknowledged the things he found "amusing," and fun to do. The trouble was, Alex reminded herself, real life wasn't like that. And there was generally a lot more "unpleasant" than "amusing" in life. But not in Coop's world. He wouldn't allow the bad stuff in. He just pretended to himself and everyone else that the bad stuff didn't exist. It made for some very odd perceptions and experiences. And he didn't "do" broke either. He did it, but he didn't acknowledge it. He just went on living, and spending, and playing. And in spite of everything, they had a lovely, relaxing evening. In Alex's eyes, it was more than a little surreal.

She called the hospital to check on Jimmy's condition, but she didn't mention it to Coop. There was no change. And hope was beginning to dwindle. He had been in the coma for nearly forty-eight hours. And with each passing day, the possibility of a full recovery would diminish. He had about another day to come around, maybe two, before his possibility for full recovery would be gone forever. He might survive, but not as they had known him. All she could do was pray now. And she had a heavy heart when she went to bed with Coop that night, not just because of Jimmy, but because of the piece of Coop she saw that was missing. She found it depressing. In her mind, the missing piece was huge.

She had a day off the next day, but went to the hospital anyway, to sit with Valerie and visit with Jimmy. She wore her scrubs even though she was off duty, so she'd have easy access to the inner sanctum.

"Thank you for being with me," Valerie said to her gratefully. She and Alex were alone all day. Mark had gone back to work. And Coop was doing a commercial for a national pharmaceutical company, and had insisted on taking Taryn with him.

Valerie and Alex sat for hours in the waiting room, and took turns keeping Jimmy company. They both talked to him endlessly, as though he could hear them. And it seemed fitting that Valerie was standing near his head and talking to him, while Alex stood near his foot and saw a toe move. At first, she thought it was a reflex. And then the whole foot moved. Alex glanced at the monitor, and then the nurse. She had seen it too. And then, very quietly, he reached for his mother's hand and held it. There were tears streaming down her cheeks, and Alex's, as Valerie continued talking. Very calmly, very surely, she told him how much she loved him and how happy she was that he was feeling better, although in truth there was no sign of it yet, but she acted as though it had already happened. It took another half hour for his eyes to open, and when they did, he looked at his mother.

"Hi, Mom," he whispered.

"Hi, Jimmy," she smiled down at him through her tears, and Alex had to fight back a sob that nearly choked her.

"What happened?" His voice was a croak from when they'd intubated him when he was first admitted. The tube had been taken out that morning, because he was able to breathe on his own, even though he was unconscious.

"You're a lousy driver," his mother said in answer to his question, and even the nurse laughed.

"How's my car?"

"In worse shape than you are. I'll be happy to buy you a new one."

"Okay," he said, and then his eyes closed, and he opened them again and saw Alex. "What are you doing here?"

"I'm off duty, so I dropped by to visit."

"Thanks, Alex," he said and drifted off to sleep. The attending came only minutes later to check on him.

"Bingo!" he said, grinning at Alex. "We made it." It was a real victory for the whole team, and while they

checked him, Valerie sobbed in Alex's arms in the hallway. She had thought he would die, and she was so relieved, she was completely unglued from the stress
she'd been through.

"It's okay...it's going to be okay now...." Alex
comforted her and held her. It had been a terrible ordeal for her, and a huge relief that he had made it.

Alex finally convinced Valerie to leave him later
that night, and drove her to the gatehouse. She found a
spare key at Coop's, and let her in. Coop was still on
the set of the commercial when they got there. And
Alex checked to see she had everything she needed.

"You've been so wonderful to me," Valerie said,
with tears in her eyes again. Everything made her cry
now. It had been an agonizing two days, and she was
starting to feel seriously shaken. "I wish I had a
daughter like you."

"I wish I had a mother like you," Alex said honestly,
smiling at her, before she left her. Alex was feeling
greatly relieved when she went back to the main
house. And she'd had a bath and washed her hair by
the time Coop came in at eleven, looking tired too. It
had been an endless day for him as well.

"Oh my God, I'm exhausted," he complained, as he
poured himself, Alex, and Taryn champagne. "I've
done plays on Broadway in less time than it took to
shoot that dreadful commercial." But at least they had
paid him well, and Taryn had found it interesting. It
had kept her mind off Jimmy, and she had called at
regular intervals all day to see how Jimmy was. "How
was your day, darling?" he asked Alex blithely.

"Excellent." She smiled at Taryn, who already knew.

"Jimmy woke up today. He's going to be fine, eventually. He's going to be in the hospital for quite a while, but he's going to make it." Her voice shook as she said it. It had been an emotional experience for everyone, except Coop.

"And they all lived happily after," Coop added, and smiled at her somewhat patronizingly. "You see, my darling, if you simply don't focus on those things, they take care of themselves in time. It's much easier to let God handle it, and go about your business." What he said denied entirely what she did for a living. God was in control undoubtedly, but she did her share of the work too.

"That's one way to look at it," she said quietly. But Taryn was smiling with relief.

"How's his mother?" she asked, looking concerned.

"Collapsing, but fine. I took her to the gatehouse."

"You'd think she'd rather stay at a hotel, with some service, at her age," Coop said grandly. As always, he looked as immaculate and as elegant as he had that morning, when he left to do the commercial.

"Maybe she can't afford it," Alex said practically, "and she's not as old as we expected."

Coop seemed surprised though not particularly interested in the entire drama. He'd had enough of it. "How old is she?"

"I don't know. She looks about forty-two, forty-three, forty-five tops maybe...but she must be in her early fifties."

"She's fifty-three," Taryn supplied. "I asked her. She looks amazing. She looks more like his sister."

"Well, at least we don't have to worry about her

falling and breaking a hip at the gatehouse," Coop teased. He was happy the entire story was over, and relieved for Jimmy of course, but he disliked melodrama. Now they could all go back to normal. "Well, what are we all doing tomorrow?" he asked happily. He had made some money, and he was in fine spirits. And now Jimmy was going to be fine too. Even Coop was pleased for him, and Alex was relieved to see that he cared.

"I'm working," Alex said, laughing.

"Again?" He looked disappointed. "How boring. I think you should take a day off and we'll go shopping on Rodeo."

"I'd love that," Alex smiled at him, he was so loving and boyish at times, it was hard to stay angry at him. She had been upset with him over the whole incident with Jimmy. It was a side of him that had surprised her, and recognizing what he couldn't handle and didn't feel really hurt. "I think the hospital would be a little upset if I didn't show up for work because I went shopping. That would be a tough one to explain."

"Tell them you have a headache. Tell them you think there's asbestos in the place and you're going to sue."

"Maybe I'll just go to work," Alex laughed at him. And at midnight they all went to bed. She and Coop made love, and she kissed him as he slept when she left for work the next morning. She had forgiven him his lack of sympathy for Jimmy. Some people just couldn't handle emergencies or medical problems. They were so familiar to her that it was hard for her to understand it. But not everyone could do what she did, she told herself. She felt a powerful need to make excuses for him. She was willing to give him a break on this one. In fact, for her own sanity, she needed to. Love, in her eyes at least, was about compassion, compromise, and forgiveness. Coop's definition might have been a little different. It was about beauty, elegance, and romance. And it had to be easy. Therein lay the problem. In Alex's mind, love wasn't always easy. But it had to be for Coop. It was a serious glitch.

She stopped in to see Jimmy during lunch that day. His mother had just gone to the cafeteria for a sandwich, and they chatted for a minute about how great she was. Alex said she loved her, and Jimmy agreed with her. He was lying quietly on his bed, and they were going to move him out of the ICU by the next morning.

"Thanks for hanging around while I was out cold. Mom says you were with her all day yesterday. That was nice of you, Alex. Thank you."

"I didn't want her to be alone here. That's pretty scary for anyone," she said, looking at him, and then decided to brave it. He was well enough for her to ask the question that had been tormenting her since it had happened. "So what was with the accident? I assume you hadn't been drinking." She was sitting very close to him, and he took her hand in his without thinking.

"No, I hadn't... I don't know, I guess the car got out of control. Old tires... old brakes... old something..."

"Is that what you wanted?" she asked softly. "Did you make it happen or did you let it?" Her voice was almost a whisper as he paused for a long moment and looked at her.

"To be honest with you, Alex, I'm not sure.... I've asked myself the same question. I was in a daze... I was thinking about her... it was her birthday on Sunday.... I think for just a fraction of a second, I let it happen. I think I started to skid, and I just let it go, and when I tried to stop it, I couldn't, and then it was all over, and I woke up here." It was exactly what she suspected. And he looked as horrified as she felt as she listened. "It's a hell of an admission. I wouldn't ever do it again, but for that one second, I just threw it to the Fates... and fortunately, they threw it right back at me."

"You took a hell of a chance," she said sadly. It hurt her to think that he was in that much pain, and had been for a long time. It was a terrible way to learn a lesson. He had confronted all his own miseries and terrors, and lived to tell it. "I think some good therapy is in order."

"Yeah. So do I. I'd been thinking that lately anyway. I can't stand feeling like this anymore. I felt like I was drowning, and I couldn't come back up to the surface. It sounds crazy to say it," he said as he looked at his casts and the monitors, "I actually feel better now." And he looked it.

"I'm glad to hear it," Alex said with relief, "I'm going to keep an eye on you now. I'm going to ride your ass till I see you jumping for joy all the way down the drive from the gatehouse."

He laughed at the vision she'd created. "I don't think I'm going to be doing a lot of jumping." He was going to be in a wheelchair for a while, and then on crutches. His mother had already volunteered to stay and take care of him for the duration. The doctors thought that in six or eight weeks he'd be walking. He was already fretting about going back to work as soon as he could manage, which was a good sign. "Alex," he said cautiously, "thanks for caring. How did you know what happened?" he asked, impressed that she had figured out the part he himself had played in the accident. She was a very caring person.

"I'm a doctor, remember?"

"Oh yeah, that. But preemies don't drive cars off cliffs, generally speaking."

"I just figured. I don't know why, but I knew the minute Mark told me. I think I felt it."

"You're a smart woman."

"I care about you a lot," she said seriously, and he nodded. He cared about her too, but he was afraid to say it.

Alex went back to work when his mother returned with her sandwich, and she sang Alex's praises to Jimmy. Valerie was curious about her.

"Mark says she's Cooper Winslow's girlfriend. Isn't he a little old for her?" his mother asked with interest. She hadn't met Coop yet, but she knew who he was, and had heard a lot about him from both his tenants and Alex.

"Apparently, she doesn't think so," Jimmy answered.

"What's he like?" his mother asked, munching turkey on whole wheat. Jimmy was still on a soft diet, and watching her made him hungry. It was the first time in a long time that he actually remembered being hungry. Maybe what he had said was right, he thought to himself, maybe he had finally exorcised his demons. He had gone right to the edge and jumped off, and, no thanks to himself, had landed safely. Maybe in a crazy way, the accident would prove to be a blessing in the end.

"Coop is arrogant, handsome, charming, debonair, and selfish as hell," Jimmy answered his mother's question. "The only problem is, she doesn't see it," he said, looking annoyed.

"Don't be so sure," Valerie said quietly, wondering if he was in love with her, or even knew it. "Women have a way of seeing things and not choosing to deal with them until later. They file them. But it's not that they don't see them. And she's a very bright young woman."

"She's brilliant," Jimmy defended her, which confirmed his mother's suspicions about his feelings, whether or not he was aware.

"I suspect she is. She won't make a mistake. Maybe he suits her for the time being, although I must say, they seem like an odd combination, from everything I've heard about him."

But she was impressed the next day when they moved Jimmy to a private room, and Coop sent him a gigantic bouquet of flowers. She wondered if Alex had sent them for him, and then realized she hadn't. It was the kind of bouquet a man would send, and not a woman. A man who was used to knocking women right off their feet and bowling them over. It didn't even occur to Coop to send fewer than four dozen roses.

"Do you think he wants to marry me?" Jimmy teased his mother.

"I hope not!" she said, laughing at him. But she also hoped Coop didn't want to marry Alex either. She deserved better than an aging movie star, Valerie knew, after talking to her for hours. She needed a young man who loved her and cared about her and would be there for her, and would give her babies. Like Jimmy. But Valerie knew better than to say anything to either of them. They were friends, and for the moment, it was all either of them wanted.

Alex came to see Jimmy every day, when she was working, and when she wasn't. She came down to see him on her breaks, and brought him books to keep him entertained, and told him funny stories. She even brought him a remote-controlled fart machine, so he could wreak havoc with the nurses. It wasn't dignified, but he adored it. And late at night, she would come down quietly, and they spent long hours talking about things that mattered. His work, hers, his parents' marriage, his life with Maggie, the agonizing way he missed her. She told him about Carter and her sister. About her parents, and the relationship she had wanted with them as a child, and never had, because both of them were incapable of it. Little by little, they fed each other their secrets and tested uncharted waters. They were entirely unaware of it, and had anyone asked, they would have insisted it was friendship. Only Valerie knew better. She was highly suspicious of the label they put on it. The brew they were concocting was far more potent, whether or not they knew it. And she was happy for them. The only fly in the ointment, as far as she could see, was Coop.

And that weekend, she got a look at the fly for herself. She hadn't met him until then. And she had to admit, he was very impressive. He was everything Jimmy had said he was, egotistical, self-centered, arrogant, entertaining, and charming. But there was more to him than that. Jimmy just wasn't old enough to see it, or mature enough to understand it. What she saw in Coop was a man who was vulnerable, and scared. No matter how youthful he looked, or how many young women he surrounded himself with, he knew the game was almost over. He was terrified, she realized. Of being sick, of being old, of losing his looks, of dying. His refusal to deal with Jimmy's accident in any form told her that. And so did his eyes. There was a sad man behind the laughter. And no matter how charming Coop was, she felt sorry for him. He was a man who was afraid to face his demons. The rest was just window dressing. But she knew Jimmy would never have understood it if she'd tried to explain it to him. And the nonsense about the girl having the baby was just food for his ego. Even if he complained about it, she sensed instinctively that there was a part of it which flattered him, and he brought it up to torture Alex, just to remind her subliminally that there were other women who wanted his babies. It meant he was not only young, but potent.

She didn't think Alex was genuinely in love with him. She was impressed with him, and he was the attentive father she'd always wanted and never conquered. They were an interesting group, Valerie decided. And she thought Mark and Taryn were perfect for each other.

But more than anything, she found Coop's complexities fascinating. And at first glance, he appeared to be unimpressed by her. Valerie was by no means the profile of the women he courted. She was old enough to be their mother. What he did like, he told Alex later, as they lay in bed and rehashed the evening, was Valerie's graciousness, her style, her simple elegance. She had worn gray slacks and a gray sweater and a string of pearls. There was nothing pretentious about her. And the fact that she didn't try to appear young, actually made her look it. There was a distinct sense of class and breeding about her.

"It's a shame she doesn't have money," Coop said sympathetically. "She looks like she ought to have it. But then again," he laughed, "we all should." Alex was the only one in the group who did, in vast abundance, and it was wasted on her. She really didn't care whether or not she did. Just as he felt youth was wasted on the young, money was wasted on the overly philanthropic. He thought money was meant to be spent and have a good time with. Alex hid hers, or ignored it. She needed lessons in how to spend it. Lessons he could easily have given her, but hesitated to for the moment. His conscience again, damnably. He was still trying to overcome it. It was new to him, and becoming an infernal nuisance.

Coop saw Valerie again the next day, at the pool. She was sitting in the shade of his favorite tree. She had taken the day off from visiting Jimmy, and was going to see him that evening. She lay on a chaise longue in a perfectly simple black bikini, and did herself credit wearing it. She had a very reasonable body. Both Alex and Taryn were envious of her and hoped they looked half as good at her age. And when they'd said so, Valerie said she was just lucky, she had good genes, and did very little to maintain it. But she was grateful for the praise of the younger women.

Coop invited her up to the house for a glass of champagne afterwards, and she came, just to say she had seen it, and was surprised by how beautiful it was, and how restrained. There was nothing showy about the house. It was all in perfect taste, with splendid antiques and exquisite fabrics. It was definitely the house of a grown-up, as she put it, when discussing it later with Jimmy. And once again, she thought Alex was out of place there. But they seemed happy together.

She was actually beginning to think that Coop was serious about Alex. He was so solicitous, so attentive, so loving. He was obviously smitten with her, but it was hard to tell with Coop how much depth there was to anything. He kept everything in his life on the surface, particularly his emotions. But she could easily see him marrying her, even if for the wrong reasons, to prove something, or worse, to slide into the Madison money. Valerie hoped, for Alex's sake, that there was more sincerity to it than that, but it was difficult to determine. In any case, Alex didn't appear to be worried about it. She was perfectly at home with him, and happy staying at The Cottage, particularly with Taryn.

"You've got adorable friends," Valerie commented

to Jimmy that night, when she visited him at the hospital. And she told him how much she liked Coop's house, and even the gatehouse. "I can see why you love it." She did too. It had a rural quality, and one had a sense of peace there.

"Did Coop put the make on you?" he asked with interest.

"Of course not," his mother laughed at him. "I'm about thirty years too old for him. He's smarter than that. Women my age see right through him. It would do him good actually, but I haven't got the energy for a man like Coop," she said, smiling at Jimmy. "It's too much work to train them." She didn't have the energy for any man, or the desire. Those days were over for her, as she always said. She was content to live on her own, and to be spending time with Jimmy. She had promised to see him through his convalescence and he was looking forward to spending time with her. He hadn't done that in years, and he enjoyed her company. Aside from mother and son, they were best friends.

"Maybe you should give Alex a run for her money," he teased her.

"Not likely, my darling," she laughed, "she'd win hands down, and she deserves to." Whether or not it was good for her was another question which remained to be seen.

Chapter 21

By June, the romance between Taryn and Mark was progressing nicely. They carried on as discreetly as they could. Neither she nor Mark wanted to upset his children. But both Jessica and Jason were extremely comfortable with her. So much so that by the end of school, they didn't want to go to New York to see their mother. She had only seen them once since they'd been there. And when Janet called Mark to talk about it, she was insistent that they come East. What's more, she wanted them to stay with her until after the wedding. She was marrying Adam over the Fourth of July weekend.

"I'm not going," Jessica told her father stubbornly when they discussed it. And Jason had said he would do whatever she did, or didn't. Jessica was still furious with her mother. "I want to stay here with you, and see my friends. And I'm not going to the wedding."

"That's a separate issue, and we can talk about that later. Jessica, you cannot refuse to see your mother."

"Yes, I can. She left you for that asshole."

"That's between me and your mother, and it's none of your business," Mark said firmly. But it was obvious to him that Janet had really burned her bridges, or damaged them badly. And Adam hadn't helped her. He had been outspoken and overbearing with the kids, and made it obvious to them that he'd been involved with their mother before she left California. If nothing else, it was stupid of them. And it had hurt Janet badly with her children. But sooner or later, Mark felt, they had to forgive her. "You still have to see her. Come on, Jess," Mark wheedled, "she loves you."

"I love her too," Jessie said honestly, "but I'm mad at her." She had just turned sixteen, and she was in deep conflict with her mother. Jason remained more of a bystander, but it was clear that he was disappointed in her. And in truth, he was happier living with his father, and so was Jessie. "And I'm not going back to school there." He hadn't even begun to broach that, but Janet wanted them back with her as soon as possible, and in school in New York in the fall.

In the end, he had to call Janet back to discuss it with her.

"I can't sell it, Janet. I'm trying, but the kids aren't buying. They don't want to come to New York now, and they're adamant about not coming to the wedding."

"They can't do that," she said, bursting into tears as soon as she said it. "You have to make them!"

"I can't drug them and put them on a plane in body bags," Mark said, feeling frustrated with both factions. She had made her bed, and she was having a tough time lying in it. He wasn't feeling vengeful about it, or even angry. He was happy with Taryn. "Why don't you come out here and talk to them? It might make things easier for them," Mark suggested sensibly, but Janet didn't want to hear it.

"I don't have time. I'm too busy getting ready for the wedding." They had rented a house in Connecticut, and were having two hundred and fifty guests at the reception over the Fourth of July weekend.

"Well, if you care, your children aren't going to be there, unless you do something to change that. I've done everything I can."

"Force them," she said, finally getting angry. "I'll take them to court if I have to."

"They're old enough that the court is going to listen to them. They're fourteen and sixteen, they're not babies."

"They're behaving like juvenile delinquents."

"No," he defended them quietly. "They're hurt. They think you lied to them about Adam. And you did. He made it obvious to them that you left me for him. I think his ego was talking. But they heard him loud and clear."

"He's not used to children." She defended him, but she knew Mark was right.

"Honesty is a major message, and usually the best one." He had never lied to his children, and until Adam, nor had Janet. She was besotted with him. And now she did everything he wanted, including antagonize her children. "I can't help you with this, unless you do something to help too. Why don't you come out here for a weekend?"

In the end, she did. She stayed at the Bel Air for two days, and Mark convinced the kids to stay with her. Things weren't resolved at the end of it, but they had agreed to go to New York for the remainder of the month of June. She had promised not to force them to go to the wedding if they didn't want to. She was sure that once they were there, she could convince them. And Jessica had told her in no uncertain terms that they were coming back to LA to go to school. And Jason agreed with her. Janet knew that she couldn't force them to do otherwise, but she told Mark that if she agreed, they had to set up a regular visiting schedule for them to come to New York for weekends, once a month, if not more often. He agreed, and promised to try to convince the children. They thought it was a major victory that she had agreed to let them continue living with their father, and so did Mark. And they left for New York the following week, in much better spirits. They were going to be gone for four weeks, and as soon as they left, Taryn moved to the guest wing to stay with him. Things were going very smoothly. She and Jessica were nearly best friends now. Jessica felt entirely different about Taryn than she did about Adam, and so did Jason. But Taryn had been honest with them so far, and hadn't broken up their parents' marriage, which was a definite advantage.

Taryn had never liked anyone's children before, and she was surprised to see how comfortable she was with Mark's kids. She found them respectful, and funny and loving and easy, and she was developing a deep affection for them, which they reciprocated freely.

"You know, if they're going to stay with me permanently," he said to Taryn thoughtfully, a few days after they'd left, "I should look for a house. I can't stay here forever. We should really have our own place." There was no hurry, but he said he would start looking sometime that summer. And if the house he bought needed remodeling, they still had the guest wing until February. It was a great arrangement, and he had to admit he'd be sorry to leave.

Talking about it, even tentatively, brought up questions about him and Taryn.

"How would you feel about living with us?" he asked her seriously. Life had worked out so unexpectedly for them. Five months earlier he had been devastated by Janet leaving him, and now he had found this wonderful woman, who seemed like a perfect fit, not only for him, but his children.

"That sounds interesting," she said as she leaned over and kissed him. "I think I could be talked into it, under the right circumstances." She was in no hurry to get remarried, and Coop had told her she could have the guest wing, if Mark ever moved, or the gatehouse, if Jimmy did. But in truth, she preferred to live with Mark and his children, in whatever location. "You have to be sure your children won't mind, Mark. I don't ever want to be the intruder."

"That would be Adam, not you, sweetheart." He smiled ruefully. He thought it highly unlikely that his children were going to attend their mother's wedding, and he wasn't sure he blamed them. That was a big bite for them to swallow.

The time Mark and Taryn spent together while the children were gone only solidified their relationship, and strengthened their resolve to do something about it in the near future.

Things were moving along at such a fast clip that Taryn spoke to her father about it. He wasn't surprised, but he was faintly disappointed.

"I'd love to see you with someone more exciting," he said honestly, as though she'd been in his life since her childhood. He felt very protective of her. In three months, she had not only moved into his heart and his life, but he wanted her to stay at The Cottage with him.

"I don't think I want 'someone more exciting,' in fact I know it," Taryn confided in him. She was a sensible woman. "I have an exciting father, I don't need an exciting husband. I want someone peaceful and reliable and stable. Mark is all of those things, and he's a good person." Even Coop couldn't deny it, although talking about tax law bored him to extinction.

"What about his children? Don't forget our genetic horror of offspring. Could you tolerate living with those juvenile delinquents?" He wouldn't have admitted it to anyone, but lately he had found them far less disruptive, and almost pleasant. Almost. Within limits.

"I really like them. No, more than that. I think I love them."

"Oh God, not that." He rolled his eyes in mock horror. "This could be fatal. Worse yet," he added, realizing yet another detail. "The little monsters would be my grandchildren. I'll kill them if they ever tell anyone that. I will never be anyone's grandfather. They can call me Mr. Winslow." She laughed, and they chatted about it for a while. She and Mark had actually talked about getting married the following winter. And they both suspected that the children would have no objection to their wedding.

"What about you and Alex?" Taryn asked him after they'd exhausted the subject of her plans with Mark. Everything seemed to be in good order, and she was obviously happy.

"I don't know," Coop said, looking troubled. "Her parents just invited her to Newport, and she refused to go. I think she should. But apparently, I couldn't go with her. Her father is not enthused about the relationship. I can imagine why, more than Alex can. I don't know, Taryn. I don't think I'm being fair to her. That's never bothered me before. I must be getting senile, or just plain old."

"Or growing up," she said gently. She knew all his frailties by now, or many of them, but she loved him. He was very different from the father she'd grown up with, but he was also a very decent person. He had lived in a different world all his life, which had centered around him, and spoiled him. It wasn't surprising that his character hadn't developed in some areas. It never had to. But in an odd way, Alex had forced him to look at things he never had before, and challenge his entire belief system and values. And so had Taryn. And whether he liked it or not, it had changed him.

He was still thinking about it that afternoon when he went down to the pool by himself for a swim. Taryn and Mark had gone out, and Alex was at work as usual. Jimmy had just come home from the hospital a few days before, and was still in bed at the gatehouse, and his mother was with him. Coop was glad to have some time to himself, to think quietly, and he was surprised when he ran into Valerie at the pool, quietly swimming. She had her hair in a knot on top of her head, wore little or no makeup, as usual, and a plain black bathing suit, which showed off her youthful figure. There was no denying she was a good-looking woman, beautiful even, he conceded. Just older than he liked them. And so far at least, he'd found her easy to talk to. She was sensible, and had an uncomplicated view of life that seemed to cut right through the fog that seemed to confuse others, and sometimes even him.

"Hello, Cooper," she said with a smile, as he sat down in one of the lounge chairs, and decided not to swim. He preferred watching her, although he was a little sorry to see her, because he had a lot on his mind. Alex. And Charlene's DNA test was only a few weeks away now. That was a whole other problem.

"Good afternoon, Valerie. How's Jimmy?" he asked politely.

"He's all right. Frustrated that he can't walk yet. He's asleep. It's hard helping him get around with those casts." And he was heavy for her.

"You should get him a nurse. You can't do all that yourself." It seemed foolish but admirable of her.

"I like taking care of him. I haven't had a chance to in a long time. And it's probably my last chance." And Coop realized he'd been tactless. She probably couldn't afford to pay for a nurse for Jimmy. Although she had style, it was obvious that they didn't have much money. The only evidence to the contrary was the fact that Jimmy paid a stiff rent at the gatehouse, but Coop suspected he did so out of insurance money Maggie must have had, and that would run out sooner or later. Everything else he saw suggested that he, and his mother, lived on a shoestring. Albeit in her case, a silk one. Valerie O'Connor was a very distinguished woman.

"Is Alex working?" Valerie asked pleasantly, as she got out of the pool and came to sit beside him. She wasn't going to stay long. She didn't want to intrude on him. She thought he looked distracted.

"Naturally. The poor girl works too hard, but she loves it." And in his own way, he admired her for it. She certainly didn't have to, which made it even more noble, or more foolish, depending on how you chose to see it.

"I saw one of your old movies last night," Valerie said easily, and told him which one. She had seen it in the middle of the night when she was taking care of Jimmy. "You're a remarkably good actor, Coop." It had surprised her. "It was an excellent movie." And a far cry from the cameos and commercials he was doing now. "You were a very serious actor, and still could be."

"I'm too lazy to be," he said honestly, with a tired smile. "And too old. You have to work awfully hard to make movies like that. I'm too spoiled now."

"Maybe not," she said, looking at him with more faith than he had in himself. But she'd been impressed by the caliber of the movie. She had never seen it before, nor heard about it. She figured he must have been about fifty when he made it, and he was embarrassingly handsome, and still was. But in his younger years, he had been even more amazing. "Do you enjoy your work, Coop?"

"I used to. The things I do now aren't very challenging, Valerie." On any level. It was all about easy and fast, and quick money. He had sold out so long ago, it was hard to remember back to when he hadn't. "I keep waiting for the right part to come along. But nothing has in a long time." He sounded sad about it, and somewhat discouraged.

"Maybe if you shake the trees a little bit, you'll surprise yourself. The world deserves to see you in a great film again. I really enjoyed that one."

"I'm glad to hear it." He smiled at her and they sat in silence for a while, as he thought about what she had said to him. He knew there was truth to it, and what she had said made him think about it. "I'm sorry about your boy," he said finally. "That must have been terrifying for you." For the first time, as he looked at her, he almost understood it. She was a truly devoted mother.

"It was. He's all I have," she said honestly. "My life wouldn't be worth a damn if I lost him." Because of his newfound relationship with Taryn, he could almost glimpse the agony it would be for him now if he lost her. And after all the years Valerie had shared with her son, the pain of such a loss didn't bear thinking. It was his first glimpse of compassion since Jimmy's accident, and Valerie could sense it, and was grateful to him.

"How long have you been widowed?" he asked comfortably. He was curious about her.

"Ten years. It seems like forever." She smiled at him, she was a woman who had made peace with herself and the hand life had dealt her. She had surrendered to life's forces and was comfortable with them. There was nothing pathetic about her. In fact, to Coop, she seemed like a very strong woman. He had judged her correctly. "I'm used to it now."

"Do you ever think about remarrying?" It was an odd conversation between the two of them, as they sat beneath the trees at the pool on a warm June day, thinking about life and what it meant to them. She was just old enough to be able to see things from his vantage point, but not so old she had lost her zest for life, or appreciation of having fun or being happy. Talking to her was comfortable for him, and she seemed surprisingly young to him, despite her wisdom. She was seventeen years younger than he was. As opposed to the forty that separated him from Alex.

"I don't even think about remarrying," Valerie said honestly. "I haven't been looking. I always figured if there was another man out there for me, he'd find me, and he hasn't. I don't mind. I've already had a good one. I don't need another one."

"Maybe someone will surprise you sooner or later."

"Maybe," she said easily. But she didn't seem to care one way or the other, and he found that appealing. He hated desperation. "You have a lot more energy for those things than I do." She smiled, thinking to herself that if she applied the same age difference as he, she would have to be dating Mark's son Jason. But she didn't say it.

"What are you doing for dinner tonight?" he asked suddenly. He was at loose ends, with Alex working, and he was lonely. It was difficult for him at times being faithful to one woman, who was so often busy. In the past, he had always dated several women, so he never had solitary nights as he did now. He would have been even lonelier without Taryn. She had been a godsend for him.

"Cooking for Jimmy," she smiled at him comfortably. "Would you like to join us? I'm sure Jimmy would love to see you." Coop had dropped by the gatehouse once since he'd gotten home. He had exited quickly, and explained to Alex later how much he hated sickrooms.

"I can have Spago send us dinner if you like," he offered, suddenly grateful for the invitation. He liked her, and enjoyed their budding friendship. She was almost like a sister to him.

"I make much better pasta than they do," she said proudly, and he laughed out loud.

"I won't tell Wolfgang you said that, but I'd love to try it."

Jimmy was surprised to see him when he appeared for dinner that night. His mother had forgotten to tell him Coop was coming. And Jimmy was a little uncomfortable with him at first. He had been spending a lot of time with Alex, when she visited him, and he had told her all of his secrets, and knew a great many of hers now. He wasn't sure if Coop knew, or if he was jealous of him. But Coop seemed far more interested in talking to his mother. And he agreed with her readily about the quality of her pasta.

"You should open a restaurant," he said grandly. "Maybe we should turn The Cottage into a spa or a hotel," he said. Abe had been threatening him again that if he didn't have a windfall of some kind soon, he would have to sell it. He was beginning to run out of steam and bravado fighting with him. And contrary to what Abe thought, Coop didn't see Alex as the optimal solution. Nor would her father.

Jimmy went to bed right after dinner, and after Valerie settled him, she came back and sat in the living room with Coop and they talked for hours. About Boston, and Europe, the films he'd made, the people he knew, and they were both surprised to discover they had a number of friends in common. Valerie said she led a quiet life, but Coop was surprised to find she knew some very racy people. All she said was that her husband had been a banker, but she didn't elaborate on it, and Coop didn't ask her. He just enjoyed her company, and they were both startled to discover that it was two in the morning when he finally left her, and he was in excellent spirits. He had had a wonderful evening with her.

Alex had called him several times that night, and was surprised to find him out. He hadn't said anything to her about it. But she had noticed that he had been restless recently, and she didn't know what to do about it. It never occurred to her to call and check on him at two in the morning, nor that he might have gone up to the gatehouse to have dinner with the O'Connors. But after five months in the relationship with him, it seemed to be stalling.

Coop lay in bed awake for a long time that night, thinking about things he and Valerie had said. He had a lot to think about, and decisions to make. He fell into a fitful sleep finally, dreaming about Charlene and the baby.

Chapter 22

Things got considerably worse for Coop after his dinner with Jimmy and Valerie. He had a meeting with Abe the next day, who told him that if he didn't turn things around in the next three months, there was no question in his mind that Coop had to sell The Cottage.

"You owe back taxes, you owe stores, you owe hotels, you owe your tailor in London eighty thousand dollars. You owe jewelers, you owe just about everyone on the planet. And if you don't pay what you owe to the IRS by the end of the year, not to mention your credit cards, they're not going to give you a chance to sell The Cottage, they're going to seize it and sell it for you." Things were even more dire than Coop had suspected, and for once he heard him. The months he had spent with Alex had somehow improved his hearing. "I think you ought to marry Alex," Abe said sensibly, but Coop was offended by the suggestion.

"My love life has nothing to do with my financial circumstances, Abe," Coop said with dignity. But his accountant thought his scruples foolish in the extreme. He had a golden opportunity. Why not take advantage of it? Marrying Alex would have provided him a windfall he needed desperately.

Alex had just worked three days straight when she came home exhausted one night. She'd been covering for two other people, and had had a string of emergencies, babies coding, mothers getting hysterical, a father who had threatened a doctor with a gun when his baby died unexpectedly, and was subsequently arrested. She felt as though she'd seen it all and then some by the time she got to The Cottage. Mark and Taryn were away for two days, and all Alex wanted to do was take a bath and go to sleep in bed next to Coop. She didn't even have the energy to describe to him what she'd been through.

"Bad day?" he asked casually, and she shook her head. She was near tears from sheer exhaustion. She wanted to see Jimmy, but she was too tired to visit him. She had promised to go up and see him in the morning. He was getting stir-crazy being stuck in the gatehouse with his mother. Alex called him as often as she could, but in the past two days she hadn't even had time to do that. She felt like she'd been a hostage on another planet.

"Bad three days," she explained, as Coop offered to cook her dinner. "I'd be too tired to eat it," she said honestly. "All I want to do is jump into the tub and go to bed. I'm sorry, Coop. I'll be better tomorrow."

But in the morning, he seemed strangely quiet. He sat staring into space at the breakfast table. She made him bacon and eggs, and poured him a glass of orange juice in his favorite Baccarat goblet. And after he ate it, he looked at her with an unhappy expression.

"Are you okay?" she asked quietly. She was feeling much better after a night's sleep and a good breakfast. But she was a lot younger than he was, and recovered quickly.

"I have something to say to you," he said, looking anguished for a moment.

"Is something wrong?" He didn't answer her, and she didn't know why, but she'd had the feeling they'd been losing altitude lately.

"Alex ... there are things you don't know about me. Things I didn't want to tell you. I didn't want to tell me either," he smiled sadly. "I have enormous debts. I'm afraid I'm a bit like the prodigal son, and have spent it all on 'riotous living.' The problem is, unlike the prodigal, I have no father to come home to. My father is long gone, and he had no money anyway. He lost it all in the Depression. And I'm up the creek, as they say. Taxes, debts, I have to pay the piper one of these days. I may even have to sell The Cottage."

She wondered for a minute if he was asking her for money. It wouldn't have upset her if he had. They were close enough by now for him to be honest with her. She preferred that to secrets between them, even if the truth was unpleasant. She knew about all this anyway, from her father. "I'm sorry to hear it, Coop. But it's not the end of the world. There are worse things." Like death, and bad health, and cancer, and what had happened to Maggie.

"Not for me. My lifestyle is important to me. So much so that I've sold my soul for it occasionally, making bad movies, or just spending money I didn't have, so I could go on living the way I wanted, the way I felt

I deserved. It's not something I'm proud of, but I did it." He was making a clean breast of his situation. He knew he had to. It was the voice of his conscience speaking, in his case a country never before heard from. It was all very unfamiliar to him.

"Do you want me to help you?" she asked, looking lovingly at him. She had truly come to love him, whether or not he wanted to have children with her. She had decided to make that sacrifice for him, if he asked her to. She thought he was worth it.

But he startled her with his answer. "No, I don't. That's why I'm talking to you. Marrying you would be the easiest way out for me. And the hardest in the long run. If I married you, I would never know for sure why I did it. For you. Or your money."

"Maybe you don't have to know. They come as a package. Fully loaded. You don't have to select options."

"To be honest with you, I'm not even sure if I love you. Not enough to marry you anyway. I love being with you, I have fun with you. I've never known anyone like you. But you're a solution for me. The answer to all my prayers and problems. And then what? The whole world will call me a gigolo, and they'd be right probably. And so would you eventually. And without a doubt, your father. Even my accountant thinks I should marry you. It's a lot easier than working to pay back taxes. That's not who I want to be, Alex. And maybe I do love you, because I care about you enough to tell you that's not who I want you to marry."

"Are you serious?" She looked horrified. "What are

you saying to me?" She thought she knew but she didn't want to hear it.

"I'm too old for you. I'm old enough to be your grandfather. I don't want babies. Yours, Charlene's, or anyone else's. I have a daughter now, through the grace of God. She's a grown woman and a nice one, and I never did a damn thing for her. I'm too old and too poor and too tired, and you're too young and too rich. We have to end this." She felt as though her breakfast had just gotten stuck in her throat as she listened.

"Why? I'm not even asking you to marry me. I don't need to get married, Coop. And telling me I'm too rich is discrimination." He smiled at her answer, but there were tears in her eyes, and his. He hated to do this, but he knew he had to.

"You should get married, and have babies. Lots of them. You'd be a terrific mother. And any minute that bitch Charlene is going to turn my life into an absolute swamp of scandal. I can't do anything about it, but I can at least spare you the embarrassment of swimming through it with me. I can't do this to you. Any of it. I won't let you solve my financial problems. And I'm serious, if I marry you, I'll never know why I did it. To be honest, more than likely, it would be for the money. If I didn't have these problems, I probably wouldn't even be thinking about getting married. I'd just be playing." He had never been as candid with anyone, but he felt he owed it to her.

"Don't you love me?" She sounded like a little girl who had just been dropped off at the orphanage, which was what she felt like. He had rejected her. Just as her parents had. And Carter. She felt the weight of the world on her as she looked at him, and he was as honest as he had promised himself he would be.

"I don't know, to be honest with you. I'm not even sure I know what love is. But whatever it is, it shouldn't happen between a girl your age and a man mine. It's not natural, and it's not right. It isn't the correct order of things. And marrying you for what you can do for me won't change that. It only makes matters worse. For once in my life, I want to have some dignity, and not just act as though I have it. I want to do the right thing, for both of us. And the right thing in this case is setting you free, and cleaning up my own mess, no matter what it takes to do it." It had been a Herculean effort for him to say what he had to her, and it nearly broke his heart looking at her. All he wanted to do was put his arms around her and tell her he loved her, because he did, enough not to ruin her life by staying with her. "I think you should go home now, Alex," he said sadly. "This is hard for both of us. But trust me, it's the right thing to do here." She was crying openly, as she cleared away their breakfast. And afterwards, she went upstairs and packed up her things. And when she came down, he was sitting in the library, looking morbid. He hated doing it, but he knew he had to. "It's a terrible thing, a conscience, isn't it?" She had given him one, like a gift from her, and so had Taryn. He wasn't sure he was grateful to them. But now that he had one, he knew he had to use it.

"I love you, Coop," she said, looking at him, hoping he would change his mind and beckon to her, and ask her to stay with him, but he didn't. He couldn't.

"I love you too, little one...take care of yourself." He made no move toward her. She nodded, and walked out the front door. She felt as though her life as a fairy princess was over. She was being sent away from home, into the darkness and loneliness. It was impossible for her to understand why he had done it. She couldn't help wondering if there was someone else. And there was finally. There was Coop. He had himself now. He had found the piece of him that had always been missing. It was the piece he had always been afraid to find.

Alex drove up the driveway in tears, and as the gate opened, she knew without a doubt that she had just turned into a pumpkin. Or she felt that way anyway. But she was who she had always been. It was Coop who had turned into a prince finally. A real one.

Chapter 23

Jimmy couldn't understand why he hadn't heard from Alex. She hadn't called, she hadn't come to visit. And Valerie said she hadn't seen Alex at the pool all week. She hadn't run into Coop either. And when she did finally, he looked grim. She almost hesitated to talk to him. She just swam quietly, until he finally said something to her. He asked about Jimmy.

"He's better. He complains constantly. He's getting sick of me. It'll do him good when he can get around on crutches." Coop only nodded. And then Valerie asked after Alex. There was an interminable silence. And then he looked at Valerie, and she saw something in his eyes she hadn't previously. He looked desperately unhappy, which was very unlike him. Coop had always been able to hide everything, even from himself. He had been brilliant at it. But no longer. He was no longer a god, he was a mortal. And mortals suffered. Sometimes a great deal.

"I'm not seeing her anymore," he said unhappily, as Valerie paused, while drying her hair with a towel. She could see how much it had upset him to say what he just did.

"I'm so sorry." She didn't dare ask him what had happened. He had told Taryn, and Taryn had had lunch with Alex, and then told Coop how unhappy Alex was. She felt sorry for both of them, but she thought Coop had made the right decision, especially for Alex. It would take her time to see it. And it had made him feel better when Taryn said that. He needed her full support now.

"I'm sorry too," Coop told Valerie honestly. "Giving her up was like giving up the last of my illusions. It's better this way." He didn't explain to her about his debts, or the fact that he didn't marry her for her money. It was enough to know it, and that he hadn't done it. Virtue was its own reward, or something like that. He told himself that often late at night, but he missed her anyway. And he had no desire to run out and find another woman, particularly a young one, which was a first for him.

"It's a bitch being a grown-up, isn't it?" she asked sympathetically. "I just hate it."

"So do I," he smiled at her. She was a nice woman. And so was Alex, which was why he'd refused to take advantage of her. Maybe for the first time in his life he really had been in love.

"Do you want to have dinner with us?" Valerie asked generously, and he shook his head. For once in his life, he didn't want to see anyone. He didn't want to talk or play or party. "You and Jimmy can sit and feel sorry for yourselves and growl at each other."

"I'm almost tempted," he laughed. "Maybe in a few days." Or a few years. Or a few centuries. He was surprised by how much he missed her. She had become a delicious habit. Too delicious. In time, he would have choked on her. Or hurt her badly, and he didn't want to do that either.

Valerie didn't say anything to Jimmy for a few days, but when he started fuming about Alex's silence again, she finally relented.

"I think she's got some heartaches of her own right now," Valerie said gently.

"What does that mean?" Jimmy snarled at her. He was sick of being stuck in a wheelchair and having casts on his legs. And he was angry at Alex. She had completely forgotten about him.

"I think she and Coop stopped seeing each other. In fact, I'm sure of it. I saw Coop at the pool a few days ago and he told me. I think they're probably both very upset about it. I suspect that's why you haven't heard from her."

Jimmy sat very quietly when he heard it. And after thinking about it for a few days, he called her at the hospital but they told him she was off duty. He didn't have her number at her studio. And when he paged her, she didn't answer. It was another week before he reached her at work.

"What's happening to you? Did you die or something?" he barked at her. He had been snapping at his mother all morning. And he missed talking to Alex. She had been the only one he opened his heart to, and then she disappeared.

"Yeah, I died...sort of....I've been busy." She sounded awful, and near tears. She had been crying for two weeks.

"I know," his voice softened as he spoke to her. He

could hear that she was hurting. "My mother told me what happened."

"How does she know?" Alex sounded startled.

"I think Coop told her. He saw her at the pool or something. I'm sorry, Alex. I know you must be unhappy about it." He thought it was a good thing for her, but he didn't want to say that and upset her more.

"I am. It's complicated. He had some sort of crisis of conscience or something."

"It's nice to know he has one." Even after what had happened, Jimmy didn't like him. Particularly if he had hurt Alex in the process. But pain was unavoidable in those situations. The peeling away of two lives that had become one, even briefly, was inevitably painful. "They're taking my casts off next week, and giving me smaller ones I can walk on. Can I come and see you when they do?"

"Sure. I'd like that." She didn't want to come and see him at The Cottage, and risk running into Coop. It would be too painful for her, and maybe even for him.

"Can I call you sometime? I don't know how to reach you. You're always busy at work, and I don't have your home number."

"I don't have one. I sleep in a laundry basket on a pile of dirty clothes," she said, feeling and sounding pathetic.

"That sounds attractive."

"It isn't. Oh shit, Jimmy, I'm miserable. I guess he's right, but I think I really loved him. He says he's too old for me, and he doesn't want kids. And . . . he has a lot of other problems, and he doesn't want me to take care of them for him. I think he thought he was being noble. What a dumb idea."

"I think he was being decent," Jimmy said honestly, "and he was doing the right thing. He's right. He is too old for you, and you should have kids. When you're fifty, he'll be ninety."

"Maybe that doesn't matter," she said plaintively. For the moment, she still missed him. She had never known anyone like him.

"Maybe it does. Do you really want to give up having kids? And even if you could have talked him into it, he would never have participated in that with you." She knew Jimmy was right. When Jimmy had had his accident, Coop had entirely removed himself, because going to see him at the hospital was "unpleasant." In the long run, she needed a man who was willing to do both pleasant and unpleasant. And Coop would never do that. She hadn't liked that side of him when she'd seen it.

"I don't know. I just feel like shit." It was comfortable opening up to Jimmy again. She had missed his friendship. The only one she'd spoken to since it had happened was Taryn, who had been very understanding, but also thought Coop had done the right thing. And in some part of her, so did Alex. It just didn't feel good.

"You'll probably feel like shit for a while," Jimmy said sympathetically. He knew it well. He had been there after Maggie. But ever since the accident, he was feeling a lot better. It had been a kind of epiphany for him. "When I get my casts off, I'll take you to dinner and a movie."

"I'm lousy company," she said, feeling sorry for herself, and he smiled.

"So am I a lot of the time. I've been biting my mother's head off. I don't know how she stands me."

"I suspect she loves you." They both knew she adored him.

He promised to call Alex again the following day, and when he did, she sounded a little better. He called her every day until they took his casts off. And to celebrate, he took her out to dinner. His mother drove them, and she was relieved to see that Alex looked better than she had expected. It had been a hard blow, but maybe the right one in the long run. It was hard to say, but she hoped so. Coop had talked to her about it again. He had thrown himself into doing a series of commercials, which distracted him. And for the moment, he was worried about Charlene's DNA test. The last thing he needed now was a baby to support, not to mention Charlene, whom he was still furious with.

"I swear, Valerie," he had told her the day before, "I'm never going out with another woman." He was positively fuming and she had laughed at him.

"Why is it that I don't believe you? If you were ninety-eight and on your deathbed, I wouldn't believe you if you made a statement like that. Coop, your whole life has been about women." Over the past weeks, they had become friends, and he was surprisingly open with her, and she with him.

"True," he said pensively, reconsidering. "But in most cases, the wrong ones. Alex wasn't the wrong one, and if I'd never known about her money, it might have been different. I knew about it from the first moment I met her. It was always a factor in how I felt about her. I was never able to separate the two elements. What I felt for her, and what I needed from her. It was too confusing in the end." He had reexamined it a thousand times, but always wound up in the same place. Confused. And then, finally, he was sure he had done the right thing. He had even admitted once to Valerie that Alex had been too young. A first for him.

"I still think you did the right thing, Coop," she said honestly. "Although I'd understand it if you married her, she's a very special girl and she loves you. You could do a lot worse." But she hoped he didn't marry her. For Alex's sake.

"I love her too. But the truth is I didn't *want* to marry her. Not really. And I certainly didn't want to have babies with her. I felt I *had* to marry her, or should, because I needed the money. It's what my accountant wanted me to do." Given what he said, she still thought he'd made the right decision for both of them.

"What are you going to do now to solve those problems?" Valerie asked him with concern.

"Make a great movie," he said thoughtfully, "or a lot of very bad commercials." He had already told his agent that he was willing to take some very different parts than the ones he'd played previously. He was willing to consider playing an older man, or someone's father. He no longer expected to play the leading man. His agent had been dumbstruck, and it had nearly killed Coop to say it. But his agent was more hopeful for him than he'd been in the last decade.

It was the first of July before Coop looked like himself again, and Alex finally seemed more cheerful. Valerie had driven Jimmy to see her at the hospital several times, and one weekend that she knew Coop was away, Alex had actually come to the gatehouse to have dinner, with Mark and Taryn. The kids were coming home after the Fourth of July. They had finally agreed to go to their mother's wedding. They still said Adam was an asshole, but they were doing it for their mother. And Mark was proud of them.

"We're getting engaged," Mark said with a look of pride at Taryn. They were both feeling a little shy about it, but it was easy to see that they were both excited, and very much in love.

"Congratulations!" Alex said, feeling a pang. She still missed Coop and the time they'd spent together. She had never expected it to end so quickly, and it still hurt a lot that it had.

Jimmy was hobbling around the room on his crutches, and his mother was trying to talk him into going to their house on Cape Cod later that summer.

"I can't get away from work, Mom. I have to go back sooner or later." He had already promised them to go back the following week on crutches. He couldn't do home visits. But he could at least see people in his office. Valerie was going to drive him to work, and she was planning to stay with him until he was fully walking again, and able to drive.

"I feel like a kid with my mother driving me everywhere, and taking me to the bathroom," he confessed to Alex with a rueful grin.

"Be grateful you have her," Alex scolded him. They all had a nice evening together, and afterwards as she drove home, she wondered what Coop was doing. She knew he had flown to Florida for two days, to do a commercial on a sailboat. But he hadn't called her. He said he thought it was best if they didn't talk for a while, although he hoped they'd be friends one day. For the moment, it wasn't a cheering prospect. She was still in love with him.

Mark's kids came home after the Fourth of July. And three days later, Alex saw on her calendar that it was the day for Charlene's DNA test. They were supposed to get the results in ten days, and she wondered what was going to happen, or when she would hear about it. But two weeks later to the day, Coop called her. He was ecstatic, and had wanted to share it with Alex. The moment he heard, he'd picked up the phone to call her.

"It's not mine!" he said exuberantly, after he asked Alex how she was doing. "I thought you'd want to know, so I called you. Isn't that marvelous? I'm off the hook."

"Whose is it? Do you know?" Alex was happy for him, although it tugged at her heart to hear his voice again.

"No, and I don't give a damn. All I care about is that it's not mine. I've never been so relieved in my life. I'm too old to have children at my age, legitimate or otherwise," he said for Alex's benefit. He wanted to remind her, and perhaps himself, that he was not the right man for her, in case she was mourning for him. He missed her too, but every day he was more certain that he had done the right thing in ending it with her. And he was more adamant than ever that she belonged with a man who wanted to have children with her.

"I'll bet Charlene is disappointed," Alex said pensively, still absorbing what he'd said. She knew it was a huge relief to him, and how worried he'd been about it for months.

"Probably more like suicidal. The father is probably a gas station attendant somewhere, and she won't be getting support and an apartment in Bel Air. Couldn't happen to a more deserving woman." They both laughed, and Coop sounded more relaxed than he had in months. And the following week Alex saw in the tabloids in the grocery store a front-page piece that said COOP WINSLOW LOVE BABY NOT HIS! She knew it had to have been planted by his press agent. Coop was vindicated. Which left him footloose and fancy free, with his bills still to pay, and Alex still lonely for him. But he had made it clear again when he called that he wasn't coming back to her, not only for her sake, but for his. It no longer seemed right to him to be with a woman forty years younger than he. Times had changed. So had he.

"Okay, okay," she said when Jimmy chided her for working more than usual. He could never see her. "So I still miss him. There aren't a lot of other people like him."

"That could be a good thing," Jimmy teased her. He had started working again and was feeling better than he had in a long time. He was sleeping well, and claimed he was getting fat on his mother's cooking, but he didn't look it. He had another month of physical therapy ahead of him, before he finally got his final casts off. He insisted on taking her to dinner and a movie, with his mother still acting as chauffeur. But he was in much better spirits, and as time wore on, so was Alex. She felt more like her old self again, and she enjoyed spending time with him. Maggie had been gone for six months by then, and Coop for one, and they were both healing from their emotional wounds.

"You know," Jimmy said to her one night over Chinese dinner. He had taken a cab for once. His mother had a dinner date, and he didn't want to impose on her. Alex had said she would drive him back to the gatehouse. "I think you should start dating."

"Really?" she said with a look of amusement. "And who appointed you as the guardian of my love life?"

"That's what friends are for, isn't it? You're too young to go into mourning for a guy you dated for four or five months, however long it was. You've got to get out there in the world, and start again." He sounded almost fatherly about it. They always had a good time together, and there wasn't a single subject between them that was sacred. She was completely open with him, just as he was with her. They shared a special bond of friendship that meant a lot to both of them.

"Well, thank you, Dr. Strangelove. And for your information, I'm not ready."

"Oh, bullshit. Don't give me that crap. You're just chicken."

"No, I'm not. Okay, I am," she amended, "and besides I'm too busy. I don't have time for a relationship. I'm a doctor."

"I'm not impressed. You were a doctor when you went out with Coop. So what's different?"

"Me. I'm wounded." But her eyes were laughing as she said it. She just hadn't found anyone she wanted to date yet, and Coop was admittedly a tough act to follow. He had been wonderful to her, even if it hadn't been a relationship meant to last for a lifetime. She was beginning to see that, although she still wished it had.

"I don't think you're wounded. I think you're lazy and scared."

"What about you?" She turned the tables on him, as they polished off their dim sum, and she ate the last of his pot stickers.

"I'm terrified. That's different. Besides, I'm in mourning." He said it seriously, but he didn't look nearly as devastated as he had when she'd met him. He looked healthier again. "But I'll go out with someone one of these days too. My mother and I have been talking a lot about it. She went through it when my dad died, and she said she made a big mistake not getting back out in the world again, and now I think she regrets it."

"Your mom is a gorgeous woman," Alex said admiringly. She had enormous affection for her and thought Jimmy was very lucky, and said so frequently.

"Yeah, I know. I think she's lonely as hell though. I think she loves being here with me right now. I told her she should move out here." And he meant it.

"Do you think she will?" Alex asked with interest.

"Honestly, no. She likes Boston, she's comfortable there. And she loves our place on the Cape. She usually spends the whole summer there. She's going as soon as I get my casts off. I think she can hardly wait.

She loves to putter around fixing the place up while she's there."

"Do you like to go?" Alex was curious about it.

"Sometimes." He had a lot of memories of Maggie there, which were going to be hard for him to deal with, he knew. He had decided to give it a rest until the following summer. By then, he thought it would be easier for him to handle, and his mother said she understood. She was always very sympathetic, and understanding about whatever he did. Particularly now. She was just grateful he was alive.

"I hate our place in Newport. It looks like Coop's place, only bigger. I've always thought that was stupid for a beach house. When I was a kid, I wished we had something simple, like the other kids. I always had the biggest and the best and the most expensive. It was embarrassing." And the place in Palm Beach was even bigger, and she hated that too.

"I can see that was very traumatic for you," Jimmy teased her as they sipped their tea, and she complained that she'd had too much to eat. They were like two kids kidding around with each other. "I mean look at you now, you never wear decent clothes anymore. I don't think you own a pair of jeans that's not ripped. You drive a car that looks like you bought it in the junkyard, and from what you tell me, your apartment looks like you furnished it in a dumpster. It's obvious that you have a psychotic phobia about anything decent or expensive." He didn't realize it, but he could have made the same speech to Maggie, and had often.

"Are you complaining about the way I look?" She looked vastly amused and not the least bit insulted.

"No, you actually look pretty good, considering that you live in hospital pajamas ninety percent of the time. The rest of the time you look great. I'm complaining about your car and your apartment."

"And my love life, or lack of one. Don't forget that. Anything else you want to complain about, Mr. O'Connor?"

"Yeah," he said looking into her eyes, and noticing that they looked like brown velvet. "You don't take me seriously, Alex." His voice sounded strange when he said it.

"What am I supposed to take seriously?" She looked startled.

"I think I'm falling in love with you," he said softly, not sure of what her reaction would be, and terrified she would hate him for it. His mother had encouraged him to tell her when they'd had a serious conversation about it the night before.

"You're *what*? Are you crazy?" She looked stunned.

"That's not exactly the response I was hoping for. And yeah, maybe I am. I hated it when you were going out with Coop. I always thought he was the wrong guy for you. I just wasn't ready to be the right guy," he said honestly as she looked at him in amazement. "And I'm not sure I am yet. But I'd like to be one day. Or at least apply for the job.

"It may be hard for me at first. Because of Maggie. But maybe not as hard as I think. It's kind of like getting the casts off my legs and walking again. Same thing. But you're the only woman I've ever known that I feel about the way I felt about Maggie. She was a hell of a woman, and so are you.... I don't know what I'm saying, except that I'm here and I care about you, and I'd like to see what would happen if we both give this a chance. And now you probably think I'm a lunatic, because I'm not making sense, and I sound like a total jerk," he was stumbling all over the place as Alex stretched out a hand to touch his.

"Hey, it's okay," she said softly, "I'm scared too... and I like you too... I always did.... I was terrified when I thought you would die after the accident, and all I wanted was for you to wake up from the coma and come back... and you did... and now Coop's gone. I don't know what'll happen either. Let's just go slow, okay? ... And we'll see...."

He was sitting there smiling at her, not sure what either of them had said, or what they felt, other than that they liked each other. But maybe it was enough. They were both good people, and they deserved the right person in their lives. Whether or not they proved to be the right ones remained to be seen, but it was a beginning at least. It was a promise to promise to try to promise to maybe if they were lucky fall in love with each other one day. They had each opened their doors, and were standing on the threshold of a new beginning. It was all either of them could have hoped for, or asked for at that point in time. And for now, it was enough. Neither of them was ready for more.

And when she drove him back to the gatehouse after dinner that night, they felt both comfortable and awkward, hopeful and scared. And when she helped him out and up the stairs, he turned to her with a smile, and then leaned down and kissed her. He almost slipped and fell, and she yelled at him as she helped him into bed.

"Are you crazy to kiss me there, you could have fallen down the stairs and killed me, and yourself!" He laughed, watching her. He had always loved everything about her, and even more so now.

"Stop yelling at me!" he tossed back at her good-naturedly.

"Then don't do dumb things like that," she said as he kissed her again. And a few minutes later, she left, and called back up the stairs from the living room, "Tell your mother I said thank you!" For what she had given them, for encouraging Jimmy to live again, and finally let go of Maggie, at least a little. There were no promises, no guarantees. But there was hope for both of them. They were young and life had everything in store for them. Alex smiled to herself as she drove home, thinking of him. And in his bedroom at the gatehouse, Jimmy looked pensive and smiled too. Life was a perilous road at times, fraught with demons and miseries. But his mother had been right. It was time to give life another chance. Time for a new beginning.

Chapter 24

While Alex and Jimmy were at the Chinese restaurant, Coop was out with Valerie that night. He had promised to take her to L'Orangerie. She had been nursing Jimmy for nearly two months, and Coop thought she deserved at least one decent evening out. And he appreciated her friendship. Besides which, he'd been lonely since Alex left. In the past, he had always rushed into other romances to heal his "*chagrins d'amour,*" but this time he had wanted to spend some time alone. It was yet another first for him.

It was also the first time he'd been out to a restaurant in a month, and Valerie proved to be excellent company. They seemed to share the same points of view on a multitude of subjects.

They liked the same operas, the same music, the same cities in Europe. He knew Boston almost as well as she did, and they both loved New York. She had spent time in London with her husband before Jimmy was born, and Coop loved going there. They even liked the same food, and the same restaurants.

They shared an easy, relaxing evening, and talked about Taryn and Mark. He told her the story of how

Taryn had come into his life. And she talked about Jimmy and his father and how much alike they were. They seemed to touch on everything that mattered to either of them. And he talked about Alex.

"To be honest, Valerie, I was crazy about her, but I don't think it was ever right. I'm not sure she's old enough to realize it yet, but I think we'd have made each other unhappy in the end. I'd been having second thoughts about it for the last month, but I didn't want to give her up, selfishly." It had actually felt better to him not to be selfish for once, in the end. He and Valerie even talked about Charlene, and what an embarrassing mistake that had been. There was nothing hidden between them. Alex had taught him that. And the honesty was familiar to him now, and comfortable with Valerie. He was even candid about the financial stress he was in. He had sold one of his Rolls-Royces recently, which was a big step for him. At least, for once in his life, he was facing things. Liz would have been proud of him, and Abe nearly was. And his agent said he was chasing an important part for him. But he always said that.

"Maybe it isn't so bad being a grown-up," he confessed to Valerie, contrary to what he'd said after leaving Alex a month before. "It's a novelty for me. I've never been a grown-up before." But his lack of responsibility had always been part of his charm. There was just a high price to pay for it at some point. And the piper still had to be paid. "I wanted to go to Europe this summer." He had talked to Alex about the Hotel du Cap, but she couldn't get away from work. And he couldn't afford it anyway. "But I'm going to stick around and hustle work."

"Would you like to come to Cape Cod for a few days when I go back, Coop? I have a comfortable old house there. It was my grandmother's, and I don't run it as well as she did. It's a lot harder these days. The place is falling apart, but it has a lot of charm. I've spent my summers there since I was a child." The house meant a lot to her and she liked the idea of showing it to Coop. She was sure he'd appreciate it.

"I'd like that very much," he said with a warm smile. He enjoyed being with her. You could see that she was a woman who had suffered a great deal, but at the same time, she had learned from it, and made the best of it. She wasn't sad or depressed or pathetic. She was peaceful, calm, and wise. And it did him good just being with her. He had felt that about her from the first. He enjoyed her as a friend, and could easily imagine their friendship growing into more in time. He had never been attracted to a woman her age, or not in a long time. But he could see a lot of merit in it now. He had developed a strong distaste for women like Charlene, and he didn't want to hurt or disappoint anyone, as he had Alex. It was finally time to play with kids at least a little closer to his age. She was, after all, nearly twenty years younger, but it was a vast improvement over what he'd been doing in recent years, with girls half Valerie's age, or a third of his own.

"Is there anyone in your life, Valerie?" he asked her with gentle curiosity. He wanted to make sure there was no one waiting for her in Boston or Cape Cod before he embarked on anything, or even approached it with her, and she shook her head as she smiled at him.

"I haven't wanted to be involved with anyone since my husband died. It's been ten years." He looked shocked.

"That's a terrible waste," he said sympathetically. She was a beautiful woman and she deserved to have someone in her life.

"I'm beginning to think so too," she admitted, "and I was afraid Jimmy would do the same thing. I've been on his back a lot about that. He needs time, but he can't mourn Maggie forever. She was a wonderful girl, and a great wife for him. But she's gone. He's going to have to face that one day."

"He will," Coop said confidently. "Nature will push him, if nothing else does," he laughed. "It did me. A few too many times, I'm afraid," and then he looked serious. "But I've never had a great grief like that in my life." He had enormous respect for both of them. They had come a long way, and in his own way so had he. He just hoped Alex recovered quickly, and wasn't bitter about the disappointment he'd been for her. He knew how badly Carter had hurt her, and he didn't want to add to her scars. He hoped she was finding her way, or would soon.

It was a pleasant, easy evening for both of them. And they walked for a while afterwards, when they got back to The Cottage. The grounds were so peaceful and beautiful on a warm, summer night. They sat next to the pool for a while and talked. They could hear laughter coming from the guest wing. He knew Taryn was there with Mark and the kids, although she was sleeping in the main house again, now that the kids were home.

"I think they'll be good for each other," Coop said, talking about them, and Valerie agreed. "It's funny how things work out, isn't it? I'm sure he was devastated when his wife left. And now he's got Taryn, and his children want to live with him. I'm sure he never expected any of that to happen. Fate is a wondrous thing sometimes."

"I was telling Jimmy that tonight. He has to trust that things are going to work out for him. Even if differently than he once thought they would."

"And what about you, Valerie? Are things working out for you?" he asked her gently, as they held hands, sitting in two chairs by the pool. He could see her blue eyes in the moonlight, and her dark hair shone.

"I have everything I need," she said, content with her fate. She didn't ask or expect a great deal from life. She had Jimmy. He had lived. That was enough for her for now. She didn't dare ask for more.

"Do you? That's a rare thing. Most people wouldn't say they have everything they need. Maybe you're not asking for enough."

"I think I am. Maybe someone to share it with. But if not, that's all right too."

"I'd like to come to Cape Cod to visit you, if you really meant what you said at dinner," he said quietly.

"I did. And I'd like that too."

"I love old houses. And I've always liked the Cape. It has a wonderful old-fashioned quality to it. It doesn't have the grandeur of Newport, which has always seemed a little out of place to me, although the houses are magnificent." He would have liked to see the Madison place, although that was not to be, for now anyway. Maybe one day, when he and Alex had become friends as he hoped they would. But he liked the idea of visiting Valerie on Cape Cod. He was ready for a simple holiday in a comfortable place, with a woman he could talk to, and whom he liked. He couldn't think of anything nicer than visiting her. It was easy for him too, knowing he wanted nothing from her, nor she from him. Whatever they gave each other, if they did, would be from the heart and nothing more. There were no motives to question, nothing to be gained. It was all very clean and very pure.

They sat in silence for a little while, and then he walked her home. He left her at her front door, and smiled down at her. He wanted to go slow this time. He was in no rush. They had a lifetime ahead of them, and she smiled up at him. She felt the same way too.

"I had a lovely time, Valerie. Thank you for having dinner with me." He meant every word of it and more.

"I had a lovely time too. Goodnight, Coop."

"I'll call you tomorrow," he promised, and she waved and walked through the front door. It was a development she hadn't expected, and a friendship she hadn't anticipated. But one she was grateful for. She didn't need more than that just now, and didn't know if she ever would. But for now, this was something special for them.

Chapter 25

Coop had meant to call Valerie, as he'd promised to, the next day. But he got a call from his agent at nine in the morning instead. His agent asked him to come to the office as soon as he could. Whatever it was he had to tell Coop, he didn't want to say on the phone. Coop was irritated by the mystery and cloak-and-dagger of it all, but he turned up at eleven anyway, and the agent said nothing to him, and handed him a script.

"What is it?" Coop looked blasé. He'd seen a million scripts before.

"Read it, then tell me what you think. It's the best damn script I've ever read." Coop expected another walk-on, or a cameo where he played himself. He'd seen too many of them by now, but it was all they'd offered him in years.

"Are they willing to write me in?" Coop asked.

"They don't need to. This one's written for you."

"How much are they offering?"

"Let's discuss it when you've read the script. Call me back this afternoon."

"Who do I play?"

"The father" was all he would say. Not the leading man. But Coop didn't complain. He was in no position to.

Coop went home and read it, and was duly impressed. It was admittedly a potentially extraordinary part, depending on who the director was, and how much money they were willing to put into it. Having read it, Coop needed to know more.

"Okay, I read it," Coop said when he called back. He sounded interested, but he wasn't leaping for joy yet, there was too much he still didn't know. "Now tell me the rest."

The agent reeled off the names. "Schaffer is the producer. Oxenberg directs. The leading man is Tom Stone. Leading lady either Wanda Fox or Jane Frank. They want you for the father, Coop. And with a cast like that, you'll win an Oscar for sure."

"What are they offering?" Coop said, trying to sound calm. He hadn't been associated with names like that in years. It was one of the best films he'd ever been associated with, if he took the part. But he was sure they weren't going to pay him much. It was all for glory, but even at that, it might be worth it. They were shooting in New York, and LA, and he assumed, given the size of his part, it would be a three-to-six-month shoot. He had nothing else to do, except a bunch of commercials he didn't want to do anyway. "How much?" he repeated to the agent, bracing himself for bad news.

"Five million dollars, and five percent of the box office. How does that sound, Coop?" There was a long, stunned silence from Coop's end.

"Are you serious?"

"I am. Someone's looking out for you, Coop. I never thought I'd have a picture like this to offer you. It's yours, if you want it. They want to hear from us today."

"Call them. I'll sign it tonight, if they want. Don't let this one get away." Coop could hardly catch his breath he was so stunned. He couldn't believe his incredible good luck. At last.

"They're not going anywhere, Coop. They're desperate for you. You're perfect for the part, and they know it."

"Oh my God," Coop said, and he was shaking when he hung up the phone. He went to tell Taryn, because he didn't know who else to tell. "Do you realize what this means?" he asked her. "I can keep The Cottage, pay my debts, put some money away for my old age." It was a dream come true, a reprieve, his last chance. His ship had come in. And then he stopped and looked at Taryn. It also meant he could tell Alex he could support himself, but the funny thing was, he no longer wanted to call her. Instead, he rushed to the front door, and Taryn called after him.

"Congratulations, Coop! Where are you going?" But he didn't answer her. He strode down the path to the gatehouse and knocked on the front door.

Jimmy was at work, but Valerie was there. She opened the door wearing black linen slacks and a white T-shirt, and she stared at Coop. He looked like a madman, with wild eyes, and he'd been running a hand through his hair. She'd never seen him look like that, no one had. But he didn't care. He knew he had to tell her.

"Valerie, I just got an incredible part, in a film that's going to take all the Oscars next year. And even if it doesn't, I can take care of all my, err...responsibilities....It's a miracle, truly. I have no idea what happened. I'm going to my agent's office to sign the deal." He was almost stuttering he was so excited, and she smiled broadly at him.

"Good for you, Coop! No one deserves it more."

"I'm sure someone does," he said, laughing, "but I'm glad I got it instead. It's exactly what you said. I'm playing the father instead of the leading man."

"I'm sure you'll be fabulous," she said sincerely, as he stood talking to her and grinned.

"Thank you. Will you have dinner with me tonight?" He had to celebrate with her. And he was going to invite Jimmy, Taryn, and Mark. For a moment, he was sorry not to invite Alex, but he knew it wasn't a wise thing to do, yet. Maybe he could in time. But he was going to call and tell her he was out of the woods.

"Are you sure you want to have dinner with me again? You just had dinner with me last night. I might wear thin."

"You have to have dinner with me," he said, trying to look stern, but unable to, he was smiling too much.

"All right. I'd love to."

"And bring Jimmy."

"I can't. He's going out." She knew he was seeing Alex again. They were exploring new facets of an old relationship, and she knew he couldn't bring Alex along, it would be too hard for her. "But I'll tell him you asked." She knew he wouldn't want to go. He would rather be with Alex than with Coop, which made sense. He had no animosity toward him, he was just more interested in pursuing his own love life, which seemed reasonable and healthy to her.

"I'll call you when I get back, and tell you where we're going. Spago, I think," Coop called over his shoulder as he hurried back down the path with a wave.

Five minutes later he was in the car on the way to his agent's office, and an hour later, he was home again. He had signed the deal. He told Valerie and Taryn they had a reservation at Spago at eight o'clock. And then he called Alex at the hospital. She came to the phone right away. It was the first time he had called her in nearly a month, since Charlene's DNA results. Her heart pounded as she answered, and her hand shook, but she tried to sound calm for him.

He told her what had happened, and she told him how happy she was, as he told her all the details, and then there was a long silence. He knew what she was thinking, and what the answer was. He had thought about it all the way home, although he had been tempted for a minute or two.

"Does this change anything between us, Coop?" she asked, holding her breath. She wasn't even sure what she wanted now, but she knew she had to ask.

"I thought about it a little while ago, Alex. And I'd love to say yes. But it doesn't. It's not right between us. Even with my debts paid, I'm too old for you. People would always think I was after your money. And it's not right for a girl your age to be with a man like me. You need a husband and babies, and a real life, maybe with someone from your own world, or someone who does the same kind of work you do. I think if we tried to make this work permanently, it would be a huge mistake. I'm so sorry if I hurt you, Alex. I learned a lot from you, but that's a poor excuse to have done it at your expense. Maybe it wasn't about the money. But it just doesn't feel right. Maybe we both need people closer to our own age. I don't know why, but all my instincts tell me that we both need to walk away from this before we make a real mess of it. If it's any consolation, you've taken a piece of my heart with you. Just keep it close to you, like a locket, or a lock of hair. But let's not go back and make a big mistake we'll both regret. I think we both need to go forward instead of back."

In light of the time they'd spent together and what she'd felt for him, she had hoped he would say something different to her, but she didn't disagree with him. She just didn't want to lose. But she had thought about it a lot in the past weeks too, and her conclusions weren't very different than his. She missed him terribly, and she'd had a wonderful time with him, but something in her gut stopped her from trying to talk him into it, or even wanting to go back herself. But she had felt compelled to ask.

In truth, she wanted to explore things with Jimmy now. That felt right to her. In a funny way, more than it ever had with Coop. She and Jimmy had the same passions, the same love for kids, so much so that it spilled over into their work. Jimmy was fascinated by what she did. Coop had always been squeamish about it. And she had never really belonged in Coop's world. She had had fun being in it with him, but she had always felt like a visitor, a tourist, she couldn't really imagine living there for good. In fact, she had more in common with Jimmy than she'd ever had with Coop. Although whether or not it ever worked out with Jimmy was something else. Neither of them could be sure of that yet. But for whatever reason, in the end, it hadn't worked with Coop. For him at least, and maybe he'd been right. It was easier now to move forward, and not back, just as he said.

"I understand, Coop," she said quietly. "And I hate to say I agree, but I think I do. My head does, and my heart will catch up eventually." A part of her hated to let him go, maybe because he was the loving, happy-go-lucky father she'd never had, and hers had never been.

"You're a brave girl," he said generously.

"Thank you," she said solemnly. "Will you invite me to the premiere?"

"Yes. And you can come watch me get an Oscar at the Academy Awards."

"It's a deal." She smiled, happy for him.

She felt better after talking to him. It was as though his windfall had set them both free. He needed that so desperately, not only to pay his bills, but for his peace of mind, and self-respect. Now he could do whatever he wanted to. She was truly pleased for him. And she felt better that night when Jimmy met her at work in a cab. She was driving after that. They were going out for dinner and a movie, and he noticed her mood as soon as they got into her car.

"You look happy. What's up?"

"I talked to Coop today. He got a big part in a

movie, and he sorted out a lot of stuff." Jimmy looked
instantly panicked although he also knew his mother
was having dinner with him. But he didn't want to
mention it to Alex.

"What kind of stuff? About you two?"

"Yeah, that and other things." She didn't want to
tell Jimmy about his debts. She thought she owed that
much to Coop. "I think we've both figured out that it
wasn't right between us. It was fun, but in the long
run, we both needed something different." She felt
freer and more at ease than she had since he left.

"What do you mean you needed something different? Like what?" He looked stressed.

"Like you, dummy," she said, smiling at him.

"Is that what he said?"

"Not specifically. I figured that much out for myself.
I'm a doctor, you know," she said, as he relaxed. She
had worried him for a minute or two. Coop was a for-
midable opponent for any man, and Jimmy felt at a serious disadvantage compared to him. He was ten feet
tall and had so goddam much charm. But what Jimmy
had to offer meant more to her. He had a tenderness of
soul and gentleness of spirit that had captured her
heart. And Coop was right, she needed someone with
more in common with her than they had shared. In
some ways, she and Jimmy were the answer to each
other's prayers.

As promised, Coop and Valerie and Mark and
Taryn had dinner at Spago that night. Their mood was
ebullient, and Coop was practically euphoric he was
so pleased. People stopped to talk to him, and the
news was already leaking out. There was going to be

an article about it in the trades the next day. He was already the man of the hour around town.

"When do you start shooting?" Mark asked with interest.

"We go on location in New York in October. And we should be back here by Christmas. We'll shoot in a studio here after that." He had two months to play before he went to work. "I'd like to go to Europe in September, before I start," he said, looking at Valerie. Maybe they could go after his visit to Cape Cod. He could afford to now, and he was hoping to invite her. "How does that sound to you?" he asked Valerie softly, a little while later, while the others were talking to each other.

"Interesting," she said with a Mona Lisa smile. "Let's see how Cape Cod goes." There was a lot they still didn't know.

"Don't be so sensible," he chided her, but she was smart. He had the feeling that he had finally met the woman of his life. "I'd love to go to the Hotel du Cap."

She looked tempted, and they both laughed. They both felt the same nearly irresistible pull. But if it was right, it would unfold. They didn't have to rush into it. And later, while they took a walk on the grounds again, Valerie said as much to him, and Coop agreed. It was just that there was so much happening, he felt like a kid in a candy store, and he wanted to share it with her.

He told her about his conversation with Alex that afternoon, and said that he felt liberated after talking to her. They both knew he'd done the right thing by ending it with her, painful though it had been.

"I think she and Jimmy are starting to see each other," Valerie said cautiously. She didn't want to be indiscreet, but she didn't want Jimmy to feel awkward with him, particularly now. Coop looked pensive for a minute, and then he sighed and looked at her. For an instant, all his male jealousies had been aroused, and then he calmed down.

"I think that sounds right, Valerie. For both of them. And this is right for us." He smiled at her, and took her hand, and he kissed her that night when he left her at her door. It was a world full of new beginnings for all of them. It was funny the way things worked out the way they were meant to eventually, if you waited long enough. It had been a long wait for Valerie, and not as long for Coop, but they had found each other, and the right movie had even found him. It all felt like destiny as he kissed her again, and then she slipped quietly into the gatehouse, thinking of him. Cooper Winslow was not who she'd expected, but she was glad he had come along. She didn't even feel like Cinderella with him. She felt like herself, but a woman falling in love with her best friend. It was the same feeling he had as he walked down the path to the main house. What he was looking forward to now was their time on Cape Cod.

Chapter 26

Jimmy's casts came off on schedule in early August, and news of Coop's upcoming movie was all over the papers by then. He was a hero around town. Everyone was congratulating him, and suddenly he had more offers for work. But he was determined to get out of town with Valerie for a few weeks. And after that, he was going on to Europe, whether she went with him or not. She said she would decide after Cape Cod.

Jimmy was walking comfortably again by the time they left. He was seeing a lot of Alex, and things were going well for them. Mark and Taryn were taking the kids to Tahoe for two weeks. Only Jimmy and Alex were staying in town, because they both had to work.

Valerie made one of her memorable pasta dinners the night before they left. Coop was flying with her to Boston, and then they were driving to the Cape. Alex hadn't come to dinner, she had to work anyway. But Valerie had gone to the hospital that afternoon to have lunch with her and say goodbye before she left. But Mark and Taryn and the kids had come to dinner, and Coop was pretending to growl at them. He asked Jason if he'd broken any windows lately, and Jason looked mortified, and then Coop invited him onto the set when they were shooting in LA, and the boy looked thrilled. Jessica asked if she could come too, and bring some of her friends.

"I don't suppose I have a choice in the matter anyway," he said, looking pained, with a glance at Taryn and Mark. "Something tells me we're going to be related sometime in the next few months. I will do anything you want, as long as you promise never to refer to me as your grandfather, step or otherwise. My reputation has taken a lot of hits over the years, but I don't think it would survive that. They'll be giving me parts for ninety-year-olds," he said ruefully, and everyone laughed. But Jessica and Jason were slowly getting used to him. They were crazy about Taryn and willing to accept him as part of the deal. There was a possibility that they were all going to wind up related, one way or another, sooner or later, which was an exotic idea. Even he and Alex if she and Jimmy became a serious thing, and he and Valerie stayed together, which he hoped they would. It was all a little incestuous, but everyone seemed to have gotten something out of it, even Mark's kids.

"I hope the toilets flush this year when you get to Marisol," Jimmy teased as they finished dessert, and Coop looked across the table at him with a puzzled expression, as Valerie scolded Jimmy for frightening Coop.

"It's not as bad as all that. It's just a very old house."

"Wait a minute, back up. . . . Who is Marisol?" Coop asked with a strange look in his eyes.

"Not 'who,' 'what,'" Jimmy corrected him. "That's

my mom's house on the Cape. It was built by my great-grandparents, and it's a combination of their names. Marianne and Solomon." Coop looked as though he'd been struck by a thunderbolt as he stared at them.

"Oh my God. Marisol. You didn't tell me that," he said to Valerie, as though he'd just been told she'd been in prison for the last ten years. That might have been easier to absorb.

"Tell you what?" she said innocently, pouring him another glass of wine. Her dinner had been excellent, but he wasn't thinking about that now.

"You know exactly what I mean, Valerie. You lied to me," he said, looking stern, and the others looked faintly concerned. Something was happening that none of them understood. But she did.

"I did not lie to you. I just didn't explain it to you. I didn't think it mattered." But she knew it did, and was afraid it would.

"And your maiden name is Westerfield, I assume." She made a kind of humming sound in answer, and nodded her head. "You fraud! Shame on you! You pretended you were poor!" He looked shocked. The Westerfield fortune was one of the largest in the world, surely in the States.

"I did not pretend anything. I didn't discuss it with you," Valerie said nervously, while trying to appear calm. But she had been worried about his reaction for a while. It was a lot for him to swallow at one gulp.

"I went to Marisol once. Your mother invited me when I was making a film near there. The place is bigger than the Hotel du Cap, and if you turned it into a hotel, you could charge more. Valerie, that was a very dishonest thing to do." But he didn't look as angry as she had feared he would. The truth was that the Westerfields were the biggest banking family in the East. They were the Rothschilds of America in the early days, and related to the Astors and the Vanderbilts and the Rockefellers and half the blue bloods in the States, if not the world. The Westerfields made the Madisons look like paupers by comparison, but the difference was that Valerie was a grown-up, and didn't have to answer to anyone. Somehow, the circumstances were such, now that his finances were in order, or about to be, that it didn't seem like such a shocking alliance after all. And she wasn't a young girl, but he was stunned that she had never said anything to him. She was the most unassuming woman in the world. He had presumed she was a widow living on a small income. But it explained why Jimmy had been able to rent the gatehouse so easily. It explained a lot of things, about the people she knew and the places she'd been. But he'd never seen anyone as unpretentious and discreet as she was. He sat there and stared at her for a long moment, absorbing it, and then he sat back in his chair and laughed. "Well, I'll tell you one thing, I don't feel sorry for you anymore." But he wasn't going to let her support him either. If they married, he was going to be supporting her. That was the way he wanted it to be. She could be as discreet as she wanted on her own budget, but their extravagances, and there would be many of them, would be paid for by him. "And I'm calling a plumber, if my toilet doesn't flush at Marisol, you little witch. What would you have done if I didn't get this movie?" He'd have been in the same boat as he had been in with Alex in that case. But Valerie was more mature. It wasn't just about the money with Alex, it was about their age, and not having kids, and being perceived as a gigolo, and Arthur Madison disapproving of him. But none of that seemed relevant with Valerie, because she was the right woman for him. And he was back on his feet financially, in fact better than he'd ever been.

"If you call a plumber at Marisol," Jimmy warned him with a grin, "my mother will have a fit. She thinks it's part of the charm, along with the roof that leaks, and the shutters that fall off. I damn near broke my leg last year when the south porch caved in. My mother loves fixing the place up herself."

"I can hardly wait," Coop groaned. But he already knew he loved the place. He had fallen in love with it when her mother had invited him there. It seemed to go on forever, with houses and boathouses and guest houses, and a barn full of antique cars he could have spent the entire weekend in. It was one of the most famous houses in the East. The Kennedys had often visited there when they were in residence at Hyannis Port, and the President had stayed there. Coop was still shaking his head when the others left.

"Don't ever lie to me again," he scolded Valerie.

"I didn't. I was being discreet," she said, looking demure, with a decided look of mischief in her eye.

"A little too discreet perhaps?" he said, smiling at her. In a way, he was glad he hadn't known before. It was better like this.

"One can never be too discreet," she said primly.

But he loved that about her. He loved her elegance and her simplicity. It explained the distinction he had felt. She was an undeniable aristocrat even in white shirt and jeans. And suddenly he realized what it meant for Alex too. Jimmy was exactly the man she needed, he was part of her world, and at the same time, as much of a renegade as she. Even Arthur Madison couldn't object to him. And suddenly Coop felt pleased. Things had worked out exactly as they were meant to. Not only for him, but for her too. Even if she didn't know it yet, she was on the right track. And as Valerie cleared the table, and put the dishes in the dishwasher, Coop glanced at her.

"Does Alex know?"

"Knowing Jimmy, probably not." Valerie smiled at him. "It matters even less to him than it does to me." It didn't matter to them because it was part of them, right down to their bones. They hadn't made it up, or invented it, or acquired it, or married it. They were born to it, so they could live any way they chose. Richly, or poorly, or quietly or noisily. It was entirely up to them. And Alex was cut from the same cloth. It meant nothing to her, and she liked living as though she were poor.

"How do I fit into all that?" Coop asked Valerie honestly, pulling her close to him. She really was the woman of his life, whether she knew it yet or not. But he was determined to convince her of it eventually. Not for the money, but simply because of who she was and what she meant to him.

"You fit into it very comfortably, I suspect. You're used to all that. In fact, we might not be quite elegant enough for you." He had lived very well for a very long time. In fact, he was very spoiled. And now, with the movie he'd just landed, he could afford to indulge himself, and her. And he had every intention of doing just that.

"I'll adjust," he said, laughing at her. "I can see I have my work cut out for me. I'm going to spend all my money repairing your old house."

"Don't," she smiled, "I like it the way it is, falling apart and crumbling, with things falling down all over the place. It has charm that way."

"So do you," he said, holding her tight, "and you're not falling down or crumbling." But he knew that when she did, he would still love her. And he was likely to crumble first, because he was, after all, seventeen years older than she. She was in fact a younger woman, and a very wealthy woman. But not too young. And no matter how rich she was, he no longer cared, because he had money of his own. It had taken a Westerfield to bring him down, and capture him. But the job had been done at last, and done well.

"Will you marry me?" he asked her, as Jimmy tiptoed softly upstairs, smiling to himself. It was funny how much better he liked Coop now, now that Alex wasn't involved with him. He was beginning to think he was a pretty good guy.

"Eventually, I suspect," Valerie answered him with a smile. He kissed her then, and then he left the house. They were leaving at the crack of dawn the next day.

The driver took them to the airport in the Bentley the next morning. Coop had four suitcases with him, and he'd had a hard time getting it down to that. But he was going on to Europe afterwards. Valerie only had one. But she had packed in a hurry when she left.

Coop had said goodbye to Taryn when he left the house. And Valerie hugged Jimmy tight, and then kissed him and told him to take care at least ten times.

"Take good care of yourself, Jimmy," she said and then both men hurried her out the door so they didn't miss the plane.

They left for the airport in high spirits, and both of them slept on the plane. And when they woke up, they were nearly there. She told him some of the history he didn't know about the house. It fascinated him and he couldn't wait to see it again, and share it with her. As he remembered it, it was an elegant, charming, romantic old estate, with exquisite grounds.

He rented a car at the Boston airport, and they drove slowly up the Cape. And when they got there, Marisol was exactly as he remembered it, only better now. Because he was there with her.

He helped her hammer things, and fix screens, and repair wicker furniture. They were there for three weeks, and he'd never been happier, although he'd never worked as hard in his life. But he loved doing it with her, and she worked as hard as he. She always had a hammer and nails in her pocket, and a swipe of paint somewhere on her face. He loved her and every minute that they shared.

On Labor Day weekend, they flew to London and spent three weeks there. He went straight from there to New York to start working on his movie. And Valerie went back to Boston for a few days and then joined him in New York. They lived at the Plaza for the

duration of his location shoot. And she flew back to
California with him just before Thanksgiving. Taryn
and Mark were married by then. They had gotten married at Lake Tahoe with only Jason and Jessica with
them the week before. There was much to celebrate.
Alex and Jimmy were living at the gatehouse by then.
She had turned his bedroom into a laundry basket,
and given up her studio. She had almost finished her
residency, and been promised a permanent position on
staff as a neonatologist at UCLA. She and Jimmy were
talking about getting married. But he hadn't met
Arthur yet.

Coop had them all for Thanksgiving dinner, even
Alex, and it was easy to see how happy she and Jimmy
were. Wolfgang sent over a turkey, which Paloma
served wearing the leopard sneakers which she wore
with a new pink uniform. The rhinestone glasses had
been retired for the winter months, and much to
everyone's relief, she liked Valerie. A lot. And Valerie
liked her.

The tabloids carried the story the week before
Christmas. As did *People* magazine, *Time, Newsweek,*
the respectable newspapers and wire services, and
CNN. The headlines were pretty much the same
everywhere. WIDOWED EASTERN HEIRESS MARRIES MOVIE
STAR. Others gave him top billing. COOPER WINSLOW
MARRIES WESTERFIELD HEIRESS. In either case, the photographs showed them both happy and smiling at a
small reception they gave. His press agent delivered
the photographs to the press. And the following day,
Valerie came down the stairs from his bedroom with
an armful of towels she'd found in the linen closet.

"This works out really well, Coop," she said distractedly. He had a week off before he started shooting again in LA, and he was trying to talk her into going to Saint Moritz for the week, but so far she didn't seem interested. She was happy at home with him, and so was he. More than he'd ever been.

"What's that?" He was looking over changes in the script. The movie was going very well, and he already had offers for others in the spring. His rates had gone up of course, so Abe was pleased.

"I just found a stack of monogrammed towels I don't think you use, and since I'm a *W* again, I thought maybe we could send them to Marisol. We need towels desperately there."

"I suspect that's why you married me," he said as he grinned at her. "God forbid you should buy new towels for Marisol. Could I order you some as a wedding present?"

"Of course not. These are fine. Why buy new towels when old ones will do?"

"I love you, Valerie," he said, as he smiled at her, and then got up and came across the room to her. He put his arms around her and forced her to put the towels down. "You can have all the towels you want. Maybe we can find you some old monogrammed sheets too. If not, we can pick some up at Goodwill."

"Thank you, Coop," she said, and kissed him. It had been a fine year indeed.

ABOUT THE AUTHOR

DANIELLE STEEL has been hailed as one of the world's most popular authors with over 500 million copies of her novels sold. Her many international bestsellers include *Answered Prayers, Sunset in St. Tropez, The Kiss, Leap of Faith, Lone Eagle, Journey, The House on Hope Street, The Wedding,* and other highly acclaimed novels. She is also the author of *His Bright Light,* the story of her son Nick Traina's life and death.

Introducing an exciting way to learn more about
DANIELLE STEEL

Visit the Danielle Steel website at
www.daniellesteel.com

 Finally, a website completely devoted
to Danielle Steel and her books

Log on, and you'll find

❖ *The News Page* featuring the latest bulletins on current Danielle Steel bestsellers, upcoming novels, and other news

❖ *The Danielle Steel Bookshelf* featuring all of Danielle Steel's novels, with excerpts from each one and a 4-6 minute audio sample from audio editions

❖ *Hot Off the Press* featuring a chapter excerpt from Danielle's latest bestselling book

❖ *The Screening Room* featuring information on movie and TV tie-ins

❖ *The Trivia Contest*: win a limited edition of one of her bestselling novels

❖ *The Guest Book*: add your name to Danielle's electronic mailing list or send her an e-mail letter

❖ *The Danielle Steel Scrapbook*: never-before-aired audio and video interviews, photographs, and more, available only on the Danielle Steel website

 www.daniellesteel.com

Dell